In the few stolen moments
she'd had with him,
she'd shared more
intimacy than
she had with
any man…

Where Dreams Begin

"At least tell me this...are you taken?" he asked. "Married. Betrothed. Otherwise committed to someone."

"Oh, I...yes I am." A widow Holly might be, but she was as married to her husband's memory as she had been during his life.

But she couldn't move. They stood together, breathing, clasped in awareness and stirring passion while a few sweet strains of music drifted to them from the ballroom.

The stranger's hot breath fanned her ear. "Kiss me again."

"You don't understand," she whispered shakily. "This isn't like me...I don't do these things."

"We're strangers in the darkness," he whispered back. "We'll never be together like this again. No, don't pull away. Show me how an evening can be magical."

"I'm sorry," she gasped. "I never should have..." And she fled. Her feet could not take her away fast enough from the scene, the memory of which she knew would cause her shame and pleasure for the rest of her life.

LISA KLEYPAS

WHERE DREAMS BEGIN

AVON BOOKS
An Imprint of HarperCollinsPublishers

AVON BOOKS
An Imprint of HarperCollins*Publishers*
10 East 53rd Street
New York, New York 10022-5299

Copyright © 2000 by Lisa Kleypas
Inside cover photo by Sigrid Estrada
Library of Congress Catalog Card Number: 00-90035
ISBN: 0-380-80231-7
www.avonromance.com

First Avon Books paperback printing: August 2000
First Avon Books special printing: February 2000

Avon Trademark Reg. U.S. Pat. Off. and in Other Countries, Marca Registrada, Hecho en U.S.A.
HarperCollins® is a trademarks of HarperCollins Publishers Inc.

Printed in the U.S.A.

WCD 10 9 8 7 6 5 4 3 2 1

To the Avon Ladies, for giving me their love and support after the flood, and letting me know that when everything disappears, true friends remain.

And to Nancy Richards-Akers, a beautiful, talented woman who was taken from us too soon. I will miss her friendship and all the wonderful stories she had yet to write.

One

London, 1830

She had to escape.

The rumble of sophisticated chatter, the blaze of chandeliers that splashed hot wax onto the dancers below and the profusion of smells that heralded the lavish supper to come, all overwhelmed Lady Holly Taylor. It had been a mistake to attend a grand social event so soon after George's death. Of course, most people would not consider three years to be "soon." She had gone through the year and a day of Deep Mourning, barely venturing from the house except to take garden walks with her small daughter Rose. She had worn black bombazine and covered her hair and face with veils that symbolized her separation from her husband and the unseen world. She had taken most of her meals alone, covered all mirrors in the house with black crepe and written letters on black-banded paper, so that every interaction with the outside world would bear the signs of her grief.

Second Mourning had come next. She had still worn all-black clothing, but had relinquished the protective veil. Then, on the third year after George's death, Holly had undergone Half Mourning, which had allowed her to wear

1

gray or mauve, and to participate in small, inconspicuous women's activities, such as tea with relatives or close female friends.

Now that all stages of mourning were finished, Holly had emerged from the dark and comforting shelter of the grieving period into a bright social world that had become terribly unfamiliar. True, the faces and the scene were exactly as she remembered . . . except that George was no longer with her. She felt conspicuous in her aloneness, uncomfortable in her new identity as the Widow Taylor. Like everyone else, she had always regarded widows as somber figures to be pitied, women who wore an invisible mantle of tragedy no matter what their outward attire suggested. Now she understood why so many widows who attended events like this always looked as though they wished they were somewhere else. People approached her with sympathetic expressions, offered a small cup of punch or a few consoling words and left with a discreet air of relief, as if a social duty had been performed and they were now free to enjoy the ball. She herself had done the same thing to widows in the past, wanting to be kind and yet reluctant to be affected by the desolation in their eyes.

Somehow it had not occurred to Holly that she would feel so isolated in the midst of a large gathering. The empty space beside her, where George should have been, seemed like a painfully obvious gap. Unexpectedly, a feeling akin to embarrassment came over her, as if she had stumbled into a place where she did not belong. She was half of something that had once been whole. Her presence at the ball only served as a reminder that a dearly loved man had been lost.

Her face felt stiff and cold as she inched her way along the wall toward the door of the drawing room. The sweet riot of melody the musicians played did not cheer her, as her friends had hopefully suggested . . . the music only seemed to mock her.

Once Holly had danced as lightly and swiftly as the other young women here tonight, feeling as if she were flying in George's protective arms. They had been made for each other, and people had once commented with admiring smiles. She and George had been similar in size, with her own diminutive stature matched by her husband's less-than-towering frame. Although George had been average in height, he had been wonderfully fit, and so very handsome with his golden brown hair and alert blue eyes, and a dazzling smile that was never long in hiding. He had loved to laugh, dance, talk . . . no ball or crush or dinner party had ever been complete without him.

Oh, George. A wet aching pressure grew behind her eyes. *How lucky I was to have you. How lucky we all were. But how am I supposed to go on without you?*

Well-meaning friends had pressured her to come here tonight, intending that this should begin the days of freedom from the smothering rituals of mourning. But she wasn't ready . . . not tonight . . . perhaps not ever.

Her gaze scored across the crowd, locating various members of George's family as they socialized and ate delicacies from gilded Sevres porcelain plates. His older brother, William, Lord Taylor, was escorting his wife to the drawing room, where a quadrille was about to begin. Lord and Lady Taylor were a well-suited couple, but their tepid affection did not begin to approach the genuine love that she and George had shared. It seemed that everyone in George's family—his parents, his brothers, and their wives—had finally recovered from his death. Enough that they could take part in a ball, laugh and eat and drink, allow themselves to forget that the most beloved member of the family was in an early grave. Holly did not blame them for their ability to carry on, now that George was gone . . . in fact, she envied them. How wonderful it would be to escape the invisible mantle of grief that covered her from head to toe. If not for her daughter Rose, she would never have a moment's respite from the constant ache of loss.

"Holland," came a murmur from nearby, and she turned to see George's youngest brother, Thomas. Although Thomas had the same attractive features, blue eyes and amber-streaked hair that all the Taylor men shared, he lacked the mischievous spark, the slow dazzling smile, the warmth and confidence that had made George so irresistible. Thomas was a taller, more somber version of his charismatic brother. He had been a steady source of support ever since George's death from typhoid fever.

"Thomas," Holly said brightly, forcing a smile to her stiff lips, "are you enjoying the ball?"

"Not especially," he replied, while sympathy flickered in the azure depths of his eyes. "But I believe I'm navigating it better than you, my dear. There's a pinched look on your face, as though one of your megrims is starting."

"Yes, it is," Holly admitted, suddenly aware of the persistent pain in her temples and the back of her skull, the throbbing that warned of worse pain to come. She had never had a megrim in her life until George's passing, but they had started after his funeral. The severe headaches appeared unexpectedly and often drove her to bed for two and three days at a time.

"Shall I escort you home?" Thomas asked. "I'm certain that Olinda would not mind."

"No," Holly said swiftly, "you must stay here and enjoy the ball with your wife, Thomas. I'm perfectly able to return home unescorted. In fact, I would prefer it."

"All right." He smiled at her, and the similarity of his

features to George's made her heart wrench painfully and caused the throbbing in her head to sharpen. "At least allow me to send for the family carriage."

"Thank you," she said gratefully. "Shall I wait in the entrance hall?"

Thomas shook his head. "I fear there is such a crush of vehicles outside that it may take several minutes for ours to come to the forefront. In the meanwhile, there are several quiet places for you to wait. As I recollect, there is a nice little parlor that opens onto a private conservatory. You'll find it past the entrance hall, along the hallway to the left of the curving staircase."

"Thomas," Holly murmured, touching his sleeve lightly and managing a wan smile. "What would I do without you?"

"You'll never have to find out," he replied gravely. "There is nothing I would not do for George's wife. The rest of the family feels the same. We'll take care of you and Rose. Always."

Holly knew she should have taken comfort in his words. However, she could not rid herself of the troubling awareness of being a burden for George's family. The annuity left to her at George's death was so small as to be inconsequential, making it necessary for her to sell the elegant white-columned house they had occupied. She was grateful for the Taylors' generosity in giving her two rooms in their family residence. She had seen the way other widows were shunted aside, or compelled to marry again, just so a family could be rid of them. Instead, the Taylors treated her as a beloved guest and, even more, as a living monument to George's memory.

As Holly moved along the wall of the drawing room, her left shoulder blade suddenly met the hard, gilded edge of the ornately molded doorframe. Blindly she darted through the open doorway, into the keyhole-shaped entrance hall of the mansion belonging to Lord Bellemont, the earl of Warwick. The town estate was designed for house parties in which politics were plotted, marriages were engineered and fortunes were changed. Lady Bellemont possessed a well-deserved reputation as an expert hostess, inviting the perfect mixture of aristocrats, politicians and accomplished artists to her balls and soirees. The Taylors liked and trusted Lady Bellemont, and had deemed it appropriate for Holly to reenter society at the first ball of the new Season.

The circular space of the entrance hall was flanked by two immense curving staircases. Conveniently situated on the ground floor, the main rooms of the mansion branched into clusters of parlors and visiting areas that opened onto outdoor conservatories or small paved gardens. Anyone wishing for a small private meeting or romantic rendezvous could find a secluded place with no difficulty.

Breathing easier with every step that took her farther away from the crowded drawing room, Holly strode along the hallway toward the parlor that Thomas had suggested. The skirts of her corded silk evening dress, dyed in a shade of blue so dark as to approximate black, swished heavily around her legs as she walked. The hem of the gown was weighted with wadded and stitched bunches of silk and crepe that gave it the currently fashionable fullness, so different from the light, floating skirts of the gowns that had been in style before George had died.

The parlor door was half-open, and the room was unlit. However, clear icy light filtered through the windows, illuminating the parlor just enough that Holly could see without the aid of a candle. A pair of curving French armchairs and a table occupied one corner, while a few musical instruments reposed in mahogany stands nearby.

Fringed velvet swags shrouded the windows and the top of the fireplace mantel. The thick carpet underfoot, patterned with floral medallions, muffled her footsteps.

Slipping inside the shadowy, quiet space, Holly closed the door, put a hand to the snug banded waist of her gown and gave a long sigh.

"Thank God," she whispered, relieved beyond measure to be alone. How strange . . . she had become so accustomed to solitude that she was uncomfortable in a crowd. She had once been socially adept, fun-loving, at ease in any situation . . . but that had been because of George. Being his wife had given her a confidence that she now sorely lacked.

As she wandered deeper into the room, a cool draft wafted over her, making her shiver. Although her boat-shaped neckline was modestly high, nearly covering her collarbone, her throat and the tops of her shoulders were exposed to the open air. Seeking the source of the breeze, Holly realized that the parlor opened onto a conservatory leading to the outside gardens, and that the French doors had been left ajar. She went to close the doors, then hesitated with her hand on the cold brass knobs as an odd feeling came over her. As she stared through the frosted-glass door panes, she felt her heartbeat escalate to an uncomfortable speed, until it pounded and throbbed in every limb.

She had the feeling of being poised at the edge of a cliff with endless air below her. The urge to withdraw quickly into the safety of the parlor, perhaps even back to the over-heated clamor of the drawing room, came over her in a strong surge. Instead, she gripped the doorknobs tightly in her palms until they turned slick and hot in her perspiring palms. The night lured her outward, away from everything safe and known.

Trembling a little, Holly tried to summon a laugh at her
own foolishness. She stepped forward, intending to fill her
lungs with a blast of bracing air. Suddenly a huge, dark
shape appeared before her . . . the towering form of a man.
Holly froze in utter surprise. Her nerveless hands slipped
from the doorknobs, while shock sent prickles all over her
body. Perhaps it was Thomas appearing to inform her that
the carriage was ready. But he was too tall, too massive
to be her brother-in-law, or any other man of her acquaintance.

Before she could utter a word, the stranger reached inside and pulled her across the threshold. With a small cry,
Holly stumbled forward, dragged unwillingly out of the
parlor and into the night. Momentum brought her full
against him, and she was nothing but a tumble of silk and
stiff limbs in his arms. He handled her easily, his strength
so great that she was as helpless as a kitten in his large
hands.

"Wait—" she gasped in bewilderment. His body was as
hard as if he were wrought of steel instead of flesh. The
cloth of his coat was smooth beneath her perspiring palms.
Her nostrils were filled with the scents of starched linen,
tobacco, brandy, an utterly masculine mixture that reminded her somewhat of how George had smelled. It had
been so long since she had been held like this. In the past
three years she had not turned to any man for comfort, had
not wanted any embrace to interfere with the memory of
the last time her husband had held her.

She was not allowed any choice about this, however. As
she spluttered a protest and writhed against his solid body,
he bent his head and murmured close to her ear.

The sound of his voice stunned her . . . a deep purring
rumble, like the voice of Hades as he dragged an unwilling
Persephone down to his underworld kingdom. "You took

your sweet time about getting here, my lady."

He thought she was someone else, she realized. Somehow she had stumbled onto someone else's romantic rendezvous. "But I—I'm not—"

Her words were crushed into silence as he covered her mouth with his. She jerked in startled reaction, amazed and horrified and abruptly furious . . . he had taken away George's last kiss . . . but that thought was burned away in a sudden blaze of sensation. His mouth was so hot, pressing and demanding until her lips were forced apart. She had never been kissed like this, his mouth imparting a message of such lurid desire that she wilted from the heat. She turned her head to escape him, but he followed the movement, angling his head more intimately over hers. The pounding of her heart increased to a deafening roar, and she whimpered in instinctive fear.

Holly sensed the exact moment when the man realized that she was a stranger. She felt him go still with surprise, his breath stopping. Now he would release her, she thought hazily. But after the long hesitation, he changed his grip, his arms still secure but no longer crushing, and one large hand slid up her back to cradle the bare nape of her neck.

She had been a married woman—she had thought herself to be experienced and worldly-wise. But this stranger kissed her in a way no one ever had, invading her, tasting her with his tongue, making her shiver and recoil. The subtle hint of brandy flavored his sleek, warm mouth . . . and there was something else . . . some intimate essence that lured her strongly. She eventually found herself relaxing against his hard body, accepting the tender ravishment of his kiss, even answering the exploration of his tongue with timid touches of her own. Perhaps it was the suddenness of the encounter, or the concealing darkness around them, or the fact that they were utterly unknown to each

other . . . but for a feverish moment she became someone
else in his arms. Compelled to touch him somewhere, anywhere, she reached around his neck and felt the smooth,
hard nape of his neck, and the thick, short locks of hair
that curled slightly against her fingertips. His vast height
made it necessary for her to rise on her toes to reach him.
She slid her palm to his lean cheek, discovering the grain
of heavy close-shaven bristle.

He seemed intensely affected by her touch, his breath
puffing like steam on her cheek, his pulse hammering in
the soft place beneath his jawbone. Holly craved the hard,
deliciously masculine texture of him, absorbing his scent
and taste greedily before she came to a sudden awareness
of what she was doing.

Horrified, she broke away with a muffled cry, and at
this first sign of unwillingness, the stranger released her.
His encompassing arms fell from her as she stumbled toward the sheltering shadows of the conservatory. She finally stopped in the lee of the winged statue wedged
against the stone wall, where there was no further retreat
possible. He followed her, though he made no move to
touch her again, stopping so close that she could almost
feel the animal heat emanating from his body.

"Oh," she whispered shakily, wrapping her arms around
herself, as if she could contain the sensations that continued to spill from every nerve. "Oh."

It was too dark for them to see each other's faces, but
the man's large form was silhouetted by the shimmer of
moonlight. He was wearing evening clothes—he must be
a guest at the ball. But he did not have the slender, elegant
build of a gentleman with abundant leisure time. He had
the tremendous, iron-hard muscles of a day laborer. His
shoulders and chest were too deep, his thighs too developed. Aristocratic gentlemen did not usually possess such

obvious muscles. They preferred to distinguish themselves from those who had to earn a living through physical labor.

When he spoke, the gravelly undertone of his voice seemed to set off pleasurable vibrations along her spine. His accent lacked the clicking precision that a nobleman would have possessed. He was from the lower classes, she realized. How could such a man be attending a ball like this?

"You're not the lady I was expecting." He paused and added with a touch of gruff amusement, fully cognizant of the fact that it was too late for apologies, "I am sorry."

Holly strove to reply coolly, although there was a betraying tremor in her voice. "Quite all right. You merely assaulted the wrong woman. I'm certain the same mistake could have happened to any lurker in the shadows."

She sensed that her response had surprised him, that he had expected her to erupt in a fit of hysterics. A soft catch of laughter escaped him. "Well. Maybe I'm not as sorry as I thought."

As she saw his hand lift slowly, she thought he meant to take her in his arms again.

"Don't touch me," she said, shrinking back until her shoulders were pressed flat against the wall. Instead, he braced his hand on the stone beside her head and leaned closer, until she felt imprisoned by the muscular cage of his body.

"Should we introduce ourselves?" he asked.

"Definitely not."

"At least tell me this . . . are you taken?"

"Taken?" Holly repeated blankly, shrinking backward until her shoulder blades met the hard wall.

"Married," he clarified. "Betrothed. Otherwise committed to someone."

"Oh, I . . . yes. Yes, I am." A widow she might be, but

she was as married to George's memory as she had been to him during his life. At the thought of George, Holly wondered bleakly how her life had come to this, that her splendid, beloved husband should be gone and she was here in the shadows, talking with a stranger who had practically assaulted her.

"Forgive me," he said, keeping his voice gentle. "I had arranged to meet with someone else . . . a lady who is obviously not able to keep her promise. When I saw you coming through the doors, I mistook you for her."

"I . . . I wanted to be alone somewhere while my carriage was brought 'round."

"Leaving the ball early? I don't blame you. These affairs are damned dull."

"They don't have to be," she murmured, remembering the way she had once laughed and danced and flirted with George until the early hours of the morning. "It depends on one's choice of companionship. With the right partner, an evening like this could be . . . magical."

The wistfulness must have been evident in her voice, for he reacted unexpectedly. She felt the heat of his fingertips brush her shoulder, throat, until he found the side of her face and curved his palm against her cheek. She should have jerked away from the touch, but she was shocked by the pleasure of his warm, cradling hand on her face.

"You're the sweetest thing I've ever touched," came his voice from the darkness. "Tell me who you are. Tell me your name."

Holly took a deep gulp of air and pushed away from the wall, but there was nowhere to go. His powerful masculine form was everywhere, surrounding her, and without intending to, she walked straight into his arms. "I must go," she gasped. "My carriage is waiting."

"Let it wait. Stay with me." One hand clasped her waist,

the other slid behind her back, and a shudder of unwilling excitement went through her. "Are you frightened?" he asked as he felt the involuntary tremor.

"N-no." She should be protesting, fighting to break free of him, but there was an insidious delight in being held against his hard, sheltering body. She kept her hands between them, when all she wanted was to fold herself inside his embrace and lay her head on his broad chest. A trembling laugh escaped her. "This is madness. You must release me."

"You can walk out of my arms anytime you want."

But she still didn't move. They stood together, breathing, clasped in awareness and stirring passion while a few sweet strains of music drifted to them from the ballroom. The ball seemed another world away.

The stranger's hot breath fanned her ear and stirred the little wisps of hair around it. "Kiss me again."

"How dare you suggest—"

"No one will know."

"You don't understand," she whispered shakily. "This isn't like me. . . . I don't do these things."

"We're strangers in the darkness," he whispered back. "We'll never be together like this again. No, don't pull away. Show me how an evening can be magical." His lips brushed the rim of her ear, unexpectedly soft and entreating.

The situation was far beyond Holly's ordinary experience. She had never understood why women behaved recklessly in these matters, why they would take risks and break vows for the sake of fleeting physical pleasure . . . but now she knew. No one in her life had ever affected her like this. She felt empty and frustrated, she wanted nothing more than to be swallowed up in his embrace. It had been easy to be virtuous when she had always been sheltered from temptation. Now she truly understood the weakness of her own character. She tried to bring George's image to mind, but to her despair, she couldn't summon his face. There was only the star-filled night, and the gleam of moonlight in her dazed eyes, and the solid reality of a stranger's body.

Breathing hard, she turned her head, just a small movement, but it brought her mouth against the burning heat of his. Dear Lord, he knew how to kiss. He used his hand to urge her head to his shoulder, anchoring her firmly as his lips slanted over hers. The feel of his mouth was exquisite as he possessed her with slow, teasing kisses, using the tip of his tongue to entice her. She surged against him in an awkward movement, wobbling on her toes as she tried to press herself deeper into the hard masculine shelter of his body. He steadied her, one arm sliding around her back, the other locking around her hips. It had been so long since she had felt physical pleasure of any kind, much less this voluptuous abandonment.

The searching kisses become deeper, more sensuously aggressive, and Holly answered helplessly, while for some reason the sensation of being held in passion made her eyes sting and water. She felt a few tears leak from the outside corners of her eyes and slide to her trembling chin, while she continued to respond to him with a sort of desperate yearning that she couldn't begin to control.

His gentle fingers slid to her cheek and felt the wetness there. Slowly his mouth withdrew from hers, leaving it moist and kiss-softened. "Ah," he breathed, his lips dragging tenderly over the wet surface of her skin. "Sweet lady . . . tell me why a kiss makes you cry."

"I'm sorry," she gasped. "Let me go. I never should have . . ." She struggled away from him, relieved that he made no attempt to follow her as she fled back to the parlor and toward the main rooms. It seemed her feet could not take her fast enough away from the scene, the memory of which she knew would cause her both shame and guilty pleasure for the rest of her life.

Lady Bellemont, a pretty, vivacious woman of forty-five, giggled as she was led to the window of her own front parlor by a strong masculine hand on her arm. She was accustomed to receiving the greatest deference from every man of her acquaintance except for this one, who seemed to treat countesses and serving maids alike. It intrigued her to be handled so familiarly by this tall and charismatic male, who seemed not to recognize the great social barrier that existed between them. Despite the disapproval of her husband and friends, or perhaps because of it, she had decided to become friends with him. After all, a woman should never be too predictable.

"All right," Lady Bellemont said with a laughing sigh, "show me who has managed to excite so much interest in you."

Together they stared at the row of carriages and the bustling assortment of footmen outside, while the waltz music from the nearby drawing room swirled through the open doorway of the parlor. The small guest who was currently departing turned to thank the footman who helped her into the carriage. The golden light from the outside lamps caught her full in the face.

Lady Bellemont heard the man beside her catch his breath. "There," he said, his voice deepening. "That one. In the dark blue gown. Tell me who she is."

The face belonged to Lady Holland Taylor, a young woman who was well-known to Lady Bellemont. Somehow it seemed that the grief of widowhood, which usually took such a toll on a woman's beauty, had only enhanced

Lady Holland's looks. Her figure, which had always tended toward plumpness, was now trim and tidy. The severity of her hairstyle, gleaming brown locks pulled tightly into a coil atop her head, only served to emphasize the uncommon prettiness of her features . . . a straight little nose, a soft, ripe-looking mouth, and clear brown eyes the color of scotch whiskey. Since her husband's death, the sparkling liveliness of her character had been replaced by an air of quiet melancholy. She had the perpetual expression of being absorbed in some beautiful, sad dream. And after all she had lost, who could blame her?

Men would have swarmed around the attractive young widow like bees in the vicinity of a particularly lush flower. However, Lady Holland seemed to wear an invisible sign proclaiming "touch-me-not." Lady Bellemont had observed the widow's behavior this evening, wondering if she was interested in catching another husband. But she had refused all offers to dance and had seemed oblivious to the various men who endeavored to attract her attention. Clearly the widow did not want another man, not now, and likely not ever.

"Oh, my dear friend," Lady Bellemont murmured to the man beside her, "for once your taste is impeccable. But that lady is not for you."

"She's married," he said rather than asked, his black eyes as expressionless as slate.

"No, Lady Holland is widowed."

He glanced at Lady Bellemont with an interest that seemed casual, but she sensed the tremendous fascination coiled beneath his calm exterior. "I've never seen her before."

"That is not surprising, my dear. Lady Holland's husband passed on to his reward three years ago, just before you arrived on the scene. This is the first social event she has attended since coming out of mourning."

As Lady Holland's carriage pulled away from the mansion and rolled along the drive, the man's gaze flickered back to the vehicle and held until it was gone from sight. He reminded Lady Bellemont of a cat staring at a bird that had ascended too far in the air for him to reach. She sighed in friendly sympathy, having come to understand his ambitious nature. He would be forever reaching for things he was not born to possess and would never be able to have.

"George Taylor was the epitome of everything a gentleman should be," Lady Bellemont remarked in an effort to explain the situation. "Intelligent, handsome and born to an exceptional family. He was one of three sons born to the late Viscount Taylor."

"Taylor," he repeated, not especially familiar with the name.

"Their breeding and bloodlines are remarkable. George had the looks of the family, and more charm than should be allotted to one man. I believe every woman who met him fell a little bit in love with him . . . but he adored his wife, and made no secret of it. They had an extraordinary marriage, one that could never be equaled. It has been confided in me by one of the Taylors that Holly will surely never marry again, as any future relationship would be inferior to what she once had with George."

"Holly," he repeated softly.

"A pet name used by family and very close friends." Lady Bellemont frowned a little, troubled by his apparent interest in Lady Holland. "My dear, I can assure you that there are many charming and *attainable* ladies present here tonight. Let me introduce you to a few who would be thrilled to receive your attention—"

"Tell me everything you know about Lady Holland," he said, staring at her intently.

Lady Bellemont made a face and sighed. "Very well. Tomorrow you may come to tea and we'll discuss—"

"Now."

"In the middle of a ball that I am giving? There is a time and a place for—" She broke off and laughed as she found herself being pulled unceremoniously to a nearby settee. "My dear, I find your masculine qualities quite charming, but it is possible to be a bit *too* masterful—"

"Everything," he repeated, and flashed her a crooked grin of such roguish appeal that she felt her heart give an extra beat. "Please."

And suddenly Lady Bellemont felt there was nothing she would rather do than spend the rest of the evening ignoring her social responsibilities and telling him anything and everything he wished to know.

Holly crossed the threshold of the Taylor family mansion like a rabbit retreating to the safety of its burrow. Although the Taylors did not possess the abundance of funds necessary to keep the house perfectly maintained, Holly loved every elegant, gently worn inch of the place. The faded tapestries and frayed Aubusson carpets were comfortingly familiar. Sleeping under the ancient roof gave one the feeling of resting in a beloved grandparent's arms.

This dignified house fronted with pediments and columns and rows of small, neat windows was where George had lived as a child. It was easy to imagine the boisterous boy he must have been, running up and down the central staircase, playing on the gently sloped lawns outside, sleeping in the same nursery where Holly's own daughter Rose now rested.

Holly was glad that the townhouse where she and George had lived during their short, lovely marriage had been sold. That place contained the happiest and the most agonizing memories of her life. She would rather stay here, where her grief was dulled by pleasant images of George in his childhood. There were paintings of him as a boy, places where he had carved his name in the woodwork, trunks of toys and dusty books that must have occupied him for hours. His family . . . his mother, his two brothers and their wives, not to mention the servants that had attended George since infancy, were nothing but kind and loving. All the affection that had once been lavished on George, the favorite of the family, was now given to her and Rose. She could easily see spending the rest of her life here, in the mellow world the Taylors provided.

It was only at odd moments that Holly felt constrained by this perfect seclusion. There were times when she sat with her needlework and found herself drifting into strange, wild fantasies that she couldn't seem to control. There were also moments when she felt some irrepressible emotion that she had no means to release . . . she wanted to do something scandalous, scream in church, go somewhere in a shocking red dress and dance . . . or kiss a stranger.

"Dear Lord," Holly whispered aloud, realizing that there was something wicked inside her, something that must be battened down and tightly secured. It was a physical problem, the need of a woman for a man, the dilemma that every widow faced when there was no longer a husband to visit her bed. She had loved George's caresses, and she had always anticipated the nights when he would come to her room and stay until morning. For the past three years, she had fought the unspeakable need she felt since his death. She confided her problem to no one, as she was well aware of society's view on female desire. That it should not exist at all. Women must live as an example to men and use their virtue to tame a husband's base instincts. They must submit to their husbands, but never encourage a man's passion, and they certainly must not display any sign of physical desire themselves.

"Milady! How was the ball? Did ye enjoy yerself? Did ye dance? Were there people ye remembered from before?"

"Fine, yes, no, and many," Holly replied, forcing herself to smile as her servant, Maude, appeared at the threshold of her two-room suite and welcomed her inside. Maude was the only maidservant that Holly had been able to retain after George's death. The others had either been absorbed into the Taylor household, or dismissed with good references and as much severance pay as Holly had been able to spare. Maude was an attractive, buxom woman in her early thirties, possessed of boundless energy and unfailing high spirits. Even her hair was exuberant, with blond curls springing insistently out of the tight coils she pinned it in. She worked hard each day, primarily serving as a nanny to Rose, and also functioning as lady's maid to Holly when necessary.

"Tell me how Rose is," Holly said, heading to the small fire on the grate and extending her hands toward its inviting warmth. "Did she go to sleep easily?"

Maude laughed ruefully. "I'm sorry to say she didn't. She was chattering like a little bird about the ball, and how pretty ye look in yer blue gown." She took Holly's pelisse and folded it neatly over her arm. "Although, if ye ask me, yer new gowns still look like mourning—they're all so frightfully dark. I wish ye'd had one made in yellow or that pretty light green all the fine ladies are wearing—"

"I've been wearing black and gray for three years," Holly interrupted wryly, standing still as the maid began on the back buttons of her dark blue gown. "I can't suddenly burst into a rainbow of colors, Maude. One has to ease into these things slowly."

"Ye're still mourning fer the poor master, milady." The constricting gown eased from Holly's shoulders. "I think part of ye still wants to show it to the world, 'specially to any gentlemen that might wish to court ye."

Holly's cheeks immediately took on a glow that had nothing to do with the fire's heat. Thankfully Maude was behind her and did not notice the gathering blush. Uncomfortably Holly reflected that there was at least *one* man she had made no effort to keep at bay. In fact, she had all but encouraged the rogue to kiss her a second time. Even now, the memory of his mouth on hers was still vivid. He had turned an ordinary evening into something dark, sweet and strange. He had seized her boldly and yet he had been so . . . tender. Ever since the moment she had left him, she had not been able to stop wondering who he was and what he looked like. It was possible she might meet him again and never realize he was the stranger that had kissed her.

But she would know his voice. Closing her eyes, she remembered the low masculine whisper, curling around her like smoke: *Sweet lady . . . tell me why a kiss makes you cry.* She swayed slightly, and was recalled to reality as Maude spoke in concern.

"Ye must be tired, milady. 'Twas yer first ball since the master passed on. . . . Is that why ye came home early?"

"Actually, I left because one of my megrims had started, and—" Holly broke off, puzzled, and rubbed her temples absently. "How strange," she murmured. "It's gone. Once they start, there's usually no stopping them."

"Shall I bring the tonic the doctor gave ye, in case it comes back?"

Holly shook her head, stepping out of the circle of her dress. "No, thank you," she replied, still bewildered. It

seemed that the episode in the conservatory had chased
away any hint of a headache. What a strange antidote for
the megrims, she thought ruefully. "I don't believe I'll
have further problems tonight."

With Maude's help, she changed into a white cambric
night rail and a lace-trimmed pelisse that buttoned up the
front. After tucking her feet into a pair of worn slippers,
Holly bade the maid good night and headed up the narrow
stairs leading to the nursery. The light from the candle she
carried sent a flickering glow over the narrow rectangular
room.

A child-sized chair covered in rose velvet and trimmed
with silk fringe occupied one corner, next to a miniature
tea table bearing a chipped and much-used toy tea service.
A collection of old perfume bottles filled with colored water were carefully arranged on the lower shelves of the
bookcase. At least a half-dozen dolls were scattered
throughout the nursery. One doll was seated on the chair,
and another perched on a battered rocking horse that had
once belonged to George. And another was clasped in
Rose's arms as she lay sleeping.

Holly smiled as she approached the bed, feeling a rush
of love as she watched her child in slumber. Rose's little
face was innocent and peaceful. The little girl's dark lashes
rested on the sweet roundness of her cheeks, and her mouth
hung slightly open. Kneeling by the bed, Holly touched
one of her daughter's hands, smiling at the faded splotches
of blue and green that had lingered despite vigorous wash-
ings. Rose loved to paint and draw, and her hands were
forever stained with pigment. At four years of age, the
child's hands still retained a trace of dimpled baby-
plumpness.

"Precious hands," Holly whispered, and pressed a kiss
to the back of one. Standing, she continued to stare at her

daughter. When the child was born, everyone, including Holly, had thought she resembled the Taylors. However, Rose had turned out to be a nearly identical replica of herself, small, dark-haired and brown-eyed. She favored George in character, possessing the same innate charm and intelligence.

If only you could see her now, my darling, Holly thought longingly.

In the year after their daughter's birth, the last twelve months of George's life, Holly and George had often watched their daughter sleeping. Most men would not have displayed such keen interest in their own children, considering it unmanly. Children were part of the feminine world, and a man had little to do with them, other than to occasionally ask about their progress or dandle them on his knee for a minute or two. However, George had been openly fascinated by his daughter, enchanted by her, and had cuddled and played with her in a way that had delighted Holly. His pride in Rose had known no limits.

"We're linked forever in this child," George had said one evening, as he and Holly stood over their infant in her lace-trimmed cradle. "We made her together, Holly . . . such a natural, simple thing for two people to have a baby . . . but it almost defies my comprehension." Too moved for words, Holly had kissed him, loving him for regarding Rose as the miracle that she was.

"What a father you would have had, Rose," she whispered. It grieved her to know that her daughter would grow up without the security and protection a father would have provided. . . . But no man could ever replace George.

Two

Zachary Bronson needed a wife. He had observed the kind of ladies that men of wealth and social position were wedded to—composed, quiet-voiced women who managed a household and every detail of a man's life. The servants of a well-run household seemed to work together like the mechanism of a clock . . . completely *un*like his own. Sometimes his servants seemed to get things right, whereas at other times they made his life into a farce. Meals were often late, linens and silver and furniture were never spotless as they were in other wealthy households, while supplies were either overly abundant or nonexistent.

Zachary had hired a succession of housekeepers until he had realized that even the best ones still needed the overall direction provided by a lady of the house. And God knew his mother hadn't the slightest notion of how to give orders to a servant, other than to timidly ask a maid for a cup of tea or for assistance in dressing.

"They're servants, Mother," Zachary had told her patiently, at least a hundred times. "They *expect* you to ask for things. They *want* you to. They wouldn't have jobs otherwise. Now, stop looking so damned apologetic when you need something, and ring the bellpull with some authority."

But his mother only laughed and stammered, and protested that she hated to put someone to any bother, even if they were paid for it. No, his mother was never going to improve in this area—she had lived in humble circumstances for too long to be any good at managing servants.

Part of the problem was that his servants, like his money, were all new. Other men of means had inherited a household of experienced servants that had lived and worked together for years, even decades. Zachary had been forced out of necessity to hire his all at once. A few were rank newcomers to the profession, but most were servants who had been dismissed from their previous positions for various reasons. In other words, he was now the employer of the greatest accumulation of alcoholics, unwed mothers, bunglers and petty thieves in west London.

Friends had advised that the right sort of wife could do wonders with his household management problem, leaving him free to do what he did best—make money. For the first time in his life, Zachary found the idea of marriage to be sensible and even appealing. However, he had to find the right sort of woman and convince her to accept his suit, and this was hardly a simple task. He had specific requirements for any woman he would consider taking to wife.

For one thing, she must be blue-blooded, if he was ever to gain access to the high social circles he aspired to. In fact, considering his own lack of breeding and education, she had better compensate by having bloodlines that dated back to William the Conqueror. However, she must not condescend to him—he would not have a wife that looked down her aristocratic nose at him. She must also be independent, so that she would not mind his frequent absences. He was a busy man, and the last thing he needed was someone else tugging at him and trying to usurp what little spare time he still possessed.

Beauty was not required. In fact, he did not want a wife so lovely that other men would be staring and drooling and forever trying to seduce her. Moderate attractiveness would suit him perfectly. Good mental and physical health was imperative, as he wanted her to bear strong, intelligent children. Social skills were also important, as she would have to serve as his wedge into a society that was obviously reluctant to accept him.

Zachary was well aware that many aristocrats secretly mocked him for his low birth and his rapidly built fortune, claiming that his mind was bourgeois and mercantile, that he had no understanding of style, elegance and good breeding. They were correct in this assessment. He knew his limitations. However, he took a grim satisfaction in the fact that no one could afford to mock him openly. He had made himself into a force to be reckoned with. He had sunk his financial tentacles into banks, businesses, real estate, investment trusts . . . it was likely that he had some kind of monetary affiliation, whether large or small, with every man of means in England.

The nobility would not want him to marry one of their precious daughters. Marriage to an aristocrat meant the alignment of one great family with another, the mixing of blue blood with blue. One did not breed a splendidly pedigreed animal with a mongrel. Except that this particular mongrel had enough money to purchase whatever he wanted—even a highborn bride.

Toward this end, he had arranged for a meeting with Lady Holland Taylor. If his invitation proved alluring enough, she would be coming for tea. Zachary had calculated that it would take one day for the elusive widow to consider the idea, a second day for friends and family to talk her out of it, and the third for her curiosity to get the better of her. To his satisfaction, she had accepted his invitation. He would see her today.

He walked to the front window of his library, the large room set on the northeast corner of his gothic mansion. The house was designed in a style his architect had called a "cottage orné," a term Zachary had come to believe meant pretentious and overpriced. However, it was much admired by the *ton,* or at least much remarked on, and it made the statement Zachary had intended—that he was a man of consequence, a man to be reckoned with. It was a massive wedding cake of a house loaded with spires, towers, arches, conservatories, and glittering French doors. The twenty-bedroom building lounged insolently on a huge sprawl of land west of London. Artificial lakes and lush groves of trees graced the landscape, not to mention gardens, parks, follies, and walks both serpentine and straight, depending on the visitors' taste.

He wondered what Lady Holly would think of the estate, if she would deem it heaven or horror. She probably had the good taste that most ladies of her station possessed, the kind of taste that he admired but could not seem to emulate. His own taste was for styles that would conspicuously display his success—he couldn't help it.

The chiming of the long-case clock in the hall alerted him to the time, and he stared through the window at the long circular drive at the front of his home. "Lady Holly," he said softly, filled with biting anticipation, "I'm waiting for you."

In spite of the Taylors' collective objections, Holly had decided to accept Mr. Zachary Bronson's unexpected invitation to tea. She had not been able to resist. Since the night of the Bellemont ball, life had returned to its usual serene pace, but the rituals of life in the Taylor household had somehow lost their comforting magic. She was tired of needlework and letter writing and all the genteel pursuits that had occupied her for the past three years. Ever since those stolen kisses in the Bellemonts' conservatory, she had felt terribly restless. She wanted something to happen, to alter the predictable flow of her life.

Then had come Mr. Zachary Bronson's letter, with an opening sentence that had instantly fascinated her:

Although I have never had the honor of making your acquaintance, I find that I have need of your assistance in a matter that concerns my household. . . .

How could a man like the notorious Mr. Bronson possibly need *her* help?

All of the Taylors considered it an ill-advised decision to meet him. They had pointed out that many ladies of consequence did not condescend to accept introductions to him. Even an innocuous tea might cause a scandal.

"A scandal? From a simple afternoon tea?" Holly had responded skeptically, and George's eldest brother, William, had explained.

"Mr. Bronson is not an ordinary man, my dear. He is a social climber—nouveau—he is vulgar in breeding and manner. There are rumors about him that have shocked and appalled *me,* and as you know, I am a worldly man. No good could come of your association with him. Please, Holly, don't expose yourself to harm or insult. Send a refusal to Bronson at once."

In the face of William's certainty, Holly had considered rejecting Mr. Bronson's invitation. However, her curiosity was overwhelming. And the thought of remaining enshrouded in safety while one of England's most powerful men had asked to meet her . . . well, she just had to find out why. "I believe I shall be able to withstand his corruptive influence for at least an hour or two," she said lightly. "And if I find his behavior objectionable, I will simply leave."

William's blue eyes—the same shape and color her husband's had been—flashed with disapproval. "George would never have wanted you to be exposed to such a nefarious character."

The simple statement devastated her. Holly lowered her head, while emotion tugged at the tiny muscles of her face. She had sworn to live the rest of her life as her husband had wished. George had protected her from everything that wasn't seemly and good, and she had trusted his judgment in all things. "But George is gone," she whispered, and glanced up at William's set face with tear-filled eyes. "I must learn to rely on my own judgment now."

"And if your judgment proves to be faulty," he retorted, "I am obligated by the memory of my brother to intercede."

Holly smiled faintly, reflecting that ever since the day she had been born, there had been someone to protect and guide her. First her loving parents, then George . . . and now George's family. "Allow me to make a few mistakes, William," she said. "I must learn to make decisions now, for Rose's sake as well as my own."

"Holly . . ." His tone was threaded with mild exasperation. "What could you possibly gain from visiting a man like Zachary Bronson?"

Anticipation curled inside her, making her realize how badly she needed to escape the blanketing security of the Taylor household. "Well," she said, "I expect to find out soon."

*   *   *

The information that the Taylors had managed to glean about Mr. Bronson had clearly not eased their minds as to the lack of wisdom Holly displayed in agreeing to meet him. Friends and acquaintances had been eager to share what little knowledge they had about the elusive newcomer to London society. Zachary Bronson was called a merchant prince in many circles, and this term was not intended as flattery. He was outrageously, incomprehensibly rich, and he displayed nearly as much vulgarity as wealth.

Eccentric, interested not in money but in the power it brought, Bronson happily outwitted and destroyed competitors in the manner of a lion set among the Christians. He did not conduct business as a gentleman, accepting all the usual unspoken understandings and limitations. If one did not spell out every letter of an agreement, it was reported, Bronson would take ruthless advantage. Gentlemen were reluctant to enter into business with him, and yet they were compelled to by the hopes that they might receive a mere fraction of the tremendous profits that flowed his way.

Bronson had started as a pugilist, someone said. A common street fighter. And then he had eventually gotten himself hired as the captain of a steamship and acquired increasing numbers of routes. His toughness and shrewd manipulations had either bankrupted his competitors or caused them to merge with him.

Bronson's budding fortune had exploded when he began selling stock to the public at inflated prices, and he had turned to real estate. Since there had been little available land to purchase in England, he had bought thousands of acres of farmland in America and India. The size of his farms dwarfed the acreage that had been in British aristocrats' possession for centuries, and the massive quantity of goods he produced and imported had multiplied his fortune yet again. Now Bronson had invested in the development of a locomotive railroad in Durham, upon which a steam carriage was reputedly able to pull loaded wagons at the rate of twelve miles an hour. Although everyone knew that steam power would never replace horses for general transportation purposes, the experiment was eagerly followed because of Mr. Bronson's patronage.

"Bronson is dangerous," said Lord Avery, an elderly friend of the Taylors' who had been invited to supper. Avery sat on the boards of several banks and insurance companies. "Every day I see the wealth of England being transferred from fine families and gentlemen farmers to opportunists like Bronson. If he is allowed to mingle with us, become one of us, merely because he has amassed a fortune . . . well, it will be nothing less than the end of first society as we know it."

"But should not achievement be rewarded?" Holly had asked hesitantly, knowing that a respectable woman must never enter into political or financial discussions. However, she was unable to resist. "Should we not recognize Mr. Bronson's accomplishment by welcoming him into our society?"

"He is not fit for our society, my dear," Avery responded emphatically. "The nobility is the product of generations of breeding, education and refinement. One cannot *buy* a place in first society, which is exactly what Mr. Bronson is attempting to do. He has no honor, no good blood and, from what I understand, the bare minimum of education. I liken Bronson to a trained monkey—he has but one trick, and that is the knack for playing with numbers until he somehow ends up multiplying a small amount into a great one."

The other guests and the Taylors nodded at the explanation.

"I see," Holly murmured, and applied her attention to the food on her plate, while thinking to herself that there had been a trace of envy in Lord Avery's tone. Mr. Bronson might have just one trick—but what a trick it was! Every well-bred man at the table would have loved to possess Bronson's Midas-like abilities. And the disparaging talk about him did not accomplish the purpose of deterring her from meeting Mr. Bronson. In fact, it made her all the more curious.

Three

Holly had never seen anything like Zachary Bronson's London estate, the opulence of which might have made a Medici envious. The entrance hall, lavishly paved with Rouge Royal marble and lined with shimmering gold-covered columns and priceless tapestries, rose two floors in height. Massive crystal chandeliers hung from the silver-and-gold-coffered ceiling, illuminating an astonishing amount of Roman statuary. Huge malachite vases stuffed with palms and luxuriant ferns framed each of the four exits leading from the central hall.

A surprisingly youthful butler led Holly through the hall toward the library suite. "Suite?" Holly had repeated, perplexed, and the butler explained that Mr. Bronson's private collection of books, manuscripts, antique folios and maps was too large to be contained in just one room. Holly repressed the urge to turn circles as she stared at her surroundings. Both sides of the hallway had been covered in blue silk, to which hundreds of glittering glass butterflies had been affixed. The entrance door to the library was flanked by a pair of paintings—Rembrandts—each of which was finer than the grandest works of art the Taylors possessed.

Having been brought up to consider that simple surroundings offered the most relaxation and repose, Holly thought the place was in horrendously bad taste. But it was so spectacular in its sheer excess that it brought a wondering smile to her face. Recalling that Bronson had reputedly begun his career as a prizefighter, she felt an admiration that bordered on awe, that one man could achieve so much.

The butler led her to a room that was flooded with light from the intricate leaded-glass ceiling. The walls were covered in green velvet and a great quantity of triple-hung paintings that appeared to be portraits of venerable ancestors. Rows and rows of glass-fronted bookshelves contained intriguing collections of volumes. How tempting it was to take a book and recline on one of the luxuriously overstuffed leather chairs, and lean back against one of the plush rug-covered pillows. Passing a glossy brown globe that must have measured six feet in diameter, Holly paused and touched it tentatively.

"I've never seen a library as magnificent as this," she said.

Although the butler struggled to look impassive, his expression contained a mixture of amusement and pride. "This is merely the library *entrance,* my lady. The main room is just ahead."

Holly accompanied him to the next room, and stopped at the threshold with a slight gasp. The library looked like something from a palace, too spectacular to belong to one family. "How many books does it hold?" she asked.

"Nearly twenty thousand volumes, I believe."

"Mr. Bronson must love to read."

"Oh, no, my lady, the master hardly ever reads. But he is quite fond of books."

Suppressing a laugh at the incongruous statement, Holly wandered farther into the library. The main room soared upward three stories in height, to a ceiling elaborately frescoed with angels and heavenly scenes. The shining parqueted floor beneath her feet emanated a fresh scent of beeswax that mingled pleasantly with the smells of book leather and vellum, underlaid with the faint pungent trace of tobacco. A roaring fire burned in a carved green marble fireplace that one could have parked a carriage in. At the far end of the room, there was a mahogany desk so massive that it must have required the combined strength of a dozen men to move it. The man who was seated behind it rose to his feet as the butler announced Holly's name.

Although she had met nobility and even royalty with perfect confidence, Holly felt a little nervous now. Perhaps it was because of Mr. Bronson's reputation, or the splendor of her current surroundings, but she was actually a bit breathless as he approached her. She was glad she had worn her nicest day gown, a coffee-colored Italian silk, its high neck trimmed with vanilla lace, its full sleeves gathered at the elbows with bands of fabric.

Why, he's young, Holly thought in surprise, having expected a man in his forties or fifties. However, Zachary Bronson could not be older than thirty. Despite his elegant clothes—black coat and dark gray trousers—he reminded her of a tomcat, tall and large-boned, lacking the polish of aristocrats she was accustomed to. The spill of thick black hair over his forehead should have been slicked back with pomade, and the knot of his cravat was too loose, as if he had been tugging at it unconsciously.

Bronson was handsome, although his features were blunted and his nose looked as though it had once been broken. He had a strong jaw, a wide mouth and laugh lines at the corners of his eyes that betrayed a ready sense of humor. She received a strange shock of awareness as she met his gaze. His eyes were a shade of brown so deep they

appeared black, giving his alert stare a penetrating quality
that made her distinctly uncomfortable. The devil must
have eyes like that, audacious, knowing . . . sensuous.

"Welcome, Lady Holland. I didn't think you would
come."

The sound of his voice caused Holly to stumble a little.
When she recovered her balance, she froze in place and
stared at the carpeted floor. The room seemed to spin
around her, and she concentrated hard on retaining her
balance when her entire body was shaken by panic and
confusion. She knew that voice, would have known it anywhere. He was her stranger, the man who had spoken to
her so tenderly and kissed her with an intimacy that had
left an indelible brand on her memory. The hot blood of
shame flooded her face, and it seemed impossible to look
back up at him. But the silence compelled her to say something.

"I was very nearly dissuaded," she whispered. Oh, if she
had only listened to George's family and stayed behind the
safe walls of the Taylor estate!

"May I ask what made you decide in my favor?" His
tone was so polite, so bland, that she glanced upward in
surprise. The dark eyes were reassuringly devoid of mockery.

He didn't recognize her, she thought with sudden wild
hope and relief. He didn't know that she was the woman
he had kissed at the Bellemont ball. Licking her dry lips,
she made an attempt at normal conversation. "I . . . don't
really know," she said. "Curiosity, I suppose."

That elicited a quick grin. "That's as good a reason as
any." He took her hand in a welcoming grip, his long
fingers engulfing hers completely. The warmth of his palm
sank through the delicate weave of her glove. Holly nearly
swayed at a sudden flash of memory . . . how hot his skin

had been the evening of the Bellemont ball, how hard and warm his mouth had been as he had kissed her—

She withdrew her hand with a sound of discomfort.

"Shall we have a seat?" Bronson gestured to a pair of Louis XIV armchairs arranged beside a marble-topped tea table.

"Yes, thank you." Holly was grateful at the prospect of occupying a chair instead of relying on the uncertain support of her own legs.

After she was seated, Bronson occupied the chair opposite hers. He sat with both feet on the floor, muscular thighs spread apart as he leaned slightly forward. "Tea, Hodges," he muttered to the butler, then returned his attention to Holly and gave her a disarming grin. "I hope it will be acceptable to you, my lady. Taking refreshments at my home is a bit like playing roulette."

"Roulette?" Holly frowned quizzically at the unfamiliar term.

"A gamble," he explained. "On a good day, my cook is unsurpassed. On a bad one . . . well, you could break a tooth on one of her biscuits."

Holly laughed suddenly, losing some of her nervousness at the disclosure that Bronson had household complaints just as ordinary men did.

"Surely with a little management—" she began, then stopped suddenly as she realized she had been about to give him unasked-for advice.

"There is no real management in my household, my lady. We all muddle along without direction, but that is something I want to discuss with you later."

Was that why he had summoned her to his estate? To receive her thoughts on the smooth running of a household? Of course not. He must suspect she was the woman he had encountered at the Bellemont ball. He was toying with her, perhaps. He would ask her a few sly questions to see if she would rise to the bait.

If so, the best defense was to bring everything out into the open right now. She would simply explain that he had surprised her that evening, that she had behaved completely unlike herself because he had caught her off guard.

"Mr. Bronson," she said, having to drag each word from her clenched throat, "there is something I sh-should tell you . . ."

"Yes?" He stared at her with keen black eyes.

Suddenly Holly found it impossible to believe that she had kissed this large masculine creature, that she had embraced him and caressed the shaven bristle of his jaw . . . that he had kissed the tears from her cheeks. In the few stolen moments they had met, she had shared more intimacy with him than she ever had with any man except George.

"Y-you . . ." Her heart slammed repeatedly against her ribs. Damning herself for a coward, Holly abandoned the attempt at confession. "You have a very beautiful home."

He smiled slightly. "I thought it might not be to your taste."

"It isn't, exactly. But it serves its purpose magnificently."

"And what purpose is that?"

"Why, to announce to everyone that you have arrived."

"That's right." He gave her an arrested stare. "A few days ago some pompous baron called me an 'arriviste.' I didn't realize what it meant until just now."

"Yes," Holly said with a gentle smile. "You're a recent arrival to society."

"It wasn't a compliment," he said dryly.

Guessing that he must have received hundreds of subtle set-downs from the peers he had encountered so far, Holly

felt a touch of sympathy. It was hardly Bronson's fault
that he had come from less-than-stellar beginnings. However, the English aristocracy felt as a whole that a man
should never "rise above his buttons." People in the serving class, or the working class, could never elevate themselves to the upper levels of society, no matter how great
their fortunes might be. And yet Holly rather thought that
achievement alone should be enough to make a man like
this acceptable to "first society." She wondered if George
would have agreed with her, or what he would have
thought about this man. She truly had no idea.

"In my opinion your accomplishments are worthy of admiration, Mr. Bronson," she said. "Most of English nobility are merely retaining wealth that was granted to their
families by ancient kings as a reward for service. You have
made your own wealth, and that requires great intelligence
and will. Although the baron was not paying you a compliment by calling you an arriviste, it should have been
one."

He stared at her for an unaccountably long moment.
"Thank you," he finally muttered.

To Holly's surprise, her words had caused a tide of color
to creep up from Bronson's collar. She guessed that he
was not accustomed to such direct praise. She hoped he
would not think she was trying to flatter him for some
reason. "Mr. Bronson, I was not being unctuous just now,"
she said.

A smile tugged at the left side of his mouth. "I'm sure
you would never be unctuous . . . whatever that means."

Two maids arrived bearing huge silver trays, and they
busied themselves with arranging the tea table. The stout
maid, who set out little plates of sandwiches, toast and
biscuits, seemed nervous and was inclined to giggle as she
performed her task. The smaller one fumbled with the sil-

verware and napkins and deposited the cups and saucers on the wrong side of the place setting. They struggled to set the kettle properly over a small flame, nearly overturning it. Secretly pained by the inept service when the girls clearly required a few words of direction, Holly made her face into a polite mask.

She was surprised by the maids' obvious lack of training. A man of Mr. Bronson's position should have the very best of service. A well-trained servant was quiet and efficient, making himself or herself part of the scenery. In Holly's experience, a housemaid would certainly never draw attention to herself and would rather be shot than giggle in front of a guest.

When at last the preparations were made and the maids had left, Holly began to unbutton the wrists of her little gray gloves and tug them neatly from her fingertips. She paused as she felt Mr. Bronson's intent gaze on her, and looked up with an inquiring smile. "Shall I?" she asked, gesturing toward the tea service, and he nodded, his attention immediately returning to her hands.

There was something in Bronson's eyes, some disquieting glow that made Holly feel as if she were unbuttoning her blouse instead of simply removing her gloves. It was an ordinary thing to bare one's hands before a gentleman, and yet the way he stared at her made the task seem strangely intimate.

She rinsed the Sevres teapot with boiling water to warm it, then poured the liquid into a china bowl. Expertly she measured and spooned the fragrant tea leaves into the teapot and added hot water. While the tea steeped, Holly arranged a selection of sandwiches and biscuits on the plates and made idle conversation. Bronson seemed content to follow her lead.

"You have filled your library with a lovely collection of portraits, Mr. Bronson."

"Other peoples' ancestors," he replied dryly. "Mine weren't the kind to sit for paintings."

Holly had heard of other men with newly made fortunes doing the same thing—hanging portraits of strangers in their homes to give the impression of an illustrious family lineage. However, Zachary Bronson was the first man in her experience who had openly admitted to it.

She handed him a small plate and napkin. "Do you reside here alone?"

"No, my mother and younger sister Elizabeth also live here."

Holly's interest was piqued. "I don't believe anyone has mentioned before that you have a sister."

Bronson seemed to answer with great care. "I've been waiting for the right time to bring Elizabeth out in society. I'm afraid—circumstances being what they are—things might be difficult for her. She hasn't been taught how to . . ." He paused, clearly searching for a word to describe the intricate knowledge a young woman was expected to have of manners and social skills.

"I see." Holly nodded in immediate understanding, her brows knitting together. Difficult indeed, for a girl who had not been rigorously trained in such matters. Society could be merciless. On top of that, the Bronson family was undistinguished in every area but money, and the last thing they needed was a plague of fortune hunters to descend on Elizabeth. "Have you considered sending her to finishing school, Mr. Bronson? If you like, I could recommend one—"

"She's twenty-one," he said flatly. "She would be older than all the other girls—she informs me that she would 'rather die' than attend one. She wants to live at home."

"Of course." Deftly Holly poured the tea through a small silver strainer with a bird-shaped handle. "Do you prefer your tea strong, Mr. Bronson, or shall I add a splash of water?"

"Strong, please."

"One lump or two?" she asked with a pair of delicate tongs hovering over the sugar bowl.

"Three. And no milk."

For some reason Holly felt an irresistible smile come to her face. "You have a sweet tooth, Mr. Bronson."

"Is there something wrong with that?"

"Not at all," Holly replied softly. "I was just thinking that you would enjoy one of my daughter's tea parties. For Rose, three lumps is the absolute minimum."

"Maybe I'll ask Rose to pour for me one day, then."

Holly wasn't certain what he meant by that, but the intimacy it implied, the promise of familiarity, made her uneasy. Tearing her gaze from his, she returned her attention to the tea. Having prepared a cup for Bronson, she set about finishing her own, adding a touch of sugar and a generous splash of milk.

"My mother pours the milk in first," Bronson remarked, watching her.

"Perhaps you might suggest to her that it is easier to judge the tea by its color when the milk is added last," Holly murmured. "The nobility tends to disparage people who pour the milk in first, as it is usually done by nannies and servants and . . ."

"People of my class," he said wryly.

"Yes." Holly forced herself to meet his gaze. "There is a saying among the peerage when a woman hasn't sufficient breeding . . . they say she is rather a 'milk-in-first' sort."

It was presumptuous of her to offer such advice, no

matter how helpfully intended, and some would have taken offense. However, Bronson accepted it comfortably. "I'll tell my mother," he said. "Thank you."

Relaxing a little, Holly reached for a biscuit. It was delicate, sweet and slightly spongy, a perfect accompaniment to the crisp tea. "The cook is having a good day," she pronounced after swallowing a bite.

Bronson laughed, the sound quiet and deep, utterly attractive. "Thank God," he said.

The conversation was easy and companionable after that, although it was strange to Holly, being alone with a man who was neither a relative nor a long-held acquaintance. Any trace of self-consciousness was soon submerged by her fascination with Zachary Bronson. He was an extraordinary man, with an ambition and drive that made all other men she had known seem like weak, passive creatures.

She sipped her tea as she listened to him describe the latest experiments with the steam carriage, or locomotive, in Durham. He talked about feed pumps injecting hot water into boilers, and the steam blasts that were channeled through the smokestack at the top of the vehicle, and various attempts to improve the draft in the furnace to increase power. Someday soon, he claimed, the locomotive would be used not only to carry freight, but livestock and even human passengers, and rail lines would cross through every town of importance in England. Holly was skeptical but fascinated. It was the kind of subject that a gentleman rarely discussed with a lady, as ladies were thought to be far more interested in matters of family, society and religion. But it was refreshing to hear something other than society gossip, and Bronson managed to explain the technical subjects in a way that Holly could easily understand.

Zachary Bronson came from a world so different from

her own, a world of businessmen, inventors, entrepreneurs
. . . It was so clear that he would never fit comfortably into
a stodgy aristocracy steeped in centuries of tradition. However, it was also clear that he was determined to make a
place for himself in first society, and heaven help anyone
who tried to deter him.

It must be exhausting to live with him, Holly mused,
wondering how his mother and sister dealt with his relentless energy. He had such an active brain and so many
interests, and his obvious appetite for life amazed her. One
wondered if he ever made time to sleep. She couldn't help
comparing him to George, who had loved long, lazy walks,
and reading quietly with her beside the hearth on rainy
afternoons, and lounging with her in the mornings to watch
their baby play. She couldn't imagine Zachary Bronson
ever sitting still to watch something as mundane as a child
learning to crawl.

Somehow the conversation was gently steered into more
personal matters, and Holly found herself describing her
life with George's family, and the facts of her widowhood.
Usually when she discussed George with someone who
had known him, her throat became tight and her eyes
misted with tears. However, Bronson had no knowledge
of George, and for some reason it was much easier for
Holly to discuss her husband with a stranger.

"George was never sick," she said. "He never had fevers
or headaches—he was always fit and healthy. But then one
day he began to complain of fatigue, and pains in his
joints, and he was unable to eat. The doctor diagnosed it
as typhoid fever, which I knew was exceedingly dangerous, but many people live through it. I convinced myself
that with good nursing and a great deal of rest, George
would recover." She stared at the empty cup in her saucer
and traced her finger around the delicate gilded edge. "Day

by day he shrank before my eyes. The fever turned to delirium. In two weeks he was gone."

"I'm sorry," Bronson said quietly.

I'm sorry was something people always said. There really wasn't anything else to say. But there was a gleam of warmth in Bronson's black eyes that conveyed genuine sympathy, and she felt that he truly understood the magnitude of her loss.

A long silence extended between them, until Bronson spoke again. "Do you like living with the Taylor family, my lady?"

She smiled faintly. "It's not really a matter of like or dislike. It is the only choice available to me."

"What of your own family?"

"My parents are still supporting three remaining daughters and trying to find good matches for them. I did not want to add to their burden by returning home with my child. And in abiding with the Taylors, I feel somewhat closer to George."

Bronson's wide mouth tightened at the last sentence. Glancing at her empty cup and plate, he stood and extended a hand to her. "Come walk with me."

Startled by his abruptness, Holly obeyed automatically, taking his proffered hand. Her fingers tingled at the warm shock of his touch, and her breath caught in her throat. Pulling her upward, Bronson tucked her hand in the crook of his arm and escorted her away from the tea table. He had touched her far too familiarly—not even George's brothers would dare to reach for her bare hand. But it seemed that Mr. Bronson did not know better.

As they walked, Bronson had to adjust his long strides to match her short ones, and she suspected that he seldom walked at this slow a pace. He was not the kind of man to meander.

The library suite opened to a huge private art gallery, sided by long windows that displayed a view of the formal gardens outside. The gallery was filled with a stunning collection of Old Masters. There were works by Titian, Rembrandt, Vermeer and Botticelli, all striking in their rich color and romanticism. "What, nothing by Leonardo da Vinci?" Holly asked lightly, knowing that Bronson's private collection was undoubtedly the most impressive in England.

Bronson gazed at the rows of paintings and frowned as if the lack of a da Vinci were a glaring omission. "Should I buy one?"

"No, no, I was only jesting," Holly said hastily. "Really, Mr. Bronson, your collection is magnificent, and more than complete. Besides, a da Vinci would be impossible to acquire."

Making a noncommittal sound in his throat, Bronson focused on a bare place on the wall, clearly considering how much it would take to put a da Vinci there.

Holly slipped her hand from the crook of his arm and turned to face him. "Mr. Bronson . . . won't you tell me why you've invited me here today?"

Bronson wandered to a marble bust mounted on a pedestal, and rubbed a bit of dust from it with his thumb. He slid Holly an assessing sideways glance as she stood in a rectangle of sunlight from the tall window.

"You were described to me as the perfect lady," he said. "Now, having met you, I agree completely."

Holly's eyes widened, and she thought in a flurry of guilt and nervousness that he would never have made such a statement if he were aware that she was the woman who had wantonly responded to his kiss a few nights ago.

"You have an impeccable reputation," he continued, "you are received everywhere, and you have knowledge and influence that I need. Badly. So I would like to employ you as a sort of . . . social guide."

Stunned, Holly could only stare at him. It took a half-minute for her to find her voice. "Sir, I am not seeking employment of any kind."

"I know that."

"Then you will understand why I must refuse—"

He stopped her with a subtly restraining gesture. "Hear me out first."

Holly nodded for the sake of courtesy, although there was no possibility that she would accept his offer. There were times when a widow was forced to seek genteel employment out of financial necessity, but she was far from that state. George's family would never hear of it, and neither would her own. It was not the same as entering the working class, but it would most definitely alter her status in society. And to be employed by a man like Zachary Bronson, no matter how rich he was . . . the fact was, there were people and places that might no longer receive her.

"I need some polish," Bronson continued evenly. "I need introductions. No doubt you'll hear me referred to as a social climber, which I assuredly am. I've come damned far on my own, but I need help to get to the next rung. Your help. I also need someone to teach Elizabeth how to be . . . well, like you are. Teach her how to do the things that London ladies do. It's the only way for her to land a decent match."

"Mr. Bronson," Holly said carefully, staring hard at the marble bench beside him, "I am sincerely flattered. I wish I could help you. However, there are many others who would be much more suitable than I—"

"I don't want anyone else. I want you."

"I cannot, Mr. Bronson," she said firmly. "Among my many reservations, there is my daughter to consider. Taking care of Rose is the most important responsibility in the world to me."

"Yes, there is Rose to consider." Bronson slid his hands in his pockets, deceptively relaxed as he paced around the bench. "There's no delicate way to put this, Lady Holland, so I'm going to be blunt. What are your plans for your daughter's future? You'll want to send Rose to expensive schools . . . travel the continent . . . give her a dowry to attract titled suitors. But in your current circumstances, you won't be able to provide those things for her. With no dowry, she'll only be able to land a member of the lesser gentry—if that." He paused and added silkily, "If Rose had a large dowry, combined with her good bloodlines, she would someday land the kind of aristocratic husband that George would have wanted her to have."

Holly stared at him, stunned. Now she understood how Bronson had been able to conquer so many business opponents. He would stop at nothing to get his way—he was using her own daughter to convince her to do what he wanted. Zachary Bronson could be completely ruthless when it served his purpose.

"I estimate that I'll need your help for approximately a year," he said. "We could draw up a contract to our mutual satisfaction. If you dislike working for me—if you find that for any reason you want to end the arrangement—just say the word, and you can leave with half the amount I'm offering."

"And how much is that?" Holly heard herself ask, her mind buzzing with agitated thoughts. She was unbearably curious to know what he thought her services were worth.

"Ten thousand pounds. For one year's employment."

A sum at least a thousand times more than a governess made in a year. It was a fortune, enough for a generous dowry for her daughter, enough for a private house, including servants. The thought of having her own home made Holly nearly dizzy with longing. But the idea of involving herself closely with this man, and the reaction of her family and friends . . .

"No," she said quietly, nearly choking on the word. "I am sorry, Mr. Bronson. Your offer is very generous, but you must find someone else."

He did not seem at all surprised by her refusal. "Twenty thousand, then," he said, and flashed her a roguish smile. "Come, Lady Holland. Don't tell me you're planning to return to the Taylor family and spend the rest of your life as you've spent the last three years. You're an intelligent woman—you need more than needlework and gossip to sustain you."

Unerringly he had hit upon another vulnerable point. Life with the Taylors had indeed become monotonous, and the thought of no longer being dependent on them . . . on anyone . . . Holly twisted her hands together tightly.

Bronson rested his weight on one leg and braced his knee against the bench. "Just say yes, and I'll have the money placed in trust for Rose. She'll never want for anything. And when she marries a peer, I'll throw in a carriage and a team of four for her wedding present."

Accepting his offer would be a step into the unknown. If Holly said no, she knew exactly what kind of life she and Rose would have. A safe one, if not always comfortable. They would manage well enough, and they would bask in the love and approval of everyone they knew. If she said yes, there would be an uproar of surprise and condemnation. There would be ugly comments and rumors that would take years to die down, if ever. But what a future Rose would have! And there was something inside Holly, something reckless and wild, the same terrible im-

pulsiveness she had been struggling with ever since her
husband's death.

Abruptly she lost the struggle.

"I would do it for thirty thousand," she said, listening
to her own voice as if she somehow stood outside the
scene.

Although Bronson's expression did not change, she
sensed his tremendous satisfaction, like that of a lion settling down to enjoy his kill. "Thirty," he repeated, as if
the figure were outrageous. "I think twenty is sufficient for
what I'm asking, don't you?"

"Twenty for Rose, ten for me," Holly replied, her voice
growing steadier. "Social influence is like currency—once
expended, it is not easily regained. I may not have much
left after this year is through. If I accept your offer, the
ton will gossip and spread rumors about me. They may
even imply that I am your . . ."

"Mistress," he supplied softly. "But they would be
wrong, wouldn't they?"

She colored and continued in a rush. "No one in the *ton*
can distinguish rumor from fact. Therefore, the loss of my
respectability is worth an additional ten thousand pounds.
And I—I want you to invest it and manage it for me."

Bronson's dark brows raised slightly. "You want me to
manage your money?" he repeated, practically purring.
"And not Lord Taylor?"

Holly shook her head, thinking of William, who was
responsible but extremely conservative with investments.
Like most men of his station, William's talent was to con-
serve funds, not to multiply them. "I would prefer you to
take care of it," she said. "The only condition is that I
don't want you to make any investments that could be
considered immoral."

"I'll see what I can do," Bronson said gravely, laughter dancing in his devil-black eyes.

Holly took a deep breath. "Then you agree to thirty? And if I leave your employment early, I may retain half?"

"Agreed. However, in return for the extra money you're demanding, I'm going to ask for a concession."

"Oh?" she asked warily.

"I want you to live here. With me and my family."

Holly stared at him in amazement. "No. I couldn't."

"You and Rose will have your own suite of rooms, a carriage and horses provided for your exclusive use and the freedom to come and go as you choose. Bring your own servants, if you wish. I'll take care of their salaries for the next year."

"I don't see why it is necessary—"

"Teaching the Bronsons to behave like gentlefolk is going to require more than a few paltry hours a day. Once you get to know us, you'll have no doubt of it."

"Mr. Bronson, I just couldn't—"

"You can have your thirty thousand, Lady Holland. But you'll have to move away from the Taylors to get it."

"I would rather take less and not live here."

Bronson grinned suddenly, seeming not at all perturbed by her scowl. "The negotiations are over, my lady. You'll live here for a year and accept thirty thousand pounds, or there is no bargain."

Filled with nervous trepidation, Holly felt herself tremble all over. "Then I accept," she said breathlessly. "And I would like the carriage and team of four you promised for Rose to be written into the contract."

"All right." Bronson extended a hand, grasped her small one and shook it firmly. "Your hand is cold." He retained her fingers in his for a moment longer than necessary. His lips curved with a smile. "Are you frightened?"

It was the same thing he had asked her in the conservatory the night he had kissed her. She felt much as she had then, overwhelmed by an extraordinary event she had never anticipated. "Yes," she whispered. "Suddenly I'm afraid I may not be the kind of woman I've always thought I was."

"Everything will be all right," he said, his voice low and gentle.

"You can't pr-promise such a thing."

"Yes, I can. I have a good idea of what your family's reaction will be to this. Don't lose your courage."

"Of course not," she said with an attempt at dignity. "You have my word that I will keep to our bargain."

"Good," he murmured, while his gaze held an unnerving glitter of victory.

Lady Holly's carriage departed along the drive, the sun striking the black-lacquered vehicle with a blinding gleam. Zachary nudged the curtains of a library window apart and watched until the carriage was no longer visible. He was filled with the same explosive energy that he always felt after making a deal that was clearly to his advantage. Lady Holland Taylor would be living under his roof, with her daughter. It was a situation that no one, including himself, would have ever believed possible.

What was it about her that affected him so deeply? He had been aroused from the moment she had entered the room, aroused and fascinated as he had been by no other woman in his life. That moment when she had removed her gloves, exposing her delicate pale hands, had been the erotic highlight of his entire year.

He had known many great beauties and women of great talent, both in bed and out. He couldn't fathom why one small widow should have such an effect on him. Perhaps it was the warmth that shone through her demure exterior. She was clearly a lady, but without the airs and pretensions he had seen in other women of her class. He liked the direct, friendly way she had spoken to him, as if they were social equals. She was luminous, warm and far too refined for the likes of him.

Troubled, Zachary jammed his hands into the pockets of his trousers, bunching the hem of his coat. He wandered through the library suite, glancing absently at the priceless collection of volumes and artwork he had amassed. Ever since childhood, he had been aware of an endless, nagging urgency inside, the drive to achieve and conquer. He was filled with a dissatisfaction that drove him to work, plot and plan long into the night when other men were sleeping. It always seemed that there was one more object to acquire, one more deal to construct, one last mountain to climb, and then perhaps he would be happy. But he never was.

Somehow in the company of Lady Holly Taylor, he had felt like an ordinary man, one who was able to relax and enjoy himself. During the hour that she had visited him, all his usual aggression had vanished. He had felt almost . . . content. That had never happened to him before. The feeling was impossible to dismiss, and he wanted more of it. He craved Lady Holly's presence in his home.

And he craved her presence in his bed. Remembering the precise moment when she had realized he was the man who had kissed her, Zachary felt a smile tugging at his lips. She had turned scarlet, and her entire body had seemed to tremble. For a moment he had even wondered if she might faint. He wished she had—it would have given him an excuse to hold her again. But she had regained her composure and held her silence, clearly hoping that he would not recognize her. One would think she had committed a far greater crime than exchanging a hasty kiss with a stranger in the dark. For all her social knowledge, she was not sophisticated. He wasn't certain why that aroused him so.

She had a quality of innocence that married women didn't usually possess, as if she wouldn't recognize sin or depravity even if it was staring her in the face.

She had cried the second time he had kissed her, and now he knew why. He was certain she had not been kissed or caressed by anyone since the death of her husband. Someday, he thought, she would weep in his arms again. But the next time, it would be from pleasure, not grief.

Four

Holly berated herself all the way home for her impulsiveness. As the carriage bumped and rolled and jiggled over the unevenly paved streets of London, she decided that she would write Mr. Bronson a letter as soon as she arrived back at the Taylors' home. She would explain that she had made the decision too hastily, that it was clearly not in her best interests, not to mention Rose's, for her to alter their lives so radically. What had she been thinking, to agree to employment with a family she didn't know, a family that was clearly beneath her in society, a man who was known by everyone as an unscrupulous, mercenary scoundrel? "I've gone mad," she whispered to herself.

However, the anxiety she felt over the decision was countered by a strange, mounting reluctance to return to the dull existence she had known for the past three years. For some reason the home that had been such a comforting haven since George's death now seemed like a prison, and the Taylors like very kind and well-meaning gaolers. It was unfair of her, she knew, to feel this way.

Everything will be all right, Mr. Bronson had murmured to her just before she left his estate. He had known that she would second-guess her decision, that even the fortune

55

he had offered would not be enough to convince her to work for him, unless . . .

Unless there was something wild and reckless in her, something that would not allow her to retreat from this leap into the unknown. And the truth was, she wanted to take Rose and Maude and leave the Taylors. She wanted to break from the predictable path she had always followed until now.

What was the worst thing that could happen to her if she did so? She would face social disapproval . . . Well, what did that matter? The one person whose approval had mattered most to her was dead. The reaction of George's family was a concern, of course, but she could always insist that she did not want to be a burden to them any longer. There was Rose to consider, but Holly knew that she could persuade her daughter to look upon this as an adventure. And Rose would have such a magnificent dowry someday, and she would indeed be looked on as a highly desirable match for some well-titled peer.

Holly groaned and covered her face with her hands, knowing that she was not going to renege on her promise to Zachary Bronson. Because all her reasoning boiled down to one thing—she wanted to work for him.

Although everyone in the Taylor household, including the servants, was clearly eager to know what had transpired during the tea with Zachary Bronson, Holly said very little. In reply to the multitude of questions, she said that Bronson had been a gentleman, that his house was remarkably grand and that the conversation was perfectly pleasant. Rather than make a general announcement that she would be leaving soon, Holly decided that it would be easiest to break the news to George's brothers and let them tell the rest of the family. After supper, she asked to meet

William and Thomas in the library, and they agreed, both of them surprised by the unusual request.

Port was brought for the brothers and a cup of tea for Holly, and she sat in a heavy leather chair by the fire. Thomas occupied the chair next to her, while William stood and leaned an elbow on the white marble mantel. "Well, Holly," William said in a quiet, friendly way, "out with it. What in God's name did Bronson want with you? I think we've been kept in suspense long enough."

Faced with the two men who looked so achingly similar to her husband, their blue eyes containing identical expressions of curiosity, Holly felt the teacup tremble in the saucer she held. She was unexpectedly glad that she would no longer live here. Perhaps it would be better, easier, not to be surrounded by so many constant reminders of George. *Forgive me, my darling,* she thought, wondering if George was watching over her right now.

Slowly, taking care not to sound uncertain, Holly explained that Bronson wished to employ her as a social guide and instructor for his family, for the period of a year.

For a moment the Taylor brothers stared at her in surprise, and then Thomas burst out laughing. "I'll just bet he wants to hire you," Thomas gasped between spurts of laughter. "To think he could employ one of us—George's wife, no less! I hope you told the arrogant ape that you have far better things to do than teach him manners. Wait until I tell the fellows about this—"

"How much did he offer?" William asked, not sharing Thomas's amusement. As the elder and more perceptive of the brothers, he had seen something in Holly's face that gave him cause for concern.

"A fortune," Holly said softly.

"Five thousand? Ten?" William pressed, setting his glass of port on the mantel and turning to face her fully.

Holly shook her head, refusing to name the sum.

"More than ten?" William asked in disbelief. "You told him you couldn't be purchased, of course."

"I told him . . ." Holly paused to swallow a burning mouthful of tea, then set the cup and saucer on a nearby table. She folded her hands in her lap and spoke without looking at either of George's brothers. "I've lived here for three years, and you both know of my concern about being a burden on the family—"

"You're not a burden," William interrupted swiftly. "We've told you that a thousand times."

"Yes, and I appreciate your kindness and generosity more than I could ever say. However . . ."

As she paused in a silent search for words, both brothers wore identical expressions of disbelief as they realized what she was trying to convey. "No," William said softly. "Don't tell me you're considering his offer."

Holly cleared her throat nervously. "I accepted his offer, actually."

"My God," William exclaimed. "Didn't you hear a word Lord Avery said about him last night? He's a wolf, Holly. And you're as helpless as a lamb. He preys upon people far more knowledgeable and worldly than you. If you don't think of yourself, at least think of your daughter—have you no motherly instinct to protect her?"

"I *am* thinking about Rose," Holly said fiercely. "She's all I have left of George—she's all I think about."

"She's all that we have left of George, too. It would be cruel, a sin, to take her away from the only family she's known."

"You have your own wives and children to protect and look after. I have no husband. I have no means of providing for myself. And I don't want to be dependent on you forever."

William looked as though she had struck him. "Has it been so terrible, living here? I didn't realize our company was so unpleasant for you."

"Of course it hasn't. I didn't mean . . ." Holly sighed in frustration. "I will always be grateful for the way you've sheltered me since . . . but I must think of the future." She glanced at Thomas, who remained in the chair beside her. Although she hoped for an ally, Thomas was obviously in agreement with his older brother.

"I cannot conceive that this is happening," Thomas said, his tone containing not anger, but anguish. "Holly, tell me how to stop this. Tell me what it is about Bronson's offer that made you accept. I know it isn't the money. You're not the kind to be swayed by that. Is it the family? Has someone said or done something to offend you? To make you feel as though you're not welcome?"

"No," Holly said instantly, feeling horribly guilty. "Dear Thomas, I don't believe I could have survived George's death without your help. It's just that lately I—"

"Bronson will want more than etiquette lessons from you," William interrupted coldly. "I hope you realize that."

Holly threw him a look of rebuke. "I find that remark distasteful, William."

"You need to know what to expect, living in the household of a man whom all society knows is not a gentleman. You'll be at his mercy, and your desire for his money will lead you to do things you can't begin to imagine."

"I'm not a child."

"No, you're a young widow who has gone three years without the attentions of a man," William said with a brutal bluntness that caused her to gasp. "You'll never be as vulnerable as you are right now, and therefore any decision you make should not be trusted. If it's money you want, we'll find some way to increase your income. I'll find some investment that will earn greater interest for you. But I won't allow you to take a shilling from that unscrupulous bastard Bronson. I won't let you do this to yourself, or to my brother's child."

"Enough, William," Thomas snapped. "She needs sympathy, and instead you are doing your utmost to bully and alienate her—"

"It's all right, Thomas," Holly said calmly. Although part of her wanted to allow George's brothers to make the decision for her, another part of her remembered the teasing challenge in Zachary Bronson's eyes, and his admonition not to lose her courage. "I understand that William is concerned for my welfare. He doesn't want me to make a mistake. I have had the luxury of being protected by the both of you ever since George died. And I will always be grateful. But I want to step out from beneath your wing. I want to make choices. I even want to make a few mistakes."

"I don't understand," Thomas said slowly. "Why are you doing this, Holly? I never thought that money was so important to you."

Before Holly could reply, she was interrupted by William's cold, flat voice.

"For the first time I'm glad my brother is dead. I'm glad he can't see what is happening to you."

Holly turned white with shock. She expected to feel a blow of pain from his words, but instead there was only numbness. Unsteadily she came to her feet and backed away from the two of them. "There is nothing to be gained by discussing this further," she said with difficulty. "I have made my decision. I will leave within the week. I would like to take my servant Maude with me, if I may."

"You're going to live with Bronson," William said softly, undercutting his brother's protests. "Now I understand exactly what is going on. Yes, take Maude with you, by all means. But what of Rose? Will you discard her as easily as you have discarded my brother's memory, and leave us to take care of her? Or will you bring her with you, and allow her to watch you become a rich man's paramour?"

No one had ever spoken to her in such an insulting way. To hear it from a stranger would have been bad enough, but for it to come from George's brother was nearly unendurable. Steeling herself not to cry, Holly strode to the door. "I would never leave Rose for any reason," she said over her shoulder, her voice shaking only a little.

She heard the two brothers arguing as she left, Thomas berating William for his cruelty, and William responding in the clipped tones of a man suppressing great anger. What would George have wanted her to do? Holly wondered, and knew the answer immediately. He would have desired her to remain in the shelter of his family's home.

Holly paused at a window overlooking a small courtyard. The deep sill was scarred by a thousand tiny nicks and scratches. One of the servants had told her that George used to stage battles between his toy soldiers at this very window. She pictured his small hands manipulating the little painted iron men, the same hands that in manhood had caressed and held her. "I'm sorry, darling," she whispered. "After this year is through, I'll live exactly the way you wanted me to. And Rose will want for nothing. Just this one year, and then I'll keep all my promises to you."

Five

Lady Holly emerged from the carriage, stepping lightly to the ground with the assistance of a footman. As Zachary watched her, he was aware of a peculiar sensation in his chest, a deep throb of pleasure. She was here at last. His gaze drank in the sight of her. She was perfectly turned out, her little hands encased in gloves, her dark brown hair smooth and shining beneath a small-brimmed hat trimmed with a wisp of a veil at the front. Zachary was tempted to disarrange her demure facade, plunge his hands into her hair and unfasten the prim row of buttons at the neck of her chocolate-hued gown.

Another brown dress, Zachary thought, a frown working between his brows. The signs of her continued mourning—"slight mourning," as such austere garments were called—caused him a stab of annoyance. He had never personally known a woman who had chosen to grieve so long. His own mother, who had undoubtedly loved his father, had been more than ready to relinquish her smothering dark mourning garb after a year, and Zachary had not blamed her for an instant. A woman did not bury all her needs and instincts along with her husband, much as society would like to pretend otherwise.

Excessively devoted widows were much admired, kept

on pedestals as examples for others of their sex to follow. However, Zachary suspected that Lady Holly did not cling to mourning because it was the fashion, or because she wished to earn admiration. She sincerely grieved for her husband. Zachary wondered what kind of man had inspired such passionate attachment. Lord George Taylor had been an aristocrat, to be certain. One of Holly's own kind, someone well bred and honorable. Someone completely unlike himself, Zachary thought grimly.

A maidservant and a child descended the movable steps placed at the carriage door, and Zachary's attention lingered on the little girl. As he watched her, a smile came unbidden to his lips. Rose was a doll-like replica of her mother, with the same pretty features, and long brown curls adorned with a pale blue bow at the crown of her head. Appearing a bit anxious, Rose clutched something in her hands—something that sparkled like jewelry—as she stared at the grandeur of the house and grounds.

Zachary thought that perhaps he should remain in the house and receive Lady Holly in the parlor, or even the entrance hall, rather than greet them outside. What the hell, he thought grimly, and strode down the front steps, deciding that if he made a faux pas, Lady Holly would certainly let him know.

He approached Holly as she murmured instructions to the footmen who unloaded trunks and valises from the carriage. The brim of her hat lifted as she glanced at Zachary, and her mouth curved with a smile. "Good morning, Mr. Bronson."

He bowed and gave her an assessing glance. Her face was strained and pale, as if she had not slept for several nights, and Zachary understood at once that the Taylors must have put her through hell. "That bad?" he asked softly. "They must have convinced you that I'm the devil incarnate."

"They would prefer that I work for the devil," she said, and he laughed.

"I'll try not to corrupt you beyond recognition, my lady."

Holly rested her fingertips on her child's tiny shoulder and urged her forward. The note of motherly pride in her voice was unmistakable. "This is my daughter Rose."

Zachary bowed, and the little girl bobbed a perfect curtsy. Then Rose spoke without taking her eyes from his face. "Are you Mr. Bronson? We've come to teach you your manners."

Zachary flashed a grin at Holly. "I didn't realize when we struck our bargain that I was getting two of you."

Cautiously Rose reached up for her mother's gloved hand. "Is this where we're going to live, Mama? Is there a room for me?"

Zachary sat on his haunches and stared into the little girl's face with a smile. "I believe a room right next to your mother's has been prepared for you," he told her. His gaze fell to the mass of sparkling objects in Rose's hands. "What is that, Miss Rose?"

"My button string." The child let some of the length fall to the ground, displaying a line of carefully strung buttons . . . picture buttons etched with flowers, fruit or butterflies, ones made of molded black glass and a few of painted enamel and paper. "This one is my perfume button," Rose said proudly, fingering a large one with velvet backing. She lifted it to her nose and inhaled deeply. "Mama puts her perfume on it for me, to make it smell nice."

As Rose extended it toward him, Zachary ducked his head and detected a faint flowery fragrance that he recognized instantly. "Yes," he said softly, glancing up at

Lady Holly's blushing face. "That smells just like your mama."

"Rose," Holly said, clearly perturbed, "come with me— ladies do not remain talking on the drive-"

"I don't have any buttons like that," Rose told Zachary, ignoring her mother's words as she stared at one of the large solid gold buttons that adorned his coat.

Gazing in the direction of the child's dainty finger, Zachary saw that a miniature hunting landscape was engraved on the surface of his top button. He had never looked closely enough to notice before. "Allow me the honor of adding to your collection, Miss Rose," he said, reaching inside his coat to extract a small silver folding knife. Deftly he cut the threads holding the button to his coat and handed the object to the excited little girl.

"Oh, thank you, Mr. Bronson," Rose exclaimed. "Thank you!" Hurriedly she began to thread the button onto her string before her mother could offer an objection.

"Mr. Bronson," Holly spluttered, "a gentleman does not pull out w-weapons in the presence of ladies and children—"

"It's not a weapon." Casually he replaced the knife in his coat and rose to his feet. "It's a tool."

"Nevertheless, it's not—" Holly broke off as she saw what her daughter was doing. "Rose, you must return that button to Mr. Bronson this instant. It is far too fine and costly for your collection."

"But he gave it to me," Rose protested, her short fingers working frantically until the button was safely knotted on her string.

"Rose, I insist—"

"Let her keep it," Zachary said, grinning at Holly's perturbed expression. "It's just a button, my lady."

"It looks to be solid gold, and part of a matched set—"

"Come with me," he interrupted, crooking his arm invitingly. "My mother and sister are waiting inside."

Frowning, Lady Holly took his arm. "Mr. Bronson," she said in a crisp undertone, "I have tried very hard to ensure that my child is never indulged or spoiled. Therefore—"

"You've succeeded," he said, walking her up the front steps while the maidservant followed behind with Rose. "Your daughter is delightful."

"Thank you. But I have no wish for Rose to be caught up in your extravagant lifestyle. And I want my instructions concerning her to be followed to the letter. She must have a disciplined, well-ordered life just as she did at the Taylor estate."

"Of course," he said at once, trying to look chastened and humble, while the jaunty jangle of Rose's button string dragged the ground behind them.

Holly's trepidations were not calmed as she entered the house and saw once more how impossibly opulent it was. *Good Lord,* she thought with a pang of worry, *how are ordinary people to live here?* She glanced back at Maude, who stared speechlessly at the two-story gold columns that lined the entrance hall, and the gigantic chandeliers that shed sparkling light over the scene.

"Listen, Mama," Rose exclaimed, and began to make peeping noises that rebounded from one side of the cavernous hall to the other. "It echoes in here!"

"Hush, Rose." Holly glanced at Mr. Bronson, who seemed to bite back a smile at her daughter's antics.

A heavyset woman in her forties appeared, rather brusquely identifying herself as the housekeeper, Mrs. Burney. Wearing a look of bemusement, Maude accompanied Mrs. Burney up the baroque top-lit staircase to the upstairs rooms, where she would oversee the unpacking of the trunks.

Holly kept Rose by her side as they proceeded to a circuit of ornate receiving rooms. They entered a parlor decorated with alternating panels of embossed green velvet and gold panels, and French furniture covered in gold leaf. Two women awaited them, both rising anxiously to their feet. The younger, a tall, strikingly attractive girl with a mass of unruly black curls pinned atop her head, came forward. "Welcome, Lady Holland," she exclaimed, smiling broadly, although her gaze flickered over Holly in a wary survey.

"My sister Elizabeth," Bronson murmured.

"I couldn't believe my ears when Zach told us you would be coming to live here," the girl exclaimed. "You're very brave to take on the lot of us. We'll try not to make it an ordeal for you."

"Not at all," Holly replied, liking Bronson's sister at once. "I only hope to be of assistance to you, and perhaps offer some guidance when required."

"Oh, we'll require a great deal of guidance," Elizabeth assured her with a laugh.

There was a definite likeness between Bronson and his younger sister. They possessed the same black hair, flashing dark eyes and roguish smiles. They also shared the same sense of barely repressed energy, as if their active brains and supreme physical health would not allow them to relax for more than a few minutes.

It would not be difficult for Elizabeth to attract suitors, Holly thought. However, Elizabeth would require a strong partner, as the combination of her brother's wealth and her own robust spirit would prove intimidating for many men.

Elizabeth grinned, seeming to understand the thoughts behind Holly's discreet assessment. "The only reason Zach wants me to acquire some polish is to make it easier for him to engineer a marriage between me and some well-heeled aristocrat," she said bluntly. "However, I should warn you that my idea of a good match is vastly different from Zach's."

"Having heard some of your brother's views on the subject," Holly said evenly, "I am entirely prepared to take your side, Miss Bronson."

The girl laughed in delight. "Oh, I do like you, my lady," she exclaimed, and turned her attention to the child that waited patiently beside Holly. "Why, you must be Rose." Her voice gentled as she continued. "I think you're quite the prettiest little girl I've ever seen."

"You're pretty too, like a gypsy," Rose said frankly.

"Rose," Holly said reprovingly, afraid that Elizabeth would take exception to the remark, but the young woman laughed.

"What a darling you are," she exclaimed, sinking to her knees and examining Rose's button string.

As Rose proceeded to demonstrate the wonders of her button collection to Elizabeth, Holly turned her attention to the other woman in the room, who seemed as if she would prefer to shrink back into the corner. Bronson's mother, she thought, and felt a surge of kindly sympathy as she saw how uncomfortable the woman was as her son made the introductions.

It was clear that Mrs. Paula Bronson had once been a beautiful woman, but years of work and worry had taken their toll. Her hands were permanently rough and reddened from physical toil, and her face was heavily lined for a woman her age. The locks of hair that were twisted tightly and pinned at the back of her head had once been jet-black, but were now streaked liberally with silver. The beauty of her bone structure remained, however, and her eyes were warm and velvety brown. Overcome with apparent shyness, Paula managed a murmur of welcome.

"Milady," she said, forcing herself to meet Holly's gaze, "my son has a way of . . . of making people do things they don't want to do. I hope you are not here against your will."

"Mother," Zachary muttered, his black eyes gleaming with amusement. "You make it sound as though I dragged Lady Holland here in chains. And I never make people do things they don't want to do. I always give them a choice."

Throwing him a skeptical glance, Holly approached his mother. "Mrs. Bronson," she said warmly, taking the woman's hand and pressing gently, "I assure you, I have every wish to be here. I take great pleasure at the prospect of being useful. For the past three years I've been in mourning and . . ." She paused, searching for the right words, and Rose interrupted with what she considered to be a salient comment.

"My Papa's not coming to live here with us because he's in heaven now. Isn't that right, Mama?"

The group was suddenly silent. Holly glanced at Zachary Bronson's face and saw that it was expressionless. "That's right, darling," she answered her daughter softly.

The mention of George had cast a pall over the scene, and Holly searched for words to dispel the sudden awkwardness. However, the longer the silence stretched, the more difficult it seemed to break. She couldn't help reflecting in a flash of despair that if George were alive, she would never be in this position, coming to live in a house of strangers, accepting employment from a man like Zachary Bronson.

Suddenly Elizabeth broke the pause with a bright, if slightly forced, smile. "Rose, let me show you upstairs to your new room. Do you know that my brother has bought the contents of an entire toy shop for you? Dolls and books, and the biggest doll house you've ever seen."

As the little girl squealed with delight and followed her at once, Holly stared at Zachary Bronson with rapidly dawning disapproval. "An entire toy shop?"

"It was nothing like that," Bronson said immediately. "Elizabeth is prone to exaggeration." He threw a warning glance at Paula, silently demanding that she agree with him. "Isn't that right, Mother?"

"Well," Paula said uncertainly, "actually, you did rather—"

"I'm certain Lady Holland will want a tour of the house while her belongings are unpacked," Bronson interrupted hastily. "Why don't you take her around?"

Clearly overwhelmed by shyness, Mrs. Bronson gave a noncommittal murmur and sped away, leaving the two of them alone in the parlor.

Faced with Holly's disapproving stare, Zachary shoved his hands in his pockets, while the toe of his expensive shoe beat a quick, impatient rhythm on the floor. "What harm is there in an extra toy or two?" he finally said in an excessively reasonable tone. "Her room was about as cheerful as a prison cell. I thought a doll and a handful of books would make the place more appealing for her—"

"First of all," Holly interrupted, "I doubt that any room in this house could be described as a prison cell. Second . . . I will not have my daughter spoiled and overwhelmed, and influenced by your taste for excess."

"Fine," he said with a gathering scowl. "We'll get rid of the damned toys, then."

"Please do not swear in my presence," Holly said, and sighed. "How am I to remove the toys after Rose has seen them? You don't know very much about children, do you?"

"No," he said shortly. "Only how to bribe them."

Holly shook her head, her displeasure warring with sudden amusement. "There is no need to bribe Rose—or me, for that matter. I gave you my word that I would not break our agreement. And please do not tap your foot that way . . . it is not good deportment."

The impatient rhythm ceased at once, and Bronson gave her a darkly ironic glance. "Anything else about my deportment you'd like to change?"

"Yes, actually." Holly hesitated as their gazes met. It felt odd to give directions to a man like this. Especially a man as powerful and physically imposing as Bronson. However, he had hired her for this specific purpose, and she would prove herself equal to the challenge. "You mustn't stand with your hands in your pockets—it isn't good form."

"Why?" he asked, removing them.

Her brow puckered thoughtfully. "I suppose because it implies that you have something to hide."

"Maybe I do." His intent gaze remained on her face as she approached him.

"I was schooled excessively on proper carriage of the body," Holly said. "Ladies and gentlemen must appear composed at all times. Try never to shrug your shoulders or shift your weight, and keep your gestures to a minimum."

"This explains why aristocrats are always as stiff as corpses," Bronson muttered.

Smothering a laugh, Holly regarded him gravely. "Bow to me, please," she commanded. "When you greeted us outside, I thought I detected something . . ."

Bronson glanced at the doorway of the parlor to make certain they were not being observed. "Why don't we start the lessons tomorrow? I'm sure you want to unpack and accustom yourself to the place—"

"There's no time like the present," she assured him. "Bow, please."

Muttering something beneath his breath, he complied.

"There," Holly said softly, "you did it again."

"What did I do?"

"When you bow, you must keep your gaze on the person you're addressing—you must not hide your eyes, even for an instant. It seems a little thing, but it's quite important." Only servants and inferiors bowed with their gaze downcast, and being unaware of this fact would put a man at an instant disadvantage.

Bronson nodded, taking the point as seriously as she had intended. He bowed again, this time staring steadily at her. Holly suddenly felt breathless, unable to stop staring into the midnight depths of his eyes . . . so wicked and dark they were.

"That's much better," she managed to say. "I think I'll spend the rest of the day making a list of the subjects we'll need to study: deportment, rules of conduct in the street and in the home, rules for calling and for conversation, ballroom etiquette and . . . do you know how to dance, Mr. Bronson?"

"Not well."

"We'll have to begin right away, then. I am acquainted with an excellent dancing master who will instruct you on the finer points of the allemande, the reel, the quadrille and waltz—"

"No," Bronson said immediately. "I'll be damned if I'll learn how to dance from some fop. Hire him for Elizabeth, if you like. She doesn't know any more about dancing than I do."

"Then who will teach you?" Holly asked, making her voice very patient.

"You."

She shook her head with a protesting laugh. "Mr. Bronson, I am not qualified to instruct you in the intricacies of dancing."

"You know how, don't you?"

"There is a vast difference between knowing how to do something and teaching someone else. You must allow me to hire a proficient dancing master—"

"I want you," he said stubbornly. "I'm paying you a fortune, Lady Holland, and I expect to get my money's worth. Whatever I learn over the next several months, I'm going to learn from you."

"Very well. I will do my best, Mr. Bronson. But do not blame me if you attend a ball someday and can barely manage the figures of a quadrille."

Bronson smiled. "Don't underestimate your abilities, my lady. I've never met anyone with such a knack for telling me what to do. Except my mother, of course." He crooked his arm for her to take. "Come with me to the gallery—I want to show you my da Vinci."

"What?" Holly asked, startled. "You have no da Vinci, Mr. Bronson. At least, you hadn't as of last week, and no one could possibly—" She broke off as she saw the gleam in his eyes. "You've acquired a da Vinci?" she asked faintly. "How . . . where . . ."

"The National Gallery," he replied, walking her toward the library and the gallery beyond. "I had to trade a few of my other paintings and promise to build them an alcove for a Roman statuary collection. And technically the painting still isn't mine—I paid a king's ransom just to get them to loan the damn thing to me for a period of five years. You should have been at the negotiations. It's difficult enough to make deals with bankers and London business-men, but as it turns out, museum directors are the greediest bastards of all—"

"Mr. Bronson, your language," Holly reproved. "Which painting did you acquire?"

"A Madonna and child. They said it was a superb exam-ple of some Italian art technique for light and shadow—"

"Chiaroscuro?"

"Yes, that was it."

"Good Lord," Holly said, bemused. "You have a da Vinci. One wonders if anything is beyond your financial reach." There was something in his manner—a touch of boastfulness, a boyish enthusiasm—that caused a warm, unexpected pang in her heart. Zachary Bronson was a ruth-less man whom many people doubtless feared. However, she sensed a vulnerability in his need to belong to the society that was so determined to reject him. Being an intelligent man, he had acquired all the trappings—the house and lands, the Thoroughbreds and paintings and well-tailored clothes—but his ultimate goal was still far away.

"Unfortunately there are still a few things I can't buy," Bronson said, as if he could read her thoughts.

Holly stared at him in fascination. "What do you want most?"

"To be a gentleman, of course."

"I don't think so," she murmured. "You don't really want to be a gentleman, Mr. Bronson. You just want the appearance of being one."

Bronson stopped and turned to face her, his brows arched in ironic amusement.

Holly's breath caught as she realized what she had just said. "Forgive me," she said hastily. "I don't know why I—"

"You're right. If I really were a gentleman, instead of merely trying to ape one, I'd never be a success at business. Real gentlemen don't have the heads or the guts for making money."

"I don't believe that."

"Oh? Name one true gentleman of your acquaintance who can hold his own in the business world."

Holly thought for a long moment, searching silently through a list of men who were known for their financial acumen. However, the ones who could truly be called entrepreneurs, successful in the way Bronson meant, had lost the sheen of honor and integrity that had once defined them as true gentlemen. Uncomfortably she reflected that a man's character was easily damaged by the quest for financial glory. One couldn't sail through stormy waters without suffering some weathering.

Bronson smiled smugly in the face of her silence. "Exactly."

Frowning, Holly walked beside him, now declining to take his arm. "Increasing one's wealth should not be the ultimate goal in a man's life, Mr. Bronson."

"Why not?"

"Love, family, friendship . . . those are the things that matter. And they most definitely cannot be purchased."

"You might be surprised," he said, and she couldn't help but laugh at his cynicism.

"I only hope that someday, Mr. Bronson, you will encounter someone or something for which you would gladly give up your fortune. And I hope that I'll be there to witness it."

"Maybe you will," he said, and steered her down another long, gleaming hallway.

*   *   *

Although Holly always awakened gladly to the sight of her daughter bouncing into bed for a good-morning kiss, today she resisted being pulled from slumber. Mumbling drowsily, she burrowed further into her pillow, while Rose cavorted around her.

"Mama," the little girl called, climbing beneath the warm covers, "Mama, wake up! The sun is out, and it's a lovely day. I want to play in the gardens. And visit the stables. Mr. Bronson has lots of horses, did you know that?"

Maude chose just that moment to enter the room. "Mr. Bronson has lots of *everything,*" came the maid's wry observation, and Holly emerged from her pillow with a smothered laugh. Busily Maude poured a hot basin of water at the marble-topped washstand and set out Holly's silver-backed brush and comb set, along with various toiletries.

"Good morning, Maude," Holly said, feeling unaccountably cheerful. "Did you sleep well?"

"Yes, and so did our Rose. I suspect she exhausted herself playing with all those toys. How did ye fare, milady?"

"I had the most wonderful rest." After the past several nights of tossing and turning, waking up in the middle of each night beset with doubt, Holly had finally succumbed to a deep slumber. She supposed it was only natural that she would relax, now that they were under Mr. Bronson's roof and there was no more opportunity for second-guessing. And they had been given a lovely suite of rooms, large and airy, decorated in beige and rose and gleaming white paneling. The windows were swathed in frothy Brussels lace, and the French armchairs had been covered with Gobelin tapestry. The bed had been carved with a curling shell motif that matched the huge armoire on the other side of the room.

It pleased Holly that Rose's room was located right next to hers, instead of being relegated to an upper floor where nurseries were usually located. The little girl's room had been filled with child-sized cherrywood furniture, and bookshelves filled with beautifully illustrated volumes, and a mahogany table loaded with the largest doll house Holly had ever seen. Every detail of the toy was astonishingly perfect, from the tiny Aubusson rugs on its floors to the thumbnail-sized wooden hams and chickens hanging from the kitchen ceiling.

"I had a splendid dream last night," Holly remarked, yawning and rubbing her eyes. She sat up and began to stack a pile of downy pillows. "I was walking in a garden filled with red roses . . . they were so large, with velvety petals, and they seemed so real that I could actually smell them. And the most remarkable thing was, I could gather as many armfuls as I wished, and there were no thorns."

"Red roses, ye say?" Maude glanced at her, eyes bright with interest. "They say to dream of red roses means ye'll soon have luck in love."

Holly gave her a startled glance, then shook her head with a wistful smile. "I've already had that." Glancing at the child cuddling by her side, she kissed the top of Rose's curly dark head. "All my love is for you and your papa," she murmured.

"Can you still love Papa when he's in heaven?" Rose asked, reaching across the embroidered silk counterpane for the doll she had brought into the room with her.

"Of course I can. You and I still love each other even when we're not together, don't we?"

"Yes, Mama." Rose beamed at her and brought the doll forth. "Look—one of my new dolls. This is my favorite."

Holly regarded the doll with an admiring smile. Its head, arms and feet were made of china covered in a high-gloss finish, and the delicately painted features glowed beneath a cap of real hair that had been attached a strand at a time. The doll was dressed in a lavish silk gown adorned with buttons, bows and ruffles, and little red shoes had been painted on her feet.

"How lovely," Holly said sincerely. "What is her name, darling?"

"Miss Crumpet."

Holly laughed. "I have a feeling you and she will enjoy many tea parties together."

Rose hugged the doll and regarded Holly over its little head. "May we invite Mr. Bronson to one of our tea parties, Mama?"

Holly's smile faded as she replied, "I don't think that will be possible, Rose. Mr. Bronson is a very busy man."

"Oh."

"That Mr. Bronson is a strange one," Maude chatted, bringing a ruffled white pelisse from the armoire and holding it as Holly slipped her arms through the sleeves. "I was talking with some of the servants this morning—I had to fetch the hot water myself, as no one ever seems to come when the bell is pulled—and they had a few things to say about him."

"Such as?" Holly asked idly, concealing a flare of curiosity.

Gesturing for Rose to come to her, Maude dressed the little girl in a fresh white chemise and underdrawers, and thick cotton stockings. "They say he's a good master and that no one wants for anything here. But the house isn't run well. The housekeeper, Mrs. Burney, and all the servants know that Mr. Bronson hasn't the slightest idea of what goes on in real gentlefolks' households."

"And so they take advantage of his lack of knowledge

in this area," Holly concluded, shaking her head in disapproval. Instantly she made up her mind that if she accomplished nothing else during her time here, she would at least ensure that the servants received some instruction. Zachary Bronson certainly deserved proper service from his own employees.

However, Maude's next words dispelled all trace of charitable feeling. Settling a ruffled white dress over Rose's head, the maid ensured that the child's ears were covered before she continued. "They say, milady, that Mr. Bronson is quite wild. He's given parties here sometimes, with drinking and gambling and harlots in every corner, and the guests were all very bad *ton*. After the goings-on at one of these evenings, they even had to replace carpets and furniture in some of the rooms—"

"Maude!" Rose wriggled impatiently beneath the tent of white ruffles.

"And they say Mr. Bronson is the randiest gentleman of all," Maude said, seeming to relish Holly's expression of quiet horror. "He doesn't scruple between washwomen and duchesses, he'll chase anything in skirts. One of the maids, Lucy, says she once saw him with two women at once." Realizing that Holly didn't understand her meaning, Maude added in a whisper, "In *bed,* milady!"

"Maude," came Rose's voice from the enveloping dress. "I can't breathe!"

While Maude jerked the dress down and busied herself with tying a blue sash at Rose's waist, Holly sat in stricken silence and contemplated the information. Two women at once? She had never heard of such a thing, couldn't imagine how or why it would be done. A decidedly unpleasant feeling crept over her. It seemed that Zachary Bronson was well acquainted with depravity. Uneasily she wondered how she was ever to influence a man like him. Doubtless it was folly to even try. Well, Bronson would have to change his ways. There would be no bad *ton* invited here, and no gambling or licentious behavior of any kind. The first time she witnessed a hint of something scandalous occurring, she, Rose and Maude would leave the estate at once.

"The master was a prizefighter, had ye heard?" Maude asked Holly, reaching for a comb to attack the snarls in Rose's hair.

The little girl sighed and waited with tremendous patience, her gaze fixed longingly on Miss Crumpet. "Are you almost finished?" she asked, eliciting a laugh from the maid.

"I will be after I've combed these rats from yer hair, miss!"

"Yes, I'd heard something like that," Holly said, her brow wrinkling curiously.

"For two years or so, the footman James told me," Maude reported. "A bare-knuckle fighter, Mr. Bronson was, and he took home a purse every time he was let into the rope ring. Can ye believe James actually saw him fight once, long before Mr. Bronson gained his fortune? James says Mr. Bronson is the finest figure of a man he ever saw, with arms ye couldn't close yer hands around and a neck thick as a bull's. And he fought cool as ye please, never putting himself in a passion. The perfect champion of the fist."

Holly's dismay rose with each word the maid spoke. "Oh, Maude . . . I must have been mad to bring us here. It's hopeless to try to teach him anything about etiquette."

"I don't think so, milady," came Maude's reply, as she cheerfully flipped aside the blond curls that had escaped the front of her coiffure. "After all, the master brought himself all the way from the rope ring to the fanciest estate in London. Surely being a gentleman is only one more step away."

"But it's the biggest step of all," Holly said wryly.

Rose picked up her doll and came to the bedside. "I'll help you, Mama. I'll teach Mr. Bronson all about his manners."

Holly gave her daughter a loving smile. "You're very sweet for wanting to help, darling. But I want you to have as little to do with Mr. Bronson as possible. He's . . . not a nice man."

"Yes, Mama," Rose said dutifully, heaving a disappointed sigh.

As Maude had indicated, no amount of bellpulling could summon a servant to the room, and Holly finally gave up with a sigh of frustration. "If we wait for a servant to bring Rose's breakfast to the nursery, she'll starve," she murmured. "I'll have a talk with Mrs. Burney this morning, and perhaps she will explain why not one out of a household of eighty servants can manage to climb the stairs."

"They're no good, milady," Maude said darkly. "Not a blessed one of them. When I passed through the servants' hall this morning, I saw one housemaid with a belly out to here—" she indicated an advanced pregnancy—"and another giving kisses to a sweetheart—right there in the hall, mind ye—and another girl was sleeping upright at the table. One footman was going about with his hair half-powdered, and another was charging about complaining as how no one had washed his livery breeches on laundry day—"

"Please, no more," Holly begged in laughing dismay, holding up her hands in a helpless gesture. "There is so much to be done that I hardly know where to begin." She bent down to her perplexed daughter and kissed her soundly. "Rose, darling, why don't you bring Miss Crumpet downstairs, and we'll try to find some breakfast?"

"Breakfast with you?" the little girl asked in delight. Like most children of her station, she was accustomed to taking her morning meal in the nursery. Eating with adults was a privilege usually granted to children of appropriate age, as well as highly developed manners.

"Just for this morning," Holly said with a laugh, gently straightening the huge blue bow atop her daughter's head. "And I sincerely hope that you'll set a good example for the Bronsons to follow."

"Oh, I will!" Holding Miss Crumpet firmly, Rose began to instruct the doll on the importance of ladylike behavior.

Holly somehow managed to guide her daughter and maidservant to the breakfast room, from which an appetizing aroma drifted. The breakfast room, with its tall windows overlooking the sumptuous gardens and walls paneled in gilded fruit motifs, was charming. A side table fitted with plate-warmer drawers had been weighted with domed silver trays and a tiered stand with revolving china compartments. Six small round tables gleamed beneath a crystal chandelier.

Elizabeth Bronson was already seated at one of the tables, lifting a delicate china cup to her lips. As she saw Holly, Maude and Rose enter the room, she gave them a glowing smile. "Good morning," she said cheerfully. "Why, Rose, are you going to share breakfast with us? How delightful. I hope you'll sit beside me."

"And Miss Crumpet, too?" Rose asked, holding up her new doll.

"Miss Crumpet shall have her own chair," Elizabeth said grandly, "and the three of us shall discuss our plans for the day."

Wriggling with delight at being treated like a grown-up,

Rose headed for the girl as fast as her short legs would take her. Quietly Maude went about preparing a breakfast plate for the child, as if to demonstrate to the household how a properly trained servant should go about her duties.

Holly wandered to the sideboard, where Zachary Bronson was filling his plate with a selection of eggs, cold meats, breads and vegetables. Although he was dressed in the gentlemanly attire of a charcoal-gray morning coat, black trousers and a dove waistcoat, there was something a bit piratical about him. She supposed he would never completely be able to rid himself of the street-seasoned air that lurked beneath his well-groomed facade. His assessing dark gaze caused a tickling flutter just beneath her lower ribs. "Good morning," he murmured. "I hope you rested well?"

Remembering the scandalous allegations of his wild behavior, Holly responded with a polite, rather distant smile. "Very well, thank you. I see we've joined you in time to start breakfast together."

"I started a while ago," Bronson replied cheerfully. "This is my second plate."

Holly felt her eyebrows inch upward as she saw the mountain of food he intended to consume.

The housekeeper entered the room just at that moment, and Holly gave her an inquiring glance. "Good day, Mrs. Burney ... as you can see, I've brought my daughter downstairs for breakfast, as no one seems able to answer the bellpull. I wonder if perhaps the mechanism is broken?"

"We've a very busy household, milady," the housekeeper replied, her face expressionless except for the taut pull of displeasure around her eyes and mouth. "The maids can't answer the bell every instant after it is pulled."

Resisting the temptation to ask if the maids *ever* answered the bell, Holly resolved to take up the matter with Mrs. Burney later in the day. The housekeeper set out more silver and left the room.

Having loaded his own plate, Bronson lingered at the sideboard as Holly chose a few delicacies for her own breakfast—a slice of toast, a spoonful of eggs, a tidbit of ham. "I have business to attend to this morning," he remarked. "I'll be able to start our lessons after lunch, if that's pleasing to you."

"That will be fine," Holly said. "In fact, why don't we plan a similar schedule every day? I will instruct your sister during the morning hours, and your lessons will take place during Rose's afternoon nap."

"I won't always be available during midday," Bronson replied.

"Perhaps on those occasions, you and I could meet during the evening hours, after Rose's bedtime," Holly suggested, and Bronson nodded in agreement. With those arrangements settled, Holly handed Bronson her plate. "You may carry my plate to the breakfast table, sir. On the occasions when a footman is not available to perform this service, a gentleman may offer his assistance to a lady."

"Why should I carry a woman's plate when she is perfectly capable of carrying it for herself?"

"Because a gentleman must act as a lady's servant, Mr. Bronson. He must make all possible concession for her convenience and comfort."

One of his dark brows arched. "You ladies have things rather easy."

"Hardly," Holly replied, matching his dry tone. "We spend every other minute of our lives bearing children, managing the household accounts, attending the sickroom when necessary, supervising the mending and laundry and meals and planning our husbands' social schedules."

Bronson stared at her with laughing dark eyes. "Is that what I can expect of a wife? I'd like to get one soon, then."

"Someday I'll instruct you as to the rules of proper courtship."

"I can hardly wait," he replied softly.

Bronson carried their plates to the same table that Elizabeth and Rose occupied. Before Holly could instruct him as to how to seat a lady, Rose glanced at Bronson with bright, inquiring eyes and asked a question that nearly caused Holly to faint.

"Mr. Bronson," the little girl chirped innocently, "why did you sleep with two women at your party?"

Stunned, Holly realized that Rose had overheard her earlier conversation with Maude.

Maude paused in the act of filling the child's plate, the fine china slipping from her hands and clattering on the sideboard.

Elizabeth choked on a mouthful of food, somehow managed to swallow and concealed her crimson face with a napkin. When she was able, she glanced at Holly with eyes brimming with equal parts of dismay and mirth, and spoke in a strangled murmur. "Excuse me—my right shoe is pinching—I believe I'll change into another pair." She fled the scene hastily, leaving the rest of them to stare at Bronson.

Of all of them, Bronson was the only one who showed no visible reaction, save for a thoughtful quirk of his mouth. He must have been a very, very good card player, Holly thought.

"At times the guests become very tired at my parties," Bronson said to the child, his tone matter-of-fact. "I was merely helping them to rest."

"Oh, I see," Rose said brightly.

Holly managed to find her voice. "I believe my daughter is finished with her breakfast, Maude."

"Yes, milady." The maid rushed forward in a panic to gather up the child and quit the mortifying scene.

"But Mama," Rose protested, "I haven't even—"

"You may take your plate to the nursery," Holly said firmly, seating herself as if nothing untoward had occurred. "Right this minute, Rose. I want to discuss something with Mr. Bronson."

"Why don't I ever get to eat with the big people?" the child asked sullenly, accompanying Maude from the room.

Bronson seated himself beside Holly, his wary gaze fastened on her disapproving face. "Apparently the servants have been talking," he muttered.

Holly made her voice as cool and brisk as possible. "Mr. Bronson, there will be no more 'helping ladies to rest' at this house as long as we are in residence, in ones or twos, or any number. I will not have my daughter subjected to an unwholesome atmosphere. Moreover, although the servants owe you respect as a matter of course, it would help immensely if you behave in a manner *worthy* of their respect."

Rather than look ashamed or embarrassed, Bronson returned her steady stare with a growing scowl. "Your task is to teach me a few points of etiquette, my lady. How I conduct my private life is my own concern."

She picked up her fork and pushed a few yellow egg curds around her plate. "Unfortunately, you cannot separate your private life from your public one, sir. No one is able to check his morals at the door like a hat, and pick them up when he leaves."

"I can."

Amazed by his cool assertion, Holly let a disbelieving laugh escape. "Apparently you like to think so!"

"Don't try to tell me that every moment of your private life could stand up to public scrutiny, my lady. Hasn't your halo ever slipped just a little?"

Discovering that she was gripping her fork as if it were a defensive weapon, Holly set the utensil down. "What exactly are you asking?"

"You've never had too much to drink? Gambled all your pin money? Cursed like a sailor when you can't hold your temper? Laughed in church? Said something nasty about a close friend behind her back?"

"Well, I . . ." Earnestly she searched her memory, conscious of his expectant stare. "I don't think so."

"Never?" Bronson seemed perturbed by the answer. "Spent too much at the dressmaker's?" he asked, as if hoping beyond hope that she had once committed some grievous mistake.

"Well, there is one thing." Holly smoothed her gown over her lap. "I am much too fond of cakes. I am quite capable of eating an entire plate of them at one sitting. I can't seem to help myself."

"Cakes," he muttered with obvious disappointment. "That's your only fault?"

"Oh, if we're discussing weaknesses of character, I have several," she assured him. "I am self-indulgent, opinionated and I battle a great streak of vanity. But that is not the point of this conversation, Mr. Bronson. We are talking about *your* personal habits, not mine. And the fact is, if you wish to have the appearance and manner of a gentleman, you must never allow your lower nature to rule over your higher one."

"I don't have a higher nature, Lady Holland."

"No doubt it is more convenient—and pleasurable—to pretend so. However, a man is never his own master until he is able to control his lustful impulses. And when such behavior is excessive, it causes degeneration of the mind and body."

"Degeneration," he repeated gravely. "With all due respect, I've never noticed any harmful effects, my lady."

"Well, you will someday. It is unhealthful for a man to indulge any excessive appetites, whether for food, spirits or . . . or . . ."

"Sexual activity?" he supplied helpfully.

"Yes. Therefore I hope that you will practice temperance in all areas from now on. I think you will be pleased to discover the positive effects it will have on your character."

"I'm not a choirboy, Lady Holland. I'm a man, and men have certain needs. If you care to refer to our contract, there was no mention of the activities in my own bedroom—"

"Then if you must have your harlots, bring them elsewhere," Holly said. Although she did not raise her voice, it was threaded with steel. "Out of consideration for your mother and sister, and my daughter . . . and me. I insist on an atmosphere of respect and decency, and I will not remain under the same roof with such goings-on."

Their gazes held for a challenging moment. "You're telling me that I can't lie with a woman in my own house," he said, as if he couldn't believe her audacity. "In my own bed."

"Not as long as I am residing here, sir."

"A man's sexual habits have nothing to do with being a gentleman. I could tell you the names of at least a dozen so-called 'gentlemen,' highly respected souls all, who are frequent guests at the same bordellos I choose to visit. In fact, I could tell you the most remarkable practices they are known for—"

"No, thank you," Holly interrupted hastily, pressing her

hands over her burning ears. "I see your tactic, Mr. Bronson. You are trying to distract me with tales of other mens' disgraceful behavior to divert attention from your own. However, I have set my terms, and I insist that you abide by them. And if you bring one woman of low character to this house and have intimate relations with her, I will break off our arrangement at once."

Bronson plucked a slice of toast from a delicate silver rack and proceeded to heap it with marmalade. "For what I'm having to put up with," he said darkly, "I'd better learn a hell of a lot from you."

"I've promised to instruct you to the best of my ability. And please do not gesture with that utensil."

Grimacing, Bronson set the spoon back into the crystal preserves dish. "Instruct all you like, my lady. Just don't try to reform me."

He was an incorrigible scoundrel, and yet his unrepentant wickedness held a certain charm. Holly wondered why she found him so strangely likable. Perhaps she had been surrounded by honorable men for a little too long.

"Mr. Bronson," she said, "I hope someday you'll understand that the sexual act can be so much more than you understand it to be. It is an elevated expression of love . . . a communion of souls."

Bronson responded with a low laugh, as if he were mightily entertained by the notion that she might know something about physical intercourse that he did not. "It's a simple bodily need," he countered. "No matter how many minstrels and poets and novelists have tried to make it seem otherwise. And it happens to be one of my favorite pastimes."

"Do it all you like, then," she said tartly. "Just not in this house."

He gave her a smile designed to cause annoyance. "I intend to."

Six

As Zachary rode to town at a breakneck pace, he tried to gather his thoughts in preparation for a board meeting. The day was one he had anticipated for a long time. He would be signing a deal, along with two co-owners of a massive soap factory, to improve the factory as well as build new housing for many of their employees. Zachary's co-owners, both of them born into the aristocracy, had resisted such expenditures, pointing out that production at the factory was at such a profitable level that no improvements were needed. They had called Zachary's insistence on making the improvements a waste of money. After all, they had both remarked, factory workers were accustomed to the squalid conditions they lived and worked in and would expect nothing else.

It had taken a great deal of stubbornness and bullying for Zachary to make his partners understand his view, that the workers would be even more productive if their daily lives weren't such a damned misery. He knew exactly why his partners had finally caved in to his demands. They considered themselves too refined and gentlemanly to involve themselves in the dirty concerns of factory life. They preferred to leave all that to him, which was fine. More than fine. He would manage the business to his satisfaction, and see that they all made money in the future. In fact, he would make certain their annual profits would double, and their factory would eventually be a model for all others in London. "Just sign and keep your mouth shut," one of the partners had advised the other in Zachary's presence. "We've done well enough with Bronson so far, haven't we? He's taken my original investment and made it into the largest source of income my family has ever known. Why quibble with success?"

The upcoming meeting, and his plans for the factory, were all that Zachary should be thinking about. However, his mind was filled with Lady Holly: the air of sweet earnestness that tempted him to ruffle and tease her, and the sad, secretive mouth that sometimes curved into an unexpectedly dazzling smile.

Zachary found her irresistible, though he was not certain precisely *why*. He had encountered nice women before, kind and virtuous women whom he had admired. But he had never felt the barest stirring of desire for any of them. Goodness did not excite him. Innocence in any form was not titillating in the least. He preferred to spend his time with sexually experienced women, the ones with naughty gazes and adventurous souls, the ones whose manicured hands strayed beneath the tables at dinner parties. He was especially fond of women who had a strong command of swear words and dirty language, women who might appear ladylike on the outside but were decidedly abandoned in the bedroom.

Lady Holly was none of those things. In fact, taking her to bed would not be an adventure in any sense of the word. Why, then, did the very thought of it cause him to break out in a sweat? Why was he aroused by the mere fact of being in the same room with her? She was pretty, but he had known women of great beauty before. Her figure was pleasing but not spectacular, and she did not possess the long, elegant lines that were currently so admired. In fact, she was short. A grin tugged at his mouth as he imagined her naked between the silk sheets of his enormous bed. He could imagine no more desirable activity than chasing that short, curvaceous figure from one corner of the mattress to the other.

But that would never happen. To his great regret, Zachary acknowledged that he liked Lady Holly far too much to seduce her. She would be devastated by the experience. Any temporary pleasure she felt would soon be overwhelmed by guilt and remorse. And she would hate him for it. Better to leave her as she was, content with the happy memories of her late husband, keeping herself for George Taylor until they met again in the next world.

Zachary could get physical satisfaction from other women, but no one else could supply him with what Holly could. She was intelligent, principled and fascinating, and as long as he didn't misbehave too badly, he could have her company for a year. That was far more important than one night's tumble, no matter how pleasurable it might be.

At Holly's suggestion, she and Elizabeth strolled in the five-acre garden outside, temporarily delaying their lessons until they became better acquainted. "This is my favorite place to walk," Elizabeth said, guiding her to a "wilderness path" that was far less structured and formal than the rest of the garden. Walking along a trail paved with limestone, Holly enjoyed the huge drifts of snowdrops all around them. The path was lined with ornamental trees and bunches of winter honeysuckle that flooded the air with fragrance. Lush topiaried hedges were heavily interspersed with rosy splashes of cyclamen and scarlet clematis, luring Holly farther along the curving path.

As she conversed with Elizabeth, Holly realized that the girl was truly extraordinary. Elizabeth's high-spirited nature did little to conceal her acquaintance with the more unpleasant facts of life. Here was no schoolroom miss who viewed the world through narrow blinders, but a girl who had been born in poverty, the kind of poverty that stripped away all girlish illusions. Her dark eyes were rather too seasoned for a young woman her age, and she seemed to have no desire to please anyone save herself. Both would be extremely off-putting to most prospective suitors, except that Elizabeth also happened to possess a wild, romantic beauty that most men would find irresistible.

Pushing back dark curls that kept tumbling into her face, Elizabeth began the conversation with what Holly would soon discover was her habitual bluntness. "I hope you don't think too badly of my brother, Lady Holland."

"I regard him as an interesting challenge." Holly quickened her step to match the girl's long, lazy strides.

"You don't dislike him, then?"

"Not at all."

"That's good," Elizabeth said with obvious relief. "Because I would understand if you considered him to be perfectly rotten. Zach has many bad habits, and he's a bit wild, not to mention arrogant beyond belief . . . but underneath he's the gentlest man that ever lived. You'll probably never see that side of him—he only shows it to Mama and me. But I did want you to understand that he is definitely worth helping."

"If I didn't believe that, I would never have accepted the position he offered." They walked up a gentle slope toward a pair of long rectangular ponds. It was early enough that white mist still hovered over the water and frost still clung to the leaves of the hedges. Breathing deeply of the morning air, Holly cast a smile toward Elizabeth. "I find it remarkable that your brother has accomplished all this," she said, gesturing at the spectacular beauty all around them.

"Zach does whatever is necessary to get what he wants," Elizabeth replied, slowing her pace as they crossed a stone bridge leading to a topiary garden. "No matter what the cost to himself. I never knew my own father—there's only been Zach to take care of Mama and me. All during my childhood, Zach worked at the docks to support us. But there was never enough money for a decent life. Then Zach turned to prizefighting. He was good at it, of course, but the fights were so brutal . . . Just hearing the accounts of them afterward made me physically ill." Pausing at a topiary shaped like three balls standing atop each other, Elizabeth scrubbed her fingers through the riot of dark curls on her forehead. She sighed at some painful memory. "After a fight, Zach would come into the smelly old lodging house where we lived . . . and, oh, the way he looked. All bloody and battered, his body just black and purple with bruises. He couldn't stand to be touched, even to let Mama and me rub liniment on him. We begged him not to do it anymore, but once he's made up his mind about something, he won't be swayed."

Holly meandered to a cone-shaped hedge. "How long did his prizefighting last?"

"About two years, I think." A heavy swath of curls dropped from the pile on Elizabeth's head, and she scowled. "Oh, this wretched hair . . . there's nothing to be done with it." She reached up, twisted the offending locks and pinned them back into the unruly mass. "By the time I was twelve," she continued, "we moved out of the lodging house and into our own little cottage. Then Zachary became part-owner of a steamship and started acquiring more wealth, and . . . well, he seems to have the Midas touch. Zach has accomplished almost every goal he's set for himself. Except . . . he hasn't changed much since his prizefighting days. Often he behaves as if he's still in the rope ring. Not that he's physically violent, but . . . can you understand what I mean?"

"Yes," Holly murmured. Zachary Bronson was still struggling and striving, unable to let go of his tightly coiled aggression. Now it was being applied to the world of business rather than pugilism. And he was horribly self-indulgent, taking his pleasure with many women in order to reward himself for all he had been deprived of. He needed someone to tame him enough that he could live comfortably in a civilized society. However, that person would certainly not be herself—all she was capable of was polishing the surface a little.

"Zach wants to marry, and marry well," Elizabeth said wryly. "Tell me truthfully, Lady Holly, do you know any woman that would be able to manage him?"

The question made Holly uncomfortable, because she did not. And she knew that none of the legion of sheltered young girls coming out this Season would have any idea of how to handle a man like Bronson.

"I thought so," Elizabeth said, reading the answer in Holly's face. "Well, we've our work cut out for us, don't we? Because Zachary also wants *me* to marry, and not just any old baron or viscount will do." She gave a merry, unrestrained laugh. "He won't rest until he's foisted me off on a duke!"

Holly seated herself on a small marble bench and stared at the girl expectantly, not sharing her amusement. "Is that what you want for yourself?"

"Good God, no!" Elizabeth's laughter quieted somewhat, and she strode around the topiaries. Her restless energy would not allow her to sit. "What I want is impossible

. . . so I shall probably become a spinster, and travel 'round the world for the rest of my days."

"Tell me," Holly insisted gently. "What is it that you dream of?"

Elizabeth flashed her a strangely defiant glance. "It's simple, really. I want a man who will love me, without having an eye on my brother's damned fortune. An honest, decent man who is strong enough to deal with my brother. But I'll never have that, no matter how many manners you might try to teach me."

"Why not?"

"Because I'm a bastard," Elizabeth blurted out. She gave a sudden shaky laugh at Holly's blank face. "Zach didn't tell you? Of course not—he thinks that ignoring the fact will make it go away. But the truth is, I am the result of a brief affair my mother had long after her husband died. A scoundrel came into her life, seduced her with pretty words and a few paltry gifts, and he disappeared when he tired of her. I never knew him, of course. But I was a terrible burden on the family, until Zachary grew old enough to start taking care of us."

Holly felt a wave of compassion as she saw the girl's shamefaced expression. "Elizabeth, please come here." She indicated the seat next to her.

After a long hesitation, the girl complied. She stared at the scenery before them, her profile set, her long legs stretched out before them. Holly spoke with extreme care. "Elizabeth, illegitimacy is hardly an unusual circumstance. There are many such offspring of the aristocracy that have found places for themselves in good society."

"Well," Elizabeth said gruffly, "it doesn't exactly add to my appeal, does it?"

"It's not something one would wish for," Holly admitted. "But neither does it have to ruin all chance of making a good marriage." She reached out and patted the girl's long, slender hand. "Therefore, I wouldn't count on becoming a spinster just yet."

"I'm not going to marry just anyone," Elizabeth said. "He'll be a man worth having, or I'll remain unattached."

"Of course," Holly replied equably. "There are many things worse than having no husband, and one of them is having a bad or insufficient husband."

Elizabeth laughed in surprise. "I've always thought your kind believed that any marriage, no matter how good or bad, is better than no marriage at all."

"I've seen too many unhappy unions, in which an ill-suited husband and wife cause each other terrible misery. There must be liking and respect between two partners."

"What kind of marriage did you have, my lady?" As soon as the question left her lips, Elizabeth flushed, fearing she might have given offense. "I'm sorry—do you mind my asking—"

"No, of course not. I take great pleasure in talking about my late husband. I want to keep him alive in my memory. We had the most wonderful marriage imaginable." Smiling wistfully, Holly stretched out her short legs and regarded the worn front edges of her shoes. "Looking back on all of it now, it almost seems like a dream. I'd loved George always—we were distant cousins, and during my childhood I had only brief glimpses of him. George was a handsome young man, and he was very kind, and he was adored by his friends and family. I was a plump child, and very shy, and I doubt I ever exchanged more than ten words with him. Then George went on his Grand Tour, and I didn't see him for the longest time. When he returned four years later, I was eighteen. We met at a ball." Smiling, Holly put her hands to her warm cheeks, finding that the pleasurable memory still caused her to blush. "George asked me to dance, and I thought my heart would stop. He had a sort of quiet charm and confidence that I found irresistible. For the next few months he courted me most ardently, until my father gave his consent for us to marry. We had three years together. There wasn't a day of our marriage that I didn't feel loved and cherished. Rose was born not long before George died. I am so thankful he was able to spend a little time with her."

Elizabeth seemed enthralled by the story. "Oh, Lady Holland." She stared at Holly with sympathy and wonder. "How lucky you were to have such a man."

"Yes," Holly said softly. "I certainly was."

They were both quiet for a minute, staring out at the rustling flower beds beyond the topiaries, until Elizabeth seemed to shake her private thoughts away. "Let's make the most of the bad material you've been given to work with, Lady Holland," she said briskly. "Shall we return to the house and begin our lessons?"

"Certainly." Holly stood and brushed her skirts. "I thought we might begin with sitting, standing and walking."

That drew a burst of laughter from the young woman. "I thought I already knew how to do those things!"

Holly smiled. "You do them quite well, Elizabeth. However, there are a few little things . . ."

"Yes, I know. I swing my arms when I'm walking. As if I'm in a rowing competition."

The description caused Holly to smile. "I assure you, it's not nearly that bad."

"You're very diplomatic," Elizabeth said with a grin. "But I know very well that I have all the feminine grace of a soldier under the command of his drill sergeant. It will be a miracle if you can help me."

They began the walk back to the mansion, and Holly

hurried to keep up with Elizabeth's ground-covering strides. "For one thing," she said breathlessly, "you might try slowing a bit."

"Sorry." Instantly Elizabeth checked her free pace. "I always seem to be in a hurry, even when there's nowhere for me to go."

"My governess always taught me that gentlemen and ladies should never walk fast—it's a mark of vulgarity."

"Why?"

"I don't know why." Holly laughed ruefully. "In fact, I don't know the reasons for many of the things I plan to teach you . . . it's just the way things are done."

They chatted amiably as they returned to the house, and Holly reflected that she hadn't expected to like Zachary Bronson's sister so much. Elizabeth was entirely worthy of being helped, and so deserving of love. But she needed a very particular sort of man to marry, one who was neither too weak nor too controlling. A strong man who would appreciate Elizabeth's lively spirit and not try to crush it. The girl's natural ebullience was part of what made her so attractive.

There ought to be someone, Holly mused, sorting through a list of her acquaintances. She would write a few letters this evening, to friends she hadn't communicated with in far too long. It was time to step back into the flow of society and renew old friendships, and become *au courant* with all the news and gossip. How strange, that after the past years of solitude, she was suddenly eager to rejoin the circles she had once belonged to. A sense of buoyant lightness filled her, and she was hopeful, excited, as she had not been since . . .

Since George had died. Suddenly uneasiness seeped through her, dispelling the warm anticipation. She felt guilty for enjoying herself. As if she had no right to happiness now that George was no longer with her. For the duration of her mourning, he had been in the forefront of her thoughts every minute of the day . . . until now. Now her mind was being filled with new thoughts and ambitions, and she was mingling with people he had never known.

I won't ever let go of you, dearest darling, she thought fiercely. *I will never forget one moment of what we had. I just need a change of scene, that's all. But I'll spend the rest of my life waiting to be with you again—*

"Lady Holland, are you all right?" Elizabeth had stopped near the entrance of the mansion, her glowing brown eyes filled with concern. "You've become so quiet, and you're flushed—oh, I was walking too fast again, wasn't I?" She hung her dark head contritely. "Forgive me. I'm going to hobble myself, see if I don't."

"No, no . . ." Holly laughed self-consciously. "It's not you at all. It's difficult to explain. My life has moved at a very slow pace for the past three years. A very slow pace. Now everything seems to be changing very quickly, and it's a bit of a struggle for me to adjust."

"Oh." Elizabeth looked relieved. "Well, that's what my brother does to people. He meddles and fiddles with their lives, and turns everything upside down."

"In this case, I'm glad he did. I'm happy to be here, and to be of use to someone other than my daughter."

"No happier than we are, my lady. Praise heaven that someone will try to make this family a bit more presentable. The only thing I regret is that I won't be able to watch you teach Zach about etiquette. To my mind, that would be jolly good entertainment."

"I wouldn't mind if you wished to join our lessons," Holly said, taking to the idea instantly. She wasn't looking forward to being alone with Zachary Bronson, and having his sister accompany them might dispel the tension that seemed to shred the air whenever he was near.

"Zach would mind," Elizabeth said dryly. "He made it clear that his sessions with you were to remain strictly private. He has a lot of pride, you know. He never allows his weaknesses to be exposed, and he doesn't want anyone, even me, to discover how little he knows about being a gentleman."

"Being a gentleman is quite a bit more than a few lessons on manners," Holly replied. "It is a condition of character . . . it means being noble, kind, modest, courageous, self-sacrificing and honest. Every minute of the day. Whether one is in the company of others or completely alone."

There was a brief silence, and then Holly was surprised to hear Elizabeth snicker. "Well," the girl said, "just do your best with him."

The lessons with Elizabeth went very well, as Holly instructed her in the art of sitting in a chair or rising gracefully. The trick was to keep the body from inclining too far forward during either process, and managing one's skirts with one hand without exposing a provocative glimpse of ankle. Elizabeth's mother Paula came to watch the proceedings, sitting quietly in the corner of a plush settee. "Come practice with us, Mama," Elizabeth urged, but the shy older woman declined with a smile.

There were several moments of hilarity, as Elizabeth resorted to antics that Holly suspected were designed to amuse her mother . . . walking and sitting with exaggerated stiffness, then swooping about theatrically, until all three of them were laughing. Toward the end of the morning, however, Elizabeth mastered every nuance of posture and movement, until Holly was more than satisfied.

"Perfect. How graceful you are, Elizabeth," Holly exclaimed.

The young woman flushed, clearly unaccustomed to such straightforward praise. "I'll forget every bit of this by tomorrow."

"We'll practice until everything becomes second nature," Holly replied.

Folding her long, slender arms across her chest, Elizabeth lounged in a chair, her legs sprawled in a completely unladylike manner. "Lady Holland," she asked with a smile, "have you ever thought that all these manners and social rules were invented by people with entirely too much time on their hands?"

"You may be right," Holly said with a laugh.

As Holly left the Bronson women in search of her daughter, she continued to ponder the question. Everything she knew about first society and the behaviors associated with gentlefolk had been instilled in her since birth. She had never thought to question those long-ago lessons until now. Many of the social graces, such as courtesy and self-composure, were undoubtedly necessary for a civilized society. But as for the countless little affectations that Elizabeth had been referring to . . . was it truly important how a person sat or stood or gestured, or what phrases were fashionable and what clothes were in style? Or was it really all just a way for certain people trying to prove themselves superior to others?

The idea that a man like Zachary Bronson might be inherently equal to a man like . . . well, like one of the Taylors, or even her dear George . . . it was a provocative notion. The great majority of aristocrats would immediately dismiss the idea. Some men were born with blue blood, with generations of noble ancestors behind them, and this made them better, finer than ordinary men. This

was what Holly had always been taught. But Zachary
Bronson had started in life with no advantage whatsoever,
and he had made himself into a man to be reckoned with.
And he was trying very hard to better himself and his
family, and soften the coarseness of his own character.
Was he really so inferior to the Taylors? Or to herself?

These ideas would never have occurred to her had she
not agreed to work for Bronson. For the first time, Holly
realized that this year of closeness with Bronson and his
family might change her, just as it would change them.
And that troubled her. Would George have approved?

After a pleasant afternoon of reading books and taking
a walk in the gardens together, Holly and Rose sat in the
library and waited for Zachary Bronson. Rose devoured a
snack of milk and buttered bread, and proceeded to play
on the floor while Holly sipped tea from a flowered china
cup. A blazing fire in the huge green marble fireplace mingled with the shafts of afternoon light coming through the
velvet-draped windows.

Not daring to sit at Bronson's huge masculine desk,
Holly occupied a chair at a nearby side table as she made
a few notes regarding the proper forms of address for the
various tiers of aristocracy. The subject was a complicated
one, even for those who had been born into the peerage,
but it was important for Bronson to understand it thoroughly if he desired to mingle successfully with the *ton*.
She concentrated so hard on the task before her that she
would not have noticed Bronson's entrance into the room
were it not for her daughter's delighted exclamation.

"There he is, Mama!"

Glancing upward, Holly tensed at Bronson's approach,
while her nerves responded to his presence with a strange,
pleasurable jangle. He was such a large, vital man, bring-

ing the fresh scent of outdoors with him. As he stopped close to her and bowed, she couldn't help noticing the alluring fragrance that clung to him, a masculine blend of horses and starched linen and sweat. With his swarthy complexion and sparkling black eyes, and the shadow of bristle beneath his close-shaven skin, he seemed more potently virile than any other man of her acquaintance. Bronson smiled at her, his teeth gleaming white in his tanned face, and Holly realized with renewed surprise that he was handsome. Not in a classical sense, and not in a poetic or artistic sense . . . but he was definitely attractive.

Holly was perturbed by her own reaction to him. He was not at all the kind of man she should find appealing, not after having known and loved someone like George. Her husband had been faultless in his easy confidence and his golden good looks. Holly had even been amused by the way women stared and swooned over George. It had not been George's dazzling looks, however, that had made him so compelling. It was his utter refinement, both of character and manners. He had been polished, courteous, a gentleman from the inside out.

Comparing George to Zachary Bronson was like comparing a prince to a pirate. If one spent ten years doing nothing but drilling rules and rituals into Bronson's head, anyone would still glance at him and immediately proclaim him a scoundrel. Nothing would ever dispel the rascally gleam in his black eyes or the heathen charm of his smile. It was all too easy to picture Bronson as a bare-knuckle fighter, stripped to the waist as he pummeled an opponent in the rope ring. The problem was, Holly felt a thrill of shameful unladylike interest in the image.

"Good afternoon, Mr. Bronson," she said, gesturing for him to take a seat next to her. "I hope you will not object if Rose plays in the corner during our discussion today. She has promised to be very quiet."

"Naturally I wouldn't object to such charming company." Bronson smiled at the petite child, who sat on the carpeted floor with her toys. "Are you having tea, Miss Rose?"

"Yes, Mr. Bronson. Miss Crumpet asked me to pour. Would you like a cup, too?" Before Holly could restrain her, the little girl hastened to Bronson with a doll-sized cup and saucer no bigger than his thumbnail. "Here you are, sir." A tiny concerned frown adorned her brow. "It's only 'air tea,' but it's quite delicious if you're good at pretending."

Bronson accepted the cup as if it were a great favor. Carefully he sampled the invisible brew. "A bit more sugar, perhaps," he said thoughtfully.

Holly watched while the two prepared the cup to Bronson's satisfaction. She had not expected Bronson to interact so comfortably with a child. In fact, not even George's brothers, Rose's own uncles, had displayed such ease with her. Children were seldom part of a man's world. Even the most doting father did little more than view his child once or twice a day and inquire after his or her progress.

Glancing at Holly briefly, Bronson caught her perplexed expression. "I was coerced into more than a few tea parties by Elizabeth when she was no bigger than Rose," he said. "Although Lizzie had to make do with shingles for plates and an old tin cup instead of china. I always swore I'd get her a proper toy tea set someday. By the time I could afford one, she was too old to want it any longer."

A maid entered the room, evidently having been requested to bring a tray of refreshments, and Bronson rubbed his hands in anticipation. Bearing a huge silver tray laden with a coffee service and a plate of confections, the maid awkwardly unloaded the pots and dishes onto the small table.

Quietly asking the girl's name, Holly murmured a few suggestions to her. "You may set the tray on the sideboard, Gladys," she said, "and carry the dishes here one or two at a time. And serve from the left, please."

Clearly taken aback by the unexpected advice, the girl looked askance at Bronson. He smothered a grin and spoke gravely. "Do as Lady Holland says, Gladys. I'm afraid no one is exempt from her authority—not even me."

Nodding at once, Gladys complied with Holly's instructions. To Holly's surprise, the maid set out a plate piled high with miniature round cakes, each one covered with a delicate sheen of pale pink icing.

Holly sent Bronson a reproachful glance, knowing that he had ordered the treat specifically for her enjoyment. "Mr. Bronson," she said, recalling their conversation much earlier in the day, "I can't fathom what reason you have for plying me with cakes."

Bronson settled back in his chair, looking completely unrepentant. "I wanted to see you wrestle with temptation."

Holly couldn't repress the laugh that bubbled to her lips. The insolent rogue! "I fear you're a wicked man," she said.

"I am," he admitted without hesitation.

Still smiling, Holly grasped a pair of forks and expertly grasped a delicate cake in a scissor hold that did not damage its fragile shape. She placed it on a small china plate and handed it to her daughter, who exclaimed happily and proceeded to devour the confection. After serving herself and Bronson, Holly gave him the pages of notes she had made.

"After the success I had with your sister today, I am feeling rather ambitious," she said. "I thought you and I might start on one of the most difficult subjects of all."

"Titles and rules of peerage," Bronson muttered, staring at the long columns written in neat script. "God help me."

"If you can learn this," Holly said, "and eventually do a decent quadrille, the battle will be mostly won."

Bronson picked up one of the pink-iced cakes with his fingers and ate most of it in one bite. "Do your worst," he advised out of the side of his mouth that wasn't stuffed.

Making a mental note to do something about his primitive eating style at some later date, Holly began to explain. "I'm certain you're already aware of the five titles of peerage: duke, marquess, earl, viscount and baron."

"What about knights?"

"Knights are not peers, and neither are baronets." Holly lifted a fork to her lips, swallowed a spongy morsel of cake and closed her eyes in a brief moment of pleasure as the crisp, delicate icing dissolved at once on her tongue. She took a swallow of tea, then became aware that Bronson was staring at her strangely. His face was smooth and suddenly taut, and the coffee-dark eyes were as alert as those of a cat watching for movement in the grass.

"Lady Holland," he said, his tone underlaid with gravel, "there's a speck of sugar on your . . ." He stopped suddenly, apparently too preoccupied to find any more words.

Holly explored the left corner of her mouth with the tip of her tongue, discovering a fleck of sweetness. "Thank you," she murmured, dabbing at the spot with her napkin. She made her tone brisk as she continued, wondering why he seemed a bit uncomfortable and distracted. "Now, back to the peerage. Only an actual peer can be considered to have the title by right. All other titles, including those possessed by the peer's eldest son, are merely courtesy titles. If you turn to the third page I gave you, there is a little chart that I hoped might make things clear . . ." Holly slipped from her chair and went to Bronson's side of the table, leaning over his shoulder as he riffled through the sheaf of paper. "There. Does that make sense to you, or am I creating a hopeless muddle?"

"No, it's clear enough. Except . . . why are there no courtesy titles in these two columns?"

Holly forced herself to concentrate on the paper he held, but it was difficult. Their heads were very close together, and she was strongly tempted to touch his hair. The thick, rumpled locks needed to be brushed and smoothed with a drop of pomade, especially the place where an unruly swath sprang over his forehead. So different from George's silky blond hair. Bronson's locks were as black as midnight, a bit coarse, curling slightly at the ends and the nape of his neck. His neck was thick with muscle, and it looked as hard as iron. She almost brushed the tempting surface with her fingers. Horrified by the impulse, she curled her hand into a fist as she answered him. "Because children of dukes, marquesses and earls are able to prefix their names with 'Lord' or 'Lady,' but children of viscounts and barons are merely 'Mr.' or 'Miss'."

"Like your husband," Bronson muttered, not taking his eyes from the list.

"Yes, that is an excellent example. My husband's father was a viscount. He was known as Viscount Taylor of Westbridge or more simply, Albert, Lord Taylor. He had three sons, William, George and Thomas, all three of whom were "Mr. Taylor." When the viscount passed away a few years ago, his eldest son William assumed his title and became William, Lord Taylor."

"But George and his brother never became 'lords.' "

"No, they both remained 'Mr.' "

"Then why are you called 'Lady Holland'?"

"Well . . ." Holly paused and laughed ruefully. "Now

we're treading on more complicated territory. I am the daughter of an earl. Therefore, I have had the courtesy title 'lady' since birth."

"And you didn't lose it when you married George?"

"No, when a peer's daughter marries a man who is not a peer, she is allowed to keep her own courtesy title. After I married, I still derived my rank from my father rather than from George."

Bronson turned his head and stared at her intently. Looking into his fathomless eyes at close range gave Holly a small, warm shock. She could see the glints of brown in the midnight depths. "So your rank was always higher than your husband's," he said. "In a way, you married down."

"Technically," she admitted.

Bronson seemed to savor the information. Holly had the impression that for some reason the idea pleased him. "What would happen to your rank if you married a commoner?" he asked idly. "Like me, for example."

Flustered by the question, Holly drew away from him and resumed her seat. "Well, I . . . I would remain 'Lady Holland,' but I would take your surname."

"Lady Holland Bronson."

She started a little at the strange sound of her own name being joined with anything other than Taylor. "Yes," she said softly. "In theory, that is correct."

Busily she fussed with her skirts and smoothed them over her lap as she sensed him staring at her. Glancing upward, she saw the look in his eyes, a raw glitter of masculine interest. A surge of something like anxiety drove her heart to a faster beat. When had a man ever looked at her this way? George's blue eyes had contained love and tenderness when he beheld her, but never this look of sexual appraisal . . . heat . . . appetite.

Bronson's gaze moved to her mouth, her breasts, then

back to her face, bringing a wash of prickling warmth to her skin. It was the kind of intimate stare that no gentleman would give a lady. He was doing it to fluster her, Holly thought. He was amusing himself by deliberately unsettling her. Yet he did not seem amused. A frown drew the thick slashes of his brows together, and he seemed as troubled, more troubled, than she.

"Mama!" Rose's laughing voice cut through the uncomfortable silence. "Your cheeks are all red!"

"Are they?" Holly asked unsteadily, bringing her cool fingers to her hot face. "I must be sitting too close to the fire."

Tucking Miss Crumpet beneath one arm, Rose went to Bronson. "I'm only a 'Miss,' " she informed him, having listened to their discussion of the peerage. "But when I marry a prince someday, I'll be 'Princess Rose,' and then you may call me 'Your Highness.' "

Bronson laughed, his tension seeming to dispel. "You're already a princess," he said, scooping the little girl up and setting her on his knee.

Caught by surprise, Rose let out a squealing laugh. "No, I'm not! I don't have a crown!"

Bronson appeared to take the point seriously. "What kind of crown would you like, Princess Rose?"

"Well, let me think . . ." Rose screwed up her small face in deep concentration.

"Silver?" Bronson prompted. "Gold? With colored stones, or pearls?"

"Rose does not need a crown," Holly intervened with a touch of alarm, realizing that Bronson was more than ready to purchase some ostentatious headpiece for the child. "Back to play, Rose—unless you would care to take an afternoon nap, in which case I'll ring for Maude."

"Oh, no, I don't want a nap," the little girl said, immediately sliding from Bronson's knee. "May I have another cake, Mama?"

Holly smiled fondly and shook her head. "No, you may not. You'll spoil your dinner."

"Oh, Mama, can't I have just one more? One of the little ones?"

"I've just said no, Rose. Now please play quietly while Mr. Bronson and I finish our discussion."

Obeying reluctantly, Rose glanced back at Bronson. "Why is your nose crooked, Mr. Bronson?"

"Rose," Holly reproved sharply. "You know very well that we never make observations about a person's appearance."

However, Bronson answered the child with a grin. "I ran into something once."

"A door?" The child guessed. "A wall?"

"A hard left hook."

"Oh." Rose stared at him contemplatively. "What does that mean?"

"It's a fighting term."

"Fighting is bad," the little girl said firmly. "Very, very bad."

"Yes, I know." Lowering his head, Bronson tried to look chastened, but his air of repentance was far from convincing.

"Rose," Holly said in a warning tone. "There'll be no further interruptions, I hope."

"No, Mama." Obediently the child returned to her play area. As she walked behind Bronson's chair, he surreptitiously handed her another cake. Grabbing the tidbit, Rose hurried to the corner like a furtive squirrel.

Holly gave Bronson a look of reproof. "I won't have my daughter indulged, sir. She'll become accustomed to all your extravagances, and after this year is through, she'll have a difficult time returning to her normal existence."

Mindful of the small imp playing nearby, Bronson kept his tone low. "It won't hurt her to be spoiled a little. They're only children for a short time."

"Rose must not be sheltered from the realities and responsibilities of life—"

"Is that the prevailing thought in child-rearing these days?" he asked lazily. "It explains why most of the aristocratic children I've seen are pale, repressed creatures with sullen expressions. I suspect many parents are just a little too eager to expose their brats to 'reality.' "

Instantly offended, Holly opened her mouth to disagree, but found to her chagrin that she could not. The Taylors reared their own children with an eye toward proving a "good stiff preparation for life," and frequently encouraged Holly to do the same with Rose. Discipline, constant moral training, and deprivation were all methods employed to make a child properly obedient and well-mannered. Not that it worked, of course. The Taylor children were little hellions, and Holly thought that Rose might have been, too, had she not been far more gentle with her daughter than the Taylors had advised. And yet their views were common for noble families and shared by most people of their rank.

"Childhood should be wonderful," Bronson said abruptly. "Worry-free. Happy. I don't give a damn if anyone agrees with me or not. I only wish . . ." Suddenly his dark gaze dropped to the papers before him.

"Yes?" Holly prompted gently, leaning forward.

Bronson answered without looking at her. "I wish I could have made it that way for Lizzie. She went through hell during her childhood years. We were poor and dirty and starving most of the time. I failed her."

"But you're not that much older than Elizabeth," Holly

murmured. "You were only a child yourself, with a great burden of responsibility."

Bronson reacted with a dismissive gesture, clearly wanting no excuses to be made for himself. "I failed her," he repeated gruffly. "The only thing I can do is try to make things right for her now, and for my own children when I have them."

"And you'll spoil my daughter unmercifully in the meantime?" Holly said, a faint smile curving her lips.

"Maybe I'll spoil you as well." There was a teasing edge to his voice, but his gaze contained a flash of challenge that stunned her. She did not know how to react. Indignation or rebuke would only earn his mockery. Yet she could not allow him to play with her this way. Cat-and-mouse-games were not her forte, and she did not enjoy them.

She made her voice crisp and unruffled. "You've already given me a handsome salary, Mr. Bronson, which I intend to earn by educating you thoroughly in the social graces. Now, if you'll refer to the second page of notes, we will discuss the differences between correct forms of address in correspondence and conversation. For example, you would never refer to a man as 'The Honourable' in person, but you would on paper—"

"Later," Bronson interrupted, lacing his long fingers together and settling them against his lean midriff. "My brain is filled with titles. I've had enough for today."

"All right. Shall I leave you, then?"

"Do you *want* to leave?" he asked softly.

She blinked at the question, then felt her throat tighten with a catch of laughter. "Mr. Bronson, I wish you would stop trying to disconcert me!"

A mocking smile appeared in his eyes. "Now, what is so disconcerting about a simple question?"

"Because if I said yes it would be rude, and if I said no—"

"—then it might imply a liking for my company," he finished for her, his white teeth flashing in a grin. "Go, then. God knows I wouldn't force you to make such a damning admission."

Holly remained in her chair. "I'll stay if you'll tell me about the time you broke your nose."

Bronson's smile lingered as he touched the angled bridge of his nose reflectively. "I got this while sparring with Tom Crib, the former coal porter they called the 'Black Diamond.' He had fists as big as hams and a left hook that made you see stars."

"Who won?" Holly asked, unable to resist.

"I outlasted Crib after twenty rounds and finally knocked him down. It was after that fight that I got my name—'Bronson the Butcher.' "

The obvious masculine pride he took in the name made Holly feel slightly queasy. "How charming," she murmured in a dry tone that made him laugh.

"It didn't improve my looks much, having Crib smash my beak," he said, rubbing the bridge of his nose between thumb and forefinger. "I wasn't a pretty sort to begin with. Now I'll definitely never be mistaken for an aristocrat."

"You wouldn't have anyway."

Bronson pretended to wince. "That's as painful a jab as any I received in the rope ring, my lady. So you don't exactly fancy my beat-up mug, is that what you're saying?"

"You know very well that you're an attractive man, Mr. Bronson. Just not in an aristocratic way. For one thing, you have too many . . . that is, you're too . . . muscular." She gestured to his bulging coat sleeves and shoulders. "Pampered noblemen don't have arms like that."

"So my tailor tells me."

"Isn't there any way to make them, well . . . smaller?"

"Not that I'm aware of. But just to satisfy my curiosity, how much would I have to shrivel to pass for a gentleman?"

Holly laughed and shook her head. "Physical appearance is the least of your worries, sir. You need to acquire a proper air of dignity. You're far too irreverent."

"But attractive," he countered. "You did say I was attractive."

"Did I? I'm certain I meant to use the word 'incorrigible.' "

A shared smile caused a mixture of delight and heat to ripple over Holly. Hurriedly she dropped her gaze to her lap, breathing a little faster than normal. She felt odd, barely contained, as if the pressure of excitement within her would cause her to leap from her chair. She didn't dare look at Bronson, fearing her own reaction if she did. He made her want to . . . well, she wasn't certain what. All she knew was that the memory of his kiss, the sweet, warm invasion of his mouth, was suddenly at the forefront of her mind. She turned scarlet and folded her hands tightly together, repressing herself.

"My fighting career didn't last for long," she heard Bronson say. "I only did it to make enough money to acquire interest in a steamship."

"Really?" Holly asked, finally able to look at him once more. "I rather wonder if you didn't enjoy it a little."

"Yes, I did," he admitted. "I like to compete. And to win. But there was too much pain and too little profit from prizefighting. And I soon learned that there are ways to down a man without bloodying your hands."

"My goodness, Mr. Bronson. Must you lead your life as if it's a constant battle for supremacy?"

"How else should I behave?"

"You could try relaxing a bit and enjoying what you've accomplished."

His dark, cinnamon-flecked eyes mocked her. "Did you ever play king of the mountain when you were a child, Lady Holly? Probably not—it's hardly a game for respectable little girls. You find a pile of dirt or refuse and compete with your comrades to see who can fight his way to the top. And that's the easy part."

"What is the difficult part, Mr. Bronson?"

"Staying there."

"I'll bet you managed to stay there from sunrise to nightfall," she said softly. "Kicking and pummeling all the boys who tried to replace you."

"Only until suppertime," he confessed with a sudden grin. "I was always defeated by my stomach."

Holly let out a sudden peal of unladylike laughter. She couldn't seem to hold it in, not even when her daughter, clearly surprised by the sound, came to stand by her chair. "What is it, Mama?"

"Mr. Bronson," Holly explained, "was just telling me a story about when he was a little boy."

Although Rose had no idea what the joke was, she began to laugh, too.

As Bronson watched them both, his brown eyes were lit with a peculiar warm glow. "I believe the two of you are the prettiest sight I've ever seen."

Holly's amusement faded, and she stood in sudden consternation, obliging Bronson to stand as well. *I shouldn't be here,* was the uppermost thought in her mind. *I should never have agreed to work for him, no matter what the enticement.* She realized now how inexperienced and sheltered she was, otherwise he wouldn't be able to throw her off balance so easily. If she didn't guard herself against him, he was going to play havoc with her emotions. Was it because she had been so long without a man that she was so flustered by his attentions? Or was it because he was so unlike any other man she had ever known?

Worst of all was the feeling that any enjoyment of his company, and any appreciation of his robust, street-seasoned handsomeness, was a betrayal of George.

For a moment Holly remembered the days of utter despair after her husband had died, and the black wish that had consumed her. She had wanted with all her heart to die along with him. It was only the love and concern Holly felt for her infant daughter that had kept her sane. Instead, she had vowed to honor George by spending the rest of her life loving only him, thinking only of him and his wishes. It had never occurred to Holly that such a vow might be difficult to keep. But here was an utter stranger, gently wooing her away from propriety a step at a time.

"Mr. Bronson," she said a bit unsteadily, "I—I will see you at supper."

Bronson's face wore an expression of seriousness identical to her own. "Let Rose eat with us," he said. "Don't any upper-class children have supper with their families?"

Holly took a long moment to answer. "In some country homes the children are allowed to eat *en famille*. However, in most well-to-do households the children take separate nursery meals. Rose has become accustomed to the arrangement at the Taylors' mansion, and I should dislike to change a familiar ritual—"

"But there she had other children to eat with, didn't she?" Bronson pointed out. "And here she has to take most meals by herself."

Holly glanced into her daughter's small face. Rose seemed to be holding her breath, waiting with silent excitement to see if her unexpected champion would succeed at gaining her a place at the adults' dinner table. It would be easy for Holly to insist that Rose adhere to the traditional mealtime separation between grown-ups and children. However, as Bronson and the little girl both stared at her expectantly, Holly realized with a flash of amused despair that yet another boundary was to be broken.

"Very well," she said. "If Rose behaves well, she may take meals with the family from now on."

To Holly's surprise, Rose flew to Bronson with an exclamation of happiness and threw her arms around his leg. "Oh, Mr. Bronson," she cried, "thank you!"

Grinning, Bronson disentangled her little arms and sank to his haunches. "Thank your mother, princess. I only asked. She was the one who gave permission."

Bouncing back to Holly, Rose decorated her face with kisses.

"Darling," Holly murmured, trying not to smile, "let's go upstairs and change your pinafore and wash your face before dinner. We can't have you looking like a ragamuffin."

"Yes, Mama." Rose's small hand took hers, and she skipped eagerly as she led Holly away.

Seven

As Holly began to correspond with a number of friends, many of whom she had not seen since George's funeral, she was surprised by their responses to the information that she was working and residing at the London estate of Mr. Zachary Bronson. Naturally many of the reactions were disapproving, even offering her a place in their own homes if she was truly that destitute. However, an unexpected majority expressed great interest in her new situation and inquired if they might come to call on her at Bronson's estate. It seemed that a great many ladies were eager to view Bronson's home and, more than that, encounter the man himself.

Bronson did not seem surprised by the fact when Holly mentioned it to him. "It happens all the time," he said with a cynical smile. "Women of your class would go to the guillotine before marrying a mongrel like me . . . but a surprising number want to be my 'friend.' "

"You mean they are willing to . . . with *you* . . . ?" Holly paused in dismayed wonder. "Even the married ones?"

"Especially the married ones," Bronson informed her dryly. "While you were secluded in mourning at the Taylors' house, I've entertained a great many fine ladies of London between my sheets."

119

"A gentleman does not boast of his sexual conquests," Holly had said, flushing at the information.

"I wasn't boasting. I was stating a fact."

"Some facts are better kept to yourself."

The unusual sharpness of her tone seemed to interest him to no end. "There's a strange expression on your face, Lady Holly," he said silkily. "It almost looks like jealousy."

A wave of rising annoyance nearly choked her. Zachary Bronson had a talent for rousing her temper more easily than anyone she had ever known. "Not at all. I was merely reflecting unpleasantly on the number of diseases one must catch from such a dedicated pursuit of gallantry."

" 'Pursuit of gallantry,' " he repeated with a low laugh. "That's the prettiest way I've ever heard it put. No, I've never caught the pox or any other affliction from my whoring. There are ways a man can protect himself—"

"I assure you, I do not wish to hear about them!" Horrified, Holly had clapped her hands over her ears. As the most sexually indulgent creature of her acquaintance, Bronson was all too willing to discuss intimate subjects that a gentleman should never admit to knowing. "You, sir, are a moral abyss."

Rather than look shamed, he actually grinned at the remark. "And you, my lady, are a prude."

"Thank you," she said crisply.

"That wasn't meant as a compliment."

"Any criticism of yours, Mr. Bronson, I will definitely receive as a compliment."

Bronson had laughed, as he did whenever she attempted to provide the smallest tidbit of moral instruction. He was interested only in the superficial lessons of how to behave like a gentleman. And when it suited him, he would be more than ready to shed his mannered facade. However, try as she might, Holly could not dislike him.

As the days of Holly's residence at the Bronson estate lengthened into weeks, there were many things she learned about her employer, including the fact that he had many personal qualities to admire. Bronson was honest about his flaws and remarkably unpretentious about his background and lack of education. He possessed a strange sort of modesty, constantly downplaying his tremendous innate intelligence and his considerable achievements. He often used his sly charm to make her laugh against her will. In fact, he seemed to delight in provoking her until her temper began to show, then he made her laugh in the midst of her frustration.

They spent many evenings together, sometimes with Rose playing at their feet as they talked. Occasionally they conversed alone into the night, after the lateness of the hour had caused Elizabeth and Paula to retire. As the coals glowed in the hearth, Bronson would ply Holly with glasses of rare wine and regale her with vulgar but fascinating tales of his own life. In return, he insisted on hearing stories of Holly's childhood. Holly had no idea why mundane details of her past should interest him so, but he persisted in asking until she told him about ridiculous things, like the naughty childhood cousin who had once tied her long hair to the back of her chair, or the time she had deliberately dropped a wet sponge on a footman's head from an upstairs balcony.

And sometimes he asked about George. About their marriage . . . even what it had been like to give birth.

"You know I can't discuss such a thing with you," Holly protested.

"Why not?" Bronson's alert black eyes were softened by the light of the fire. They were sitting in the private family parlor, a cozy jewel box of a room that was swathed in rich olive velvet. It seemed that the world outside this small, elegant room was very far away. Holly knew that it was wrong for the two of them to be secluded in this intimate atmosphere. Too close . . . too private. However, she couldn't seem to make herself leave. There was a wicked part of her that wanted to stay despite the dictates of propriety.

"You know very well that it's indecent," she told him. "I fault you very much for asking such a question."

"Tell me," he insisted lazily, lifting a wine goblet to his mouth. "Were you a good little soldier or a screaming banshee?"

"Mr. Bronson!" She threw him a look of utter rebuke. "Have you no delicacy at all? Or even a thimbleful of respect for me?"

"I respect you more than I've ever respected another human being, my lady," he said readily.

Holly shook her head, fighting the reluctant smile that pulled at her lips. "I was not a good soldier," she admitted. "It was horribly painful and difficult, and worst of all was that it only lasted twelve hours and everyone said it was an easy birth, and I was given hardly any sympathy at all."

His laughter contained a trace of delight at her rueful complaint. "Would you have had more children? If George had lived?"

"Of course. A married woman has no choice in such matters."

"Doesn't she?"

Perplexed, she met his shrewd gaze. "No, I . . . What do you mean?"

"I mean there are ways to prevent unwanted pregnancy."

Holly regarded him with horrified silence. Good women shunned any discussion of such matters. In fact, the subject was so forbidden that there had never been a mention of it between she and George. Oh, there had been whispers she had inadvertently heard from other women, but she had promptly removed herself from the vicinity of such inappropriate discussion. And here was this unscrupulous man daring to say such things to her face!

"Now I truly have offended you," Bronson remarked, trying to look penitent, but she sensed the amusement lurking just beneath his facade. "Forgive me, my lady. There are times I forget someone could be so sheltered."

"It's time that I retired for the evening," Holly said with great dignity, deciding that her only recourse was to ignore the distasteful exchange as if it had never occurred. "Good night, Mr. Bronson." She rose to her feet, and Bronson followed immediately.

"There's no need to leave," he coaxed. "I'll behave from now on. I promise."

"It's late," Holly said firmly, retreating to the door. "Again, sir, good night—"

Somehow he reached the threshold before she did, without any appearance of haste. His large hand pressed lightly on the door, closing it with a quiet click. "Stay," he murmured, "and I'll open a bottle of that Rhenish wine you liked so much the other evening."

Frowning, Holly turned to face him. She was prepared to point out that a gentleman did not argue with a lady when she wished to leave, nor would it be proper for them to remain in the room with the door closed. But as she stared into his dark, teasing eyes, she found herself relenting. "If I stay, we'll find some proper subject to discuss," she said warily.

"Anything you like," came his prompt reply. "Taxes. Social concerns. The weather."

She wanted to smile as she saw his deliberately bland expression. He looked like a wolf trying to pretend he was a sheep. "All right, then," she said, and returned to the settee. He brought her a fresh glass of wine, something dark and full-bodied, and she sipped the rich vintage with deep appreciation. She had come to like the outrageously expensive wines he stocked, which was unfortunate, as they would someday no longer be available to her. In the meantime, however, she might as well enjoy the benefits of residing at his estate: the wines, the beautiful artwork, and most sinfully luxurious of all . . . his company.

Several years ago she would have been frightened of being alone with a man like Zachary Bronson. He did not treat her with the carefully protective courtesy she had always been given by her father, and the polite young gentleman who had courted her, and the impeccable man she had married. Bronson used coarse language in front of her, and discussed subjects no lady should be interested in, and did not try to conceal the more unpleasant facts of life.

He kept her wine glass liberally filled as they talked, and as the night deepened, Holly curled into the corner of the settee and let her head droop to the side. *Why, I've drunk too much,* she thought in surprise, and somehow did not experience the horror or embarrassment that should have accompanied such a realization. Ladies never drank too much, only allowed themselves a few drops of watered-down wine now and then.

Contemplating her nearly empty glass in puzzlement, Holly moved to set it on the small table beside the settee. The room seemed to sway suddenly, and the glass began to tilt in her hand. Deftly Bronson reached out, caught the wobbling crystal stem and set it aside. As Holly stared at his handsome face, she felt rather light-headed and loose-tongued, and strangely relieved and free in the way she always felt when Maude had helped her out of a particularly confining gown at bedtime.

"Mr. Bronson," she said, her words seeming to float aimlessly out of her mouth, "you've let me drink far too much of that wine . . . As a matter of fact, you *encouraged* me, which was very wrong of you."

"You're not all that intoxicated, my lady." His mouth twitched with amusement. "You're just a little more relaxed than usual."

The statement was patently untrue, but for some reason it reassured her. "It's time I retired for the evening," she announced, lurching upward from the settee. The room seemed to spin, and she felt herself falling, sinking through the air as if she had stepped off a cliff. Bronson reached out and caught her easily, stopping the wayward tumble. "Oh—" Holly clutched at his forearms as he steadied her. "I seem to be a trifle dizzy. Thank you. I must have tripped on something." She bent to peer fuzzily at the carpet, searching for the object that had impeded her, and she heard Bronson's soft chuckle.

"Why are you laughing?" Holly demanded as he lowered her back to the settee.

"Because I've never seen anyone get so tipsy from three glasses of wine." She made a move to rise, but he sat beside her, preventing the halfhearted attempt at escape. His hip was perilously close to hers, causing her to shrink hard against the back of the settee. "Stay with me," Bronson murmured. "The night is half-gone already."

"Mr. Bronson," she asked suspiciously, "are you trying to compromise me?"

His white teeth flashed in a grin, as if he were teasing her, but there was a disturbing hot glimmer in his gaze. "I could be. Why not spend the next few hours with me on this settee?"

"Talking?" she asked faintly.

"Among other things." He touched the curve of her jaw

with his forefinger, leaving a streak of fire along the sensitive curve. "I promise you would enjoy it. And afterward we'll blame it on the wine."

She could hardly believe he had dared to suggest something so outrageous. "Blame it on the wine," she repeated in indignation, and giggled suddenly. "How many times have you used that phrase in the past, I wonder?"

"This is the first time," he assured her easily. "I rather like it, don't you?"

She frowned at him. "You've propositioned the wrong woman, Mr. Bronson. There are a hundred reasons why I would never do *that* with you."

"Tell me a few." His black eyes were wickedly inviting.

She waggled an unsteady finger in his face. "Morality ... decency ... self-respect ... the responsibility to set an example for my daughter ... not to mention the fact that any indiscretion with you would make it impossible for me to stay."

"Interesting," he mused. Holly inched backward as he leaned over her, until her head was resting heavily on the arm of the settee and she was stretched out beneath him.

"What's interesting?" she asked, drawing a deep breath, and then another. The air in the room had become very warm. Her arm felt heavy as she reached up to push back a strand of hair that clung to her damp forehead. She let her elbow rest above her head, moist palm turned upward. She had drunk far too much ... she was intoxicated ... and while this fact did not especially bother her at present, she knew in the back of her mind that it would be a matter of great concern to her later.

"You listed every reason except the one that truly matters." Bronson's face was very close, and his mouth—surely the most tantalizing mouth she had ever seen, full-lipped and wide and promising—was so close that she felt his breath gently touch her cheek. The smell of his breath was pleasantly infused with wine and his own intimate flavor. "You forgot to say that you don't desire me."

"Well, that . . . that's a given," she faltered.

"Is it?" Rather than look offended, he seemed faintly amused. "I wonder, Lady Holly, if I could possibly make you want me."

"Oh, I don't think . . ." Her voice was extinguished into a feeble gasp as she saw his head lower toward hers, and her body tingled with a shock of realization. She closed her eyes tightly, waiting, waiting . . . and she felt his mouth descend to the delicate inside of her wrist. The velvet slide of sensation sent an erotic shiver down her arm, and her fingers twitched involuntarily. He let his mouth linger on the soft, thin skin of her wrist, encouraging the tiny pulse to beat madly. Holly's entire body drew tight as a bow, and she wanted to lift her knees and curl around him. Her lips felt swollen and warm, tautly anticipating the pressure of his kiss. He lifted his head and stared at her with eyes as dark as hellfire.

Reaching for something nearby, he held it before her. The crystal wine glass glittered in the firelight, a few remaining sips of burgundy liquid swirling in the bottom. "Finish the wine," he suggested softly, "and let me have my way with you. And in the morning we'll both pretend that you don't remember."

It frightened her, the extent to which she was tempted by the sinful offer. He was mocking her, she thought dizzily . . . surely he couldn't truly be propositioning her. He was waiting to see what her response would be, and then no matter what she said, no or yes, he would make jest of her.

"You're wicked," she whispered.

The smile had left his eyes. "Yes."

Breathing shakily, she passed a hand over her eyes as if trying to clear away the wine-soaked fogginess. "I . . . I want to go upstairs. Alone."

A lengthy silence stretched between them, and then Bronson replied in a light, friendly tone, all intensity safely banked, "Let me help you."

His hands cupped beneath her elbows, and he guided her to her feet. Once she had gained purchase, she found that the room had stopped its heady swaying. Relieved, Holly pushed herself away from his hard, inviting body and made her way to the door. "I'm perfectly able to go to my room unescorted," she said, throwing him a beseeching glance.

"All right." He came to open the door for her, glancing up and down her disheveled form.

"Mr. Bronson . . . this will be forgotten by tomorrow morning." Her voice contained an anxious questioning lilt.

He gave a short nod, watching as she sped away as fast as her wobbling knees would allow.

"Like hell I will," Zachary murmured as soon as Holly had disappeared from sight. He had gone too far with her—he had known it even as he was allowing himself to cross the invisible barriers between them—but he hadn't been able to stop himself. He couldn't seem to control his hunger for her. It was a special agony to be placed under the power of a virtuous woman. The only consolation was that she didn't seem to understand how completely he was in her thrall.

He chafed and fretted over the situation, having never experienced anything like this before. In his arrogant self-confidence, he had always known that he could seduce any woman he wanted, no matter what her station. He was even certain that he could have Holly in his bed, given enough time to melt her defenses. But the moment he slept with her, he would lose her. There would be no way to convince her to stay afterward. And the extraordinary fact was, he wanted her company even more than he wanted to bed her.

Whenever Zach had imagined the woman that might finally capture his attention, his emotions, all his waking thoughts, he had always been certain she would be worldly, bold . . . his sexual equal. He had never considered the possibility of losing his heart and head to a demure widow. Inexplicably Holly worked on him like a drug, exciting and sweet, and like a drug, her absence left him with emptiness and craving.

He was no fool. It was obvious that Lady Holly was not meant for him. Better to pluck some far more available fruit on the tree. But there she hung, tempting and exquisite, always out of reach.

In an effort to quench the desperate craving in his loins, Zachary had turned to other women. As a member of the most exclusive, ridiculously high-priced brothel in town, he was able to purchase a night with any beautiful prostitute of his choice. Lately he had frequented the place almost nightly.

In the evenings Zachary would experience the simmering delight of being with Holly, just looking at her, reveling in the sound of her voice. Then, when she had retired to her solitary bed, he would ride to London and spend the next several hours in complete debauchery. Unfortunately the skill of a prostitute provided only temporary relief from his desire. For the first time in his life, he was beginning to recognize that true passion was not easily satisfied, that there was a difference between the needs of his cock and the organ that resided two feet above it. It was not a welcome discovery.

* * *

"You're building another house?" Holly asked in surprise, standing beside a long library table as Bronson unrolled a set of plans and secured them at the corners with brass weights. "But where . . . and why?"

"I want the grandest country house England has ever seen," Bronson said. "I've bought land in Devon—three estates that will be merged into one. My architect has drawn up plans for the house. I want you to see them."

Holly regarded him with a wry smile. Like a coward, she had pretended not to remember the strange, seductive scene that had transpired the previous evening, and to her infinite relief, Bronson did not indicate by a word or glance that anything untoward had occurred. Instead, he had launched her into a discussion of one of his many developing projects. Privately she decided that her shocking behavior of the night before was all a result of too much wine, which she resolved to avoid in the future. "Mr. Bronson, I would very much like to see the plans, but I must warn you, I am not at all knowledgeable in such matters."

"Yes, you are. You know what the aristocracy admires. Tell me your opinion of the place."

His broad hand moved gently over the plans, smoothing out wrinkles and deftly weighting the paper. As Holly inspected the inked sketches of the various fronts of the house, she was very aware of Bronson standing at her side. He braced his hands on the plans and leaned over the drawings.

Holly tried to concentrate on the plans, but she was distracted by Bronson's nearness. She couldn't help noticing the way his upper arms bulged against the seams of his coat, the way his thick black locks curled on the back of his neck, the close-shaven grain of his beard on his swarthy skin. He was fastidious without being foppish, smelling of starch and soap rather than cologne, his clothes well tailored but cut a bit loose in an effort to conceal the swell of ungentlemanly muscles. Perhaps he was not ideally suited for the drawing room, but there was something powerfully attractive about his sheer manliness.

"What do you think?" he asked in a low rumble.

Holly concentrated for a long time before replying. "I think, Mr. Bronson," she said slowly, "that the architect has designed what he thinks you wish to see."

The house was ostentatious, wasteful, and too formal by far. It jutted in heavy awkwardness from the Devon landscape. Visible, yes. Grand, without question. But "elegant" and "appropriate" were not words that could ever be applied to this overweening homage to old-fashioned taste. "It's very large," she continued, "and anyone who saw it would have no doubt that the owner was a man of great means. However . . ."

"You don't like it."

Their gazes met as they stood close together, and Holly felt a spill of warmth inside as she stared into his intent black eyes. "Do *you* like it, Mr. Bronson?" she managed to ask.

He grinned at the question. "I have bad taste," he said flatly. "My only virtue is that I know it."

She opened her mouth to argue the point, but closed it abruptly. When it came to matters of style, Bronson did indeed have appalling taste.

A quiet laugh vibrated in his throat as he saw her expression. "Tell me what you would change about the house, my lady."

Lifting a corner of the top sketch and surveying the sprawling first-floor plan beneath, Holly shook her head helplessly. "I wouldn't know where to begin. And you must have gone to great expense to have these plans drawn up—"

"That expense is nothing compared to having the damn place built."

"Yes, well . . ." Holly paused thoughtfully, chewing on her lower lip as she considered what to tell him. His gaze flickered to her mouth, and she gave an uneasy start. "Mr. Bronson, would it be too presumptuous of me to suggest another architect? Perhaps you might commission another set of plans based on a different concept and then decide which you prefer. I have a distant cousin, Mr. Jason Somers, who is becoming known and admired for his designs. He is a young architect with modern sensibilities, although I don't believe he's ever been given a project quite so large as this."

"Fine," Bronson said immediately, his gaze still on her mouth. "We'll send him to Devon at once to see what he makes of the property."

"It may take some time before Mr. Somers is able to oblige you. From what I understand, his services are much in demand, and his schedule is constantly filled."

"Oh, he'll go to Devon without delay, once you mention my name," Bronson assured her cynically. "Every architect dreams of landing a patron like me."

Holly couldn't help laughing. "Does your arrogance know no limits?"

"Wait and see," he advised. "Somers will deliver a set of plans to me within a fortnight."

As Bronson had predicted, Jason Somers did indeed come to the estate with a bundle of sketches and partial floor plans in a remarkably short time—sixteen days, to be exact.

"Elizabeth, I'm afraid we'll have to cut the morning lesson short today," Holly murmured, glancing out the window as she saw Somers's modest black carriage traveling along the drive toward the house. Her cousin drove himself, handling the ribbons with clear expertise. "The architect is arriving, and your brother has insisted that I attend the meeting with them."

"Well, if you must . . ." Elizabeth said with apparent regret, shrugging her shoulders.

Holly suppressed a smile, knowing that Elizabeth's sorrow at canceling the lesson was entirely false. The girl had little patience for their current subject, the rules of correspondence. As an energetic young lady with a passion for riding, archery and other physical pursuits, Elizabeth found the act of putting pen to paper exceedingly tiresome.

"Would you like to meet Mr. Somers?" Holly offered. "His work is quite good, and I'm certain your brother would have no objection—"

"Dear me, no. I've better things to do than view the sketches and scratchings of some stuffy old architect. It's just a beautiful morning; I think I'll go for a ride."

"Very well. I'll see you at midday, then."

Taking leave of the girl, Holly descended the grand staircase with an eager step. She found herself smiling at the prospect of seeing her distant cousin. The last time they visited had been at a family gathering at least five years earlier, when Jason was barely out of his teens. A warm-natured boy with a ready sense of humor and an engaging smile, Jason had always been a family favorite. From the time he had been a small child, he had drawn and sketched compulsively, resulting in many a scolding for his perpetually ink-stained fingers. Now, however, he was in the process of building a formidable reputation for his unique style of "natural" architecture that was designed to blend into the landscape.

"Cousin Jason," Holly exclaimed, reaching the entrance hall just as he did.

Somers broke into a smile the moment he saw her, stopping to remove his hat and execute a well-practiced bow. Holly was pleased to see that in the past few years Jason had grown into a wonderfully attractive man. His heavy shock of chestnut-brown hair was cut close to his head, and his green eyes gleamed with intelligence. Although he still possessed the physical lankiness of youth, he had a surprising air of maturity for a man only in his mid-twenties.

"My lady," Jason said in a pleasantly raspy baritone. Holly gave him her hand, and he squeezed it gently. His smile turned regretful as he continued in a softer tone, "Please accept a long-overdue apology for missing your husband's funeral."

Holly regarded him fondly. There was no reason for Jason to apologize, as he had been traveling the continent at the time of George's unexpected death. Since the journey had been too long for Jason to return for the funeral, he had written a letter of condolence. Sweet, a bit awkward and wonderfully heartfelt, the letter had expressed a sincere sympathy that had touched her heart.

"No apology is necessary, as you well know," she replied softly.

The housekeeper, Mrs. Burney, came forward to take Jason's hat and coat.

"Mrs. Burney," Holly murmured, "can you tell me where Mr. Bronson is at present?"

"I believe he's in the library, milady."

"I will show Mr. Somers there." Taking her cousin's arm, Holly guided him through the house, while he carried his plans beneath his other arm.

Glancing at his surroundings as they walked, Jason

emitted a sigh that combined amazement with distaste. "Incredible," he murmured. "Excess upon excess. My lady, if this is the style that Bronson prefers, you would have done better to approach another architect. I couldn't force myself to design something like this."

"Wait until you talk with Mr. Bronson," Holly coaxed.

"All right." Jason smiled at her as they strolled together. "Lady Holly, I know it is because of your influence that I am here, and for that opportunity I thank you. But I must ask . . . what caused you to work for Bronson?" A note of amusement lightened his voice. "As you're no doubt aware, the family in general is 'not pleased.' "

"My mother has informed me of that fact," Holly admitted with a rueful smile.

Upon being informed of Holly's plans to accept employment from Bronson, her parents had made their disapproval clear. Her mother had actually questioned her sanity, suggesting that prolonged grief had undone Holly's ability to make rational decisions. Her father, however, being an exceedingly practical man, had ceased his objections once Holly had described the trust Bronson was providing for Rose's future. As the father of four daughters, three still unmarried, he was all too cognizant of the importance of a large dowry.

"Well?" Jason prompted.

"It's difficult to refuse Mr. Bronson," Holly said dryly. "You'll find out soon enough."

She brought her cousin into the library, where Bronson was waiting. To his credit, Jason showed no sign of intimidation at the sight of the brawny man rising from his massive chair. As Holly knew from her own experience, meeting Bronson for the first time was nothing if not memorable. Few men possessed his powerful larger-than-life presence. Had no one ever told Holly a single thing about

Bronson, she would have instinctively known that he was a man who shaped not only his own fate, but the destinies of other men.

Meeting Bronson's sharp black gaze directly, Jason shook his hand. "Mr. Bronson," he said in his frank, friendly way, "let me thank you at once for the invitation to your estate, and for the opportunity of showing you my work."

"Lady Holly is the one you should thank," Bronson replied. "It was her suggestion that I approach you."

Holly blinked in surprise. Something subtle in Bronson's manner had implied that her suggestions, her opinions, held great value for him. To her consternation, the implication had not escaped Jason Somers's notice. He threw her a quick speculative glance, then returned his attention to Bronson.

"Let us hope that I've justified Lady Holly's faith in me, then," Jason said, hefting the bundle of drawings a bit higher beneath his arm.

Bronson indicated his wide mahogany desk, which had been cleared, and the architect spread his drawings over the polished surface.

Though she had decided to remain neutral while viewing her cousin's work, Holly could not prevent a pleased exclamation as she leaned over the plans. With its romantic gothic overtones, the house was charming but sophisticated, with an abundance of windows—long sheets of what seemed to be undivided plate glass—to bring the landscape "inside." Large main rooms and airy conservatories would provide spectacular settings for parties, but there were also wings that allowed privacy and seclusion for the family.

Holly hoped that Bronson would appreciate the design's unpretentious style, and that he would not make the mistake of thinking elegance was synonymous with heavy embellishment. She was certain that he would at least be pleased by the abundance of modern technology, including running water on all floors, a large number of water closets and tiled shower-bath rooms, and "hot walls" to give warmth and comfort in the winter.

Bronson showed no expression as he stared at the plans, only asked a question or two that Jason hastened to answer. In the midst of the inspection, Holly became aware of someone entering the room. It was Elizabeth, dressed in a smart rose-colored riding habit trimmed in scarlet. The clothes, with their simple but dashing cut, and the feminine froth of white lace at her throat, were especially becoming. With her black curls tightly braided and topped with a scarlet hat, and her dark, heavily lashed eyes, Elizabeth looked young, fresh and exotically alluring.

"I couldn't resist having a look at the plans before I went out . . ." Elizabeth began to say, but her voice faded as Jason Somers turned and bowed. Quickly Holly made the introductions, watching with pride as Elizabeth returned Jason's bow with a perfectly executed curtsy. With the initial greeting concluded, they paused to study each other in a moment of brief but electric curiosity. Then Somers turned back to the table and focused his attention on a question Bronson had posed. He seemed not to notice Elizabeth at all.

Puzzled by his apparent indifference, Holly wondered how he or any other healthy young male could fail to be captivated by the girl's dazzling looks. As the girl joined them at the table, however, Holly noticed that Jason's gaze returned to Elizabeth in a rapid but thorough sweep. He was interested, Holly thought with well-concealed amusement, but he was clever enough not to show it.

A bit piqued by the stranger's lack of attention, Elizabeth stood between Jason and Holly and inspected the plans.

"As you can see," Jason murmured to Bronson, "I've tried to design a place that would be harmonious with the landscape. In other words, one couldn't merely take this house and set it somewhere else and have it look appropriate—"

"I know what 'harmonious' means," Bronson said with a wry smile. He continued to assess the drawings, his keen gaze noting every detail. Having some understanding of the way Bronson absorbed information, Holly knew that in a few minutes he would have nearly as great a familiarity with the floor plans as Jason Somers himself. Bronson had an astonishing memory, although he applied it only to subjects that interested him.

Elizabeth also surveyed the plans, her velvety dark eyes narrowed critically. "What is that?" she asked, pointing to a section of the drawing. "I'm not certain I like that at all."

Jason replied in a voice that seemed a shade or two deeper than usual, "Kindly remove your finger from my plans, Miss Bronson."

"Yes, but what is this . . . this misaligned thing, this odd projection—"

"It's called a wing," Jason said shortly. "And those little rectangles are what we architects like to call windows and doors."

"Your east wing doesn't match the west wing."

"Someday I would love to explain why," Jason muttered in a tone that implied just the opposite.

"Well, it looks lopsided," Elizabeth persisted.

Their gazes met in challenge, and Holly suspected that both were secretly enjoying the exchange.

"Stop provoking the man, Lizzie," Zachary muttered, ignoring the unspoken interplay. His attention was firmly secured on Holly. "What do you think of the plans, my lady?"

"I think the house would be magnificent," she replied.

He gave a decisive nod. "Then I'll have it built."

"Not merely because of *my* liking for it, I hope," Holly said, vaguely alarmed.

"Why not?"

"Because you must decide on it only as a matter of following your own taste."

"The plans look fine to me," Bronson replied thoughtfully, "although I wouldn't mind a tower here and there, and some crenellation—"

"No towers," the architect interrupted hastily.

"Crenellation?" Holly asked at the same time. Then she saw the twinkle in Bronson's eyes and realized he was teasing.

"Build it the way you've drawn it," Bronson advised the architect with a grin.

"Just like that?" Jason asked, clearly a bit stunned by the speed of decision. "Are you certain you don't want to look over the plans in private and consider the matter at your leisure?"

"I've seen all I needed to," Bronson assured him.

Holly could not help smiling at her cousin's surprise. She knew that Jason had never met a man as comfortable with his own authority as Zachary Bronson. Bronson liked to make decisions quickly, rarely wasting time to ponder difficult matters. He had once told her that while ten percent of his decisions turned out to be mistakes, and another twenty percent usually had benign results, the remaining seventy percent were generally fine. Holly had no idea how he had arrived at such figures, but she had no doubt that he could support them with evidence. It was a quirk of Bronson's, that he was fond of applying numbers and percentages to every situation. He had even once calculated that his sister Elizabeth had a ten percent chance of marrying a duke.

"Why only ten percent?" Elizabeth had asked pertly, having appeared near the end of that particular conversation. "I'll have you know that I could land anyone I wanted to."

"I calculated the number of available dukes, subtracted the ones who were too elderly or infirm and factored in the number of lessons you'll need from Lady Holland to be presentable. I also took into consideration the number of young women on the marriage market you'll be competing with." Bronson had paused and sent a sly grin to his sister. "Unfortunately, your age skewed the numbers a bit."

"My age?" Elizabeth had cried in feigned outrage. "Are you trying to say that I'm past my prime?"

"You're over twenty-one, aren't you?" Bronson pointed out, and deftly caught the small velvet cushion that his sister had hurled at his head.

"Elizabeth, a lady does not throw things when a gentleman displeases her," Holly said, laughing at the boisterous pair.

"May a lady crown her infuriating brother over the head with a fireplace poker?" Elizabeth advanced upon Bronson in a threatening manner.

"Unfortunately not," Holly answered. "And considering the hardness of Mr. Bronson's head, that effort would likely have little effect."

Bronson had pretended to look insulted, though a swift grin escaped him.

"Then how is a lady to have revenge?" Elizabeth demanded.

"Indifference," Holly replied softly. "Withdrawal."

Elizabeth flopped into a chair, her long legs splayed willy-nilly beneath her skirts. "I was hoping for something more painful."

"A bashing with an iron poker doesn't cause so much as a twinge of fear," Bronson had told his sister with a low laugh. "But Lady Holly's indifference . . ." He pretended to shiver, as if he had suddenly been thrust into an arctic blast. "That's more punishment than any man should have to bear."

Holly had shaken her head in amusement, while inwardly she had reflected that no woman could remain indifferent to a man like Zachary Bronson.

There were days, however, when Bronson did not make her smile . . . days when he could be irascible and obstinate, venting his bad temper on everyone around him. It seemed at times that demons drove him. Even Holly was not exempt from his jeers or sarcasm, and it seemed that the cooler and more courteous she became, the higher it drove his flames of discontent. She guessed that there was something he wanted but had decided was not obtainable, and whatever it was, he suffered mightily from bitter longing. Just what the "something" was, whether social acceptability or perhaps a business deal that had eluded him, was impossible to discern. Holly was certain that it was not loneliness, as Bronson did not lack for the company of women. Like the rest of the household, she was well aware of his ceaseless nocturnal activities, his frequent coming and goings, the signs of excess drinking and debauchery that showed on his face after a particularly wild evening.

His appetites for entertainment and women began to bother Holly more and more. She rationalized that he was no different from many other men in this regard. There were many aristocratic men who behaved even worse, carousing all night and sleeping off their excesses during the daylight hours. The fact that Bronson somehow managed to roam all night and work during the day was proof of a remarkably energetic constitution. But she was not easily able to shrug off his womanizing, and in a moment of raw honesty she admitted to herself that her disapproval had far less to do with morality than her own personal feelings.

The thought of Bronson in another woman's arms made her feel strangely bleak. And unbearably curious. Every evening when he left the house for a night of womanizing, her imagination ran rampant. She knew somehow that Bronson's sexual activities were different in every way from the sweet, gentle interludes she had shared with George. Although her husband had not been a virgin on their wedding night, his experience in such matters had been greatly limited. In bed, George had been respectful and kind, loving rather than lustful, and despite his warm nature, he had believed that sexual intercourse was a pleasure that should not be indulged in too often. He had never visited her bedroom more than once a week. Such occasions had been all the sweeter and more special, never to be taken for granted by either of them.

Zachary Bronson, however, had all the self-restraint of a tomcat. The way he had kissed her in the conservatory was evidence of a sexual knowledge that went far beyond her own experience, or George's. Holly knew she should be repelled by this aspect of Bronson. If only she could suppress the dreams that sometimes awakened her at night, the same tangled, erotic images that had bothered her ever since George's death. Dreams of herself being touched, kissed, held naked against a man's body . . . except that the images were more disturbing than ever before, because now the stranger in her dreams had a face. It was Zachary

Bronson's dark features above her, his hot mouth possessing hers, his hands touching her intimately.

Holly would always wake from these dreams troubled and sweating, and she was hardly able to look at Bronson the next day without flushing scarlet. She had always thought herself above such base desires, had even felt sorry for people who seemed unable to master their physical passion. She had never been troubled by lust. But there was no other word for it, this sweet ache that sometimes overwhelmed her, this terrible preoccupation with Zachary Bronson . . . this awful wish that she could be one of the women he visited to satisfy his needs.

Eight

Although Holly *wore* a gray dress today, its drabness was relieved a bit by touches of raspberry-colored piping at the throat and wrists. It was the kind of garment a nun would have been comfortable in . . . except that there was a little two-inch dip at the throat of her high-necked dress. The opening was shaped like a keyhole to reveal a glimpse of tender, pale skin. Just that little flash of skin was enough to send Zachary's imagination careening wildly. He had never been so riveted by a place on a woman's neck. He wanted to press his mouth into the sweet hollow, smell her, lick her . . . Thoughts of the soft body beneath the smothering gray fabric were almost too much to bear.

"Mr. Bronson, you seem distracted today," Holly said, and he dragged his gaze from her gown to her warm, whiskey-colored eyes. Such innocent brown eyes . . . He would swear that she had no idea how she affected him.

Holly's soft lips tilted with a smile. "I'm aware of your reluctance to do this," she said. "However, you must learn to dance, and to do it well. The Plymouth ball is only two months away."

"The Plymouth ball," he repeated, arching his brows sardonically. "This is the first I've heard of it."

"I thought it would be the perfect occasion to give your

social skills an outing. It's an annual event hosted by Lord and Lady Plymouth, always at the height of the Season. I've been acquainted with the Plymouths for many years, and they are an exceedingly gracious family. I will discreetly prevail on the Plymouths to send invitations. We'll bring Elizabeth out into society that very night, and you . . . well, there is no doubt that you will encounter many well-bred young women, one of whom might possibly capture your interest."

Zachary nodded automatically, although he knew that no woman on earth could capture his interest as intensely as Lady Holland Taylor had. He must have frowned or appeared disgruntled, for Holly gave him a reassuring smile. "I think you'll find that it's not as difficult as you might expect," she said, evidently thinking that he was worried about the dance lessons. "We'll just take things one step at a time. And if it turns out that I am not able to teach you adequately, we will consult with Monsieur Girouard."

"No dancing master," Zachary said gruffly, having taken an instant dislike to the man. He had watched the dance lessons with Elizabeth the previous morning and had strongly resisted Girouard's mistaken attempt to include him in the instructions.

Holly sighed as if her patience were being strained. "Your sister likes him well enough," she pointed out. "Monsieur Girouard is a very talented dancing master."

"He tried to hold my hand."

"I assure you, it was with no other intention than to lead you through the steps of a quadrille."

"I don't hold hands with other men," Zachary said. "And that little frog-eater looked like he was going to enjoy it."

Holly rolled her eyes and let the comment pass.

They stood alone in the sumptuously upholstered ball-room, the walls covered in pale green silk and acres of overwrought gilded carving. Rows of rich green malachite columns, fit for a Russian palace, filled the spaces between gold-framed mirrors that reached eighteen feet in height. It seemed remarkable that the ceiling could support the weight of the six massive chandeliers sparkling with carriage-loads of crystal drops. Since no music was nec-essary for Zachary to learn the basic patterns of various dances, the musicians' bower at the back of the room was empty.

Zachary saw his partner's reflection in many of the mir-rors that surrounded them. Her gray gown was incongru-ous in such an ornate setting. What would Holly look like in a ball gown? He imagined her in some low-cut garment with bare shoulders, trimmed with the frothy stuff he had seen on womens' evening dresses lately: the pretty, round shapes of her breasts rising from the bodice . . . the glitter of diamonds on her pale skin. Her dark brown hair up-swept to reveal jeweled earbobs clasped to her little ears—

"Do you remember the rules of ballroom etiquette that we discussed yesterday?" he heard her ask, and he forced his attention to the business at hand.

"Once I've asked a young lady to dance," he said in a singsong tone, "I should not leave her until I've returned her to the chaperone. After the dance is finished, I ask if she will take some refreshment. If she says yes, I find a seat for her in the refreshment room and provide every-thing she needs, and stay with her as long as she cares to sit there." He paused and asked with a slight scowl, "What if she wants to sit and fill her face for an hour? Or even longer?"

"You will remain with her until she is satisfied," Holly said. "And then you will return her to the chaperone and bow, and offer thanks for the pleasure of her company. Furthermore, you must dance with the plain girls as well as the beautiful ones, and never dance more than twice with one particular partner. And in the event of a supper dance, you must offer to escort the chaperone to the dining table, and be as agreeable and charming as possible."

Zachary sighed heavily.

"Now, on to the opening march," Holly said briskly. "When you lead the march at your own ball, you must keep the pace slow and dignified. Follow the direction of the walls, and execute the change steps at the corners." She leaned a bit closer to him and said in a conspiratorial manner, "A march is really just a walk around the room for all the ladies to display their finery. You can't make a mistake, Mr. Bronson. Just lead the couples around the sides and back through the center of the ballroom. And try to look a bit arrogant. It should pose very little problem for you."

Her gentle teasing caused a surge of pleasure inside him. The idea of performing the staid, pretentious march at a ball usually made Zachary jeer and laugh. But the notion of parading around the room to display a woman like Holly on his arm . . . well, that had some merit. It was a territorial statement that he rather liked.

"And you must never, never march with two ladies at once," Holly admonished.

"Why not?"

"For one thing, the change steps at the corners would be impossible, and for another . . ." She stopped, seeming to forget what she had been about to say as their gazes met. Blinking slowly, as if she were distracted, she forced herself to continue. "It's an honor that a gentleman does to one particular lady." She reached for his arm and took it lightly. "Let us proceed to the first corner."

They walked with great dignity, while Zachary was absurdly conscious of the sound his feet made on the gleaming parqueted floor. Upon reaching the corner, they paused while Holly explained the change steps. "I will release your arm and take your hand, and you will guide me from your left side to your right . . ." She began to execute the movement as she spoke, and Zachary obliged her. Their hands touched, and the feel of her cool little fingers sliding against his palm caused Zachary to catch his breath.

Holly stopped in apparent confusion and snatched her hand back with a slight gasp. She must have felt it, too, the exciting leap of sensation that resulted from the touch of their hands. Zachary stood staring at her down-bent head, dying to clasp his palms over her sleek, dark hair and tilt her face upward. He would never forget how it had felt to kiss her, the way her lips had clung to his, the sweet interior of her mouth, the vulnerable sound of her breathing.

"We . . ." Holly said unsteadily, "we should be wearing gloves. Ladies and gentlemen always wear gloves when they dance."

"Shall I send someone to fetch them?" Zachary was surprised by the raspiness of his own voice.

"No, I . . . I suppose that won't be necessary." She took a deep breath, appearing to compose herself. "Always bring an extra pair of gloves to a ball," she murmured. "A gentleman should never offer a soiled glove to a lady."

Not looking at him, she reached for his hand once more. Their bare fingers clasped for a brief, electric moment, and she guided him through the change steps.

"It's been so long," he heard her say in near-whisper. "I've almost forgotten how to do this."

"You haven't danced since George?" he asked.

She shook her head in wordless response.

This was his particular idea of hell, Zachary reflected silently, his mind and body on fire as the lesson on marching proceeded. He was grateful for the fashionably long hem of his coat that draped over the front of his trousers. If Holly had any inkling of how aroused he was, how close he was to crushing her against him and defiling her with his hands, mouth and every conceivable part of his body, she would probably run screaming from the ballroom.

However, the march wasn't nearly as bad as the quadrille, a tedious pattern of *glissades* and *chassés,* and all manner of foppish footwork. And the waltz turned out to be the most excruciating torment man—or woman—had ever devised.

"Stand just a little to my right," Holly said, her thick lashes lowering over her eyes, "and put your right arm around my waist. Firmly, but not too tightly."

"Like this?" Carefully Zachary fitted his arm around the neat curve of her waist, feeling unaccountably awkward. He, of all men, was well accustomed to holding a woman in his arms, but this experience was different from all others. He had never touched someone as fine as she, had never wanted so keenly to please a woman. For once her emotions were difficult to read, and he wondered if she disliked being so close to him. After all, she had been used to dancing in the slim, elegant arms of aristocratic men, not brawny, low-bred bruisers like himself. His hands felt like big paws, his feet as large and heavy as carriage wheels.

Her left hand came to rest gently on his right shoulder. His tailor had stripped every bit of padding from the shoulder of his coat in an effort to make him appear smaller, but unfortunately nothing could conceal the brutish swell of muscle.

Holly took his left hand in her right . . . Her fingers felt dainty and crushable. She was so light and sweet in his arms that it caused a pang of yearning inside him. "The man guides his partner with this hand," she said, her face upturned. "You mustn't hold my fingers too tightly ... your grasp must be firm and steady, but gentle. And keep your arm just a bit rounded."

"I'm afraid I'm going to step on you," he muttered.

"Just concentrate on maintaining the proper distance between us. If you hold me too tightly, you'll restrict my freedom of movement. If we stand too far apart, however, I won't have sufficient support."

"I don't think I can do this," Zachary said thickly. "You've taught me how to do the march, and I can muddle through a quadrille. Let's leave things at that."

"Oh, but you must learn to waltz," she coaxed. "You'll never be able to court a girl properly if you can't waltz."

His succinct reply caused her to frown in sudden determination.

"Utter all the obscenities you like, Mr. Bronson. Nothing will deter me from teaching you to waltz. And if you prove to be uncooperative, I will send for Monsieur Girouard."

The threat of the dancing master caused his scowl to deepen. "All right, dammit. What do I do next?"

"A waltz is composed of two steps, each lasting three beats. Now glide backward with your left foot—a *little* step, mind you—then draw the right foot back a bit beyond the left and turn toward the right . . ."

To say the least, it was a struggle at first. However, as Zachary concentrated on Holly's instructions and felt her glide with him in seemingly magical conformity, his lumbering steps became a bit more assured. It helped that she moved with him so easily, turning with the slightest pressure of his hand. It helped also that she seemed to be enjoying herself, although he couldn't fathom why she should like to stumble through a waltz with him.

"Keep your arm steady," she warned, her eyes sparkling as she stared into his set face. "You're moving it like a pump handle."

As she had probably intended, the comment distracted him from counting. He raised one brow in a sardonic glance that usually withered the recipient. "All I can concentrate on at the moment, my lady, is trying not to maim you with one misplaced step."

"You're doing very well, actually," she said. "Don't tell me you've never tried to waltz before."

"Never."

"You're surprisingly agile. Most beginners rest too much of their weight on their heels."

"Boxing," Zachary said, pulling her in another half-turn. "If you have lead feet in the rope ring, there's no way to duck and dodge."

Although he had not intended the comment to be amusing, Holly seemed to be greatly entertained. "I wouldn't suggest applying too many of your pugilistic skills to our dance lesson, Mr. Bronson. I should dislike to find myself engaged in fisticuffs with you."

Staring into her smiling, rosy-cheeked face, Zachary experienced a painfully sweet sensation, an ache that had less to do with the body than the spirit. She was the most adorable woman he had ever known. Not for the first time, he felt acute envy for George Taylor for having been loved by her. For having the right to touch and kiss her whenever he had wanted. For having had her turn to him for all of her needs. For being loved by her still.

From everything Zachary had been told, George Taylor had been the perfect man. Handsome, well-heeled, honorable, respectable, gentlemanly and compassionate. It seemed that he had deserved a woman like Holly, every bit as much as Zachary did *not* deserve her. Zachary knew that he was none of the things George had been. Everything he could offer her, including his own heart, was tainted.

"If only" were the two words that Zachary most loathed in the English language. They rattled in his brain unmercifully. *If only, if only . . .*

He lost the rhythm of the waltz and stopped abruptly, causing Holly to bump into him. She gave a small, gasping laugh. "Oh . . . you stopped so suddenly, I—"

Muttering an apology, Zachary steadied her with his hands. Momentum had brought her small body against his. The feel of her, even in the confining layers of her gray gown, caused his senses to riot in wild pleasure. He tried to release her, to loosen his arm, but his rebellious muscles contracted until she was caught securely against him. Her breath was rapid from exertion, and he felt the soft movements of her breasts against his chest. The moment seemed suspended in time. He waited for her to end it, to protest, but she was strangely silent. The silken fans of her lashes lifted, revealing a stricken gaze. Seared together in something that was becoming, undeniably, an embrace, they stared at each other with helpless fascination.

Eventually Holly averted her gaze, but her warm breath wafted over his chin. His mouth felt hot, dry, and he longed fiercely to press it on hers. He waited for the small hands on his shoulders to move . . . if she would raise one to his neck and urge him downward . . . if she would give only the slightest hint that she wanted him . . . but she remained frozen in his arms, neither shrinking away nor encouraging him.

An unsteady sigh escaped him, and he somehow unlocked his muscles, although his tortured body screamed a silent protest. His vision was slightly blurred. He wondered if Holly had any inkling of how close he was to snatching her up and carrying her somewhere. Anywhere. It seemed all the desire he had ever known was rushing through his body, collecting hotly in his groin. He wanted to feel her beneath him, to take his pleasure within her. And even more than that, he wanted her affection, her caresses, her whispers of love in his ears. He had never felt so much like a fool, desperately wanting something that was so clearly not for him.

All at once a cold, clear voice in his head pointed out that what he could not get from Holly, he would get from another woman. There were hundreds of women in London who would supply all the affection he wanted, for as long as he wanted. Gratefully Zachary seized on the idea like a drowning man reaching a raft. He did not need Lady Holland Taylor. He could get someone prettier, someone wittier, someone with eyes just as warm. There was nothing particularly special about her, and he would prove it to himself tonight, and the following night . . . whatever amount of time it required.

"I think that is enough for today," Holly murmured, still appearing a bit dazed. "You've accomplished quite a lot, Mr. Bronson. I'm certain you'll master the waltz in very good time."

Zachary responded with a bow, forcing a polite smile to his face. "Thank you, my lady. I'll see you for our next lesson on the morrow, then."

"You won't be taking supper at home tonight?"

He shook his head. "I've planned to see friends in town this evening."

There was a flicker in her eyes that betrayed her disapproval. He knew she didn't like his rampant socializing and sexual escapades, and he took sudden savage delight in displeasing her. Let her sleep in a chaste bed every night—he had no scruples about taking his own enjoyment where he could find it.

Holly made her way slowly to Rose's room, where her daughter and Maude were engaged in afternoon reading and playtime. She found it surprisingly difficult to bring her thoughts under control. Her mind kept summoning images of herself clasped in Zachary Bronson's arms, turning slowly in the mirrored ballroom while their joined reflections shimmered around them. Being so close to him, talking and laughing intimately for more than two hours, had ruffled her senses unbearably. She felt troubled, anxious, unhappy about something she could not identify. She was glad the dance lesson was over. There had been a delicious-awful moment when he had held her too closely and she had thought he might kiss her.

What if he had? What would her reaction have been? She was afraid to ponder that question. Bronson appealed to something deep and primitive within her. To a woman who had been taught that even her sexual attraction to her own husband should be contained within strict limits, the situation was alarming.

She should be repulsed by Bronson's coarseness, but instead she was drawn to him. He did not treat her as a fragile doll, or as a figure of sympathy. He provoked and teased and spoke bluntly to her. He made her feel vital and alive, and much too interested in the world outside her own. Instead of refining *him,* she was afraid just the reverse was happening: He was changing *her,* and none for the better.

Laughing a bit shakily, Holly passed a hand over her eyes, which felt sore and sensitive. A shower of sparks passed through her vision, and she caught her breath. "Oh, no," she murmured, recognizing the signs that heralded one of her megrims. As always, the piercing ache was appearing for no discernible reason. Perhaps if she could lie down for a little while with a cool cloth over her forehead, she could avert the coming pain.

Using the banister to aid her progress, Holly ascended the stairs, squinting against the gathering ache in her temples and the back of her neck. As she reached the suite of rooms that she and Rose shared, she heard her daughter's voice.

". . . no, that's not a trot, Maude! That's much too slow. *This* is a trot . . ."

Peeking around the doorframe, Holly watched as her daughter sat on the carpeted floor with the blond maidservant, the two of them surrounded by toys. Rose was holding one of the toys Bronson had given her, a little horse covered in leather. The horse had a cunning tail, a mane made of real horse hair and bright glass eyes. It pulled a miniature carriage and a group of dolls past buildings fashioned of blocks and books.

"Where are they going, darling?" Holly asked softly. "To the park, or to the shops on Regent Street?"

Rose looked up with a smile, her dark curls bouncing. "Mama," she exclaimed, and returned her attention to the trotting horse. "They're going to the steel refinery."

"The steel refinery," Holly repeated with amusement.

A wry smile appeared on Maude's round face. "Yes, milady. Mr. Bronson has been telling Rose about the lives of working people, and what they do at the refineries and factories he owns. I tried to tell him that a child has no need of hearing such things, but he paid me no heed."

Holly's first instinct was to be annoyed with Bronson. He had no right to talk to a sheltered child about the circumstances of the working class. On the other hand, it had never occurred to Holly that her daughter was growing up without an understanding of the differences between rich and poor, and why some people lived in fine homes while others lived in the streets and went hungry. "I suppose," she said hesitantly, "that's not a bad thing. Rose should know a little something about the world . . . that most peoples' lives are different from her own . . ."

She rubbed her aching forehead as the pain intensified to continuous jabs. For the first time, she realized that Zachary Bronson was becoming more real, more influential to her daughter than George ever would. Bronson had played hunt-the-slipper and hide-and-seek with Rose, and had sampled the jam that she "helped" the cook make one rainy afternoon, and built her a house of playing cards as they sat on the floor in front of the fire. Things her father would never be able to do with her.

Bronson never ignored Rose or dismissed her questions as silly. In fact, he treated her as if she were equally valuable, if not more so, as any other member of the household. Most adults regarded children as merely half-formed people, undeserving of rights or privileges until they came of age. But Bronson was clearly fond of the child, and Rose was in turn becoming fond of him. It was another unexpected facet of a situation that bothered Holly on many levels.

"Oh, milady," Maude said, staring at her intently. "It's yer megrims, isn't it? Ye're all white, and ye look ill down to yer toes."

"Yes." Holly let the doorframe support most of her weight and smiled wretchedly at her daughter. "I'm so sorry, Rose. I promised to take you for an afternoon walk, but I can't today."

"Are you sick, Mama?" The little girl's face wrinkled with concern, and she jumped to her feet. She came to Holly and hugged her around the waist. "You should take your medicine," she instructed, sounding like a miniature adult. "And draw the curtains together and close your eyes."

Smiling despite her growing misery, Holly allowed the small tugging hand to guide her to her bedroom. Swiftly Maude pulled the heavy drapes closed, extinguishing all trace of light, and helped Holly to undress.

"Do we have the tonic that Dr. Wentworth left the last time?" Holly whispered, flinching as Maude unfastened the buttons at the back of her gown. The slightest movement in the room caused her head to throb violently. When she had had her last attack of megrims at the Taylor household, the family doctor had given her a bottle of tonic that had sent her into merciful oblivion.

"Of course," Maude murmured, having enough experience with Holly's occasional megrims to keep her voice very soft. "I would never have left it behind, milady. I'll fetch ye a nice big spoonful as soon as ye're settled in bed."

"Thank God." Holly let out a whimpering sigh. "What would I do without you, Maude? Thank you, thank you for coming here to the Bronsons' estate with us. I wouldn't have blamed you for staying with the Taylors."

"An' let you and Rose come to this outlandish place alone?" Maude's low murmur was threaded with a smile. "Truth be told, milady, I rather like it here."

The dress slipped to the floor, followed by a set of light stays and her stockings. Left only in her chemise and pantaloons, Holly crawled into bed. She bit her lips to stifle a groan of discomfort, and eased herself back to the pillow. "Maude," she whispered, "you've had so little time off. I'll remedy that when I'm better again."

"Don't ye worry about a thing," the stout maid soothed. "Just rest yer head, an' I'll be back with yer medicine."

* * *

Dressed in a crisp blue coat and gray trousers, with a fresh black silk cravat wrapped around his throat, Zachary strode down the grand staircase as he headed out for his evening's entertainment. His mood was one not of anticipation, but determination. All the sensations roused from the afternoon's dance lesson still seethed in his body, demanding to be sated. He was primed for a good hard romp with a willing woman, and after that, perhaps a few hours of cards and drinking. Anything to help him forget how it had felt to hold Holly in his arms.

As he reached the landing midway down the stairs, however, his rapid steps slowed and halted at the sight of the disconsolate figure of Rose sitting on one of the carpeted steps. The sight of her, like a prim little doll in her ruffled muslin dress, plump calves encased in thick white stockings, tiny hands filled with her ever-present button string, made him smile. How different she was from the way his sister Elizabeth had been at this age. Rose was well-mannered, introspective, sweetly earnest, whereas Elizabeth had been a spirited little hellion. Holly had done a splendid job so far of sheltering her daughter in a safe, well-ordered existence, but in Zachary's opinion, Rose needed the influence of a father. Someone to help her understand about the world beyond park railings and neat brick-walled gardens, about children who did not wear clothes with lace collars, and people who toiled and sweated for their bread. About the ordinary business of living. However, Rose was not his daughter, and it was not his right to venture any opinions about her upbringing.

He stopped a few steps beneath her and stared at her quizzically. "Princess," he said with a smile twitching at the corner of his mouth, "why are you sitting here by yourself?"

Rose heaved a sigh, her pudgy hands sifting through the glittering buttons on the string. Locating her favorite, the perfume button, she lifted it to her nose and smelled. "I'm waiting for Maude," she said glumly. "She's giving Mama her medicine, and then we're to take supper in the nursery."

"Medicine," Zachary repeated, frowning. Why in hell did Holly have need of medicine? She had been perfectly fine not two hours ago when they had ended their dance lesson. Had she met with some kind of accident?

"For her megrims." The child rested her chin in her hands. "And now there's no one to play with. Maude will try, but she's too tired to be much fun. She'll put me to bed early. Oh, I don't like it when Mama is ill!"

Zachary regarded the child with a thoughtful scowl, wondering if it was possible for someone to develop megrims, an incapacitating case of them, in a mere two hours. What had caused them? All thoughts of his evening activities vanished abruptly. "Princess, you stay here," he muttered. "I'm going to visit your mother."

"Will you?" Rose looked at him hopefully. "Can you make her better again, Mr. Bronson?"

The innocent faith in the question somehow twisted his heart and made him laugh at the same time. He reached down and clasped his hand gently over the top of her dark head. "I'm afraid not, Rose. But I can make certain she has everything she needs."

He left her and ascended the stairs two at a time. Reaching Holly's room just as Maude was exiting, he noted the tension and concern on the maid's face. The peppery sting of anxiety filled his chest. "Maude," he said gruffly, "what the devil is the matter with Lady Holland?"

Quickly the heavyset blonde jerked a finger to her lips in a signal to keep quiet. "One of her megrims again, sir," she said in a whisper. "They come on very quick-like, an' any sound or smell or light causes her dreadful pain."

"What brings them on?"

"I don't know, sir. She's had them every now and again ever since Mr. Taylor passed on to his reward. It usually lasts a day, perhaps a bit more, and then she's back to herself."

"I'll send for a doctor," Zachary said decisively.

Maude shook her head at once. "Pardon, sir, but there's no need for that. Lady Holland has seen a specialist, an' he said there's no cure for her kind of megrims, just to rest and take her medicine until she feels better."

"I'm going to see her."

The maid's broad face registered instant alarm. "Oh, sir, I do wish ye wouldn't trouble her! Lady Holland isn't fit to speak with anyone—she's in misery, and the medicine makes her a bit out of her head. And she's not . . . well, she's not properly attired."

"I won't trouble her, Maude. Now go tend to Rose. She's sitting on the stairs by herself." Ignoring the maid's protests, Zachary pushed his way past the door and entered the bedroom. Blinking, he let his eyes adjust to the darkness and shadows. He could hear the strained sound of Holly's breathing. A faint sickly-sweet scent hovered in the air, and he sniffed curiously. Making his way to the bedside, he found a bottle and a sticky spoon at the night table. Touching his finger to the spoon, he brought it to his lips and discovered the taste of opiate-laced syrup.

Holly stirred beneath the light sheet, sensing someone's presence in the room. Her eyes and forehead were covered with a damp cloth. "M-Maude?" she whispered.

Zachary hesitated before replying. "I thought you would come away from our dance lesson with your *feet* hurting," he murmured, "not your head."

The soft rumble of his voice caused her to twitch. "Oh . . . Mr. Bronson . . . you must leave at once." She spoke groggily, clearly under the influence of the opiates. "I . . . I'm not dressed . . . and this tonic sometimes . . . makes me say things I don't usually mean to say . . ."

"In that case, I insist on staying."

A faint gasp of laughter escaped her. "Please don't make me laugh . . . hurts dreadfully."

Zachary lowered himself into the chair that had been placed by the bedside. The creak it made as it bore his weight made Holly flinch. As his gaze adapted to the lack of light, he stared at the luminous whiteness of her shoulders and the sweet curve where her throat flowed into the slope of her chest. "That medicine you're taking is full of opium, sweet lady. I would hate to see you become addicted to it. I've seen the healthiest of men turn into walking skeletons that way."

"It's the only thing that helps," she murmured, her mind clearly fogged with pain and drugs. "I'll sleep for a day or so . . . then the megrims will go away. No lessons tomorrow . . . forgive me . . ."

"Damn the lessons," Zachary said softly.

"Your language," she reproved with a weak sigh.

"How do the megrims start? Did I do something earlier—"

"No, no . . . never a reason. I start to see sparks and flashes. The pain starts on one side of my head, or my neck . . . it spreads until I'm sick and nauseous everywhere."

Cautiously Zachary moved to the mattress and sat beside her. Holly mumbled a protest as she felt the bed give beneath him. "Mr. Bronson . . . please . . . leave me in peace."

Zachary slid his fingers beneath her neck. The area between her nape and the base of her skull was so tight that he could feel the hard, contracted bands of muscle. Holly moaned at the exquisite pain of his touch. Using the fingertips of both hands, he rubbed the knotted muscles with extreme gentleness. A tear leaked out from beneath the cloth covering her eyes, and she released a quivering breath.

"Does this help?" Zachary whispered after a minute, feeling some of her tension ease.

"Yes, a little . . ."

"Shall I stop?"

Immediately one of her hands came to his wrist, her fingers curling around the side of it. "No, don't stop."

He continued to massage her neck in silence, while her breathing deepened and lengthened until he thought she might have gone to sleep. After a while she surprised him by speaking, her voice blurred and soft.

"The megrims started after George passed away. First one happened when I spent a day reading letters . . . people were so kind . . . they shared their memories . . . everyone said how surprised they were . . . no one surprised as I, though." Her tone was absent, detached, as if she spoke from the heart of a dream. "Such a healthy man. Not quite so robust as you, but still . . . very fit. Then the fever came, and George could keep nothing down but tea. He took to his bed for a week. He lost weight so quickly . . . the bones stood out on his face. The second week I became frightened when his mind began to wander. He seemed to know he was dying . . . he began to prepare. One day he sent for his dearest friend, Ravenhill . . . known since boyhood. He made Ravenhill and me promise . . ."

She sighed, seeming to float away in memory.

"What promise?" Zachary asked, staring at her lax mouth intently. "What did he make you promise?"

"Doesn't matter," Holly mumbled. "I told him yes, anything to give him peace. I asked for one last kiss. He did . . . the sweetest kiss . . . though he was too weak to hold me. A little later his breathing changed . . . the doctor said it was the death rattle. I held George in my arms and felt the life pass out of him . . . held him for a long time till he was no longer warm."

Zachary released her neck and drew the sheet protectively over her bare shoulders. "I'm sorry," he whispered.

"Later I was angry with him," Holly confessed, catching at his hand in a childlike gesture. "I've never told that to anyone."

He was very still, enclosing her fingers in a gentle grip. "Why angry, sweet?"

"Because George . . . didn't fight at all. He just slipped away . . . accepted it . . . like a gentleman. Just slipped away and left me. Wasn't in his nature to fight. How could I blame him for that? But I did."

I would have fought, Zachary thought, sternly locking the words inside himself. *I would have gone toe to toe with the devil himself to stay with you and Rose. I would go down howling and kicking before I let go of what I had.*

A weary smile touched her lips. "Now you know . . . what a bad woman I am."

Zachary remained leaning over her, watching as she drifted to sleep. She was the best woman he had ever known. His entire being was consumed with one wish, that he could somehow protect her from ever knowing another moment of unhappiness. He fought against the feeling she roused in him, this awful tenderness, but it spread until it had infiltrated every part of him. The desire to go out and find solace in another woman's body had vanished completely. All he wanted was to stay here in this dark room, guarding the sleep of Lady Holland Taylor while she dreamed of her dead husband.

Sorely troubled, Zachary moved off the bed. On impulse, he took Holly's limp hand and lifted it reverently to his lips. He kissed the backs of her fingers, the tender hollow of her palm. Nothing had ever felt as good as the silken texture of her skin against his mouth.

Setting her hand onto the covers with great care, Zachary cast a last wretched glance at her before leaving the room. He had to get out of this place, his own home. He felt confined, trapped, suffocated.

"Master?" Maude waited in the center of the hallway, staring at him with patent suspicion.

"Where is Rose?" Zachary asked curtly.

"She is in the family parlor, playing with Mrs. and Miss Bronson." Maude frowned uneasily. "If I may ask, sir, what did you do in Lady Holland's room for so many minutes?"

"I ravished her while she was unconscious," he said gravely. "It took a little longer than I expected."

"Mr. Bronson," the maid exclaimed in outrage, "that is a wicked thing to say!"

"Settle your feathers," he said with a faint smile. "I merely stayed with Lady Holly until she went to sleep. You know I would slit my own throat before causing her any harm."

Maude gazed at him speculatively. "Yes, sir," she said after a moment, "I believe I do know that."

The maid's remark caused Zachary to wonder uncomfortably if his feelings for Holly were becoming that obvious. *Dammit,* he thought savagely, and brushed past her as he strode away, overwhelmed by the need to escape.

Nine

There were clubs in London to suit any interest . . . clubs for gentlemen who were avid sportsmen, politicians, philosophers, drinkers, gamblers or skirt-chasers. There were clubs for the rich, the newly arrived, the intelligent, or the well-born. Zachary had been invited to join innumerable clubs that welcomed professional gentlemen, including highly successful merchants, barristers and entrepreneurs. However, he did not want to belong to one of those. He wanted to join a club that had no desire to accept him, a club that was so exclusive and aristocratic that members were allowed only if their grandfathers had once been admitted. Marlow's was the goal he had finally settled on.

At Marlow's a man had only to snap his fingers for something—a drink, a dish of caviar, a woman—and it was brought to him with discreet alacrity. Always the best-quality goods, in the finest surroundings, with never a mention of a man's preferences made to the outside world. The exterior of the club was unremarkable. It was located near the end of St. James's Street, one of a long line of gentlemen's retreats. The white stone and stucco facade was classical in design, pedimented and symmetrical and far from imposing. However, the interior was solidly, expensively English, every wall and ceiling covered in freshly rubbed mahogany, the floors plushly carpeted with a pattern of large octagons of crimson and brown. The leather furniture was heavy and sturdy, and the richly subdued light was spread by wrought-iron lamps and sconces. It had been designed to make a man feel comfortable, with nary a flower or frieze to be seen.

Marlow's was the Olympus of clubs, with some families applying for generation after generation without success. It had taken Zachary three years to gain entrance. With his signature mixture of financial extortion, bribery and behind-the-scenes manipulations, he had managed to get himself admitted, not as a member, but as a permanent "guest" who might come and go whenever he pleased. There were too many aristocrats whose business affairs were entwined with his, men who would lose their fortunes if he began to play with market forces. He had also bought up the debts of a few foolhardy lords, and he had not hesitated to hold those debts over their heads like a whip.

Zachary had enjoyed presenting key members of Marlow's with the choice of losing everything or allowing a mongrel such as himself to patronize the club. Most of them had unwillingly voted to allow him guest status, but there was no mistaking their keen collective desire to be rid of him. He didn't care. He took perverse enjoyment in relaxing in one of the deep leather armchairs and rustling a newspaper before him as the other men did, and warming his feet at the great stone fireplace.

Tonight Zachary especially enjoyed inflicting his presence on the club. Even George Taylor wouldn't have been welcome here, he thought darkly. In fact, the Taylors had probably never thought to apply for Marlow's. Their blood, though blue, wasn't quite blue enough, and God knew they hadn't the money. But Zachary had managed it, even if he was only a "permanent guest" and not quite a member. And now that he had forcibly wedged himself into the upper strata of society, he had made it just a little easier for the next fellow to climb the ladder after him. It was what the aristocrats feared most, that their ranks would be invaded by arrivistes, that their fine lineages would someday no longer be enough to distinguish them.

As Zachary sat before the fireplace and moodily contemplated the dancing flames, a wolf pack of three young men approached him, two seating themselves in nearby chairs, one standing in an insolent posture with one hand braced on his hip. Zachary glanced at the one who stood next to him and suppressed a contemptuous sneer. Lord Booth, the earl of Warrington, was a self-important ass who hadn't much to recommend him except a distinguished lineage. Upon the recent death of his father, Warrington had inherited a fine title and name, two handsome estates and a mountain of debt, much of it incurred by his own youthful follies. Evidently the old earl had found it difficult to curtail his son's wild spending, much of it done to impress companions that were hardly worth the effort. Now the young Warrington had surrounded himself with friends who fawned and flattered him constantly, thereby increasing his sense of superiority.

"Warrington," Zachary muttered, barely inclining his head. He acknowledged the other two, Turner and Enfield, without enthusiasm.

"Bronson," the young earl said with deceptive friendliness, "what a pleasant surprise to find you here." Warrington was a large, well-built man with a long, narrow face—clearly an aristocratic face, if not exactly a handsome one. He stood and moved with the physical confidence of a man who was proficient in athletics and sporting. "The club has not been graced with your presence for many weeks now," he continued. "One assumes you have been kept very busy with the new, er . . . circumstances in your home."

"To what circumstances are you referring?" Zachary asked softly, although he knew exactly in what direction the conversation was heading.

"Why, everyone in London knows of your new *chère amie,* the exquisite Lady Holland. May I compliment you on your remarkable—and rather surprising—show of good taste. Congratulations, my fortunate fellow."

"No congratulations are in order," Zachary said shortly. "There is no intimate relationship, nor will there be."

Warrington raised his dark brows, as if he were confronted with an obvious falsehood. "The so-called lady is residing under your roof, Bronson. Do you take us all for fools?"

"Under the same roof as my mother and sister," Zachary pointed out evenly, though inwardly his temper had exploded into cold, lethal flame. "To lend instruction and advice to the family."

Warrington laughed nastily, revealing a set of long, uneven teeth. "Oh, I'm certain there is a great deal of 'instructing' going on. Concerning how a fine lady prefers to be bedded, perhaps?"

Warrington's companions chuckled at his lame wit.

Zachary remained in his chair, appearing relaxed in spite of the burst of icy rage in his chest. He was making yet another unwelcome discovery: that any slight upon Lady Holland Taylor was sufficient to make him want to commit murder. He had known when he and Holly had signed their infernal contract of employment that there would be rumors. Even Holly had recognized the certain damage to her reputation. At the time, the idea had not bothered Zachary very much—he had been too intent on getting what he wanted. Now, however, it bothered him exceedingly. He felt little flames exploding behind his eyeballs.

"Retract the comment," he said softly. "And add an apology, while you're at it."

Warrington smiled, clearly pleased that his arrow had hit its mark. "And if I don't?"

"I'll beat it out of you," Zachary replied in deadly earnest.

"A boxing match? Excellent idea." There was no doubt that it was what Warrington had wanted all along. "If I best you, you'll give me your word that you'll leave the club immediately and never enter the place again. And if you emerge the victor, I'll come forth with a retraction and apology."

"And one more thing," Zachary said, staring at the top button of Warrington's finely tailored coat. All the buttons on the garment were large and gold, engraved with the family insignia. However, the top one was adorned with a large, sparkling white diamond that appeared to be at least two carats in weight. "If I win, I'll take that diamond button as well."

"What?" Warrington wore a perplexed expression. "Deuced strange request. What the devil do you want that for?"

"Call it a memento," Zachary replied.

The earl shook his head, as if he suspected he was dealing with a madman. "Very well. Shall we make arrangements for the morning?"

"No." Zachary had no intention of allowing the coxcomb and his cronies to publicize the event all over London, or to cast further aspersions on Lady Holly's honor. The matter would be resolved expediently. He stood and flexed his hands with anticipation. "We'll do it now. In the club cellar."

Warrington seemed momentarily perturbed by Zachary's cold, deliberate manner. "I can't do it right now without any sort of preparation. There's a difference between a properly arranged match and a common street brawl—not that you would understand such distinctions."

Suddenly Zachary smiled. "I understand that you want to make a show of your boxing skills and dispatch my arse from the club once and for all. You have your chance, Warrington. But it will happen here and now, or else we'll declare a forfeit."

"No forfeit," Warrington retorted. "I'll come to scratch whenever and wherever you desire." He turned to one of his companions. "Enfield, will you stand as my second?"

His friend nodded at once, clearly pleased to have been asked.

Warrington glanced at his other companion. "Turner, I suppose that means you'll have to stand for Bronson."

Turner, a pudgy, round-faced fellow with overlong reddish brown locks that straggled to his shoulders, frowned and folded his short arms across his chest. It was apparent that performing the duties of a second for Bronson—remaining in the corner of the rope ring to encourage and assist him—was none too appealing for Turner.

Bronson threw him a jeering smile. "Don't trouble yourself, milord," he muttered. "I have no need of a second."

To all their surprise, a new voice entered the conversation. "I'll serve as your second, Bronson, if I may."

Zachary stared in the direction of the dry, cultured voice, and saw a man seated in a corner chair. Setting aside the fresh-pressed edition of the *Times,* the man stood and approached him. The newcomer was tall and lean and blond, looking the way aristocrats were supposed to look but somehow never did. Zachary studied him thoughtfully, having never seen him at Marlow's before. With his cool gray eyes, wheat-blond hair and perfectly sculpted features, he was handsome—princely, even. His self-contained air and the watchful intelligence of his expression brought the image of a golden hawk to mind.

"Vardon, Lord Blake of Ravenhill," the man said, extending his hand.

Zachary shook his hand, discovering the man had a hard, solid grasp. The sound of the name triggered something in the back of his mind. Ravenhill, Ravenhill . . . the name Holly had spoken just a few hours ago in her drugged reminiscences of George. Ravenhill was the name of George Taylor's closest friend, a man so trusted and valued that he had been present during the last hours of George's life. Was this the same man? Why would he volunteer as Zachary's second for a fistfight? And what did Ravenhill think of the fact that George's beloved wife was now employed by a commoner like himself? Zachary stared into the man's remote silvery-gray eyes, but could discern not a single emotion.

"Why offer to stand for me?" Zachary asked, fascinated despite himself.

"My reasons are my own."

Studying him for a moment longer, Zachary gave a short nod. "Fine, then. Let's go."

Heads turned and papers rustled quietly as the members of Marlow's watched the odd procession. Realizing that some sort of altercation was about to take place, several men rose and followed as the fighters went toward the cellar stairs at the back of the club. As they descended the dark, narrow steps, Zachary caught snatches of the whispered conversation between Warrington and his companions ahead of them.

"I think you're a fool for taking on . . . bloody huge bastard . . ." Turner muttered.

". . . knows nothing of technique or discipline . . . just a street animal," came Warrington's sneering reply.

Zachary smiled with dark amusement. Perhaps Warrington had a great deal of technique and discipline. Perhaps he had undergone years of pugilistic training. That all amounted to nothing, compared to the experience Zachary had gained by standing on a street corner and taking on all comers. How many days and nights had he fought for every shilling he could get, knowing that his own mother and sister would have no food or bed to sleep in if he was defeated? Fighting had never been entertainment to him . . . It was survival . . . it was his way of life. And to Warrington it was merely a sport.

"Don't underestimate him," came Ravenhill's quiet voice behind him, as if Zachary's thoughts were somehow transparent to him. "Warrington's got a blistering right, and more speed than you might expect. I fought him a few times at Oxford and always got the stuffing knocked out of me."

They reached the cellar, which was cool, dimly lit and musty. The dirt floor was slightly damp, and the stone walls were green and slick. Endless rows of wine shelves filled half the cellar, but there was still enough room for the business at hand.

As Zachary and Warrington removed their coats and shirts, the seconds walked off the measurements of the ring and drew two furrows, one foot apart, in the center of the area. Ravenhill spoke briskly, outlining the terms of the match. "London Prize Ring Rules, each round to last until some part of a man's body touches the ground. At the end of each round, each man returns to his corner, rests for thirty seconds, and in eight seconds comes back to toe the mark again. Voluntarily dropping to a knee will result in forfeit." He glanced from Zachary's set face to Warrington's determined one. "Have I forgotten anything, gentlemen?"

"Yes," Warrington said, staring at Zachary accusingly, as if expecting him to cheat. "No headlocks."

Ravenhill replied before Zachary had a chance. "Headlocks are perfectly legal, my lord."

"That's all right," Zachary said evenly, yanking off his cravat. "I won't do headlocks if he doesn't want them." He knew what Warrington feared: that he might capture his head in an unbreakable hold and smash every bone in his face.

"A gentlemanly concession, Mr. Bronson," Ravenhill remarked, seeming to understand how it annoyed Warrington to hear the word "gentlemanly" applied to his opponent. "Very well, then, no headlocks." He extended his arms to receive Zachary's shirt, coat, waistcoat and cravat, folded the garments as deftly as a valet and set them on a wine shelf.

As the two bare-chested men turned to confront each other, Zachary saw Warrington's eyes widen with patent dismay.

"Christ," Warrington said, unable to restrain the exclamation, "have a look at him—he's a damned ape."

Zachary had been long accustomed to such comments. He knew what his body looked like, his torso rippled with muscle, scarred in some places, his arms bulging, his neck seventeen inches around and his chest thickly carpeted with black hair. It was a body meant for fighting, or for hard labor in fields and factories. Warrington, by contrast, had a lean but lanky form, with unmarked skin and trim muscles displayed by a nearly hairless chest.

Ravenhill smiled for the first time, revealing a flash of even white teeth. "I believe they used to call Bronson the 'Butcher,'" he informed Warrington, then turned to Zachary with an inquiring arch of his brow. "Isn't that correct?"

In no mood to share his humor, Zachary nodded shortly.

Ravenhill's attention returned to Warrington, and he spoke more soberly. "I might be able to persuade Mr. Bronson to abandon the fight, my lord, if you'll agree right now to retract your comment about Lady Holland."

Warrington shook his head with a sneer. "I'll offer no respect to a lady abiding under his roof."

Ravenhill sent a glance of cold encouragement to Zachary. It appeared that any insult to Holly offended him nearly as much as it did Zachary. As Ravenhill passed him on the way to the corner, he muttered something between his teeth. "Take his damned head off, Bronson."

Quietly Zachary went to the mark and waited for Warrington to do the same. They faced each other and adopted the traditional fighter's stance, left leg forward, left arm in front, elbow bent, knuckles at eye level.

Warrington opened the fight with a stinging left jab and circled to the left, while Zachary immediately gave ground. Soon Warrington unloaded more left jabs, followed by a right uppercut. Although the right failed to connect, Warrington's companions began to whoop with jubilation, clearly excited by his aggressiveness. Zachary allowed Warrington to set the pace, merely retreating and defending himself while Warrington unleashed a series of body shots. The blows hit solidly on Zachary's ribs, but it was the kind of pain he had long been impervious to, after years of bludgeoning and pounding. In return, he delivered only a series of light jabs designed to irritate, and test his opponent's range.

Finally, when Warrington's sweating face was adorned with a triumphant smirk and Turner and Enfield were cheering lustily in premature victory, Zachary threw a three-shot combination followed by a hard right cross that caught Warrington squarely in the eye.

Warrington staggered backward, clearly stunned by the power and speed of the blows. The men were instantly silenced as Warrington's legs buckled and he fell to his knees, before scrambling to rise again.

"End of the round," came Ravenhill's call, and Zachary went to his corner. He was beginning to sweat from exertion, and he brushed his hand impatiently at the wet locks of hair that fell over his forehead. "Here," Ravenhill said, giving him a clean wine towel, and Zachary blotted his face.

Warrington retreated to his own corner, while Enfield wiped his face and offered advice.

"Don't toy with him for long," Ravenhill murmured, smiling, although his gray eyes remained cool. "There's no need to drag this business out, Bronson."

Zachary handed back the towel. "What makes you think I'm toying with him?"

"It's clear the fight is yours to finish whenever you choose. But be a gentleman about it. Make your point succinctly and have done with it."

Thirty seconds had passed, and Zachary returned to the center mark for the next round. It annoyed him that Ravenhill saw through him so easily. He had indeed been planning to prolong the fight, taunting and humiliating Warrington with his superior prowess. He had intended to give the spoiled aristocrat a lengthy, painful thrashing that turned every inch of him black and blue. Instead, Ravenhill wanted him to end the fight soon and allow Warrington to walk away with a bit of pride left. Zachary knew that the recommendation was indeed the gentlemanly thing to do. But it aggravated him sorely. He didn't want to be a gentleman; he wanted to be merciless and strip away every modicum of Warrington's vanity.

Warrington came at him with renewed vigor, planting his feet and delivering three right-hand uppercuts that caught Zachary on the chin and snapped his head back. Zachary followed with two hard rib shots and a whiplike left hook to the head. The blasting blow rocked Warrington back on his heels, and he did a quick two-step to stay on his feet. Retreating, circling, Zachary waited until the other man approached once more, and they traded blows until Zachary landed a powerful straight left to the jaw. Dazed, Warrington fell to the floor and cursed as he tried to lurch to his feet.

Enfield called for the end of the round, and both opponents retreated to their corners.

Zachary swabbed at his face with the damp wine towel. He was going to be sore on the morrow—Warrington had blackened his left eye and bruised the right side of his chin. Warrington was not a bad fighter, actually. One had to give him credit for being busy in the ring, not to mention determined. However, Zachary not only outmatched him in power but was far more experienced, delivering fewer but infinitely more effective blows.

"Good work," Ravenhill said quietly. Zachary wanted to snarl that he didn't need or want his damned approval. Nor did he need the bastard's instructions on how to fight like a gentleman. However, he kept his fury in check, suppressing the emotion until it simmered coldly in his belly.

Returning for the third round, Zachary tolerated a rapid flurry of shots from Warrington, who was already tiring. Dodging at least half the blows, Zachary experienced the familiar sensation of settling in for the fight, reaching the plateau on which he could last for hours. He could box like this all day without requiring rest. It would be easy to keep Warrington occupied until the other man simply dropped in exhaustion. However, Zachary went in for the kill and landed a five-shot combination that sent Warrington to the ground.

Clearly bewildered, shaking his head in a useless effort to clear it, Warrington remained down. Turner and Enfield screamed at him to rise again, but he spat some bloody saliva and held up his hands in refusal. "Can't do it," he muttered. "Can't." Even when Enfield came forward to lift him up and lead him to the center again, Warrington refused.

Although Zachary would have liked to have inflicted further damage, he was mildly placated by the sight of Warrington's bruised and battered face, and the way he held his ribs in obvious discomfort.

"Match is finished," Warrington said out of one side of his swollen mouth. "I cede to Bronson."

After taking a minute or two to regain his strength, Warrington came forward and faced Zachary. "My apologies to Lady Holland," he said, while his companions complained and grumbled loudly. "I retract every word I said about her." He turned to Enfield. "Cut off the top button of my coat and give it to him."

"But what's he going to do with it?" Enfield complained, glaring at Zachary.

"I don't give a damn," Warrington replied curtly. "Remove the blasted thing." Turning back to Zachary, he extended his hand. "Bronson, you've got a head like an anvil. I suppose that makes you fit company for the rest of us."

Zachary was surprised by the gleam of friendly amusement in the other man's eyes. Slowly he reached out and shook Warrington's hand, the grip ginger in regard for both sets of sore knuckles. The gesture meant that Warrington recognized Zachary as an equal, or at least as someone whom he considered an acceptable member of the club.

"You've got a good right cross," Zachary replied gruffly. "As good as any I took in my prizefighting days."

Despite his swollen mouth, Warrington smiled, apparently pleased by the compliment.

Returning to Ravenhill, Zachary toweled off and donned his clothes, buttoning his shirt with difficulty and leaving his waistcoat unfastened. "Allow me," Ravenhill offered, but Zachary shook his head irritably. He hated to be touched by other men, even to the extent of refusing the services of a valet.

Ravenhill shook his head and smiled slightly. "As mild-tempered as a wild boar," he commented in a cool, dry tone. "How in God's name did you get Lady Holland to agree to it?"

"Agree to what?" Zachary asked, although he knew exactly what Ravenhill meant.

"The shy, gentle lady I knew three years ago would never have agreed to work for you. She would have been terrified of you."

"Maybe she's changed," Zachary muttered coldly. "Or maybe you didn't know her as well as you thought you did." He saw the dislike in the other man's remote gray eyes, and he experienced a strange comingling of emotions. Triumph, because Holly was indeed living with him and her life was entwined with his in a way it had never been with this superior aristocrat's. And jealousy, bitter stinging jealousy, because this man had known her before Zachary had, and for a much longer time. And Holly and Ravenhill were obviously cut of the same cloth, both of them cultured and pedigreed.

Giving his battered face one last swipe with the towel, Zachary smiled slightly at the handsome aristocrat. "My thanks, Ravenhill. I would take you as my second any-time." They exchanged a measuring glance, not hostile, but not precisely friendly. Ravenhill was not pleased with what had become of Holly, Zachary realized. His lordship was offended by the idea that his departed friend's wife was now employed by a lowbrow commoner. *Too bad for you,* Zachary thought nastily, every proprietary, primitive instinct in his body rising to the fore. *She's mine now, and there's nothing in hell that you or anyone else can do about it.*

Almost twenty-four hours to the minute since her megrims had begun, Holly felt well enough to rise from her bed. She felt weak and a bit dazed, as she always did after such an episode. It was early evening, the time when the Bronsons usually gathered in the family parlor to wait for supper to be announced. "Where is Rose?" was Holly's first question, as Maude helped her to sit up in bed.

"Downstairs with the master and his mother and sister," Maude answered, tucking supportive pillows behind her back. "They've all been doting on her while ye've been sleeping, playing games with the child and giving her extra sweets. Mr. Bronson canceled his ride to town today and spent all morning guiding her 'round the paddock on a little brown pony."

"Oh, he shouldn't have," Holly said in instant concern. "He shouldn't have neglected his business concerns—it isn't his place to take care of my child."

"He insisted, milady. I thought it a bit unseemly, and I tried to tell him there was no need. But ye know how the master is when he is set on something."

"Yes, I know." Holly sighed and clasped her hand over her sore forehead. "Oh, the extra trouble I've caused for you and everyone—"

"Now, milady, don't go fretting yerself into another megrim," Maude soothed. "The Bronsons are all quite happy, it seems, and Rose has enjoyed all the petting and spoiling. No harm done. Shall I have some victuals sent up, milady?"

"Thank you, but I would like to go downstairs and take supper with the family. I've been in bed for far too long. And I must see Rose."

With the maid's help, Holly bathed and dressed in a soft, simple gown of brown corded silk trimmed with a small collar of tea-dyed lace, and more lace edging at the sleeves. Since her scalp was still sensitive after the attack of megrims, they coiled her long, loose locks and secured them to her nape with only two pins. After checking her appearance in the dressing-table mirror to ascertain that she was tidy, Holly carefully made her way to the family parlor.

As Maude had described, the Bronsons were all there. Zachary lounged on the carpet beside Rose as they pored over a pile of painted wooden puzzle pieces, while Elizabeth read aloud from a collection of short stories. Paula occupied a corner of the long settee, contentedly mending a torn ruffle on one of Rose's white pinafores. The small group looked up in unison as Holly entered the room.

Wan and fatigued, she managed an apologetic smile. "Good evening, everyone."

"Mama!" Rose exclaimed, beaming as she hurried to Holly and threw her arms around her hips. "You're all better now!"

"Yes, darling." Lovingly Holly stroked her daughter's dark curls. "I'm sorry I took such a long rest."

"I had great fun while you were sleeping," Rose said, and proceeded to entertain her with an account of the morning's pony ride.

While Rose chattered away, Elizabeth bounded over to Holly with exclamations of sympathy and concern, and guided her to the settee. Paula insisted on covering Holly's knees with a knitted lap blanket, despite Holly's sheepish protests. "Oh, Mrs. Bronson, you're too kind. Really, there's no need . . ."

While the women fussed over her, Bronson stood and bowed in welcome. Sensing his dark, assessing gaze, Holly gave him a hesitant smile. "Mr. Bronson, I—" She broke off in surprise as she saw that his eye was shadowed with a bruise, and there was another blotch on his jaw. "What happened to your face, sir?"

Rose answered before he did, with the pride of a child who was delivering news of great significance. "Mr. Bronson ran into a left hook *again*, Mama. He was *fighting*. And he brought this to me." She pulled the end of her button string from her large apron pocket and climbed into Holly's lap to display her newest acquisition.

Cuddling her daughter, Holly examined the button carefully. It was fashioned of a huge sparkling diamond encased in rich yellow gold. Bewildered, she glanced at Elizabeth's rueful face, and Paula's tight-lipped one, before finally staring into Bronson's enigmatic black eyes. "You shouldn't have given Rose such a costly object, Mr. Bronson. Whose button is it? And why were you fighting?"

"I had a disagreement with someone in my club."

"Over money? . . . Over a woman? . . ."

Bronson's expression revealed nothing, and he gave an indifferent shrug, as if the matter were of no importance.

Considering various possibilities, Holly continued to stare at him in the tense silence that had overtaken the room. Suddenly the answer occurred to her. "Over me?" she whispered.

Idly Bronson picked a skein of thread from his sleeve. "Not really."

Holly suddenly discovered that she knew him well enough to discern when he was lying. "Yes, it was," she said with growing conviction. "Someone must have said something unpleasant, and instead of ignoring the remark, you took up the challenge. Oh, Mr. Bronson, how could you?"

Seeing her unhappiness, instead of the grateful admiration he had probably expected, Bronson scowled. "Would you rather I allowed some high-kick b—" He paused to correct himself as he noticed the rapt attention Rose was paying to the conversation. "Some high-kick fellow," he said, his tone softening a degree, "to spread lies about you? His mouth needed to be shut, and I was able and willing to do it."

"The only way to respond to a distasteful remark is to ignore it," Holly said crisply. "You did the exact opposite, thereby creating the impression in some people's minds that there may be a grain of truth in it. You should not have fought for my honor. You should have smiled disdainfully at any slight upon it, resting secure in the knowledge that there is nothing dishonorable about our relationship."

"But my lady, I would fight the world for you." Bronson said it in the way he always made such startling comments, in a tone of such jeering lightness that the listener had no doubt he was being facetious.

Elizabeth broke in then, her lips curved in a droll smile. "He'll use any excuse to fight, Lady Holly. My brother enjoys using his fists, primitive male that he is."

"That is an aspect of his character we will have to correct." Holly sent Bronson a reproachful glance, and he laughed.

A maid came to announce that dinner was ready to be served, and Rose bounced up and down in excitement. "Rosemary lamb and potatoes," she said with anticipation, evidently having gleaned the information from the cook. "My favorite! Come, Lizzie, let's hurry!"

Laughing, Elizabeth caught the child's hand in hers and allowed herself to be dragged away from the parlor. Paula smiled as she set her needlework aside and followed. Holly was slow to rise, battling a sudden wave of nausea at the thought of lamb, which did not sound at all appetizing. Unfortunately, the tonic that had relieved her megrims and caused her to sleep for a day did not come without side effects, one of them being greatly diminished appetite.

Closing her eyes for a moment, she opened them to discover that Bronson had made it to her side with astonishing speed. "Feeling faint?" he asked quietly, his gaze moving over her pale face.

"Just a bit queasy," she murmured, struggling to her feet. "No doubt I'll feel better once I eat something."

"Let me help you." His hard, strong arm slid behind her back, supporting her weight as she stood, and Holly experienced a sweet quake of familiarity. It seemed that since their dance lesson, her body had become accustomed to the closeness of his. Being in his arms felt far too natural and pleasurable.

"Thank you," she murmured, reaching up to check the coil at her nape, which felt rather loose. The pins had loosened from Rose's affectionate embrace. To Holly's dismay, the pins slid out and the mass of her hair tumbled free. She jerked away from Bronson with a small exclamation. "Oh, dear." Embarrassed by the cascade of brown locks that fell nearly to her waist, something that women never revealed to any man except their husbands, she busily gathered up the straying locks. "Pardon," she said, blushing. "I'll restore myself in no time."

Bronson was strangely quiet. In her discomfited flurry, she did not glance at his face, but it seemed to her that his breathing changed to a deeper, faster rhythm than usual. His hands lifted, reaching for her hair, and at first she thought that he was trying to help her. But instead he took her wrists in his hands, his long fingers wrapping gently around the fragile bones, and he pulled her arms to her sides.

Gasping, Holly glanced up at his dark face. "My hair . . . oh, Mr. Bronson, please . . . do let go . . ."

He continued to hold her wrists, his grip warm and light, and Holly's fingers opened and closed helplessly on nothing but air.

Her hair trailed over her shoulders and bodice in gleaming brown ripples, the lamplight striking tiny glints of gold and red in the dark strands. Bronson stared at her intently, his gaze moving along the path they made down her body, noting the way the strands parted over the gentle hills of her breasts. Holly's cheeks burned with the heat of modesty, and she pulled once more at her wrists. Suddenly he released her, allowing her to move back a few steps. But as she retreated, he followed.

Moistening her dry lips, Holly sought for something, anything, to break the seething silence between them. "Maude tells me," she said in a faltering voice, "that you went into my room last night after I took my medicine."

"I was concerned for you."

"No matter how kind your intentions, it was wrong of you. I was not in a condition to receive visitors. I don't even remember your being there, o-or what was said—"

"Nothing was said. You were sleeping."

"Oh—" Holly stopped as her shoulders bumped against

the wall, preventing further retreat. "Zachary," she whispered.

She had not intended to say his name . . . she never even used it in her thoughts . . . but somehow it had slipped out. The small intimacy shocked her, and perhaps him as well. His eyes closed for a long moment, and when his lashes lifted, his black eyes were filled with a bright, hot gleam.

"I'm not quite myself," she murmured, discovering that she was trembling all over. "My medicine . . . it's still making me a bit—"

"Shhhh." Bronson took a lock of her hair in his fingers and lifted it from her shoulder, his thumb rubbing gently over the silken strands. He moved slowly, as if he were in a dream. Staring at the shining lock in his hand, he lifted it to his lips and kissed it.

Holly's knees weakened until she could hardly stand. She was astonished by the tender, worshipful gesture, the extreme care with which he laid the lock of hair back on her shoulder.

Bronson leaned over her, his big-framed body not quite touching hers. His nearness caused her to shrink back hard against the wall. She let out a serrated breath as he deliberately placed a huge hand on either side of her head, his palms flattened on the wood paneling.

"They're waiting for us," she said faintly.

He seemed not to hear. He was going to kiss her, she thought. His tantalizing scent, the wonderful masculine spice of his skin, filled her mouth and nose as she inhaled deeply. Her empty hands flexed open and closed, shaking with the desire to pull his dark head down to hers. Confounded, she waited in sweet agony for his mouth to descend, while silent words spun through her head: *Yes, do it now, please . . .*

"Mama?" Rose's surprised giggle shredded the silence

between them. She had returned to discover why they had not yet joined the others at the dining table. "What are you doing, standing together like that?"

Holly heard her own voice as if it came from a great distance. "M-my hair came loose, darling. Mr. Bronson was helping me to repair it."

Stooping, Rose found the pins and handed them to Holly. "Here you are," she said brightly.

Bronson lowered an arm, allowing Holly to escape, though his dark gaze remained on her. Taking a deep breath, Holly stepped away and refused to look at him. "Thank you, Rose," she said, bending to hug her daughter briefly. "What a helpful girl you are."

"Hurry, please," the child requested, watching as Holly gathered her hair, twisted it in a coil and pinned it once more. "I'm hungry!"

The dinner was uneventful, but Zachary found that his normally voracious appetite had dwindled to nothing. He sat at the head of the table, noting that Holly had seated herself as far away from him as possible. Marshaling all his wits, he concentrated on keeping the conversation light, dwelling on safely neutral subjects, when all he wanted was to be alone with Holly.

Damn her . . . she had somehow taken away his ability to eat and sleep. Neither did he want to go gambling or wenching; all his desires were focused on her. Just to sit with her in a quiet parlor all evening sounded more exciting than spending a night in the bawdiest brothel in London. She aroused the most lascivious fantasies in him, and he couldn't glance at her hands or body or mouth without becoming acutely aroused. And she inspired other fantasies as well: images of tame domesticity that he had once scoffed at.

He longed for another of the intimate evenings they had shared, when everyone else had retired and they talked and drank before the fire, but it was clear that Holly was exhausted. She excused herself immediately after supper, barely looking at him, and retired early for the night.

For some reason Paula lingered at the table with him after the others had gone, sipping at a cup of tea while he drank a glass of dark reddish black port. Zachary smiled at his mother, taking pleasure in the sight of her dressed in a fine blue silk gown, her throat adorned with the pearl broach he had given her last Christmas. He would never forget the old, threadbare gowns she had once worn, the ceaseless work she had done to provide for her young children. She had been a seamstress, a washwoman, a ragseller. Now he was able to take care of her, and he would make certain she wanted for nothing.

He knew that Paula was often uncomfortable in their new circumstances, that she would have preferred to live in a small country cottage with only a cook-maid to serve her. However, he wanted her to live like a queen, and he would not allow anything less.

"You have something to say, Mother," he remarked, swirling the port in his glass. He sent her a quick, half-sided smile. "I can see it in your face. Do you have another lecture to offer about my fighting?"

"It's not about fighting," Paula said, curling her work-worn hands around the steaming teacup. Her gentle brown eyes surveyed him with both affection and admonition, "You're a good son, Zach, in spite of your wild ways. You have a good heart, and so I've held my tongue when you've kept company with whores and ne'er-do-wells, and when you've done things that you haven't even the sense to be ashamed of. But there is something I cannot be silent about, and I want you to mark every word I say."

He adopted an expression of mock alarm and waited for her to continue.

"It's about Lady Holly."

"What about her?" he asked warily.

Paula sighed tensely. "You will never have that woman, Zach. You must find a way to put all thoughts of her out of your head, or you'll bring her to ruin."

Zachary forced himself to laugh, though the sound was hollow. His mother might not be educated or polished, but she was an intelligent woman, and he couldn't dismiss her words easily. "I have no intention of bringing her to ruin. I've never touched her."

"A mother knows her son," Paula insisted. "I see how you are with her. You can hide it from the world, but not from me. Zach, it's not right. You're not meant to be with her any more than a . . . a donkey should mate with a Thoroughbred."

"I gather I'm the donkey," Zachary muttered dryly. "Well, in light of your sudden talkative mood, tell me why you've never raised any objections before when I've spoken of wanting to marry a well-born bride."

"You can have a well-born bride, if that's what you want. But Lady Holly isn't the one for you."

"What's your objection to her?"

Paula considered her words with great care. "There's a streak of hardness inside you and me and even Lizzie— and thank God for it. It's the only reason we survived those years in the East End. But Lady Holly is soft all the way through. And if she marries again, she needs a man who is soft, too. A real gentleman, like her husband was. You'll never be like that. Now, I've seen a few titled women that I've thought would suit you well enough. Take one of those, and leave Lady Holly be."

"You don't like her?" Zachary asked quietly.

"Don't like her?" Paula repeated, staring at him in surprise. "Of *course* I like her. She's the most gracious, kind creature I've ever known. Maybe the one true lady I've ever met. It's because I like her so well that I'm saying these things to you."

In the silence that ensued, Zachary applied himself to finishing his port. The truth in his mother's comments was undeniable. He was tempted to argue the case with her, but that would force him to voice things he hadn't yet dared to acknowledge even to himself. So he gave her a brief, wordless nod, a bitter recognition that she was most likely right.

"Oh, Zach," Paula murmured compassionately. "Be happy with what you have. Can't you learn how to do that?"

"Apparently not," he muttered grimly.

"There must be a word for men like you, who reach too high . . . but I don't know what it is."

Zachary smiled at her then, despite the leaden weight in his chest. "I don't, either, Mother. But I have a word to apply to you."

"What is that?" she asked suspiciously, waggling a warning finger at him.

Standing and crossing the distance between them, Zachary bent to kiss the top of her graying head. "Wise," he murmured.

"Then you'll heed my advice and forget about Lady Holly?"

"I'd be a fool not to, wouldn't I?"

"Does that mean 'yes'?" Paula persisted, but he laughed and left the room without replying.

Ten

In the weeks that followed the episode of megrims, Holly became aware of some changes in the Bronson household. The most obvious difference was the attitude of the servants. Although their service had formerly been sloppy, inconsistent and indifferent, it seemed that they had begun to take a sort of collective pride in their work. Perhaps the result of Holly's discreet education of the Bronsons on what to expect from their hired help.

"I understand your reluctance, Mrs. Bronson," Holly had murmured one afternoon, when the maids had brought a tea tray containing a pot of lukewarm water, a jug of off-scented milk and stale cakes. "However, you must send it back. There is nothing wrong in refusing unacceptable fare."

"They do so much work already," Paula protested, already fussing with the tea service as if she fully intended to make do with it. "I can't put them to more trouble, and this isn't so bad, really."

"It's terrible," Holly insisted, smothering a frustrated laugh.

"You send it back," Paula implored.

"Mrs. Bronson, you must learn to manage your own servants."

"I can't." Paula surprised Holly by catching at her hand and holding it tightly. "I used to be a rag-seller," she whispered. "Lower than the lowest scullery maid who works in the kitchen downstairs. And they all know it. How can I give them orders?"

Holly regarded her thoughtfully, feeling a surge of compassion as she finally understood the source of the woman's timidity toward everyone outside the immediate family. Paula Bronson had lived in wretched poverty for so long that she did not feel worthy of the circumstances she now found herself in. The fine house with its rare tapestries and artwork, the elegant clothes she wore, the lavish meals and expensive wines, only served to remind Paula of her humble beginnings. Yet there was no way for her to go back. Zachary had raised his family to a level of wealth far beyond anything Paula had expected or imagined. It was imperative that Paula learn to change along with her circumstances, or she would never find any comfort or happiness in her new life.

"You're no longer a rag-seller," Holly said in a purposeful voice. "You're a woman of means. You're Mr. Zachary Bronson's mother. You brought two remarkable children into the world and reared them with no help from anyone, and anyone with their wits intact will admire your accomplishment." She returned Paula's grip with a strong one of her own. "Insist on receiving the respect you deserve," she said, staring directly into the woman's troubled brown eyes, "especially from your own servants. Along this vein, there are many other things I intend to discuss with you, but for now . . ." She paused and tried to think of a curse word to give her statement emphasis. "Send the damn tray back!"

Paula's eyes rounded, and she put a hand to her mouth

to smother a bubbling laugh. "Lady Holly, I've never heard you swear before."

Holly smiled back at her. "If I can make myself swear, then you can surely ring for the maids and ask for a proper tea."

Paula squared her shoulders in determination. "All right, I'll do it!" She hurried to the bellpull before she changed her mind.

In an effort to further improve the relations between the Bronsons and their servants, Holly arranged for a brief daily meeting with the housekeeper, Mrs. Burney. She insisted that Paula and Elizabeth be present, although both were reluctant to do so. Paula was still excruciatingly shy about giving directions to Mrs. Burney, and Elizabeth had little interest in domestic matters. However, they had to learn. "The business of household management is something every lady must attend to," Holly instructed the two. "Every morning you must meet with Mrs. Burney and review the menus for the day, discuss what special chores the servants must perform, such as cleaning carpets or polishing the silver. Most importantly, you must go over the household accounts, make entries and arrange for necessary purchases."

"I thought Mrs. Burney was supposed to handle all that." Elizabeth looked disgruntled at the idea of dealing with such tedious business on a daily basis.

"No, *you* are," Holly said, smiling. "And you may as well practice along with your mother, because someday you will have your own household to manage."

To the Bronson women's amazement, their efforts were rewarded with far better service than they had been accustomed to. Although Paula was still clearly uncomfortable with giving directions to the servants, her skills were improving, and her confidence along with them.

The other significant change in the household routine was the behavior of its master. Gradually Holly realized that Zachary Bronson was no longer prowling back and forth to London every evening in search of revelry. While she wouldn't have ventured so far as to suggest that he had reformed, Bronson did seem quieter, calmer, a bit less callous and coarse. There were no further wicked dark glances or provocative discussions, no more near-kisses or disconcerting compliments. During their lessons, Bronson was sober and respectful as he applied himself to what she had to teach. He behaved perfectly even when they continued their dance lessons. And to Holly's dismay, Bronson-the-aspiring-gentleman had an appeal for her that went far beyond the pull that Bronson-the-rogue had exerted. She now saw many of the things he had kept hidden behind his sardonic, cynical facade, and she began to admire him more than she had ever dreamed possible.

He had a passionate interest in helping the poor, not merely by making charitable donations, but by increasing their opportunities to help themselves. Unlike other men of his extraordinary wealth, Bronson identified with the underclasses. He understood their needs and concerns, and he took action to improve their circumstances. In an effort to pass a bill that would shorten the workingman's labors to ten hours a day, Bronson had countless meetings with politicians and lavishly funded their favorite causes. He had abolished child labor in his own factories, and provided benefit funds for his employees, including pensions for widows and the elderly.

Other employers had resisted instituting such measures in their own companies, stating that they could not afford to provide such benefits for their workers. But Bronson was becoming so enormously rich that his success provided the best argument in favor of treating employees like men instead of animals.

Bronson used his companies to import or produce goods that improved the lives of common men, bringing affordable products to the masses, such as soap, coffee, candy, fabric and tableware. However, Bronson's business strategies were winning far more enmity than admiration among his peers. Aristocrats complained that he was trying to erase class boundaries and diminish their rightful authority, and they were almost unanimous in their bitter desire to see him brought low.

It was clear to Holly that no matter how polished Bronson became, he would never be welcomed into first society, only barely tolerated. She would be heartily sorry to see him marry a spoiled heiress who would value him only for his money and disdain him behind his back. If only there were some spirited girl who might share in his causes, who might even enjoy being married to a man of his intelligence and vigor. Bronson had much to offer a wife who had the sense to appreciate him. It would be a unique marriage, lively and interesting and passionate.

Holly had thought of introducing him to one of her three unmarried younger sisters. It would be a good match and certainly advantageous to her family to have such an infusion of wealth. But the idea of Zachary Bronson courting one of her sisters caused a deep stab of something that felt very much like jealousy. Besides, her sisters, being the unworldly creatures they were, would not be able to handle him easily. There were times, even now, when Bronson became overbearing and required a firm setdown.

The matter of the gowns, for example.

On the day that Holly had arranged to take Elizabeth and Paula to her own dressmaker, to order styles a bit more elegant than those they currently wore, Bronson had taken Holly aside and made an astonishing offer.

"You should have some new gowns made up as well," he said. "I'm tired of seeing you in all that half-mourning—gray, brown, lavender . . . No one expects it of you any longer. Order as many as you like. I'll take care of the expense."

Holly stared at him openmouthed. "Not only are you daring to complain about my appearance, you are also in-sulting me by offering to pay for my clothes?"

"I didn't mean it as an insult," he countered warily.

"You know very well that a gentleman would never pur-chase items of apparel for a lady. Not even a pair of gloves."

"Then I'll subtract the necessary amount from your sal-ary." Bronson gave her a cajoling smile. "A woman with your looks deserves to wear something beautiful. I'd like to see you in jade green, or yellow. Or red." The idea seemed to spark his imagination as he continued. "I can't imagine a finer sight in the world than you in a red gown."

Holly was not mollified by the flattery. "I most certainly will *not* order new gowns, and I'll thank you to spare me further mention of the subject. A red gown, indeed! Do you know what would become of my reputation?"

"It's already tarnished," he pointed out. "You may as well enjoy yourself." He seemed to enjoy her spluttering outrage at the comment.

"You sir, may . . . may . . ."

"Go to the devil?" he suggested helpfully.

She seized on the expression with enthusiasm. "Yes, go right at once to the devil!"

As she should have expected, Bronson ignored her re-fusal, went behind her back and ordered a selection of new gowns for her. It had been easy enough, as the dressmaker already had her measurements and knew her tastes.

On the day the boxes of finery arrived, Holly was livid to discover that fully a third of them were for her. Bronson had ordered just as many for her as he had for his mother and sister, complete with matching gloves, shoes and hats. "I won't wear any of this," Holly declared, glaring at Bronson from behind a tower of boxes. "You've wasted your money. I can't begin to describe how vexed I am with you, sir. I won't wear a single ribbon or button from any of these boxes, do you understand?" Laughing at her annoyance, Bronson offered to burn them himself, if it would serve to restore her good humor.

Holly considered giving the garments to her sisters, who were of similar build and size. However, as unmarried girls, they were consigned to wearing mostly white. These were gowns intended for a woman, a worldly one at that. Only in private had Holly allowed herself to examine the gorgeously, beautifully made garments, so different from her mourning weeds or the styles she had once worn as George's wife. The colors were rich, the styles dashing and feminine, and wonderfully flattering to a woman with her full-hipped figure.

There was the jade-green Italian silk, with its full sleeves that narrowed to neat cuffs with cunning triangular points that lay over the backs of her hands. And the dark rose watered-silk promenade dress, with its matching broad-brimmed hat trimmed with delicate white lace. The lavender-striped morning gown, with crisp white sleeves and double-flounced skirt, and the yellow silk gauze with sleeves and hem thickly embroidered with roses.

Worst of all was the red silk, an evening gown of such impeccable simplicity and elegance that it nearly broke her heart to know that it would go forever unworn. The daring scooped neckline flowed into a smooth, unadorned bodice, while the skirts cascaded in a majestic fall of red, the shade somewhere between fresh apples and rare wine. The gown's only ornamentation was a red velvet sash trimmed with silk fringe. It was the most beautiful garment she had ever seen. Had the gown been made in a more circumspect shade, even some quiet dark blue, Holly would have accepted the gift, and propriety be damned. However, Bronson, true to form, had made certain it was a color that she could never wear. He did it for the same reason he ordered her plates of cakes: He enjoyed tempting her, and watching her struggle miserably with her conscience.

Well, not this time. Holly did not try on a single gown. Instead she ordered Maude to store them in an armoire, to be given away at some future date when the opportunity presented itself. "There, Mr. Bronson," Holly murmured, turning the key in the armoire lock with a decisive click. "I may not always be able to resist your infernal temptations, but in this matter, at least, I have succeeded!"

Almost four months had passed since Holly had come to reside at the Bronson estate, and now it was time to test the results of her patient tutoring. The night of the Plymouth ball had finally arrived. It would serve as Elizabeth's introduction to society. It was also an opportunity for Zachary Bronson's newly polished manners to be displayed to the *ton*. Holly was filled with pride and hopeful anticipation, suspecting that there were many in first society who would be pleasantly surprised by the Bronsons this evening.

At Holly's suggestion, Elizabeth wore a white gown trimmed with swaths of pale pink gauze, with one fresh pink rose pinned at her waist and another fastened in the piled-up curls of her hair. The girl looked fresh and graceful, her slender figure and considerable height lending her a queenly air. Although Zachary had given his sister many gifts of jewelry in the past, Holly had looked over the priceless array of diamonds, sapphires and emeralds and realized they were too heavy and expensive for an unmarried girl. Instead, she had selected a single pearl on a delicate gold chain.

"This is all you require," Holly said, fastening the chain around Elizabeth's neck. "Keep your appearance simple and unspoiled, and save the extravagant jewels for when you're as old as I am."

Elizabeth stared at their shared reflections in the dressing-table mirror. "You make it sound as though you're decrepit," she said with a laugh. "And you look so beautiful tonight!"

"Thank you, Lizzie." Holly gave the girl's shoulders a squeeze, and turned to glance at Paula fondly. "As long as we are spreading compliments, Mrs. Bronson, I must say that you look magnificent this evening."

Paula, who was dressed in a forest-green gown adorned with sparkling beadwork at the neck and sleeves, nodded and smiled tensely. It was clear that there were a thousand things she would rather be doing than attend a formal ball.

"I'm not certain I can manage this," Elizabeth said nervously, standing before the mirror. "I'm a wreck. I'm going to make some terrible *faux pas* that everyone will talk about. Please, Lady Holly, let's forget about going anywhere tonight and try again some other time, after I've had more lessons."

"The more balls and parties and soirees you attend, the easier it will become," Holly replied firmly.

"No one will ask me to dance. They all know what I am—an illegitimate nobody. Oh, damn my brother for doing this to me! I'm going to be a wallflower tonight. I don't belong in a ball gown. I should be somewhere peeling potatoes or sweeping a street walkway—"

"You're lovely," Holly said, hugging the girl while Elizabeth continued to stare at her own alarmed reflection. "You're lovely, Lizzie, and you have very good manners, and your family is quite wealthy. Believe me, you won't be a wallflower. And not a single man who views you tonight will think you should be peeling potatoes."

It took a great deal of persuasion and stubborn insistence to force both of the Bronson women from the room. Somehow Holly managed to bring them down the grand staircase. As they descended, Holly took particular pride in Elizabeth's outward appearance of poise, despite the fact that the girl was quaking with nerves on the inside.

Bronson awaited them in the entrance hall, his black hair gleaming in the abundant light shed by the chandeliers and the silver-coffered ceiling. Although there was not a man alive whose appearance wasn't improved by the traditional formal scheme of black and white evening wear, it did Zachary Bronson particular justice. His severely simple black coat had been tailored according to the latest fashion, the collar low, the sleeves close-fitting, the lapels extending nearly to the waist. On Zachary's towering form, with his expansive shoulders and lean waist, the style was immensely flattering. His narrow white cravat and crisp white waistcoat looked snowy in contrast to his swarthy, freshly shaved face. From his neatly brushed dark hair to the tips of his polished black leather shoes, Zachary Bronson appeared to be a perfect gentleman. Yet there was something a bit dashing, even dangerous about him . . . perhaps it was the irreverent gleam in his black eyes, or the raffish quality of his smile.

His gaze went first to Elizabeth, and his smile was filled with affectionate pride. "What a sight you are, Lizzie," he murmured, taking his sister's hand and brushing a kiss on her blushing cheek. "You're prettier than I've ever seen you. You'll come away from the ball leaving a trail of broken hearts in your wake."

"More likely a trail of broken toes," Elizabeth replied dryly. "That is, if anyone is foolish enough to ask me to dance."

"They'll ask," he murmured, and gave her waist a reassuring squeeze. He turned to his mother and complimented her before finally turning to Holly.

After all the rigorous instruction in courtesy she had given him, Holly expected a polite comment on her appearance. A gentleman should always offer some small tribute to a lady in these circumstances—and Holly knew that she looked her best. She had dressed in her favorite gown, a glimmering silk of light gray, with silver beadwork adorning the low scooped bodice and the short, full sleeves. A bit of light feather padding kept the sleeves puffed out, and the gown's skirt was supported beneath with a stiffly starched petticoat. Holly had even allowed the dressmaker to persuade her to wear a light corset that trimmed her waist almost two inches. Maude had helped to arrange her hair in the latest fashion, parting it in the center and pulling the heavy mass to the back of her head. They had pinned the gleaming brown locks into rolls and curls, allowing two or three stray tendrils to dangle against her neck.

Smiling slightly, Holly stared into Bronson's expressionless face as he surveyed her from head to toe. However, the expected gentlemanly compliment was not forthcoming.

"Is that what you're going to wear?" he asked abruptly.

"Zach!" his mother gasped in horrified disapproval,

while Elizabeth jabbed him in the side in response to the
rude inquiry.

A disconcerted frown drew Holly's brows together, and
she felt a sharp stab of disappointment, coupled with annoyance. The rude, insolent boor! She had never received
a derogatory comment on her appearance from a man
before. She had always prided herself on her sense of
style—how dare he imply that she was wearing something
unsuitable!

"We are going to a ball," Holly replied coolly, "and this
is a ball gown. Yes, Mr. Bronson, this is what I intend to
wear."

Their gazes locked in a long, challenging stare, so
clearly excluding the other two that Paula pulled Elizabeth
to the other side of the hall on the pretext of discovering
a stain on her glove. Holly was barely aware of the women
drifting away. She spoke in a clipped tone that fully conveyed her displeasure.

"What, precisely, is your objection to my appearance,
Mr. Bronson?"

"Nothing," he muttered. "If you want to show the world
you're still in mourning for George, that gown is perfect."

Offended and strangely hurt, Holly sent him an outright
glare. "My gown is quite suitable for the occasion. The
only thing you don't like about it is that it is not one of
the ones you purchased for me! Did you really expect me
to wear one of those?"

"Considering it was your only alternative to wearing
mourning—or Half Mourning, whatever the hell it's
called—I thought it was a possibility."

They had never argued like this, not in deadly earnest,
in a way that ignited Holly's long-dormant temper like a
flame set to gunpowder. Whenever they debated an issue,
the words were spiced with humor, teasing, even provoc-

ative meaning, but this was the first time that Holly had ever been truly angry with him. George would never have spoken to her in the blunt, brutal manner Bronson did . . . George had never criticized her except in the gentlest of terms, and always with the kindest of intentions. In her flaring anger, Holly did not stop to wonder why she was comparing Bronson so closely with her husband, or how his opinion had come to hold such power over her emotions.

"This is not a mourning gown," she said irritably. "One would think you had never seen a gray gown before. Perhaps you've spent too much time in brothels to notice what ordinary women wear."

"Call it what you like," Bronson returned, his voice soft but stinging, "I know mourning when I see it."

"Well, if I choose to wear mourning for the next fifty years, that's my concern and none of yours!"

His broad shoulders lifted in a careless shrug, a common gesture that he knew was bound to incense her further. "No doubt many will admire you for walking around dressed like a crow—"

"A *crow*," Holly repeated in outrage.

"—but I've never been one to admire displays of excessive grief, especially public ones. There's some merit in keeping your feelings private. However, if you're so in need of sympathy from others—"

"You insufferable *swine*!"she hissed, more angry than she could ever remember being in her life. How dare he accuse her of using mourning merely as a way of gaining public sympathy for herself? How dare he imply that her grief for George was not sincere? Rage sent the blood rushing to her face, until she was hot and crimson. She wanted to hit him, hurt him, but she saw that her anger pleased him for some unfathomable reason. The cool satisfaction in his black eyes was unmistakable. Just a few minutes ago she had taken such pride in his gentlemanly appearance, but now she almost hated him.

"How could you know anything about mourning?" she said, her voice unsteady. She could not bring herself to look at him as she spoke. "You could never love someone the way I did George—it's not in you to surrender any part of your heart. Perhaps you think that makes you superior. But I feel sorry for you."

Unable to tolerate his presence a moment longer, she strode away rapidly, her stiffened petticoat batting at her legs. Ignoring Paula's and Elizabeth's worried, questioning voices, she churned up the stairs as quickly as her heavy skirts would allow, while her lungs worked like leaky bellows.

Zachary stood exactly where she left him, stunned by the argument that seemed to have flared out of nowhere. He hadn't planned to start it, had even felt a surge of pleasure the first instant he had seen Holly . . . until he had realized that her dress was gray. Gray like a shadow, a pall cast by George Taylor's ever-present memory. He had known at once that every moment of Holly's evening would be given over to regret that her husband was not with her, and Zachary would be damned if he would spend the next several hours trying to win her away from George's ghost. The silvery-gray gown, pretty as it was, had taunted him like a banner before a bull. Why couldn't he have her for just one evening, without her grief being wedged so insistently between them?

And so he had spoken carelessly, perhaps even cruelly, too wrapped up in his own annoyance and disappointment to care about what he was saying.

"Zachary, what did you tell her?" Paula demanded.

"Congratulations," came Elizabeth's sarcastic voice. "Only you could ruin the evening for everyone in a mere thirty seconds, Zach."

The few servants who had witnessed the scene suddenly busied themselves with meaningless self-appointed tasks, clearly not wanting to fall victim to his evil temper. However, Zachary was no longer angry. The moment Holly left his side, he had been flooded with a strange, sick feeling. He analyzed the sensation, unlike anything he had experienced before. Somehow he felt worse at this moment than he had after the worst beating of his prizefighting days. There was a huge block of ice in his stomach, the coldness spreading until it reached his fingers and toes. He was suddenly afraid he had made Holly hate him, that she would never smile at him or let him touch her again.

"I'll go up to her," Paula said, her tone motherly and calm. "But first I wish you would tell me what was said between you, Zachary—"

"Don't," Zachary interrupted softly. He held up his hand in a swift restraining gesture. "I'll go to her. I'll tell her . . ." Pausing, he realized that for the first time in his life, he was ashamed to face a woman. "Hell," he said savagely. He, who had never cared for anyone's opinion of him, had been utterly cowed by the words of a small woman. It would have been far better if Holly had cursed him, thrown something, slapped him. *That* he could have survived. But the quiet contempt in her voice had devastated him. "I just want to give her a minute or two to calm herself before I approach her."

"The way Lady Holly appeared," Elizabeth remarked sourly, "it will take at least two or three days before she's ready to set eyes on you."

Before Zachary could respond with an appropriately sarcastic rejoinder, Paula took her disgruntled daughter's arm and tugged her away toward the family parlor. "Come, Lizzie . . . we'll both have a relaxing glass of wine. Heaven knows we both need it."

Heaving a sigh, Elizabeth followed her, stomping away in her ball gown with all the grace of an infuriated eight-year-old. Were it not for his own turbulent emotions, Zachary would have smiled at the sight. He went to the library for a drink, stopped at the sideboard and poured something from a decanter. Downing the stuff without even tasting it, he poured another. However, the spirits failed to warm his frozen insides. His mind sorted busily through a deluge of words, grasping for an apology that would make everything right again. He could tell Holly anything but the truth—that he was jealous of George Taylor, that he wanted her to stop mourning for her husband, when it was clear that she had dedicated the rest of her life to his memory. Setting his glass down with a groan, Zachary forced himself to leave the library. His shoes felt as if they had been made with lead soles as he hoisted his feet up the grand staircase toward Holly's private rooms.

Holly nearly stumbled in her eagerness to step over the threshold of her private apartments and close herself inside. Mindful of Rose sleeping peacefully just two rooms away, she tried not to slam the door. She stood very still, with her arms tightly bunched around herself. Her mind rang with echoes of every word she had just exchanged with Zachary Bronson.

The worst part was, he hadn't been entirely wrong. The gray gown had seemed exactly right for this occasion, for just the reason he had suggested. It was elegant and stylish, but not so very different from the circumspect Half Mourning garments she had worn during the third year after George's death. No one could find fault with it, not even her own beleaguered conscience. She was more than a little afraid of fully rejoining the world without George, and this was her way of reminding everyone—including herself—of what she had once had. She didn't want to lose the last vestige of her past with George. There were already too many days that slipped by without her having thought of him. There were too many moments when she felt a heady attraction to another man, when she had once thought that only George could stir her senses. It was becoming terribly easy to make decisions for herself, on her own, without first considering what George would have wanted or approved of. And that independence frightened her fully as much as it pleased her.

Her actions of the past four months had proved that she was no longer the sheltered young matron, or the virtuous, circumspect widow that family and friends had approved of. She was becoming another woman entirely.

Stunned by the thought, Holly didn't notice her servant Maude's presence until she spoke. "Milady, is something amiss? A button loose, or a trimming—"

"No, nothing like that." Holly took a deep breath, and then another, anchoring her roiling emotions. "It appears that my gray gown displeases Mr. Bronson," she informed the servant. "He wants me to wear something that looks less like mourning."

"He *dared* . . ." Maude began in astonishment.

"Yes, he dared," Holly said dryly.

"But milady . . . ye're not going to oblige him, are ye?"

Holly stripped off her gloves, threw them to the floor and kicked off her silver slippers. Her heart was pounding with the remnants of fury, and a nerve-rattling excitement like nothing she had ever felt before. "I'm going to make his eyes fall out," she said curtly. "I'm going to make him sorry that he ever said one word about my attire."

Maude stared at her strangely, having never seen such an expression of feminine vengeance on Holly's face. "Milady," she ventured cautiously, "ye don't seem quite yerself."

Holly turned and went to the closed armoire, turning the small key in the door and opening it. She extracted the red gown and shook it briskly, giving it a quick airing. "Hurry, Maude," she said, turning her back and indicating the row of buttons that needed to be unfastened. "Help me out of this thing quickly."

"But . . . but . . ." Maude was dazed. "Ye want to wear *that* gown? I haven't had a chance to air it properly and press the wrinkles—"

"It seems to be in good condition, actually." Holly inspected the billows of glowing red silk in her arms. "But I wouldn't care if it was one big ball of wrinkles. I'm going to wear the blasted thing."

Recognizing her determination, though clearly not approving, Maude sighed gustily and set to work on the back of the gray gown. When it became apparent that Holly's prim white chemise would peek out over the low-cut bodice of the red silk, Holly stripped off her top undergarment. "Ye're going without yer chemise?" Maude gasped, thunderstruck.

Although the servant had already seen her in every stage of undress, Holly blushed all over, until even her bare breasts were pink. "I don't have any chemises cut low enough to fit beneath this." She struggled to pull the red gown over her torso, and Maude hastily moved to assist her.

When the gown was finally fastened and the red velvet sash was tied neatly at her waist, Holly went to the mahogany-framed looking glass. The succession of three mirrored ovals joined together afforded a complete view of her appearance. Holly was startled by the sight of herself clad in such rich color, the red strikingly vivid against her white skin. She had never worn anything quite as bold as this for George, a style that displayed the snowy curves of her breasts and the top third of her back. Her skirts moved in a fluid, rippling mass with each step she took, with each breath she drew. She felt vulnerable and exposed, and at the same time strangely free and light. This was the kind of gown she had worn in all her forbidden daydreams, when she had longed to escape the dullness of her ordinary life.

"At the last ball I attended," she commented, studying her reflection, "I saw ladies wearing gowns much more daring than this. Some of them were practically backless. This looks almost modest by comparison."

" 'Tisn't the style, milady," Maude replied, flatly. " 'Tis the color."

Continuing to stare at herself in the mirror, Holly realized that the gown was too spectacular to require further ornamentation. She removed all her jewelry: the diamond bracelet George had given her upon the birth of their child, the glittering earbobs that had been a wedding present from her parents and the sparkling clips that adorned her upswept hair. Everything except the simple gold band of her wedding ring. She handed the items to the maid. "There's a flower arrangement in the upstairs family parlor," she said, "and I believe it has some fresh red roses in it. Would you fetch me one, Maude?"

Maude paused before complying. "Milady," she said quietly, "I hardly recognize ye."

Holly's smile wavered, and she took a deep breath. "Is that a good thing or a bad thing, Maude? What would my husband have said, if he had ever seen me like this?"

"I think Master George would have loved to see ye in that red gown," Maude replied thoughtfully. "He was a man, after all."

Eleven

Approaching Holly's door, Zachary knocked gingerly with two knuckles of his right hand. There was no sound or response from within. Sighing, he wondered if she might have already retired to bed. It was only to be expected that she would not want to see him tonight. Silently he berated himself, wondering why he hadn't been able to keep his own damned mouth shut. While he wasn't necessarily a ladies' man, he had a certain way with women, and he had known better than to make a negative comment about Holly's appearance. Now she was probably weeping by herself in a corner of her room, too hurt and furious to even consider attending—

The door swung gently open, leaving Zachary's hand suspended in midair as he began to knock once more. Holly stood there, alone, wearing a gown that looked as if it were made of liquid flame.

Zachary gripped the doorframe with his hand to keep from falling backward. His gaze traveled over her, greedily absorbing every detail: the way her white breasts were pushed together and upward by the red silk bodice . . . the delicate angle of her collarbone . . . the soft shape of her throat, so enticing that his mouth watered in response. The startlingly simple red gown was elegant but provocative,

210

displaying just enough of Holly's pale skin to threaten his
sanity. He had never seen a woman more vibrantly, un-
reasonably beautiful in his life. The ice in his stomach
dissolved as he was filled with a raging inferno of desire.
And like a glass vessel that had been exposed to a radical
change in temperature, his self-control threatened to shat-
ter.

He stared into her velvety brown eyes. For once, he
couldn't read her mood. She looked warm, utterly inviting,
but when she spoke, her voice was crisp.

"Does this meet with your approval, Mr. Bronson?"

Unable to speak, Zachary managed a single nod. She
was still angry with him, he thought numbly. Just why she
had put on the red gown was a mystery. Perhaps she had
somehow guessed that it was the worst possible punishment she could devise. He wanted her so badly that it hurt,
a physical pain he felt everywhere in his body . . . and in
one area especially. He longed to touch her, put his hands
and mouth on her soft skin, bury his nose in the little
valley between her breasts. If only he could take her to
bed this very moment. If only she would let him worship
her, pleasure her, the way he longed to.

Holly's gaze swept over him in feminine assessment,
lingering on his face. "Come in, please," she said, gesturing for him to enter the room. "Your hair is disheveled.
I'll repair it before we leave."

Zachary obeyed slowly. She had never invited him inside her room before—he knew it wasn't right, wasn't
proper, but somehow the evening had become topsy-turvy.
As he followed her trim, silk-covered form into the
perfume-scented room, his brain rekindled sufficiently for
him to remember his apology. "Lady Holly," he began, his
voice cracking. He cleared his throat and tried again.

"What I said to you downstairs . . . I shouldn't have . . . I regret . . ."

"Indeed, you *should* regret it," Holly assured him, her voice tart but no longer outraged. "You were arrogant and presumptuous, though I don't know why I should have been surprised by such behavior, coming from you."

Usually Zachary would have responded to such an admonition with a playful retort. Now, however, he agreed with a humble nod. The sound of her skirts swishing, the movement of her legs beneath the masses of silk, filled his mind with a hot, intoxicating fog.

"Sit there, please," Holly said, gesturing to a tiny chair next to her dressing table. She picked up a silver-backed brush. "You're too tall for me when you stand."

He complied immediately, although the spindly little chair wobbled and creaked under his weight. Unfortunately, his line of vision was now perfectly level with her breasts. He closed his eyes to keep from staring at the lush mounds, but nothing would still the writhing images in his head. It would be so easy to reach out and catch her body in his hands, and bury his face between her soft breasts. He began to perspire profusely. He was in a fever, burning for her. When she spoke, the sweet sound of her voice seemed to collect at the back of his neck and in his groin.

"I regret something as well," Holly said quietly. "What I told you . . . that you were unable to love . . . I was wrong. I only said it because I was upset. I have no doubt that someday you will indeed lose your heart to someone, although I can't imagine to whom."

You, he thought with an inescapable stab of longing. *You.* Couldn't she see it? Or did she assume she was merely the target of his random lust, and no more special to him than any other woman?

In the taut silence, Zachary opened his eyes and watched

as Holly picked up a glass bottle and shook a few drops of some clear liquid into her palm. "What is that?" he asked.

"Pomade."

"I don't like pomade," he muttered.

"Yes, I'm aware of that." There was a touch of amusement in her voice. She rubbed her hands together, distributing the stuff evenly over her fingers and palms. "I'll only use a bit. But you can't go to a formal occasion with your hair falling over your forehead."

Resigned, he sat still beneath her ministrations. He felt her damp fingers moving through his hair, gently rubbing the hot scalp beneath, smoothing the pomade through his rebellious black locks. "Everyone in your family has the same hair," Holly commented, a smile lingering in her voice. "It has a will of its own. We had to use two entire racks of pins to make Elizabeth's hair behave."

Racked with pleasure and exquisite tension, Zachary couldn't reply. The feel of her hands on his head, the soft massage of her fingertips, was nothing less than torture. She combed his hair neatly, guiding it back from his forehead, and by some miracle it stayed in place. "There," Holly said in satisfaction. "Very gentlemanly indeed."

"Did you ever do this for him?" Zachary heard himself ask hoarsely. "For George?"

Holly went still. When their gazes met, he saw the surprise in her warm brown eyes. Then she smiled faintly. "Well, no. I don't believe George ever had a hair out of place."

Of course, Zachary thought. Among George Taylor's many other perfections, he'd had gentlemanly hair as well. Forcing his aching, stiff body to move, he stood and made certain his coat was buttoned to conceal the evidence of his arousal. He waited while Holly washed the traces of pomade from her hands and donned a pair of long, blinding white gloves that extended past her elbows. Such lovely elbows she had, not knobby or pointy at all, just a bit plump, perfect for nibbling.

He wondered if this was what married men did, if they were allowed to watch their wives' last preparations before going out for the evening. The scene felt cozy and intimate, and it made him hollow with yearning.

Suddenly he heard a gasp. Glancing in the direction of the sound, Zachary saw Holly's blond maid standing in the open doorway, her blue eyes as large and round as dinner plates. A lush red rose fell from her nerveless grasp onto the carpeted floor. "Oh . . . I didn't . . ."

"Come in, Maude," Holly said calmly, as if Zachary's presence in her room were an everyday occurrence.

Recovering herself, the maid scooped up the fallen rose and brought it to her mistress. They conferred for a moment, and then the maid deftly pinned the fragrant blossom amid Holly's gleaming dark curls. Satisfied with the results, Holly glanced into the looking glass, touched the rose lightly, then turned toward Zachary.

"Shall we go, Mr. Bronson?"

He was both sorry and relieved to escort her from the room. It was a continuing struggle to master his raging desires, especially with her gloved hand tucked neatly in his arm, and the damned teasing swishing of her silk skirts around his legs. She was not an accomplished temptress, and he was well aware that her experience with men was limited. But he wanted her more than he had ever wanted a woman. If having her were a mere question of money, he would have purchased entire countries for her.

Unfortunately, matters were not that simple. He could never offer her the genteel life she deserved and needed, the kind of life she'd had with George. If by some miracle she ever did accept him, Zachary knew that he would disappoint her time and again, until she finally grew to hate him. She would discover all the coarseness of his nature; she would find him increasingly repellent. She would find excuses to keep him from coming to her bed. No matter how well the union might begin, it would end in disaster. Because, as his mother had correctly pointed out, one did not mate a Thoroughbred with a donkey. Better to leave her alone and fix his attentions on some other, far more appropriate woman.

If only he could.

Stopping Holly midway down the grand staircase, Zachary descended two steps without her and turned so their faces were level. "My lady," he said seriously, "the things I said about your mourning gowns . . . I'm sorry. I had no right to make such comments." He paused with a hard, uncomfortable swallow. "Am I forgiven?"

Holly studied him with a faint smile. "Not yet."

Her gaze was teasing, almost flirtatious, and Zachary realized with a sudden rush of delight that she enjoyed having the upper hand over him. She was so pert and adorable that it took all his power not to snatch her in his arms and kiss her senseless. "Then what will you have me do?" he asked softly, and for the most delicious moment of his life, they stood smiling at each other.

"I'll let you know when I think of something, Mr. Bronson." She walked down to his step and took his arm once more.

Only to herself would Holly admit that she was surprised by the amount of eager attention her protégées were receiving at the Plymouth ball. She was thrilled by their success, and especially by the fact that they seemed to mix easily with the crowd. It seemed that her social instructions had made them more comfortable in their interactions with the *ton,* and the *ton* was appropriately impressed. "That Mr. Bronson," she overheard one dowager saying to another, "seems to have improved somewhat. He is rising in the world, but I had not thought until tonight that his manners could keep pace with his advancement."

"Surely you don't mean to say you would consider him for your daughter?" came her companion's astonished reply. "I mean, he is quite *common,* after all."

"Indeed, I would," came the emphatic reply. "He has clearly taken it upon himself to study polite accomplishments, and the results are rather pleasing. And although the man may be a bit common, his fortune is quite *un*common."

"True, true," the other dowager agreed distractedly, as they stared at Bronson's distant figure from behind their fans, like soldiers siting a military target.

While Bronson mingled among the crowd, Holly kept company with Elizabeth and Paula. Even before the dancing had begun, Elizabeth had been introduced to at least a dozen young men, all of whom apparently found her sufficiently dazzling to merit their notice. Her dance card, tucked into a paper-thin silver case that tied around her gloved wrist with a pink ribbon, would have been completely filled, except that Holly had cautioned her to reserve a few. "You'll want to rest every now and again," Holly had murmured into the girl's ear, "and besides, you might encounter a gentleman that you will want to save an extra dance for."

Elizabeth had nodded obediently, appearing a bit dazed by the scene. Lord and Lady Plymouth's cavernous drawing room accommodated at least three hundred guests, with a good two hundred more milling in the surrounding circuit of rooms and galleries. The home was called Plymouth

Court, as it was constructed around a spectacular stone and marble courtyard filled with fruit trees and exotic flowers. It was an old, settled residence, formerly a defensive castle that had progressively been expanded during the last century into a large and luxurious home. In the drawing room, pools of abundant light from the overhead chandeliers and the open fire in the great marble hearth combined to reflect off the apricot-painted walls. The crowd was bathed in a glow that caused a king's ransom worth of jewelry to sparkle madly. Dowagers and nervous young girls sat on gilt-framed furniture covered with figured silk upholstery, while groups of friends stood together against a backdrop of faded but priceless Flemish tapestries.

Holly's nose tingled pleasantly with the familiar, unique smell of a ball. It was a mixture of scents, predominantly the tang of the waxed and milk-washed dance floor and the perfume of flowers, mixed with traces of cologne, sweat, pomade and lit beeswax candles. During her three years' absence from all social events, she had forgotten this smell, but it brought back a hundred pleasant memories of herself and George.

"It all seems unreal," Elizabeth whispered, after another gentleman had introduced himself and requested a place on her dance card. "The ball is so beautiful . . . and everyone is being so nice to me. I can't believe how many destitute young men want to put their hands on a share of Zach's fortune."

"Do you think that's the reason they all want to dance and flirt with you?" Holly asked with a fond smile. "Because of your brother's money?"

"Of course."

"Some of the gentlemen that have approached you are hardly destitute," Holly informed her. "Lord Wolriche, for example, or that nice Mr. Barkham. They both come from families of considerable means."

"Then why have they asked me to dance?" Elizabeth muttered, clearly perplexed.

"Perhaps because you're pretty and intelligent and spirited," Holly suggested, and laughed as the girl rolled her eyes in disbelief.

Another man approached, this time someone familiar. It was Holly's cousin, Mr. Jason Somers, the architect that visited Zachary weekly to consult about plans and materials for the planned country estate. During these visits, Elizabeth often attended the meetings to give her unsolicited opinions regarding Somers's work, and he always responded with appropriate sarcasm. Holly had been privately amused by the encounters, suspecting that the pair's bickering concealed an underlying attraction. She wondered if Bronson had arrived at the same conclusion, but she had not yet mentioned the subject to him.

Although Bronson appeared to have respect and appreciation for Somers's architectural talents, he had not yet expressed any opinions on the young man's character. Was Jason Somers the kind of man Bronson would welcome as a brother-in-law? Holly couldn't see why not. Jason was handsome, talented and from a good family. However, he was a professional man and not possessed of a great fortune . . . yet. It would take time and many sizable commissions before he gained the wealth that a man of his gifts deserved.

Jason greeted Holly, Paula and Elizabeth with a courtly bow, but his gaze lingered on Elizabeth's suddenly flushed face. He was strikingly handsome in his black dress coat, his lanky form elegant in the crisp evening clothes, his chestnut hair gleaming with brown and gold lights beneath the bright chandeliers. Although his alert green eyes gave nothing away, Holly noted the faint tide of color that touched the crests of his cheeks and the bridge of his nose as he stared at Elizabeth. He was fascinated by the girl, Holly thought, and she glanced at Paula to see if she, too, had noticed. Paula returned the glance with a faint smile.

"Miss Bronson," Jason said to Elizabeth with extreme casualness, "are you enjoying the evening so far?"

Elizabeth fiddled with the silver dance card and made a show of adjusting the ribbon around her wrist. "Very much, Mr. Somers."

Staring at Elizabeth's down-bent head, with all the silky dark curls confined with pins, Jason spoke a bit gruffly. "I thought I should approach you before every place on your dance card was filled—or is it already too late?"

"Hmmm . . . let me see . . ." Elizabeth flipped back the silver lid and consulted the tiny pages, deliberately drawing out the moment. Holly bit back a smile, knowing that Elizabeth had followed her advice and saved a few spaces for just an occasion such as this. "I suppose I could squeeze you in somewhere," Elizabeth said, pursing her lips thoughtfully. "The second waltz, perhaps?"

"The second waltz it is," he said. "I'll be interested to discover if your dancing skills are more advanced than your architectural taste."

Elizabeth responded to the little jab by turning to Holly and adopting a look of round-eyed puzzlement. "Is that an example of witty repartee, my lady?" she asked, "or is he by chance saving that for later?"

"I believe," Holly said with a soft laugh, "that Mr. Somers is attempting to provoke you."

"Really." Elizabeth turned back to Jason. "Does that technique usually attract many girls, Mr. Somers?"

"I'm not trying to attract all that many," he said with a sudden grin. "Only one, in fact."

Smiling, Holly watched as Elizabeth clearly wondered if *she* was the one he wished to attract.

Jason turned to Paula and inquired if he might procure her some refreshment. When Paula refused with a shy smile, Jason looked back at Elizabeth. "Miss Bronson, may I escort you to the refreshment table for a cup of punch before the dancing begins?"

Elizabeth nodded, a pulse beating visibly in her throat as she took his arm.

As the pair walked away, Holly thought that they were an exceedingly well-matched pair, both of them attractive, tall and slim. It was possible that Jason, with all his youthful energy and self-confident manliness, was the perfect foil for Elizabeth. The girl needed to be courted and charmed and swept off her feet. She needed someone to banish the streak of cynicism and self-doubt that kept her from feeling worthy of a man's love.

"Look at them," Holly murmured to Paula. "A handsome pair, are they not?"

Paula managed to look both worried and hopeful at the same time. "My lady, do you think a man as fine as that would ever want to marry a girl like Lizzie?"

"I would hope—expect—that any man of good sense would want someone as special as Elizabeth. And my cousin is no fool."

Lady Plymouth, a heavyset, cheerful woman with a florid complexion, approached them with a delighted exclamation. "My dear Mrs. Bronson," she said, taking Paula's hands in her plump ones and pressing warmly. "I have no wish to rob Lady Holland of your company, but I simply must steal you away for a little while. I have some friends I would like to introduce you to, and then, of course, we must visit the refreshment table. These events become so fatiguing unless one has sufficient sustenance."

"Lady Holland," Paula said, helplessly looking back over her shoulder as she was dragged away, "if you don't mind . . . ?"

"Go on," Holly urged with a smile. "I'll watch over Elizabeth when she returns." She felt a rush of gratitude toward Lady Plymouth, having privately asked her to introduce Paula to a few ladies who would be most likely to receive her. "Mrs. Bronson is quite shy," Holly had confided to Lady Plymouth, "but she is the most pleasant-natured lady in the world, full of common sense and good will . . . If only you might take her under your wing and show her around." Her appeal had apparently touched Lady Plymouth's kind heart. Also, Lady Plymouth was hardly averse to receiving the gratitude of a man like Zachary Bronson for being kind to his mother.

Seeing that Holly was unescorted, at least three men rapidly headed toward her from different parts of the room. It was not lost on Holly that her wine-red gown was attracting more attention than she had ever received in her life. "No, thank you," she said repeatedly, as she was beset with requests for various dances. She displayed her gloved wrist and its lack of a dance card. "I'm not dancing this evening . . . thank you so much for asking . . . I'm truly honored, but no . . ." The men did not leave, however, no matter how firmly she refused. Two more appeared, bearing cups of punch to assuage her thirst, and another came with a plate of tiny sandwiches to tempt her appetite. Their efforts to capture her interest escalated rapidly, men elbowing and jostling each other in an effort to stand closer to her.

Holly's surprise at the flood of attention became tempered with a bit of alarm. She had never been so besieged. When she had been a young, white-gowned girl, her chaperones had carefully supervised all interactions with males, and as a married matron, she had been protected by her husband. But her appearance in the red gown—and no doubt the rumors and insinuations about her presence in the Bronson household—had combined to attract a great deal of masculine interest.

Only one man could have cut through the mob. All of a sudden Zachary Bronson shouldered his way into the tightly packed crowd, looking impossibly large and dark, and a bit irate. It was only now, when she saw Bronson standing amid so many other men, that Holly realized how he was able to intimidate them all by sheer virtue of his size. She felt an inappropriate but delicious thrill as he took her arm possessively and glared at the horde around them. "My lady," he said brusquely, his cold gaze continuing to survey the group, "may I have a word with you?"

"Yes, certainly." Holly gave a sigh of relief as he drew her aside to a relatively private corner.

"Jackals," Bronson muttered. "And people say *I'm* not a gentleman. At least I don't pant and slobber over a woman in public."

"I'm sure you're exaggerating, Mr. Bronson. I hardly saw anyone slobbering."

"And the way that bastard Harrowby was staring at you," Bronson continued irritably. "I think he sprained his damn neck trying to get a look down the front of your dress."

"Your language, Mr. Bronson," Holly said tartly, though inside she felt a bubbling of laughter. Was it possible he was jealous? She knew she should not be pleased by such a thought. "And I needn't remind you that my choice of attire is entirely your fault."

The musicians in the upstairs bower began to play, the bright, lively music filling the air. "The dancing will begin soon," Holly said, adopting a businesslike air. "Have you been writing your name on various young ladies' dance cards?"

"Not yet."

"Well, you must apply yourself to it at once. I will suggest a few that are well worth approaching: Miss Eugenia Clayton, for one, and by all means Lady Jane Kirkby, and that girl over there—Lady Georgiana Brenton. She's the daughter of a duke."

"Do I need a third party to make the introductions?" Bronson asked.

"At a public ball, yes. However this is a private ball, and the fact that you were invited is sufficient testament to your respectability. Remember to make conversation that is neither too serious nor trivial. Talk about art, for example, or your favorite periodicals."

"I don't read periodicals."

"Then discuss prominent people whom you admire, or social trends you find interesting . . . oh, you know very well how to make small talk. You do it with me all the time."

"That's different," Bronson muttered, staring with barely concealed alarm at the flocks of white-gowned virgins that filled the room. "You're a woman."

Holly laughed suddenly. "And what are all those creatures, if not women?"

"I'll be damned if I know."

"Do not swear," she said. "And do not say anything indelicate to one of those girls. Now go dance with someone. And bear in mind that a true gentleman would approach one of the poor girls sitting in the chairs against the wall, instead of heading for the most popular ones."

Staring at the row of disconsolate wallflowers, Zachary heaved a sigh. He couldn't fathom why it had once seemed like a good idea to marry some unformed fledgling and mold her to his liking. He had wanted a trophy, an upper-class brood mare to lend some prestige to his common bloodline. But the idea of spending the rest of his life with one of these well-bred girls seemed appallingly dull. "They all look the same," he muttered.

"Well, they're not," Holly reproved. "I remember full well how it felt to be cast out into the marriage market, and it's terrifying. I had no idea what kind of husband I might end up with." She paused and touched his arm lightly. "There, do you see that girl seated at the end of the row? The attractive one with the brown hair and the blue trim on her gown. She is Miss Alice Warner—I am well acquainted with the family. If she is anything at all like her older sisters, she will be a delightful partner."

"Then why is she sitting alone?" he asked darkly.

"She is one of a half-dozen daughters, and the family can offer practically nothing in the way of a dowry. That is off-putting to many enterprising young men . . . but it won't matter to you." Holly gave him a quick, subtle push in the back. "Go ask her to dance."

He resisted her prodding. "What will you be doing?"

"I see your sister being escorted to the refreshment room, where I believe your mother is heading as well. Perhaps I'll join them there. Now go."

He gave her an ironic glance and went off like a reluctant cat being prodded to hunt.

When it became apparent that Holly was unattended once again, several men started toward her. Realizing she was about to be mobbed once more, Holly decided instantly on a strategic retreat. Pretending not to see any of the gentleman who were headed in her direction, she sailed toward the entrance of the drawing room, hoping to find refuge in one of the surrounding galleries and parlors. She was too intent on her escape to notice the large shape that crossed her path. Suddenly she walked directly into a man's solid body. A surprised gasp escaped her. A pair of gloved hands caught her elbows, restoring her uncertain balance.

"I'm so sorry," Holly said in a rush, glancing up at the man before her. "I was in a bit of a rush. Forgive me, I should have been . . ." But her voice faded into stunned silence as she realized whom she had walked into.

"Vardon," she whispered.

The very sight of Vardon, Lord Blake, the earl of Ravenhill, caused memories to come over her in a heady rush. For a moment her throat tightened too much to allow speech or breath. It had been three years since she had seen him, not since the funeral. He looked older, more serious, and there were lines at the corners of his eyes that had not been there before. Yet he looked more handsome, if possible, maturity lending him a look of ruggedness that saved him from what might have otherwise been bland attractiveness.

His wheat-blond hair was cut the same, and his gray eyes were just as she remembered, so cool and incisive until he smiled. Then his gaze was warm and silvery. "Lady Holland," he said quietly.

A thousand memories bound them together. How many lazy summer afternoons had the three of them spent together, how many parties and musical evenings had they attended at the same time? Holly remembered how she and George had laughingly offered advice to Vardon on what sort of girl he should marry . . . or George and Vardon attending boxing matches, then coming home as drunk as parrots . . . or the grim evening when she had broken the news to Vardon that George had contracted typhoid fever. Vardon had been a steady support for Holly all through his friend's illness and eventual death. The two men had been as close as brothers, and in that light Holly had regarded Vardon as a member of the family. Now seeing Vardon like this, after he had been absent from her life for so long, brought back a sweet, intoxicating sense of what it had been like when George was still alive. Holly half-expected to see George trailing after him with a ready joke and a merry smile. But George was not there, of course. Only she and Vardon were left.

"The only reason I came here tonight is because Lady Plymouth told me that you would be attending," Ravenhill said quietly.

"It's been so long, I—" Holly broke off, her mind blank as she filled her gaze with him. She longed to talk to him about George, and about what had transpired for both of them during the past years.

Ravenhill smiled, his white teeth gleaming in his golden face. "Come with me."

Her hand slipped naturally into his arm, and she went without thinking, feeling as if she had stepped into the middle of a dream. Wordlessly Ravenhill led her from the ballroom and through the entrance hall to a long row of French doors. He guided her through the doors and out into the house's central courtyard, where the air was heady with the scent of fruit and flowers. Outside lamps adorned with festoons of lacy wrought iron shed light over the abundant greenery, and illuminated the sky above until it resembled the exact color of black plums. Seeking a measure of privacy, they walked to the edge of the courtyard, which opened onto a great formal garden at the back of the house. They found a circle of small stone benches half-concealed by a row of hedges, and they sat together.

Holly stared into Ravenhill's shadowed face with a tremulous smile. She sensed that he felt the same way she did, awkward but eager, two old friends anxious to renew their acquaintance. He looked so dear, so familiar, that she experienced a strong urge to hug him, but something held her back. His expression contained some secret knowledge that seemed to cause him discomfort . . . uneasiness . . . shame. He started to reach for her gloved hand, then drew back, resting his palms on his spread knees instead.

"Holland," he murmured, his gaze sweeping over her. "You're more beautiful than I've ever seen you."

She studied Ravenhill as well, struck by how much older he seemed, his golden handsomeness tempered by a bitter awareness of the grief that life sometimes held in store for the unsuspecting. He seemed to have lost the supreme self-assurance that had come with his privileged upbringing, and strangely he was all the more attractive for it.

"How is Rose?" he asked softly.

"Happy, beautiful, bright . . . oh, Vardon, how I wish George could see her!"

Ravenhill seemed unable to reply, staring hard at some distant point of the garden. His throat must have pained him, for he swallowed several times.

"Vardon," Holly asked after a long silence, "do you still think of George often?"

He nodded, his smile edged with self-mockery. "Time hasn't helped nearly as much as everyone assured me it would. Yes, I think about him too damn often. Until he died, I'd never lost anyone or anything that mattered to me."

Holly understood that all too well. For her, as well, life had been almost magically perfect. As a young woman, she had been untouched by loss or pain, and she had been so certain that things would always be wonderful. In her immaturity, it had never occurred to her that someone she loved could be taken away from her.

"Since boyhood, everyone thought of George as a

prankster, and I was the responsible one," Ravenhill said. "But that was only the appearance of things. In truth, George was the anchor. He had the deepest sense of honor, the greatest integrity that I've ever known. My own father was a drunkard and a hypocrite, and you know that I don't think much better of my brothers. And the friends I made at school were nothing but dandies and wastrels. George was the only man I've ever truly admired."

Filled with a wistful ache, Holly reached for his hand and squeezed it hard. "Yes," she whispered with a smile of tender pride, "he was a fine man."

"After he passed away," Ravenhill said, "I nearly went to pieces. I would have done anything to dull the pain, but nothing worked." His mouth twisted in self-disgust. "I started drinking. And drinking. I became an unholy mess, and I went away to the continent to spend some time alone and clear my head. Instead, I did even worse things. Things I'd never imagined myself doing before. If you had seen me at any time during the past three years, Holland, you wouldn't have recognized me. And the longer I stayed away, the more ashamed I was to face you. I abandoned you, after I had promised George—"

Suddenly Holly's gloved fingertips touched his lips lightly, stilling the flow of wretched words. "There was nothing you could have done for me. I needed time alone to mourn." She stared at him compassionately, scarcely able to imagine him behaving in ways that were less than proper and honorable. Ravenhill had never been one to indulge in reckless behavior. He had never been a drunkard or a skirt-chaser, had never gambled or fought, or done anything to excess. She couldn't begin to understand what his activities had been during his long absence from England, but it didn't matter.

It occurred to her that there must be many different ways

of mourning. While she had turned inward in her sorrow, perhaps Ravenhill's grief over George had turned him a bit mad for a while. The important thing was that he was back home now, and she took great pleasure in seeing him again.

"Why haven't you come to visit me?" she asked. "I had no idea you had returned from the continent."

Ravenhill flashed her a self-deprecating smile. "So far I haven't kept any of the promises I made to my best friend on his deathbed. And if I don't start to make good on them, I won't be able to live with myself any longer. I thought the best way to begin was to ask your forgiveness."

"There is nothing to forgive," she said simply.

He smiled and shook his head at her answer. "Still every inch a lady, aren't you?"

"Perhaps not quite as much a lady as I once was," she replied with a note of irony.

Ravenhill stared at her intently. "Holland, I've heard that you are employed by Zachary Bronson."

"Yes. I am acting as a social instructor for Mr. Bronson and his delightful family."

"That is my fault." Ravenhill did not appear to receive the news with the same pleasure she took in imparting it. "You would never have been driven to such lengths had I been here to fulfill my promises."

"No, Vardon," Holly said hastily, "it has truly been a rewarding experience." She fumbled for words, wondering how on earth she could explain her relationship with the Bronson family to him. "I am better for knowing the Bronsons. They have helped me in ways I can't easily explain."

"You were never meant to work," Ravenhill pointed out quietly. "You know what George would have thought."

"I am well aware of what George wanted for me," she agreed. "But Vardon—"

"There are things we have to discuss, Holland. Now isn't the time and place, but there is one thing I must ask you. The promise we gave George that day—is it still something you would consider?"

At first Holly could find no breath to answer. She had a dizzying sense of fate rolling over her in an irresistible tide. And with it came the strangest mixture of relief and dullness, as if all she had to do was accept a circumstance that she had no control over. "Yes," she said softly. "Of course I would still consider it. But if you have no desire to be bound by it—"

"I knew what I was doing then." His purposeful gaze held hers. "I know what I want now."

They sat together in a silence that required no words, while the ache of regret swirled around them. In their world, one did not seek happiness for its own sake, but received it—sometimes—as a reward for behaving honorably. Often doing one's duty brought pain and unhappiness, but one was ultimately sustained by the knowledge that he or she had lived with integrity.

"Then let us talk later," Holly eventually murmured. "Call on me at the Bronsons' home, if you wish."

"Shall I take you back to the ballroom?"

She shook her head hastily. "If you wouldn't mind, please leave me here. I just want to sit alone and think quietly for a moment." Seeing the objections in his gaze, she gave him a coaxing smile. "I promise, no one will accost me in your absence. I'm only a stone's throw from the house. Please, Vardon."

He nodded reluctantly and took her gloved hand, pressing a kiss to the back of it. When he had left her, Holly heaved a sigh and wondered why she was so confused and unhappy about fulfilling the last promise George had ever asked of her. "Darling," she whispered, closing her eyes, "you always knew what was right for me. I trust you now as much as I ever did, and I see the wisdom in what you asked of us. But if you could give me a sign that it is still what you want, I would gladly spend the rest of my life as you wished. I shouldn't see it as a sacrifice, I know, but—"

Her soulful ponderings were suddenly interrupted by an irate voice.

"What the hell are you doing out here?"

Being thoroughly a man, one whose nature was rooted in competition, Zachary had experienced jealousy before. But nothing like this. Not this mixture of rage and alarm that shredded his insides. He was no idiot—he had seen the way Holly was looking at Ravenhill in the ballroom, and he had understood it all too well. They were cut from the same cloth, and they shared a past that he'd had no part of. There were bonds between them, memories, and even more, the comfort of knowing exactly what to expect from each other. All of a sudden Zachary hated Ravenhill with an intensity that approached fear. Ravenhill was everything he was *not* . . . everything he could never be.

If only this were a more primitive time, the period of history when simple brute force overrode all else and a man could have what he wanted merely by staking his claim. That was how most of these damned bluebloods had originated, in fact. They were the watered-down, inbred descendents of warriors who had earned their status through battle and blood. Generations of privilege and ease had tamed them, softened and cultured them. Now these pampered aristocrats could afford to look down their noses at a man who probably resembled their revered ancestors more than they themselves did.

That was his problem, Zachary realized. He had been

born a few centuries too late. Instead of having to mince and prance his way into a society that was clearly too rarefied for him, he should have been able to dominate . . . fight . . . conquer.

As Zachary had seen Holly leave the ballroom, her small hand tucked against Ravenhill's arm, it had required all his will to appear collected. He had nearly trembled with the urge to snatch Holly into his arms and carry her away like a barbarian.

For a moment, the rational part of his brain had commanded him to let Holly go without a struggle. She had never been his to lose. Let her make the right decisions for herself, the comfortable decisions. Let her find the peace she deserved.

The hell I will, he had thought savagely. He had followed the pair, intent as a prowling tiger, letting nothing stand in the way of what he wanted. And now he found Holly sitting here alone in the garden, looking dazed and dreamy, and he wanted to shake her until her hair cascaded loose and her teeth rattled.

"What's going on?" he demanded. "You're supposed to be smoothing the way for Lizzie and telling me which girls to dance with, and instead I find you in the garden making calf eyes at Ravenhill."

"I was not making calf-eyes," Holly said indignantly, "I was remembering things about George, and . . . oh, I should return to Elizabeth—"

"Not yet. First I want an explanation of what is going on between you and Ravenhill."

Her small, pale face wore an expression of consternation. "It's complicated."

"Use very small words," he suggested acidly, "and I'll try to follow along."

"I'd rather discuss it later—"

"Now." He caught her gloved elbows as she rose from the bench, and glared into her moonlit face.

"There's no need to be upset." Holly gasped a little at the rough way he handled her.

"I'm not upset, I'm . . ." Realizing he was holding her too tightly, Zachary let go of her abruptly. "Tell me what you and Ravenhill were talking about, dammit."

Although his grip couldn't possibly have hurt her, Holly cupped her hands around her elbows and rubbed them gently. "Well, it concerns a promise that I made long before you and I met."

"Go on," he muttered as she paused.

"On the day George died, he expressed his fear over what was going to happen to Rose and me. He knew he wasn't leaving us very much to live on, and although his family reassured him that they would take care of us, he was terribly troubled. Nothing I said would comfort him. He kept whispering that Rose needed a father to protect her, and that I . . . oh, dear . . ." Shivering at the bleak memory, Holly sat on the bench once more and blinked hard against the rising pressure of tears. Ducking her head, she used the tips of her gloves to blot the rivulets that leaked from her eyes.

Zachary swore and rummaged through the innumerable inside pockets of his coat for a handkerchief. He found his pocket watch, his extra pair of gloves, wads of money, a gold tobacco case and a small pencil, but the handkerchief proved elusive. Holly must have realized what he was searching for, as she suddenly choked on a watery giggle. "I told you to bring a handkerchief," she said.

"I don't know where I put the damn thing." He gave her one of his extra gloves. "Here, use this."

She dabbed at her wet cheeks and nose, then held the object tightly in her hand. Although she hadn't invited him to sit beside her, Zachary straddled the bench and faced her, staring at her down-bent head. "Go on," he said gruffly. "Tell me what George said."

Holly sighed deeply. "He was afraid of what would happen to me . . . that without a husband I would be lonely, that I needed a man's guidance and affection . . . he was afraid I would make ill-advised decisions, and that others would take advantage of me. And so he asked for Vardon . . . er, Ravenhill. He trusted Ravenhill more than anyone in the world, and had faith in his judgment and sense of honor. Although Ravenhill might seem a bit cold on the surface, he is a kind man, and very fair and generous—"

"Enough about the wonders of Ravenhill." Renewed jealousy fomented inside him. "Just tell me what George wanted."

"He . . ." Holly took a deep breath and exhaled sharply, as if it were difficult to force the words out. "He asked us to marry each other after he was gone."

A scalding silenced ensued, while Zachary wondered wildly if he had heard correctly. Holly refused to look at him.

"I didn't want to be thrust upon Ravenhill, as an unwanted obligation," she finally whispered. "But he assured me that the match was sensible, and much desired on his side. That it would serve to honor George's memory, and at the same time secure a good future for all three of us— me, Rose, and himself."

"I've never heard of such a damned foolish arrangement," Zachary growled, rapidly revising his opinion of George Taylor. "Obviously you both recovered your senses and broke off the agreement, and a good thing, too."

"Well, we haven't exactly broken it off."

"What?" Unable to stop himself, Zachary grasped her jaw in one hand and forced it upward, revealing her face.

Her tears had dried, leaving her cheeks moist and flushed and her eyes glittering. "What do you mean, you haven't broken it off? Don't tell me you have some idiotic notion of actually going through with it."

"Mr. Bronson—" Holly squirmed away from him uncomfortably, seeming surprised by his reaction to the news. She handed back his wet glove, which he shoved into a pocket. "Let us return to the ball, and we'll discuss this matter at a more appropriate time—"

"*Damn* the ball, we'll talk about this right now!"

"Don't raise your voice to me, Mr. Bronson." Standing, she shook out her glimmering red skirts and adjusted her bodice. The moonlight played over the pearly skin of her bosom and sent coy shadows chasing down the lush valley between her breasts. She was so beautiful and infuriating that Zachary had to clench his hands to keep from grabbing her. He rose to his feet, swinging one long leg over the bench in an easy move. He had never been angry and aroused at the same time before—it was a novel sensation, and not a pleasant one.

"Apparently Ravenhill didn't want the match as much as he indicated," he pointed out in a low, grating voice. "It's been three deuced years since George died, and there's been no wedding. I'd say that's a damn clear sign of unwillingness."

"I thought so, too," Holly confessed, rubbing her temples. "But when I spoke with him tonight, Vardon said that it has taken him a long time to sort things out in his mind, and he still wants to honor George's wishes."

"No doubt he does," Zachary snapped, "after having a look at you in that red dress."

Holly's eyes widened, and her cheeks colored with annoyance. "I take offense at that remark. Vardon is not at all that kind of man—"

"Isn't he?" Zachary felt his face pulling into a ferocious sneer. "You have my guarantee, milady, that every man in that ballroom *including* Ravenhill would be damned happy to get under your skirts. Honor has nothing to do with what he wants from you."

Horrified by his crudity, Holly skittered to the other side of the bench and glowered at him. Her gloved fingers twitched as if she were tempted to slap him. "Is it Ravenhill we're speaking of, or you?" Suddenly realizing what she had said, she clapped her hand over her mouth and stared at him speechlessly.

"Now we're getting somewhere." He started after her in a slow, deliberate stride. "Yes, Lady Holly . . . by now it's no great secret that I want you. I desire you, I understand you . . . hell, I even *like* you, which is something I've never said to a woman before."

Clearly alarmed, Holly turned and fled down a path leading through the garden—not toward the house, but deeper toward the darkened lower lawns, where there was little chance of being seen or overheard. Good, Zachary thought in primitive satisfaction, abandoning all rationality. He followed her with no great haste, his long strides easily keeping pace with her short, frantic ones.

"You don't understand me at all," Holly said over her shoulder, her breath coming in rapid bursts. "You don't know a thing about what I need or want—"

"I know you a thousand times better than Ravenhill ever will."

She gave a disbelieving laugh, speeding through the entrance to a sculpture garden. "I've known Vardon for *years,* Mr. Bronson, whereas you and I have been acquainted for a matter of four and a half months. What could you possibly claim to know about me that he doesn't?"

"For one thing, you're the kind of woman who would kiss a stranger at a ball. Twice."

Holly stopped dead in her tracks, her small body as straight and stiff as a ramrod. "Oh," he heard her say softly.

Zachary came up behind her and stopped, waiting for her to gather the nerve to face him.

"All this time," she said in a trembling voice, "you've known that I was the woman you kissed that night. And yet you've said nothing."

"Neither have you."

Holly turned then, forcing herself to look up at him, her face scarlet with shame. "I hoped you wouldn't recognize me."

"I'll remember it until my dying day. The feel of you, the smell and taste of you—"

"Don't," she said with a horrified gasp. "Hush, don't say such things—"

"From that moment on, I've wanted you more than I've ever wanted anyone."

"You want *every* woman," she cried. Evidently deciding on a strategic retreat, she backed away from him and edged around a white marble statue.

Zachary pursued her steadily. "What do you think has been keeping me home every evening of late? I get more satisfaction from sitting in the damn parlor and listening to you read poetry than I do from spending a night with the most skilled whores in London—"

"Please," she said scornfully, "spare me your sordid compliments. Perhaps some women may appreciate your depraved charm, but I do not."

"My depraved charms are not all lost on you," he countered, reaching her just as she stumbled on a bit of gravel. He caught her from behind, his hands closing around her upper arms. "I've seen the way you look at me. I've felt the way you react when I touch you, and it's not disgust. You kissed me back that evening in the conservatory."

"I was caught off guard! I was surprised!"

"Then if I kissed you again," he said in a low voice, "you wouldn't respond? Is that what you're claiming?"

Although he couldn't see her face, he felt the tension in her muscles increase as she realized the trap she had just walked into. "Take my word for it, Mr. Bronson," she said unsteadily. "I would not respond. Now please let me—"

He spun her around and locked her against his body, and bent his head.

Twelve

Holly made a startled sound and went utterly still, paralyzed by the sensations that swept over her. Bronson kissed her in the shocking way she remembered from before, whole-mouthed, hungry, with a raw desire that made it impossible for her to withhold a response. The night seemed to close around them, the marble statuary standing like silent sentinels to ward away intruders. Bronson's dark head moved over hers, his mouth gentle but urgent, his tongue searching her in deep, hot sweeps. Her entire body seemed to burn. Suddenly she could not seem to press close enough to him. She reached inside his coat, where the heat of his body had collected, and the layers of linen were warm and male-scented. The smell of him was the most compelling fragrance she had ever encountered: salt and skin, cologne and the tang of tobacco. Stirred and excited, she pulled her lips from his and pressed her face into his shirtfront. She breathed raggedly, while her arms clutched around his hard waist.

"Holly," he muttered, sounding as shaken as she was. "My God . . . Holly . . ." She felt his big hand close around the back of her neck, flexing slowly. He tilted her head back, and his mouth covered hers once more. It wasn't enough to merely let him explore her mouth, she wanted to taste him in return. She pushed her tongue into his hot, brandy-flavored mouth. Not enough . . . not nearly enough. Moaning, she stood on her toes, pushing herself up at him, but he was too big for her, too tall, and she gasped in frustration.

Scooping her up into his arms as if she weighed nothing, Bronson carried her farther into the sculpture garden, where there was something round and flat—a stone table, perhaps, or a sundial. He sat with her in his lap, one immense arm braced behind her shoulders and neck, while his mouth continued to devour hers in delicious forays. She had never experienced such raw physical pleasure before. Compelled to touch him, she tore frantically at her right glove until it fell away. Her shaking hand groped for his hair and slid into the thick waves at the back of his neck. His muscles jumped and flexed beneath her bare fingers, his nape turning rock-hard, and he groaned into her mouth.

Breaking the kiss, Bronson bent over her, nuzzling the tender skin beneath her jaw, finding the vulnerable areas along the side of her throat. She felt his tongue touch her skin, and the sensation caused her to squirm and shiver in his lap. His mouth lingered at the hollow at the very base of her neck, where a pulse throbbed wildly.

Her gown had become disarranged, the bodice slipping so that it barely covered the tips of her breasts. Feeling the perilous down-slide of red silk, Holly came to her senses with a startled murmur, crossing her gloved arm over her nearly exposed breasts. "Please . . ." Her lips felt hot and swollen, making it difficult to speak. "I shouldn't . . . oh, we must stop this!"

He seemed not to hear her, his lips beginning a searing sojourn over her chest. He nibbled and licked at the edge of her collarbone, moving to the plump valley between her

breasts. Closing her eyes in despair, Holly bit back a protest as she felt him tug at her bodice, his strong fingers
working at the fabric. She would stop him soon, soon, but
for now the moment was unbearably sweet, and neither
shame nor honor could influence her.

She gasped as her breast popped free of the red silk
covering, the nipple budding at the caress of the cool midnight breeze. Bronson ripped off his glove, and his large,
bare hand cupped tenderly around the soft mound, his
thumb passing over the hardening crest. Holly kept her
eyes closed, unable to believe what was happening. She
felt his mouth touch her, kissing all around the sensitive
nipple, circling and teasing but avoiding the center, until
finally she groaned and arched to push it into his mouth.
His lips closed around her, tugging, his tongue stroking
the aching tip with delicate skill.

Writhing upward, she held his dark head in her arms,
while erotic sensation pulsed in every tender place of her
body. Her breath came in strange little sobs, her lungs
straining against the compression of her stays. Her clothes
seemed to bind her too tightly. She wanted to feel his skin
against hers. She wanted his taste, his touch, as she had
never wanted anything before in her life.

"Zachary," she gasped in his ear, "please stop. Please."

His hand returned to her breast, covering and gently
shaping the fullness, his palm rough against her skin. He
rubbed his mouth over hers in fierce half-kisses, until her
lips were soft and wet and pliant beneath his. Then he
raised her enough to whisper in her ear, and while his
voice was tender, his words were savage. "You're my
woman, and no man or God or ghost will ever take you
from me."

Anyone who had the slightest knowledge of Zachary
Bronson and what he was capable of would have been

alarmed. Holly went rigid with terror, not just at the prospect of being claimed so utterly, but by the flicker of fiercely joyous response she felt inside. She had striven her entire life to be moderate, reasonable, civilized, and she had never dreamed it possible that this could happen to her.

She struggled from his lap in such a panicked flurry that he was forced to release her. Her feet gained purchase, and she stood unsteadily. To her surprise, her legs were so weak that she might have fallen, had Bronson not stood and caught her waist in his hands. Blushing furiously, she restored her bodice, hiding the naked flesh that gleamed in the moonlight.

"I suspected this might happen," she said, struggling to regain some form of composure. "Kn-knowing of your reputation with women, I knew you might someday make an advance to me."

"What just happened between us was not an 'advance,' " he said thickly.

She did not look at him. "If I am to remain as a guest in your household, we must forget this incident."

"Incident," he repeated scornfully. "This has been building between us for months, since the first time we met."

"It has not," she countered, while her heart hammered in her throat, nearly choking her into silence. "I won't deny that I find you attractive, I . . . any woman would. But if you are under the misconception that I would become your mistress—"

"No," he said, his huge hands coming to the sides of her face, fingers curving around the back of her skull. He urged her face upward, and Holly quailed at the look in his dark, passionate eyes. "No, I never thought that," he said, his voice turning raspy. "I want more from you than that. I want—"

"Don't say anything else," Holly begged, closing her eyes tightly. "We've both gone mad. Let me go this instant. Now, before you make it impossible for me to stay at your estate any longer."

Although she hadn't expected the words to affect him, they seemed to make great impact. There was a long, taut silence. Slowly his hands eased their possessive grip and dropped away. "There's no reason for you to leave my home," he said. "We'll handle this however you like."

The clutch of panic began to ease from her throat. "I—I want to ignore this as if it never happened."

"All right," he said at once, although his gaze was frankly skeptical. "You set the rules, my lady." He stooped and retrieved her discarded glove, and handed it to her. Flushing, she fumbled to pull it back over her arm.

"You must promise not to interfere in the matter between Ravenhill and me," she managed to say. "I invited him to call on me. I do not wish for him to be turned away or treated rudely when he visits. I will make all decisions about my future—and Rose's—without any help from you."

She saw from the hard flexing of his jaw that he was gritting his teeth. "Fine," he said evenly. "But I want to point something out. For three years Ravenhill has gallivanted around Europe—and don't try to claim that his infernal promise to George was uppermost in his mind then. And what about your actions? You weren't thinking about the damn promise when you agreed to work for me—you know George wouldn't have approved. Hell, you and I both know he probably rolled over in his grave!"

"I accepted your offer because I didn't know if Ravenhill still desired to uphold his vows to George. I have Rose and her future to consider. When you appeared, and Ravenhill was nowhere to be found, it seemed the best choice at the time. And I don't regret it. When my employment with you is concluded, I will then be free to fulfill my obligations to George, if that turns out to be the best course of action."

"All very sensible," he observed in a soft but stinging tone. "Tell me this: If you decide to marry Ravenhill, will you let him share your bed?"

She colored at the question. "You have no right to ask such a thing."

"You don't want him that way," he said flatly.

"There is far more to a marriage than what occurs in the conjugal bed."

"Is that what George told you?" he shot back. "I wonder . . . did you ever respond to him the way you do with me?"

The question filled her with outrage. Holly had never struck anyone in her life, but her hand moved of its own accord. As if she stood outside the scene, she watched the white flash of her glove as she slapped his face. The blow was pitifully soft, insignificant except as a gesture of rebuke. It didn't seem to bother Bronson in the slightest. In fact, she saw the satisfied gleam in his eyes, and she realized in a flash of despair that she had given him his answer. With a sob of distress, she sped away from him as fast as her feet would take her.

After a while Zachary returned to the ball, doing his best to appear composed while his body ached with frustrated desire. At last he knew what it was like to hold her in his arms and feel her mouth work sweetly under his. At last he knew the taste of her skin, the throb of her pulse against his lips. Absently taking a cup of some noxiously sweet liquid from a passing servant, Zachary stood at the side of the room and stared at the crowd until he located Holly's vivid red dress. She appeared miraculously carefree and self-possessed, chatting lightly with his sister Elizabeth and making introductions to the would-be suitors that approached them. Only the arcs of bright color at the crests of her cheeks betrayed her inner turmoil.

Zachary tore his gaze from her, knowing it would cause comment if he continued to stare at her so openly. But somehow he knew that she was aware of him, despite the fact that they were separated by a roomful of people. Blindly he turned his attention to the cup of punch in his hand. He drank it in a few impatient gulps, finding the taste to be cloying and medicinal. Various acquaintances came to stand next to him, most of them partners in business ventures, and he obligingly made polite conversation, smiled at jokes he only half-heard, ventured opinions when he was barely aware of the subject matter. All his attention, his thoughts, his wilful soul, were focused on Lady Holland Taylor.

He was in love with her. Every dream, hope and ambition of his life combined was a tiny flame in comparison to the great conflagration of emotion that burned inside him. It terrified him that she held such immense power over him. He had never wanted to love anyone this way— it brought him no comfort or happiness, only the painful knowledge that he was almost certain to lose her. The thought of not having her, relinquishing her to another man, to the wishes of her departed husband, nearly brought him to his knees. Wildly he considered ways to lure her ... There were things he could offer. Hell, he would personally build a great marble monument to the memory of George Taylor, if that was her price for accepting him.

Occupied with his frantic thoughts, Zachary didn't immediately notice the nearby presence of Ravenhill. Gradually he became aware of the tall blond man standing only a few feet away, a handsome solitary figure amid the vibrant clamor of the ball. Their gazes met, and Zachary stepped closer to him.

"Tell me," Zachary said softly, "what kind of man would ask his best friend to marry his wife after he died? And what kind of man would inspire two seemingly sensible people to agree to such a damned stupid plan?"

The man's gray eyes surveyed him in a measuring stare. "A better man than you or I will ever be."

Zachary couldn't stop himself from sneering. "It seems that Lady Holland's paragon of a husband wants to control her from the grave."

"He was trying to protect her," Ravenhill said without apparent heat, "from men like you."

The bastard's calmness infuriated Zachary. Ravenhill was so damned confident, as if he had already won a competition that Zachary hadn't even known about until it was over. "You think she'll go through with it, don't you?" Zachary muttered resentfully. "You think she'll sacrifice the rest of her life simply because George Taylor asked it of her."

"Yes, that's what I think," came Ravenhill's cool reply. "And if you knew her better, you'd have no doubt of it."

Why? Zachary wanted to ask, but he couldn't bring himself to voice the painful question. Why was it a foregone conclusion that she would go through with her promise? Had she loved George Taylor so much that he could influence her even in death? Or was it simply a matter of honor? Could her sense of duty and moral obligation really impel her to marry a man she didn't love?

"I warn you," Ravenhill said softly, "if you hurt or distress Lady Holland in any way, you'll answer to me."

"All this concern for her welfare is touching. A few years late in coming, isn't it?"

The comment seemed to rattle Ravenhill's composure.

Zachary felt a stab of triumph as he saw the man flush slightly.

"I've made mistakes," Ravenhill acknowledged curtly. "I have as many faults as the next man, and I found the prospect of filling George Taylor's shoes damned intimidating. Anyone would."

"Then what made you come back?" Zachary muttered, wishing there were some way to forcibly transport the man back across the Channel.

"The thought that Lady Holland and her daughter might need me in some way."

"They don't. They have me."

The lines had been drawn. They might as well have been generals of opposing armies, facing each other across a battlefield. Ravenhill's thin, aristocratic mouth curved in a contemptuous smile. "You're the last thing they need," he said. "I suspect even you know that."

He walked away. Zachary stood watching him, stonefaced and still, while inside he writhed in anguished fury.

Holly needed a drink. A large glass of brandy, one that would calm her overwrought nerves and allow her a few hours of sleep. She had not needed to take spirits since the first year of mourning George. The doctor had prescribed a nightly glass of wine in those days of turmoil, but it had not been enough. Only strong spirits had been sufficient to calm her, and so she had sent Maude on secretive missions to fetch her glasses of whiskey or brandy when the household had settled for the night. Knowing that George's family would not approve of a lady drinking, and also aware that they would be able to detect the lowering levels of liquor in the sideboard decanters, Holly had decided to smuggle a bottle to her own room. Using Maude as intermediary, Holly had gotten a footman to purchase brandy for her, and she had stored it in the drawer of her dressing table. Now thinking longingly of that long-ago brandy bottle, she dressed for bed and waited impatiently for the Bronson household to retire.

The carriage ride back home from the ball had been nothing short of hellish. Fortunately Elizabeth had been too excited by her own success, and the flattering attentions paid her by Jason Somers, to notice the seething silence between Holly and her brother. Paula had been aware of the tension, of course, and she had sought to cover it with a stream of light chatter. Holly had forced herself to ignore Bronson's brooding stare and had made small talk with Paula, smiling and joking while inside her nerves were shattering.

When there wasn't a sound or movement to be detected in the cavernous house, Holly took a candle in a small jeweled holder and crept from her room. As far as she knew, the easiest place to find brandy was in the library sideboard, where Bronson always kept a supply of excellent French vintage.

Descending the grand staircase in her bare feet, Holly held the candle high, starting a little as the tiny flame cast eerie shadows on the gilded walls. The large house, always so busy and bustling in the daytime, resembled a deserted museum at night. Cool drafts curled around her ankles, and she shivered, grateful for the warmth of the ruffled white pelisse that fastened over her thin nightgown.

Entering the library, Holly inhaled the familiar smell of leather and vellum, and passed the huge gleaming globe on her way to the sideboard. She set the candle on the polished mahogany surface and opened a cabinet door in search of a glass.

Although there wasn't a sound or movement in the room, something alerted her to the fact that she wasn't alone. Uneasily she turned to survey her surroundings, and gasped as she saw Bronson seated in a deep leather armchair, his long legs stretched before him. He stared at her intently, his ophidian eyes unblinking. He was still dressed in his evening clothes, though his coat had been removed and his waistcoat and necktie hung loose. His white shirt was unbuttoned to the middle of his chest, revealing a wealth of thick black hair. An empty brandy snifter was held loosely in his fingers, and she surmised that he had been drinking for some time.

Holly's heart jerked violently. Air left her lungs in a swift rush, making it impossible for her to speak. Unsteadily she leaned back against the sideboard, gripping the edge with her hands for support.

Slowly Bronson rose to his feet and approached her. He glanced at the open door of the sideboard, understanding immediately what she wanted. "Allow me," he said, his voice a velvety rumble in the stillness, and he pulled out a snifter and a brandy decanter. Pouring until the snifter was a third full, he held it by the stem and used the candle flame to warm the glass bowl. An expert swirl or two, and he handed the warmed vintage to her.

Holly took the snifter and drank at once, wishing that her hand wasn't trembling visibly. She couldn't help staring at the place where his shirt hung open. George had had a smooth chest, which she had always found attractive, but the sight of Zachary Bronson in an unbuttoned shirt filled her mind with lurid, disquieting thoughts. She wanted to rub her mouth and face amid those springy dark curls, wanted to press her bare breasts against them . . .

A flaming blush covered her from head to toe, and she gulped brandy until it made her cough.

Bronson returned to his chair and sat heavily. "Are you going to marry Ravenhill?"

The brandy snifter nearly fell from Holly's hand.

"I asked you a question," he said thickly. "Are you going to marry him?"

"I don't know the answer to that."

"Of course you do. Tell me, damn you."

"I . . ." Her entire body seemed to wilt in defeat. "It is possible I will."

Bronson did not seem surprised. A soft, ugly laugh broke from him. "You'll have to explain why. I'm afraid that common bruisers like myself have trouble understanding these upper-class arrangements."

"I promised George," Holly said carefully, feeling no small amount of apprehension as she stared at him. Bronson looked so . . . well, malevolent . . . as he sat there in the darkness. Handsome, black-haired and larger than life, he could have been Lucifer seated on his throne. "If you find anything about me that is worthy of admiration or affection, then you would not wish me to behave in a way that is less than honorable. I have been raised never to break my word, once it has been given. I know that some people think a woman's sense of honor is not as strong as a man's, but I have always tried—"

"My God, I don't doubt your honor," he said roughly. "What I'm saying—what should be clear to everyone—is that George should never have asked for such a promise."

"But he did, and I gave it."

"Just like that." Bronson shook his head. "I wouldn't have believed it of you—*you,* the only woman I've ever known who is willing to stand up to me in a temper."

"George knew what would happen to me without him," she said. "He knew I would never willingly marry again. He wanted me to have the protection of a husband and, more importantly, for Rose to have a father. And Ravenhill's values and beliefs were similar to his, and George knew that Rose and I would never be mistreated by his best friend—"

"Enough," Zachary interrupted harshly. "I'll tell you what I think about good old Saint George. I think he didn't want you to ever fall in love again. And locking you into a marriage with a cold fish like Ravenhill was George's way of making certain that he would remain your one and only love."

Holly whitened at the accusation. "What a horrible thing to say. You are *completely* wrong, you know absolutely nothing about my husband or his friend—"

"I know you don't love Ravenhill. I know you never will. If you're so intent on marrying a man you don't love, then take me."

Of all the things she might have expected him to say, that was the biggest surprise of all. Clumsy with astonishment, Holly finished her brandy and set the empty snifter on the sideboard behind her. "Are you proposing to me?" she asked in a whisper.

Bronson came to her, not stopping until he had crowded her against the sideboard. "Why not? George wanted you to be protected and cared for. I can do that. And I could be a father to Rose. She doesn't know who the hell Ravenhill is. I'll take care of the two of you." He slid his hand beneath the sheath of her hair, sifting gently through the long brown locks. Holly closed her eyes and bit back a whimper of pleasure as she felt his fingers curve around the back of her neck. It seemed that her whole body responded to his touch. There was a mortifying, expectant twitch in the private place between her thighs, and she was shamed by the carnal need that pulsed so strongly inside her. She had never longed to be physically possessed by a man as much as she did this moment. "I could give you things you never even thought to want before," Bronson whispered. "Forget about your damned promises, Holly. That's all in the past. It's time to think of the future now."

Holly shook her head and parted her lips to argue. His head lowered swiftly, and he took her mouth, making her groan in pleasure as his tongue sank deeply inside her. He kissed her with a passionate expertise that sent every rational thought scattering. His mouth teased and twisted over hers, while she strained upward in helpless response. His warm hands, separated from her body by only thin layers of muslin, slid over her with shocking boldness, cupping over the shapes of her breasts, the slopes of her hips, even the full curves of her buttocks. She gasped as he squeezed her bottom gently, pulling her hips upward against his. As he kissed her, he rubbed her insistently against the rock-hard protrusion of his arousal, and Holly nearly swooned at the sensation. Not even her husband had dared to fondle her so blatantly.

She dragged her mouth from his. "You're making it impossible for me to think—"

"I don't want you to think." He pulled her hand to the front of his trousers, fitting her lax fingers over the huge, hot ridge that arched against the taut fabric. Her eyes widened at the feel of him, and she dove her head against his chest to avoid his descending mouth. He kissed the frail skin beneath her ear instead, his lips roving downward to her throat. Although the rational part of Holly's mind— what was left of it—warned stridently against such reckless sensuality, she pressed her cheek to the intriguing curls on his chest. She was enthralled by his uncompromising masculinity, every powerful, coarse, thrilling detail of him. But he was not for her. Although opposites might attract, they did not make for good marriages. One's only chance for contentment was when like married like. And she had made a binding promise to her husband in the last minutes before he died.

The thought of George abruptly sent her hurtling back to reality, and she wrenched herself free of Zachary Bronson's arms.

She stumbled to a chair and sat down hard, her legs weak and trembling. To her relief, Bronson did not follow her. For a long time the only sounds in the library were the sharp inhalations of their breathing. Finally Holly found her voice. "I can't deny the attraction between us." She paused and emitted a shaky laugh. "But surely you must know that we would never suit! I am meant for a small, quiet life—your way of living is too grand and fast for me. You would grow bored with me in a very short time, and you would long to be free of me—"

"No."

"—and I would find it such a misery, trying to live with a man of your appetite and ambition. One of us would have to change, and that would cause terrible resentment, and the marriage would come to a bitter end."

"You can't be certain of that."

"I can't take such a risk," she replied with absolute finality.

Bronson stared at her through the shadows, his head tilted a bit, as if he were relying on some sixth sense to penetrate her thoughts. He came to her and sank to his haunches before the chair. He startled her by reaching for her hand, his fingers closing over her small, cold fist. Slowly his thumb rubbed over her knotted knuckles. "There is something you're not telling me," he murmured. "Something that makes you anxious . . . even afraid. Is it me? Is it my past, the fact that I was a fighter, or is it—"

"No," she said with a laugh that caught hard in her throat. "Of course I'm not afraid of you."

"I know fear when I see it," he persisted.

Holly shook her head, refusing to debate the comment. "We must put this night behind us," she said, "or I will have to take Rose and leave right away. And I don't wish to leave you or your family. I want to stay as long as possible and fulfill our agreement. Let us agree not to speak of this again."

His eyes gleamed with black fire. "Do you think that's possible?"

"It has to be," she whispered. "Please, Zachary, tell me you'll try."

"I'll try," he said tonelessly.

She drew a trembling breath. "Thank you."

"You'd better leave now," he said, unsmiling. "The sight of you in that nightgown is about to drive me mad."

Were she not so miserable, Holly would have been amused by the remark. The tiers of ruffles that adorned her nightgown and pelisse made the ensemble far less revealing than an ordinary day gown. It was only Bronson's inflamed state of mind that made her seem desirable. "Will you be retiring now as well?" she asked.

"No." He went to fill his glass, and answered her over his shoulder. "I have some drinking to do."

Wrenched with unexpressed emotion, she tried to twist her mouth into a smile. "Good night, then."

"Good night." He did not glance back at her, his shoulders held stiffly as he listened to the sound of her retreating footsteps.

Thirteen

For the next fortnight Holly saw almost nothing of Bronson, and she realized that he was deliberately putting distance between them until they were both able to resume their previous friendship. He threw himself into his work all day, going to his town offices, rarely returning home for dinner. He stayed out late in the evenings and arose in the mornings with bloodshot eyes and lines of strain on his face. This ceaseless activity was not mentioned by the other members of the Bronson household, but Holly sensed that Paula understood its cause.

"I want you to be assured, Mrs. Bronson," Holly told her carefully one morning, "that I would never deliberately cause discomfort or unhappiness to anyone in your family—"

"My lady, it's not your fault," Paula responded with her customary frankness, reaching over to give Holly's hand an affectionate pat. "You may be the first thing my son has ever truly wanted that he wasn't able to get. To my way of thinking, it's good for him to finally learn his limits. I've always warned him about reaching too high above his buttons."

"Has he spoken to you about me?" Holly asked, flushing until even the tips of her ears felt hot.

"Not a word," Paula said. "But there was no need. A mother always knows."

"He is such a wonderful man," Holly began to tell her earnestly, afraid that Paula might be under the misconception that she didn't think Zachary was good enough for her.

"Yes, I think so, too," Paula said matter-of-factly. "But that doesn't make him right for you, milady, any more than you are right for him."

The reassurance that Bronson's mother did not blame her for the situation should have made Holly feel better. Unfortunately, it didn't. Each time Holly saw Bronson, no matter how brief or casual the encounter, she was filled with longing that threatened to overwhelm her. She began to wonder if she could really live like this for the remainder of her promised year at the Bronson home. Devoting herself to Rose and to the Bronson women, she kept herself as busy as possible. And there was much to do, especially now that Elizabeth had made her entrance into society. The great hall was filled with constantly arriving bowers of roses and spring arrangements, and the silver tray near the door was loaded daily with cards from hopeful suitors.

As Holly had predicted, the combination of Elizabeth's beauty and fortune, not to mention her irrepressible charm, had attracted many men who seemed more than willing to overlook the circumstances of her birth. It required both Holly's and Paula's efforts to chaperone the daily visits and carriage drives and picnics as various gentlemen came to court Elizabeth. However, there was one caller in particular who seemed to capture the girl's interest most strongly—the architect, Jason Somers.

There were callers with bluer blood and greater wealth, but none that possessed Jason's self-confidence and charm. He was a robust man with more than his share of talent and ambition—a man not all that unlike Elizabeth's brother. From what Holly had observed, Jason was able to balance Elizabeth's exuberant spirit with his own steady strength. It was a good match, and promised to be a happy union, if all turned out as Holly hoped.

During one of Jason's morning visits, Holly happened to see the pair as he and Elizabeth returned from a walk in the garden.

". . . besides, you're not tall enough for me . . ." Elizabeth was saying, her voice filled with effervescent laughter as they strode through the French doors and into a gallery of marble sculpture. Holly paused at the far end of the gallery where she happened to be walking. She was concealed by a towering winged rendition of some Roman god.

"Good God, woman, I'm hardly what anyone would call short," Jason retorted. "And I'm a good two inches taller than you."

"You are not!"

"Am too," he insisted, and pulled her against him with an easy strength that made Elizabeth gasp. They were matched length-to-length, Elizabeth's slender form measured against Jason's larger one. "See?" Jason said, his voice suddenly husky. The amusement faded from the girl's face, and she fell abruptly silent, staring at the man who held her, her eyes filled with shy apprehension. Holly briefly considered interrupting the scene, knowing that Elizabeth was unused to such attentions from a man. But there was a look on Jason's face that Holly had never seen before, utterly tender and desirous. He bent his head to murmur something in her ear, and Elizabeth turned pink, one of her hands creeping up to his shoulder.

Holly's own face flushed a bit as she slipped away discreetly, allowing the two a measure of privacy. Oh, how long ago it seemed that she had been courted by George in the same manner, and how innocent and hopeful she had felt. But her memories were blurred now, and she no longer found pleasure in reminiscing. Her life with George had become a distant dream.

Filled with wistfulness, Holly spent the rest of the morning playing with Rose, and then left her daughter in Maude's care. She declined lunch, as she was too dispirited to eat a bite. Instead, she selected a novel from the library and carried it with her on a walk through the gardens. The sky was overcast, and the breeze was infused with a cool mist that caused Holly to shiver and pull her brown cashmere shawl more closely around her shoulders. Pausing first at a stone table, and then at a bench sided by flower-filled urns, she finally found a spot for reading, a summerhouse about twelve feet wide. The windows were covered in little wooden shutters, and inside it was lined with cushioned benches. The seats and backs of the benches were covered with a heavy twilled green fabric that held a faintly musty but not unpleasant scent.

Curling up on one of the cushions and drawing her feet up beneath her, Holly leaned back and began to read. Soon lost in the tale of a doomed love affair—was there any other kind?—Holly failed to noticed the rumblings of thunder in the sky. The light darkened from silver-white to gray, and rain began to patter heavily on the lawn and paved walkway outside. A few errant drops blew through the shutter and fell to Holly's shoulder, finally alerting her to the worsening weather outside. Looking up from the novel, she frowned.

"Bother," she muttered, realizing that her novel reading was coming to an end. It was definitely time to return to the main house. But the rain was already heavy, and she wondered if the storm might lessen in a few minutes. Sighing, she closed the book in her lap and leaned her head against the wall as she watched the rain pelt the grassy earth and hedges. The vibrant smell of a heavy spring shower filled the summerhouse.

Her melancholy thoughts were soon interrupted as someone opened the door roughly and shouldered his way inside.

She was startled to see Zachary Bronson, his large form shrouded in a sodden greatcoat. He brought a gust of fresh rain-laden wind with him, then closed the shuttered door with the back of his shoe. Swearing beneath his breath, he struggled with a huge dripping umbrella. Retreating back against a cushion, Holly watched him with a growing smile as he endeavored to fold the ungainly contraption. He was a handsome devil, she thought with a flicker of pleasure, her gaze drinking in the sight of his rain-washed face and his coffee-black eyes and his gleaming dark hair plastered to his well-shaped skull.

"I thought you were in town," she said, raising her voice above a long rumble of thunder.

"Came back early," he replied shortly. "I managed to stay just ahead of the storm until it reached the estate."

"How did you know I was out here?"

"Maude was worried—she said you were in the garden somewhere." Triumphantly he closed the umbrella with a snap. "It was easy enough to find you—not many places to take shelter." His dark gaze settled on her face, and he returned her smile with a flashing grin. "So I'm here to rescue you, milady."

"I didn't even realize I needed rescuing," Holly said. "I was completely absorbed in my book. Perhaps the rain will ease soon?"

As if in sarcastic response, the sky turned several shades darker, and earsplitting thunder accompanied a streak of lightning as it scored across the burgeoning sky. Holly laughed suddenly and glanced at Bronson, who was smiling. "Let me take you back to the house," he said.

Holly shivered, staring at the torrential downpour. It seemed a very long way back to the house. "We'll be soaked," she said. "And the lawn has undoubtedly turned to mud. Couldn't we just wait until it stops?" Extracting a dry handkerchief from her sleeve, she stood on her toes and dabbed at the rivulets of rain on Bronson's face. Suddenly he was expressionless, standing still beneath her ministrations.

"It won't stop for hours. And I don't trust myself to be alone with you for more than five minutes." He removed his greatcoat and hung it around her shoulders. The garment was ridiculously large on her. "So unless you want to be ravished in the summerhouse," he said brusquely, staring into her upturned face, "let's go."

But neither of them moved.

Holly raised the handkerchief to his jaw, drying a few last drops of water that clung to his clean-shaven skin. She crushed the damp lace-trimmed linen in her fist, and clutched at the greatcoat to keep it from falling to the floor. She did not comprehend why being alone with him gave her such intense pleasure, why the sight of him and sound of his voice should be so comfortable and yet so stirring. The knowledge that their lives were only entwined for a temporary time caused her heart to ache. He had become important to her so quickly, so effortlessly.

"I've missed you," she whispered. She had not intended to speak the words aloud, but they pressed forth of their own accord, hanging gently amid the splashing staccato of rain. She felt almost maddened by a yearning that was deeper than hunger, sharper than pain.

"I had to stay away," Bronson said gruffly. "I can't be

around you without . . ." Falling silent, he stared at her in grim misery. He did not move when Holly pushed the coat off her shoulders, or when she brought her body against his, or even when she slid her arms around his neck. She rubbed her face against the damp collar of his shirt, and hugged him fiercely. It seemed that for the first time in days she was able to breathe fully, the dull ache of loneliness finally lifting from her chest.

A muffled groan escaped him, and he turned his head to fit his mouth against hers. His arms went around her, holding her securely. The summerhouse dissolved in a blur around her, and the smell of rain was replaced by the masculine scent of Zachary's skin. She put her hands on his hot cheeks, his neck, and his grip tightened just short of crushing her, as if he were trying to pull her inside him.

Just this once . . . the wicked thought seized her and would not let go. *Just once . . .* she would live on it, remember, savor when the days of her youth were long past. No one would ever know.

The storm pounded on the wooden structure around them, but its force was nothing compared to the violent beating of her own heart. Frantically she pulled at the knot of his necktie, tugging it loose, then worked at the buttons of his waistcoat and shirt. Zachary held still, though his powerful chest moved in deep, labored breaths.

"Holly . . ." His voice was low and unsteady. "Do you know what you're doing?"

Recklessly she pushed the shirt open, baring him from neck to navel, and her breath stopped at the sight of him. He was a magnificent creature, his body a tightly knit masterpiece of muscle and sinew. Holly touched him in awed wonder, spreading her hands on his furry chest, sliding her fingertips through to the tough muscle beneath, then stroking the hard, rippled surface of his stomach. She found the sprinkling of hair around his navel, her fingertips investigating gently, and he made a sound of pained pleasure. Catching her wrist, he pulled her hand away, holding it to the side as he stared at her. "If you touch me again," he said raggedly, "I won't be able to stop. I'll take you right here, Holly . . . do you understand?"

She moved toward him, pressed herself to his bare skin, buried her face amid the thick black curls on his chest. She felt his resistance break, his large body shuddering as he wrapped his arms around her. His mouth sought hers urgently, extracting sensations that were indecent in their sheer sweetness. A series of swift, light tugs, and the carved bone buttons of her bodice were released, the garment sagging to her elbows. After unhooking her stays, Zachary took hold of the tape that fastened the top of her chemise, wound it around his finger, and pulled. Her breasts spilled free, white and pink, the tips already contracted from the coolness of the summerhouse. Filling his hands with the round, soft weights, Zachary cradled the sensitive peaks within his palms.

"Hurry," she said in agitation. "Zachary, please, I . . . I need you." Now that she had abandoned herself in passion, she had lost all shame, all restraint. She wanted him over her, inside her, the heat of him couched between her legs.

Hushing her with his mouth, Zachary shrugged off his shirt and waistcoat, baring his gleaming sculptured shoulders. He sat on the green cushions and pulled her to his lap. Reaching beneath her skirts, he spread her knees apart and guided them to either side of his hips. Holly turned scarlet with excitement and apprehension as she settled onto his loins and felt the swollen hardness of his erection straining beneath his trousers. She could feel the immense shape of him burning against the delicate veil of her drawers. Hooking his hands beneath her arms, Zachary brought her forward and kissed the space between her breasts. She cradled his dark head in her arms, and gasped as she felt his mouth close around a tender, peaked nipple. The strokes of his tongue were soft and hot. He moved to her other breast and she felt the gentle pressure of his teeth as he tugged at her aching flesh.

Quiet, incoherent sounds filtered from her throat, and she slid lower on his body, thrusting her damp breasts into the wiry curls of his chest. The coarse silken hair teased her, stimulated her, and she rubbed herself against him with a moan of pleasure. Later she would be mortified at her own wanton actions . . . much later. For now there was only Zachary, his sleek muscled body, his amorous, marauding mouth, and she was going to savor every moment with him.

His hands slipped beneath her skirts, and he fondled the round curves of her bottom. His touch became gentle, almost lazy, drifting over her body with maddening slowness. Shakily she urged him once more to hurry, while in the back of her mind she was appalled by her own desperate need. Suddenly Zachary laughed, the sound soft and low in his throat. He untied the tape of her drawers and pulled the garment down her hips. She moved awkwardly to help him, feeling light-headed as the drawers were stripped away.

"T-tell me what to do," she begged, anxiously aware of her lack of knowledge. This reckless encounter in the midst of an afternoon storm was entirely different from the peaceful nighttime interludes she had shared with George. Zachary Bronson was so terribly experienced—jaded, even—that there seemed no possible way she could satisfy him.

"Are you asking how to please me?" His lips moved

tenderly over the rim of her ear. "You don't even have to try."

She pressed her red face against his shoulder, breathing fitfully as he widened the spread of her legs over his hips. Peals of thunder continued to rip across the sky, but the noise had lost the power to startle her. All her being was focused on the man who held her, his hard body beneath her, the masculine hand that fondled her so gently. His fingertips drew across the fragile crease of her thigh where it met the softer skin of her groin. He stroked the feathery whorls of hair, searching for the place where her intimate flesh parted . . . He found the small, secretive cove that moistened eagerly at his touch. All her muscles tightened, and she sat suspended over him in trembling astonishment. Her forehead dug into the sinewy surface of his shoulder, and she groaned his name.

She had never been taught any sort of bedroom etiquette, but she and George had both shared the same instinctive understanding that most married couples did—a gentleman accorded his wife the highest respect at all times, even in the conjugal embrace. He would refrain from touching her in indecent ways, and he would not seek to encourage her passions. Her character was to be kept untainted, and though a man should make love to his beloved with kindness, he should never touch or speak to her lewdly.

Apparently no one had ever informed Zachary Bronson of these facts. He whispered words of love and lust in her ear while he played with her unmercifully, his fingertips circling the tiny sensitive peak hidden between the folds of her sex. Aroused and perspiring, she pushed herself farther into his hand, and she gasped as she felt his finger slip inside her.

A strange, burning agitation spread throughout her body,

and she twisted against him, her hands opening and closing against his shoulder, her open mouth pressing to his neck in beseeching kisses. His throat hummed with a crooning noise, and she felt the incredible tautness of his body, his muscles tightly bunched with compressed energy. Slowly, as if he were wary of frightening her, he drew away his hand and tugged at the fastenings of his trousers. She felt the hard, heavy spring of his released flesh, and her body jerked as she felt the first scalding touch of him. He positioned her wider and wedged himself against her damp opening.

Holly quivered as she felt him ease inside her, stretching her delicate flesh. She let out a faint whistling breath through her teeth.

"Am I hurting you?" His gaze, dark as midnight, raked over her face. His hand slipped between their bodies, stroking and adjusting, spreading her so that he rubbed directly against the aching nub hidden amid the damp curls. The moment was so astonishingly intimate that she nearly wept. Her body relaxed to accommodate him, the pinching tightness easing, and suddenly there was no pain in his possession, only pleasure. Abandoning herself completely, she wrapped herself around him, her legs clamping on his hips.

Zachary's eyes closed, his brow furrowing. He took the back of her head in his hand and brought her forward, his mouth claiming hers hungrily. His other hand splayed over her hips, urging her against him in an insistent rhythm, thrusting in deep nudges that made her squirm and writhe helplessly. He kept kissing her all the while, his mouth offering, taking, consuming her with feverish heat.

She fought against the tangle of clothing between them, longing to be completely rid of her gown, wanting to feel his bare legs against hers instead of the textured broadcloth trousers. Voluptuous tension gathered inside her, while cries of need broke from her throat. A strange, wild fever had overtaken her, and she couldn't stop herself from writhing harder against him. She loved the rough, dense texture of his body, the thrusting length of him inside her, the big hands that cupped her breasts as she rode him. Then suddenly she couldn't move at all, her muscles locking as burning pleasure blossomed in her loins and spread all through her body. Paralyzed, she bit her lip and moaned as her nerves caught fire and her senses exploded.

Although she didn't entirely understand what was happening, Zachary did, for he murmured softly and cradled her in his arms, his hips continuing their steady upward drives. She began to shudder, her body tightening in delicious spasms around his invading shaft, and that was enough to send him over the edge as well. He shivered and sighed and buried himself in one last thrust. His hands gripped her buttocks, pulling her hard against his loins as he impelled himself as far inside her as possible.

Feeling drunk, Holly relaxed heavily against his chest, while the place where they were joined still glowed and throbbed. She wanted to laugh and cry at the same time, and eventually a nervous giddy sound escaped her. Zachary rubbed her bare back soothingly, and she pressed her cheek against his shoulder.

"That never happened to you with your husband," he whispered. It was a statement, not a question.

Holly nodded in perplexed wonder. It was hard to believe they could have a conversation this way, with the heat of him still lodged deep within her. But the storm was still beating outside, surrounding them in dark rain-swept privacy, and she heard herself reply in a drugged voice, "I liked making love with George . . . it was always pleasant.

But there were things he never . . . and I wouldn't . . . because it isn't right, you see . . ."

"What isn't right?" Zachary pulled a few pins from her hair and unraveled the warm coil of shining brown locks, spreading them in a curtain over her naked back.

She spoke slowly, searching for the right words. "A woman should tame a man's bestial nature, not encourage it. I told you once before what lovemaking should be—"

"An elevated expression of love," he said, playing with her hair. "A communion of souls."

Holly was surprised that he had remembered. "Yes, exactly. It should not descend into lewdness."

She felt him smile against the side of her head. "I see nothing wrong with a little lewdness now and then."

"Of course you wouldn't," she said, hiding a smile in the thick carpet of curls on his chest.

"So now you probably think your character has begun to degenerate," he mused, and her smile faded.

"I've just had illicit relations with my employer in the summerhouse. I don't think anyone would claim that as evidence of a sterling character." She tried to move off of him, gasping as the heavy length of him was pulled from inside her. Unbearable mortification swept over her as she felt the abundance of moisture seeping between her thighs, and she groped for something to blot it with. Zachary reached for his discarded coat, and for once he was able to find a handkerchief. He gave it to her, and spoke with a thread of tender amusement in his voice. "I've never seen a woman blush from head to toe before."

Glancing down, Holly saw that she had turned varying shades of pink and red over every exposed inch of skin. Snatching the handkerchief from him, she turned away from him as far as possible as she used it. "I can't believe what I've done," she said in a suffocated voice.

"I'll cherish this afternoon for the rest of my life," Zachary replied. "I'm going to have this summerhouse gold-plated, and a plaque hung over the door."

Holly whirled to face him, horrified that he might be serious, and saw the shimmering laughter in his eyes. "Oh, how can you joke about this?" She jerked and pulled at her gown, great masses of fabric wadded and crumpled around her waist.

"Here, hold still." Deftly he pulled up her undergarments and hooked her stays and helped her slide her arms back into her sleeves. The evidence of his expertise with womens' clothing was disheartening. There was absolutely no doubt that he had trysted like this with many paramours . . . She was the latest in a very long line.

"Zachary—" she began, closing her eyes as he gathered the locks of her hair in one hand and lowered his mouth to the side of her throat. His lips moved in a velvet slide across her skin, causing gooseflesh to rise. She made a despairing sound and leaned back against his solid chest. "I'm appalled by my weakness of character where you're concerned," she said. "No doubt many other women have said that to you."

"I don't remember any other women," he said.

She gave a disbelieving laugh, but he turned her to face him, his big hands moving possessively over her waist and sides and back. "What we just shared, Holly . . . I don't know if it was a communion of souls, but it was the damn closest I'm ever going to get."

"It was a moment out of time." She kept her gaze on his bare chest, her hand moving with a will of its own and stroking the hard, sleek muscles, the thick covering of hair. "It has nothing to do with our real lives. I shouldn't have . . . it's just . . . I wanted to be with you at least once. I wanted it so badly that I didn't care about anything else."

"And now you think we're going to carry on as if nothing has happened?" he asked incredulously.

Holly swallowed and shook her head, fighting the urge to curl up against his half-naked body and cry like a child. "Well, no, of course not. I—I can't stay after this."

"Holly, sweet darling, you can't possibly think I'm going to let you go." He gathered her against him, besieging her with kisses.

Holly had never known before that joy and pain could mingle like this. She clung to him, and briefly let herself respond, kissing him with fierce adoration, clutching him tightly for all the times she would never be able to hold him. Finally she tore herself away and stood, pulling at the bunched fabric of her skirts until they settled into place. She hunted for her discarded shoes, finding one in the center of the summerhouse, the other beneath a bench. Zachary moved behind her, searching for his own clothes and putting them on.

Sighing, Holly stared hard at some point far outside the rain-splattered window, where the tall hedgerows dissolved in a watery blur. "I knew before today that I would have to leave," she said, keeping her back to Zachary. "Now, after this, I certainly can't live beneath the same roof with you."

"I don't want you to leave."

"My feelings for you don't change what I must do. I've already explained why."

He was silent for a full minute, grasping the full significance of her words. "You're still planning to marry Ravenhill," he said tonelessly. "Even now."

"No, it's not that." Holly felt very cold, all the pulsing warmth of their encounter finally draining away. She tried to examine her choices, but all of them left her feeling empty and strangely fearful. It was all too natural to retreat back into the habits of a lifetime, to follow the paths that had been chosen for her long ago, first by her father and then by George. "I don't know what will happen with Ravenill. I don't even know if he'll still have me."

"Oh, he'll have you." Zachary spun her around to face him. He was huge and dark, staring at her with a sort of resigned fury. "I've had to fight for everything I've ever gotten. But I won't fight for you. You'll come to me because you want me. I'll be damned if I'll bully or beg you to have me. I suppose in the *ton*'s view, a Ravenhill is worth about a hundred Bronsons. No one will blame you for marrying him, especially when it comes out that George wanted the match. And you might even be happy for a while. But someday you'll realize it was a mistake, when it's too late for either of us to do a damned thing about it."

Holly turned white, but managed to reply calmly. "Our agreement . . . I'll return the money . . ."

"Keep the money for Rose. There's no reason for her trust to be cut in half simply because her mother is a coward."

She lowered her watery gaze to the level of his third shirt button. "You're being cruel now," she whispered.

"I think I could be a gentleman about almost anything, except for losing you. Don't expect me to take it with good grace, Holly."

Swiping her hand across her eyes, she managed one last whisper. "I want to go back to the house."

Despite the cover of Zachary's greatcoat and the shelter of the umbrella, Holly was thoroughly soaked by the time they reached the house. Zachary brought her in through the French doors connecting to a gallery filled with sculpture. The long rectangular space was shadowed and streaked with silver from the patterns the rain had made on the window. Statues were dappled and painted with gray rivulets. Dripping, his hair clinging to his head, Zachary stared down at the obdurate woman before him. She was shivering and tense, so closed away from him by her obligations and promises that they might as well have been separated by a granite wall.

Her small, pale face was surrounded by streaming tendrils of brown hair, making her look like an unhappy mermaid. He yearned to carry her upstairs and strip away her cold wet clothes and warm her with the heat of a fire, and then with his own body. "I'll talk to your mother and sister tomorrow," Holly said unsteadily. "I'll tell them that my work here is done and there's little reason to stay. Rose and Maude and I will be packed and gone by the end of the week."

"I'm leaving for Durham tomorrow," Zachary muttered. "I'll fry in hell before going through some sham of seeing you off and wishing you well, and pretending there's nothing wrong between us."

"Yes. Of course." She stood before him, her small frame held stiffly. She was so damned elusive, wounded, regretful, intractable—and so clearly in love with him. Zachary was furious that honor and common sense meant more to her than he did. She forced herself to return his gaze, and there was a perplexing glint of fear in her eyes. She was afraid to trust in any kind of future with him. He knew how to coax and badger and entice people into doing things they were reluctant to do, but he would not use those skills on her. She would have to choose him willingly, and it was clear that this was something she would never bring herself to do.

Charged with bitter defeat, Zachary longed suddenly to be away from her, before he did or said something they would both regret for eternity. "Just one more thing," he said, his voice coming out far more harshly than he had intended. "If you leave me now, don't come back. I don't give second chances."

Tears dropped from her eyes, and she turned away hastily. "I'm sorry," she whispered, and fled the gallery.

Fourteen

"*I don't understand,*" Elizabeth said unhappily. "Is it because of something I've done, or . . . have you finally decided I'm unteachable? I'll try much harder, my lady, I promise—"

"It has nothing to do with you," Holly rushed to assure the girl, reaching out to hold her hand tightly. After a sleepless night, she had arisen with bleary eyes, more resolved than ever to follow the course she had decided on. She had to, before she did things even more ill-advised than she already had. Her body felt unfamiliar to her, filled with sensations that lingered from the encounter in the summerhouse yesterday afternoon. She had never known the lure of fornication until now, never understood the power it had to ruin peoples' lives and break apart families and dissolve sacred vows. Now she knew why men and women had affairs, and why they would risk everything for the sake of them.

George wouldn't have recognized his loving, virtuous wife in the woman who had abandoned herself with Zachary Bronson. George would be horrified at what she had become. Ashamed and afraid, Holly had instructed Maude to start packing all their possessions as soon as possible. She had tried to explain to Rose, as gently as possible, that

273

the time had come for them to return to the Taylors, and of course the little girl had been upset by the news. "But I like it here!" Rose had cried angrily, her brown eyes flooding with tears. "I want to stay, Mama. *You* go back, and Maude and I will stay here!"

"We don't belong here, Rose," Holly had replied. "You know very well that we weren't planning to stay forever."

"You said it was for a year," Rose argued, snatching up Miss Crumpet and holding the doll protectively. "It hasn't been a year yet, not *nearly,* and you were supposed to teach Mr. Bronson his manners."

"He's learned everything he needed to from me," Holly said firmly. "Now stop making a fuss, Rose. I understand why you're unhappy, and it grieves me terribly, but you're not to trouble the Bronsons about this."

After Rose had stormed away and disappeared somewhere in the huge house, Holly had reluctantly asked the Bronson women to meet with her in the family parlor after breakfast. It was not easy to tell them that she would be leaving the estate in a day or two. To her surprise, she realized that she would miss Elizabeth and Paula more than she would have ever expected.

"It must be Zach," the girl exclaimed. "He's been horrid lately, as bad-tempered as a baited bear. Has he been rude to you? Is he to blame for this? I'll go see him this minute and knock some sense into him—"

"Hush, Lizzie." Paula's compassionate gaze rested on Holly's distressed face as she spoke. "You won't solve anything by charging about and making things more difficult for Lady Holly. If she wishes to leave, she will go with our affection and gratitude, and we won't repay all her kindness by tormenting her."

"Thank you, Mrs. Bronson," Holly whispered, unable to look the mother of her lover in the eyes. She had the awful suspicion that Paula, intuitive soul that she was, had guessed what had occurred between she and Zachary.

"But I don't want you to leave," Elizabeth said stubbornly. "I'm going to miss you so awfully . . . you're the dearest friend I've ever had, and . . . oh, what shall I do without little Rose?"

"You'll still see us." Holly smiled warmly at the girl, while her eyes stung with tears. "We'll remain dear friends, Lizzie, and you are welcome to visit me and Rose whenever you wish." Feeling a choking wave of emotion rising inside, she stood and wrung her hands nervously. "If you'll excuse me, I have so much packing to do . . ."

She left hastily, before they could see her tears, and the two women began to talk animatedly just as she reached the threshold.

"Did Lady Holly have some sort of falling-out with Zach?" she heard Elizabeth ask. "Is that why he's nowhere to be found and she's planning to leave?"

"It's not quite that simple, Lizzie . . ." came Paula's careful reply.

No, it was not simple at all.

Holly tried to consider what it would be like to marry Zachary, to become his wife and plunge into his ostentatious, fast-paced life. To leave behind everything she had known . . . to become a different woman, really. She ached with bitter longing, wanting him with all her being, but something inside her recoiled and shrank from the prospect. She searched blindly for the reason why, to make sense of her own fear, but somehow the truth refused to crystallize. It remained diffused and chilling inside her.

Zachary had never accepted defeat before. He'd tolerated it in small doses, perhaps, always knowing that in the larger scheme of things, he would have what he wanted.

But he'd never been truly vanquished, never known a real loss. Until this, the biggest loss of all. It made him feel vicious and a bit crazed. He wanted to kill someone. He wanted to weep. Most of all he wanted to laugh at himself for being a big sodding fool. In the nonsensical stories that Holly read aloud some evenings about Greeks and their amorous, carelessly cruel gods, mortals were always punished for reaching too high. Hubris, Holly had once explained. Too much prideful ambition.

Zachary knew he had been guilty of hubris, and now he was paying the price. He should never have let himself want a woman who was clearly not meant for him. What tormented him the most was the suspicion that he might actually still be able to obtain her, if he bullied and tormented and bribed her into it. But he wouldn't do that to her, or to himself.

He wanted her to love him as willingly and joyously as she had loved George. The very idea would have made most people laugh. It even amused him. What must Holly think when she compared him to her saintly husband? Zachary was a scoundrel, an opportunist, a rough-mannered scavenger—the definitive opposite of a gentleman. Clearly Ravenhill was the right choice, the only choice, if she wanted a life similar to the one she'd had with George.

Scowling, Zachary strode to the library in search of a packet of files and letters he intended to bring with him to Durham. A flurry of packing was going on upstairs, as Maude and the housemaids stuffed clothes and personal belongings into trunks and valises . . . and as Zachary's valet packed suits and neckties in preparation for *his* trip. Zachary would be damned if he would watch Holly leave the estate. He would go first.

Reaching his desk, he began to rifle through piles of paper, not noticing at first that someone else was there. A little peep came from the depths of his big leather chair, and Zachary swung around sharply, a question on his lips.

Rose was sitting there with Miss Crumpet, the two of them nearly lost in the deep upholstery. With a sinking heart, Zachary saw that the child's face was splotched and red, and her nose needed wiping.

It seemed that the Taylor females required an unending supply of handkerchiefs. Cursing beneath his breath, Zachary valiantly searched for one in his coat, but found nothing. He untied his linen cravat, jerked it from his neck and held it to Rose's nose. "Blow," he muttered, and she complied gustily. She giggled, evidently entertained by the novelty of using a necktie as a nose-wipe.

"You're being silly, Mr. Bronson!"

Zachary squatted down before her, staring at her eye to eye, and an affectionate grin tugged at his lips. "What's the matter, princess?" he asked gently, although he already knew.

Rose unburdened herself eagerly. "Mama says we have to go away. We're going to live at my uncle's house again, a-and I want to stay here." Her little face crumpled with childish sorrow, and Zachary nearly staggered from the impact of an invisible blow to his chest. Panic . . . love . . . yet more anguish. Although saying good-bye to Holly hadn't quite killed him, this would certainly finish him off. Somehow during the past months he had begun to love this enchanting child, with her sugar-sticky hands, her jangly button string, her long tangled curls, her brown eyes so like her mother's. No more tea parties, no more sitting in the parlor before the hearth and spinning tales of bunnies and cabbages, dragons and princesses, no more miniature hands that clung to his so trustingly.

"Tell Mama that we must stay here with you," Rose commanded. "You can make her stay, I know you can!"

"Your mama knows what's best for you," Zachary murmured, smiling faintly though he was dying inside. "You be a good girl and do as she says."

"I *am* a good girl *always*," Rose said, and began to sniffle again. "Oh, Mr. Bronson . . . what will happen to my toys?"

"I'll send every last one to you at the Taylors'."

"They won't all fit." She used a chubby hand to smear a teardrop across her cheek. "Their house is much, much littler than yours."

"Rose . . ." He sighed and pressed her head against his shoulder, his huge hand engulfing the entire top of her skull. She stayed against him and snuggled close, patting his scratchy jaw. After a while, she wriggled away. "You're squashing Miss Crumpet!"

"Sorry," he said contritely, reaching out to straighten the doll's little blue bonnet.

"Will I ever see you and Lizzie again?" Rose asked woefully.

Zachary couldn't bring himself to lie to her. "Not very often, I'm afraid."

"You'll miss me awfully," she said, heaving a sigh, and she began to fumble for something in the pocket of her pinafore.

Something went wrong with Zachary's eyes, some odd blurring and stinging that he couldn't seem to blink away. "Every day, princess."

Rose extracted a small object from the pocket and handed it to him. "This is for you," she said. "It's my perfume button. When you get sad, you can smell it, and you'll feel better. It always works for me."

"Princess," Zachary said, making his voice soft to keep it from cracking, "I can't take your favorite button." He tried to give it back to her, but she pushed his hand away.

"You need it," she said stubbornly. "You keep it, Mr. Bronson. And don't lose it."

"All right." Zachary closed his fist over the button and bowed his head over it, struggling with his unruly emotions. He had done this to himself, he thought. He had schemed and manipulated until he had gotten Lady Holland Taylor to live in his home. But he had never anticipated the consequences. If he had only known . . .

"Are you going to cry, Mr. Bronson?" the child asked in concern, coming to stand beside his knees, staring into his downturned face.

He managed to smile at her. "Just a little on the inside," he said raspily. He felt her little hand on his cheek, and he held utterly still as she kissed him on the nose.

"Good-bye, Mr. Bronson," she whispered, and she left with her button string trailing dolefully behind her.

It was still morning when his carriage was finally prepared for his departure, and there was nothing keeping him at the estate. Nothing but his own tormented heart. Pondering all that had been said between he and Holly, he realized that there was nothing to be gained by further conversation. The choices had been set out, and Holly would either go or stay according to her own desires, with no interference from him.

However, there was one bit of unfinished business remaining. Ascertaining that Holly had taken Rose out to the garden, Zachary went up to her bedroom. The blond maid, Maude was there, her arms stacked high with folded garments as she walked from the armoire to the bed. She jumped a little as she saw him standing at the entrance to the room. "S-sir?" she questioned warily, setting the folded clothes in the corner of a trunk.

"I have something to ask of you," he said curtly.

Clearly puzzled as to what he wanted, Maude turned to face him. He sensed her discomfort at being alone in the same room with him. This room, particularly, with Holly's clothes and possessions spread everywhere. There was a pile of objects on the bed: a hairbrush, a set of combs, an ivory box, a small frame covered in a leather case. He would have thought nothing of the frame, except that Maude discreetly tried to nudge it out of sight as she approached him. "Is there a chore I might do for ye, sir?" the maid asked uneasily. "Something I can fetch or mend or—"

"No, nothing like that." His gaze strayed to the frame case. "What is that?"

"Oh, it's . . . well, something personal to Lady Holly, and . . . sir, she wouldn't like it if ye—" Maude spluttered with dismayed protests as Zachary reached over and plucked the frame case from the pile.

"A miniature?" he asked, deftly shaking the object from its leather casing.

"Yes, sir, but . . . you shouldn't, really . . . oh, dear." Maude's pudgy cheeks reddened, and she sighed in patent discomfort as he stared at the little portrait.

"George," Zachary said quietly. He had never seen a likeness of the man, had never wanted to before. It was only to be expected that Holly should carry a portrait of her late husband, for Rose's benefit as well as her own. However, Zachary had never asked to view a likeness of George Taylor, and Holly had certainly never volunteered to show him. Perhaps Zachary had expected that he would feel a pang of animosity at the sight of Taylor's face, but as he stared at the miniature, he was conscious only of a surprising feeling of pity.

He had always thought of George as a contemporary, but this face was impossibly young, adorned with sideburns that amounted to a bit of peach fuzz on either side of his cheeks. Zachary was startled by the realization that Taylor couldn't have been more than twenty-four when he died, almost a full ten years younger than Zachary was now. Holly had been wooed and loved by this handsome boy, with his golden blond hair and untroubled blue eyes, and a smile that hinted of mischief. George had died before he'd barely tasted of life, widowing a girl who had been even more innocent than he.

Try as he might, Zachary couldn't blame George Taylor for trying to protect Holly, arrange things for her, ensure that his infant daughter was taken care of. No doubt George would have been anguished at the thought of his wife being seduced and made miserable by the Zachary Bronsons of the world. "Dammit," Zachary whispered, shoving the miniature back into its leather sheath. Scowling, he set the object on the bed.

Maude stared at him warily. "Is there aught I can do for ye, sir?"

He gave a single nod and reached inside his coat. "I want you to have this," he muttered, extracting a small bag weighted with gold coins. To a servant of Maude's station, it amounted to a fortune. "Take it, and promise me that if there is ever anything Lady Holland needs, you'll send for me."

The maid's face was blank with surprise. She took the bag, felt its weight in her hand, and stared at him with wide eyes. "Ye don't need to pay me to do that, sir."

"Take it," he insisted brusquely.

A reluctant smile curved her lips, and she dropped the little bag into her apron pocket. "Ye've been a good master, sir. Don't fret about Lady Holland and Miss Rose, I'll serve them faithfully, and send for ye if any trouble arises."

"Good," he said, and turned to leave. He paused and looked back at her as a question occurred to him. "Why did you try to hide the miniature from me, Maude?"

She blushed a little, but her gaze was direct and honest as she replied, "I wished to spare ye the sight of him, sir. I know how ye feel about Lady Holland, ye see."

"You do?" he said neutrally.

The maid gave a vigorous nod. "She's a dear, gentle lady, and a man would have a heart of stone not to care for her." Maude lowered her voice confidentially. "Betwixt ye and me, sir, I think that if my lady were free to choose any man for herself, she might well have set her cap for ye. 'Tis plain as day that she's fair taken with ye. But Master George took most of her heart with him to the grave."

"Does she look at his miniature often?" Zachary asked, keeping his face expressionless.

Maude's round face puckered thoughtfully. "Not so often since we came to live on yer estate, sir. To my knowledge, she hasn't taken it out at all in the past month or so. Why, there was even a bit of dust that settled on it."

For some reason the information comforted him.

"Farewell, Maude," he replied, taking his leave.

"Good luck to ye, sir," she said softly.

Returning from the garden, Holly went to her room and found her maid sorting through a pile of carefully folded stockings. "What progress you've made, Maude," she commented with a wan smile.

"Aye, milady. I'd be even further along except that the master came to the room and interrupted my chores." The words were spoken casually, and Maude continued busily with her task.

Holly felt her jaw slacken with surprise. "He did?" she

asked faintly. "Whatever for? Was he looking for me?"

"Nay, milady, he only bade me to take care of ye and Miss Rose, and I promised him I would."

"Oh." Holly reached for a linen underskirt and attempted to fold it efficiently, but it ended up in a wadded bundle that she clutched against her midriff. "How kind of him," she whispered.

Maude slid her an amused, vaguely pitying glance. "I don't think it was kindness that moved him, milady. He looked as lovesick as a green lad. In fact, he wore the same expression as ye this very moment." Seeing the damage that Holly's clutching fingers were inflicting on the neatly pressed underskirt, she clucked and reached out to rescue it.

Holly surrendered the garment without protest. "Do you have any notion where Mr. Bronson might be right now, Maude?"

"On his way to Durham, I would guess. He seemed in no mood to tarry, milady."

Holly flew to the window, which afforded a view of the front of the mansion. She made a small sound of distress as she saw Bronson's huge black-lacquered carriage rolling away along the sprawling tree-lined drive that led to the main road. Her hand flattened on the pane of glass, palm pressed hard against the coolness. Her mouth trembled violently, and she fought to contain her emotions. He was gone, she thought, and soon she would be, too. It was all for the best. She was doing the right thing for herself, and for him, too. Best to let him start a marriage with a young, unspoiled girl with whom he could share all the "firsts" with: the first vows, the first wedding night, the first child . . .

And as for herself, she knew very well that once she returned to the Taylors, it might well be her fate to stay there forever. She did not intend to hold Ravenhill to his promise to marry her—it was hardly fair to deny him all chance of finding someone he truly loved.

"Back to where I started," Holly whispered with a wobbly smile, thinking of how it would be to resume her life with her husband's family. Except that now she was sadder and a bit wiser, no longer so assured of her own moral infallibility.

She stared hard at the carriage until it reached the end of the drive and seemed to disappear in the mass of trees.

"All ye need is a bit of time, milady," came Maude's comfortingly matter-of-fact voice from behind her. "As ye well know, time takes care of pert' near everything."

Holly swallowed and nodded wordlessly, but she knew that the maid was wrong in this instance. No amount of time would soften the passion she felt—a blinding need of body and soul—for Zachary Bronson.

Fifteen

The Taylors accepted Holly's return as a prodigal daughter being welcomed back into the fold. There were comments, of course, as none of them could resist airing their collective opinion that it had been a grave mistake for her to leave in the first place. She had left with a solid gold reputation and the admiration and respect of their entire wide circle of acquaintances, and she had returned sporting a great deal of tarnish. Financially, the association with Zachary Bronson had done her a great deal of good, but morally and socially, she had fallen.

Holly didn't care. The Taylors would be able to shield her from some, if not all, of the snubs that would come her way. And by the time Rose was eighteen and possessing of an enormous dowry, there would be suitors aplenty for her, and the long-ago scandal involving her mother would have faded.

Holly made no effort to contact Ravenhill, knowing that the rumors of her new location would reach him quickly enough. He came calling not a week after she had moved back to the Taylor home, and he was welcomed eagerly by Thomas and William and their wives. Tall and blond and prosperous-looking, Ravenhill had the appearance of a knight coming to rescue a damsel in distress. As she joined him in the Taylors' formal receiving room, Holly intended to tell him that she had no need of rescuing. However, he soon let her know in his to-the-point way that George's last wishes was also his own.

"So you've left the den of iniquity," Ravenhill commented, his face serious except for the teasing glint in his gray eyes.

Holly couldn't suppress a sudden laugh as his irreverence caught her by surprise. "Be careful in your association with me, my lord," she warned lightly. "Your reputation might be damaged."

"After three years of unholy carousing in Europe, I assure you I have no reputation left to salvage." Ravenhill's expression seemed to soften as Holly smiled at him. "I don't blame you for going to live with the Bronsons," he said. "How could I, when it's my fault you were there? I should have come to you years ago, and taken care of you as I promised George I would."

"Vardon, regarding that promise . . ." Holly stopped and stared at him helplessly, her cheeks reddening as her thoughts became too entangled to voice.

"Yes?" he prompted gently.

"I know we agreed to discuss it," she said, distressed, "but now I think . . . there's no need . . . after all, you and I—"

Ravenhill hushed her gently, his long fingers touching her lips in a feather-light caress. Stunned, Holly did not move as he took her hands in a firm, warm grip. "Think of a marriage between intimate friends," he said, "who have an agreement to always communicate honestly with each other. A couple who have the same ideals and interests. Who enjoy each others' company and treat each other with respect. That is what I want. There is no reason we can't have it together."

"But you don't love me, Vardon. And I don't—"

"I want to give you the protection of my name," he interrupted.

"But it's not enough to wash away the scandal and the rumors—"

"It's better than what you've got now," he pointed out reasonably. "Besides, you're wrong about something. I do love you. I've known you since before you and George were married. I've never respected and liked a woman more. Furthermore, I believe the maxim that a marriage between friends is the best kind of all."

Holly understood that he was not referring to the kind of love she'd had with George. Neither was he offering the passionate attachment she shared with Zachary Bronson. This was truly a marriage of convenience, one that would serve both their needs and satisfy George's last request.

"What if that is not enough for you?" she asked quietly. "You'll meet someone, Vardon . . . It could be weeks after we are married, or years, but you will someday. A woman you would gladly die for. And you'll want to be with her desperately, and I'll be nothing but a millstone around your neck."

He shook his head immediately. "I'm not made that way, Holly. I don't believe there's just one person or one true love for each of us. I've had love affairs—three years of them—and I'm damn tired of all the histrionics and obsessions and ecstasy and melancholy. I want some peace." A self-mocking smile touched his lips. "I want to be a respectable married man—though God knows I'd never imagined myself saying that."

"Vardon . . ." She stared down at the brocade of the settee, using a fingertip to trace the fleur-de-lis pattern worked in gold and burgundy threads. "You haven't asked why I left Mr. Bronson's employ so abruptly."

A long speculative silence passed before he answered. "Do you want to tell me?" He didn't seem particularly eager to know the answer.

Holly shook her head, while a huff of laughter caught painfully in her throat. "Not really. But in light of your proposal, I feel obligated to confess something. I don't want to lie to you, and—"

"I don't need to hear your confessions, Holly." Raven-hill caught at her hand and squeezed, his grip steady and comforting. He waited until she brought herself to look into his regretful, brooding gray eyes. "I don't *want* to hear them," he continued, "because then I'd have to give you my confessions in return. It's not necessary, or productive. So you keep your past, and I'll keep mine. Everyone's allowed to have one or two secrets."

Holly felt a warm surge of liking for him. Any woman would be fortunate to have such a husband. It was even possible for her to envision a marriage between them. They would be a bit more than friends, albeit a good deal less than lovers. But the situation felt odd and manufactured, and she frowned as she stared at him. "I want to do the right thing, if only I knew what it was," she said.

"What *would* feel right to you?"

"Nothing," she confesssed, and Ravenhill laughed quietly.

"Let me court you for a little while, then. We can afford a bit of time. I'll wait until you're convinced this is the best choice for both of us." He paused and then pulled her hands to his shoulders, giving her a faint half-smile as if daring her to leave them there. She did, although her heart pounded in sudden panicked awareness of what he was going to do.

Ravenhill leaned forward and brushed a light kiss on her lips, lingering only a moment. There was nothing demanding in his kiss, but she sensed the wealth of sexual experience and self-assurance he possessed. She wondered if George would have matured into a man like this, if he would have acquired the same polished worldliness, if his eyes would have acquired the same faint laugh lines at the corners, if his form would have relinquished the lankiness of youth for the same solid, seasoned strength.

Ravenhill drew back, his slight smile remaining as Holly withdrew her hands hastily. "May I see you tomorrow morning?" he asked. "We'll go riding in the park."

"All right," she whispered.

Her thoughts were swamped in confusion, and she went through the motions of bidding him good-bye and seeing him out. Thankfully Ravenhill resisted the Taylors' attempts to invite him to supper, and he gave Holly a briefly ironic smile that betrayed his thoughts on her in-laws' obvious meddling.

Olinda, Thomas's tall, elegant blond wife, came to stand beside Holly as she remained in the entrance hall. "What a handsome man Lord Blake is," she exclaimed admiringly. "One never really noticed his looks when compared to George, but now that he is no longer in George's shadow . . ." Suddenly realizing that her remarks might be construed as tactless, she fell silent.

"He is still in George's shadow," Holly said softly. After all, wasn't this entire situation of George's making? It was all going according to his design. The thought should have been reassuring, but it only chafed and annoyed her.

"Well," Olinda said thoughtfully, "I suppose to you, every man in the world is inferior to George. He was so remarkable in every way. No one could eclipse him."

There was a time not long ago when Holly would have

agreed automatically. Now, however, she bit her lip and remained silent.

Sleep was elusive that night. When Holly did finally relax into slumber, it was light and restless, and she was troubled by vivid dreams. She walked through a rose garden, her feet crunching on graveled paths, her eyes squinting from the glare of harsh sunlight. Enchanted by the lush red blossoms that surrounded her, she reached for one, cupped her hand around the velvety petals and bent to inhale its fragrance. A sudden stabbing pain in her finger startled her, and she drew back hastily. There was a bleeding wound at the base of her finger, inflicted by a hidden thorn. Catching sight of a nearby fountain that splashed cool water into a marble basin, she went to soak her injured hand. But the rosebushes gathered and grew around her in a strange, living mass. The blossoms withered and dropped, and all that was left was a wall of sharp brown thorns, imprisoning her on every side. Crying out in distress, Holly shrank into a ball on the ground while the thorny branches continued to grow around her, and she held her wounded hand against the crashing, agonized beat of her heart.

The dream changed then, and she found herself lying on a thick patch of green grass, while something . . . someone . . . blocked her view of the sky and clouds overhead. *"Who is it . . . who is it . . . ?"* she begged to know, but the only reply was a soft, low laugh that curled around her like smoke. She felt a man's hands on her, gently lifting her skirts, sliding up her stiff legs, while a hot, delicious mouth pressed over hers. Moaning, she relaxed beneath him, and her sun-dazzled gaze cleared enough to reveal a pair of wicked black eyes staring into hers. *"Zachary,"* she gasped, her legs and arms and body opening to receive him, and she twisted in pleasure as she felt his weight lower over her. *"Oh, Zachary, yes, don't stop—"*

He smiled and covered her breasts with his hands and kissed her, and she groaned in excitement. "Zachary—"

Suddenly Holly jerked awake, startled from sleep by the sound of her own voice. Breathing fast, she stared dizzily at her surroundings. She was alone in bed, pillows heaped around her, sheets tangled around her knees and ankles. Sickening disappointment swept over her as the last wisps of the dream faded away. She clutched a pillow to her midriff and lay on her side, shaking and burning. Where was Zachary at this very moment? Was he sleeping and dreaming in his solitary bed, or was he sating his desires in the arms of another woman? Poisonous jealousy engulfed her. She pressed her hands to either side of her head, trying to block the images that crowded her mind. Some other woman might be holding his powerful body against hers, tangling her fingers in his thick dark hair, feeling him shudder as he took his pleasure within her.

"It doesn't matter now, I've made my choice," Holly whispered to herself agitatedly. "And he said not to come back. It's over . . . it's over."

True to his word, Ravenhill did come to court Holly, calling nearly every day. He accompanied her on rides through the park, picnics with the Taylors, and water parties with close friends. Thanks to the Taylors' determined protection, these gatherings were fairly uneventful, and Holly was sheltered from blatant snubs. One had to give her late husband's family a great deal of credit for loyalty. They closed ranks around her and defended her zealously, in spite of their own disapproval of her past actions. They did approve of her keeping company with Ravenhill, however. Having known of George's last wishes for Holly and

Ravenhill to marry, the family did its best to ensure that there were no impediments to the match.

"When you and Ravenhill are wed," William, the head of the family, told Holly matter-of-factly, "it will put to rest a large measure of the speculation concerning you and Bronson. I should do my best to hurry the procedure along, if I were you."

"I understand, William," Holly replied, though her insides had boiled in rebellion at the unwanted advice. "And I thank you for sharing your wisdom. However, it is not altogether certain that Ravenhill and I will marry."

"What?" William's blue eyes narrowed in a forbidding scowl. "Is he showing reluctance to come up to scratch? I'll have a talk with him and sort things out. Don't fret, m'dear, he'll march to the altar with you if I have to prod him at gunpoint."

"No, no," Holly said hastily, her mouth quivering in sudden amusement. "There's no need, William. Ravenhill is showing no sign of reluctance. *I* am the reluctant one, and he is allowing me the time I require to make the decision."

"What decision is there? What possible reason do you have for dragging your feet?" William stared at her impatiently. "Let me assure you, if not for this family, you would be a pariah by now. You're treading on the edge of ruin. Marry Ravenhill, for God's sake, and preserve what little social standing you have left."

Holly contemplated him thoughtfully, her heart softening as she saw the resemblance he bore to George, though his once-thick blond hair was thinning on top and his blue eyes were stern rather than merry. Taking him by surprise, Holly approached him and kissed his cheek affectionately. "You've been very kind to me, my lord. You will have my everlasting gratitude for harboring such a disreputable character as myself."

"You're not disreputable," he grumbled, "you're merely misguided. You need a man, Holland. Like most women, you require the good judgment and common sense that a husband provides. And Ravenhill's a steady sort. Oh, I know about his wild ways in Europe, but every fellow has to sow his oats at one time or another, and that's all in the past."

Holly smiled suddenly. "Why is it that my association with Mr. Bronson is called scandalous, and Ravenhill's even worse behavior is merely labeled as 'sowing oats'?"

"This is no time to discuss semantics," William said with an exasperated sigh. "The fact is, Holland, that you need a husband if you're to remain in good society. And Ravenhill is an appropriate and willing candidate. Moreover, he's the candidate that my dear brother George recommended, and if George thought that well of him, then so do I."

Reflecting on the conversation later, Holly admitted herself that William made sense. Life as Ravenhill's wife would prove far more pleasant than life as a scandal-tainted widow. Her feelings for Vardon were clear. She liked and trusted him, and they had an affinity that had been born of long acquaintance with each other. Their companionable relationship was being cemented daily by long walks and lazy afternoons, and suppers at which they jested and confided and smiled at each other over the rims of sparkling crystal wine glasses. But Holly waited in vain for some inner signal that would let her know it was time . . . time to banish Zachary Bronson from her mind and heart and proceed with George's wishes.

However, her longing for Zachary did not fade. It became even more intense, if that was possible, until she found it difficult to eat or sleep. She had not been this acutely miserable since George's death. It seemed that her vision was covered in a dull gray film, and aside from reading and playing with Rose, there was little purpose to her days. One week passed, and another, until a full month had gone by since she had left the Bronsons.

Holly awakened early after yet another sleepless night and went to the window. She pushed aside the heavy velvet drapes and stared at the street below, illuminated by the lavender light of dawn. Coal smoke drifted over the city in a gentle fog, softening the jagged horizon of buildings and homes. Inside the house, early morning noises began: maids opening shutters, lighting fires, laying the hearths and preparing breakfast trays. Another day, she thought, and felt unaccountably weary at the prospect of bathing, dressing and arranging her hair, and picking listlessly at a breakfast she had no desire to eat. She wanted to crawl back into bed and pull the covers over her head.

"I should be happy," she said aloud, puzzled by her own inner emptiness. The kind of well-ordered life she had always expected and planned for and enjoyed was easily within her reach . . . but she didn't want it any longer.

A brief memory flashed through her mind, of the occasion when she and Rose had gone to the shoemaker's for a fitting, and Holly had tried on a pair of exquisite new custom-made walking shoes. Although the shoemaker had used the same pattern as always, something about the stitching or the stiff new leather had made the shoes pinch unbearably. "They're too tight," Holly had commented ruefully, and Rose had exclaimed with delighted pride, "That means you're growing, Mama!"

Returning to this life with the Taylors, and contemplating marriage with Vardon, was exactly like trying on those tight shoes. For better or worse, she had grown out of this particular life. All those months with the Bronsons had made her, if perhaps not a better woman, at least a *different* one.

What to do now?

By force of habit, Holly went to the night table and picked up her miniature of George. The sight of his face would give her the comfort and strength, and perhaps a bit of guidance.

However, as she stared at her husband's serene young features, a startling realization came over her. The sight of George did not bring her peace. She no longer yearned for his arms, his voice, his smile. Incredible as it seemed, she had fallen in love with another man. She loved Zachary Bronson as deeply as she had ever loved her husband. Only with Zachary did she feel alive and whole. She missed his provocative, earthy conversations, and the dark-eyed glances that contained sardonic amusement or anger or knee-weakening lust. She missed the way he had seemed to fill a room with his charismatic presence, the torrent of plans and ideas that flowed from him, the boundless energy that had swept her along in a fast-moving current. Life without him was slow and dark and unbearably dull.

Realizing that she was breathing in strange little gasps, Holly put her hand over her mouth. She loved him, and it terrified her. For months her heart had resisted the inexorable pull of her growing feelings. She had been desperately afraid to have her soul torn apart by loss once again, and so it had been easier and safer not to let herself fall in love. That had been the real obstacle between herself and Zachary . . . not her promise to George, not the differences in their backgrounds, not any of the inconsequential issues she had thrown between them.

Setting down the miniature, Holly unbraided her hair

and dragged a silver-backed brush over the rumpled locks in frantic, ruthless strokes. The urge to run to Zachary was overwhelming. She wanted to dress and have a carriage readied and go to him this very minute, and try to explain why she had made such a mess of things.

But was it really the best choice for them to join their lives together? Their pasts, their expectations, their very natures were so radically different. Would any rational person advise them to marry? The notion that love would make everything all right was a ridiculous cliché, an overly simplified answer to a complicated problem. And yet . . . sometimes the simple answers were the best ones. Perhaps the small issues could be sorted out later. Perhaps all that really mattered was the truth that existed in her heart.

She would go to him, she decided resolutely. She only feared that she had burned her bridges where Zachary was concerned. He had made it clear that she should not try to come back to him. He would not welcome her.

Replacing the brush on the dressing table with great care, Holly stared into the looking glass. She was pale and tired-looking, with smudges beneath the eyes. Hardly a face to compare with the alluring beauties that Zachary was undoubtedly surrounded with. However, if there was a chance that he still wanted her, it was worth the risk of rejection.

Her heart pounded violently, and she felt weak all over. She went to the armoire and searched for one of the gowns he had bought her, one of the vibrant creations she had never worn. If he took her back, she vowed silently, she would never wear a gray dress again. Finding the jade-green Italian silk, with its stylish pointed cuffs, she shook out the gleaming skirts and laid the gown carefully on the bed. Just as she began to rummage for fresh linen undergarments, there came a quiet tap on the door and it clicked open.

"Milady?" Maude called softly, entering the room. She seemed surprised yet relieved to see that Holly was awake. "Oh, milady, I'm glad to see ye're already up and about. The housekeeper came to fetch me not five minutes ago. It seems there's someone here to see ye, an' she insists on staying till ye come down."

Holly frowned curiously. "Who is it, Maude?"

" 'Tis Miss Elizabeth Bronson, milady. She rode here herself from the Bronson estate . . . why, it must be seven miles, at least, and her without a groom for company!"

"Help me dress quickly, Maude. Oh, something must be wrong, for Elizabeth to come here at such an hour by herself!" Hurriedly she sat on a chair and began to jerk on a stocking, not bothering to keep the seams straight.

In her impatience, it seemed to take forever to dress and pin her hair up. She hastened downstairs to the Taylors' receiving room, where a maid had already set out a little coffee tray for the visitor. The rest of the family had not yet arisen, for which Holly was grateful. If any of the Taylors were awake, it would have been impossible to keep them from meddling. She felt a rush of gladness as she saw Elizabeth's tall, striking figure striding back and forth in the receiving room. She had missed the girl terribly. "Lizzie," she exclaimed.

As vibrant and beautiful and impetuous as always, Elizabeth turned and strode toward her. "My lady . . ." She seized Holly in a spontaneous hug, and the two of them laughed together.

"Lizzie, you look so well," Holly said, drawing back to view the girl's sparkling dark eyes and pink-cheeked face. Elizabeth was dressed in the height of fashion, a stylish blue riding habit with a white gauze scarf at her throat, and a little velvet hat trimmed with blue-dyed feathers. She seemed as robustly healthy as ever, but there was a pinched look of unhappiness around her eyes, and her barely suppressed frustration was almost palpable.

"I'm not," Elizabeth said, clearly eager to unburden herself. "I'm not well at all, I'm unhappy and sour and ready to murder my brother, and . . ." Her gaze swept over Holly. "Oh, my lady, you look so tired, and you've lost weight, at least half a stone!"

"It's because I no longer have your brother ordering plates of cakes for me at every turn," Holly replied with forced lightness. She gestured for the girl to join her on the settee. "Sit with me, and tell me what has impelled you to ride across town alone. You remember how often I told you that a young lady must not travel without a companion—"

"Oh, damn propriety," Elizabeth exclaimed passionately, her eyes flashing.

"I was thinking more of your safety," Holly said dryly. "If your horse picked up a stone or stumbled, you would be forced to request the help of strangers who might—"

"Damn safety," the girl interrupted. "Everything is dreadfully wrong, and I don't know how to fix things. You're the only one I have to turn to."

Holly's pulse surged in an anxious, unsteady rhythm. "Is it Mr. Bronson? Or your mother?"

"It's Zach, of course." Elizabeth scowled and fidgeted on the settee, clearly desiring to jump up and pace around the room again. "I don't believe I've seen him sober for the past month. Since you left, he's turned into a selfish monster. He hasn't a kind word to say to anyone, and he's demanding and impossible to please. He spends every night with wastrels and demimondaines, and he spends all day drinking and sneering at everyone who crosses his path."

"That doesn't sound at all like your brother," Holly said quietly.

"I haven't even begun to describe the situation. He doesn't seem to care about anyone, not me or Mama, not even himself. I've tried to be patient with him, but then this last thing happened, and now I don't—"

"What last thing?" Holly asked, trying to make sense of the rapid stream of words.

Suddenly a smile broke through Elizabeth's gloomy report. "Your cousin, Mr. Somers, proposed to me."

"He did?" Holly smiled in immediate pleasure. "So you brought him up to scratch, did you?"

"Yes, I did," the girl crowed, wriggling in joy and triumph. "Jason loves me, and I return his feelings a hundred times over. I never thought love would be so glorious!"

"My dear Lizzie, I'm so happy for you, as I'm certain your family must be."

The comment seemed to bring Elizabeth plummeting back to unpleasant reality. "There is one member of my family who is not happy," she said grimly. "Zach has forbidden the match. He says under no circumstances will he support a union between Mr. Somers and I."

"He did what?" Holly shook her head incredulously. "But why? My cousin is a perfectly respectable man with excellent prospects. What reason did your brother give for his objections?"

"Zach said that Jason isn't good enough for me! He said I must marry a man with a title and a fortune, and I can do better than a mere architect from a family of mediocre origins. It's the most appalling piece of snobbery I've ever witnessed, and from my brother, of all people!"

Holly stared at her in bewilderment. "How did you respond, Elizabeth?"

The girl's face hardened with resolve. "I told Zach the truth, that it doesn't matter whether he approves the match or not. I intend to marry Jason Somers. I don't care if Zach comes forth with a dowry or not—Jason says he will be able to provide for me, and it doesn't matter to him if I'm an heiress or a pauper. I don't need a carriage or jewels or a large house to be happy. But my lady, what kind of beginning to a marriage is this? My mother is distraught, my brother and fiancé are enemies . . . the family is being torn apart, all because of . . ." She stopped and buried her face in her hands, on the verge of frustrated tears.

"Because of what?" Holly prompted softly.

Elizabeth glanced through her fingers, dark gaze glimmering. "Well," she mumbled, "I suppose I was going to say 'because of you,' although that sounds like an accusation, and I certainly don't mean it that way. But my lady, it's a fact that Zach changed when you left. I suppose I was too self-absorbed to notice what was happening between the two of you, but now I realize . . . my brother fell in love with you, didn't he? And you wouldn't have him. I know you must have had good reason for leaving us, you're so clever and wise, and you must—"

"No, Lizzie," Holly managed to whisper. "I'm not clever or wise, not in the least."

"—and I know you're accustomed to a very different sort of man than Zach, which is why I would never dare presume that you might care for him in the same way. But I have come here to ask you something." Elizabeth bent her head and blotted a few leaking tears with her sleeve. "Please go to him," she said huskily. "Talk to him, say something to bring him to his senses. I've never seen him behave like this. And I think you may be the only person in the world he might listen to. Just make him *reasonable* again. If you don't, he's going to ruin himself and drive away everyone who cares for him."

"Oh, Lizzie . . ." Compassionately, Holly slid her arm around the girl's narrow back and held her close. They sat together for at least a minute. Finally Holly spoke in a quiet voice. "He won't want to see me."

"No," Elizabeth agreed with a sigh. "Zach doesn't allow your name to be spoken. He pretends you don't exist."

The words made Holly feel hollow and afraid. "All I can promise you is that I will try. He may refuse to speak with me, however."

Elizabeth sighed and glanced out the window at the approaching daylight. "I must be off—I have to return home before breakfast. I don't want Zach to suspect where I've been."

"You'll allow one of the Taylors' grooms to escort you back home," Holly said firmly. "It's too dangerous to ride by yourself."

Elizabeth hung her head with a wobbly, repentant smile. "All right, my lady. I'll let him come with me to the very end of the drive, as long as he takes care not to be visible from the main house." She glanced at Holly hopefully. "When will you go to see Zach, my lady?"

"I don't know," Holly confessed, while excitement and fear and hope meshed inside her. "I suppose when I can summon the nerve."

Sixteen

In the whirlwind of her thoughts, Holly had forgotten that she had agreed to go riding with Ravenhill, her would-be fiancé, that morning. Long after Elizabeth Bronson had departed, Holly sat in the receiving room with a lukewarm cup of tea in her hand. She stared into the tepid milky liquid and groped for words, the right words to convince Zachary to forgive and trust her once more. It seemed there would be no graceful way to address the subject. She would simply have to throw herself on his mercy and hope for the best. A bleak, ironic smile curved her lips as she reflected that her own social training had included a hundred polite ways to rebuff a gentleman, but no instruction on how to win one back afterward. Knowing all about Zachary's fierce pride and his formidable defenses, she knew he would not succumb to her easily. He would make her pay for the way she had fled from him—he would demand unconditional surrender.

"Good Lord, what thoughts are putting such a dour expression on your lovely face?" Vardon, Lord Blake advanced in the room, his tall, athletic form dressed in a dark riding habit. Golden-haired, quietly dashing, his movements spare and confident, he was any woman's dream of the perfect man. Staring at him with a wistful smile, Holly

302

reflected that it was time to begin burning bridges.

"Good morning, my lord." She gestured for him to sit beside her.

"You're not dressed for riding," he observed. "Am I too early, or have you changed your mind about this morning?"

"I've changed my mind about a good many things, I'm afraid."

"Ah. I sense you're leading into a gravely important discussion." He gave her a teasing smile, but the gray eyes turned watchful.

"Vardon, I'm so afraid I'll lose your friendship after you hear what I wish to say."

Gently he took her hand, turned it and bent his head to press a kiss to her palm. When his gaze returned to hers, it was serious, kind and steady. "Darling friend, you won't ever lose me. No matter what you do or say."

A month of companionship had built a great sense of trust between them, allowing Holly to speak with the blunt honesty that Ravenhill deserved. "I've decided that I don't want to marry you."

He did not blink or exhibit any flicker of surprise. "I'm sorry to hear that," he said softly.

"You deserve nothing less than a love match," she continued in a rush. "A true, passionate, wonderful love with a woman you cannot live without. And I . . ."

"And you?" he prompted, retaining her hand in a careful grip.

"I'm going to somehow gather the courage to go to Mr. Bronson and ask him to take me as his wife."

A long, thoughtful silence ensued as he absorbed the words. "You realize that if you join with him, many in the *ton* will deem it a complete fall from grace. There are circles that will no longer accept you—"

"It doesn't matter," Holly assured him with a choked laugh. "My perfect sterling reputation was cold comfort in the years after George passed away. I'll trade it gladly for the chance to be loved. I'm only sorry that it's taken me so long to realize what is truly important. Since George, I have been terrified to risk my heart again, and because of that, I've lied to myself and everyone."

"Then go to Bronson and tell him the truth."

She smiled at him, astonished by the simplicity of the answer. "Vardon, you are supposed to tell me about my duty. About honor, and what I owe to George."

"Darling Holland," he said, "you're facing an entire lifetime without George. Use your God-given sense to decide what is best for you and Rose. If you decide to cast your lot with Bronson, I'll accept your choice."

"You surprise me, my lord."

"I want you to be happy. There are few enough chances in life for that, and I wouldn't be churl enough to stand in your way."

Ravenhill's matter-of-factness, his gentlemanly acceptance of her wishes, seemed to ease the painful vise that had clamped around her heart. Holly threw him a brilliant smile of gratitude. "I wish everyone would react the same way you have."

"They won't," he assured her dryly, and they both smiled at their joined hands before Holly gently drew hers away.

"Would George have liked Mr. Bronson, do you think?" she heard herself ask.

A glint of laughter appeared in his silver-gray eyes. "Well, no. I don't think they would have had enough in common for that. Bronson is a little too raw and unprincipled to have suited George's taste. But does that really matter to you?"

"No," she confessed. "I still want Mr. Bronson."

Taking her hands, Ravenhill pulled her to her feet. "Then go to him. But before you leave, I want a promise from you."

"No more promises," she said with a groaning laugh. "They cause me such misery."

"This one I'll have from you, though. Promise me that if something goes wrong for you, ever, you'll come to me."

"Yes," Holly said, closing her eyes as she felt his warm lips touch her forehead. "And Vardon, you must believe me, in my view you have completely fulfilled the vow you made to George. You were a good, true friend to him, and an even better one to me."

He slid a strong arm around her and hugged her tightly for answer.

Holly's nerves were shredded by the time her carriage rolled to a halt at the crown of the Bronson estate drive. The footman opened the door and assisted her to the ground, while another went to knock at the door. Mrs. Burney's face was visible at the front door, and Holly suppressed a shaky laugh as she reflected that she would never have expected to feel such gladness at the sight of the housekeeper. The house, and every servant in it, seemed wonderfully familiar. She felt as if she were returning home. However, her stomach tightened with a fearful pang as she considered the possibility that Zachary Bronson might dispatch her from the estate as soon as he saw her.

The housekeeper wore a distinctly uncomfortable expression as Holly approached her. She curtsied and then stood with her hands twisted together. "My lady," she said, "it is good to see you."

"Mrs. Burney," Holly replied pleasantly, "I trust you are doing well?"

The housekeeper gave her an evasive smile. "Well enough, although . . ." Her tone lowered. "Nothing has been quite the same since you left. The master . . ." She fell abruptly silent, clearly recalling that a servant must respect the privacy of the family she or he served.

"I've come to see Mr. Bronson." In Holly's anxiety, she flushed and stammered like a girl in her teens. "I—I'm very sorry not to have given advance notice of my arrival and for coming at such an early hour, but it's rather urgent, you see."

"My lady," Mrs. Burney said softly, regretfully, "I don't know how to tell you this, but . . . the master saw your carriage from the window, and he . . . well . . . he is not receiving visitors." Her voice dropped to a whisper, and her wary gaze flickered to the footman waiting in the distance. "He is not well, my lady."

"Not well?" Holly was startled. "Has he fallen ill, Mrs. Burney?"

"Not precisely."

The housekeeper must mean that he had been drinking, then. Perturbed, Holly considered the situation. "Perhaps I should return another time," she said softly, "when Mr. Bronson is a bit more clear-headed."

Mrs. Burney's expression was brittle with distress. "I don't know when that will be, my lady."

Their gazes met. Although the housekeeper would never dare express her own opinions or wishes, Holly had the feeling Mrs. Burney was silently urging her to stay. "I would not wish to disturb Mr. Bronson, of course," Holly said. "But I fear that during my previous residence here, I may have left a few, er . . . odds and ends in my room.

Would you have any objections if I went to search for them?"

The housekeeper was clearly relieved by the suggestion. "No, my lady," she said at once, seizing on the excuse, "no objections at all. Of course you must find your belongings if you've left them here. Shall I accompany you, or are you able to remember the way?"

"I remember the way." Holly gave her a brilliant smile. "I'll just slip upstairs unaccompanied. Please, would you tell me where Mr. Bronson is, so that I may be able to avoid disturbing him?"

"I believe he is in his room, my lady."

"Thank you, Mrs. Burney."

Holly walked into the house, which had the atmosphere of a mausoleum. The massive central hall, with its towering gold columns and silver-coffered ceiling and flower-scented air, was gleaming and dark. Not a single soul was visible amid the opulent gloom. Afraid that she might encounter Paula or Elizabeth and be distracted from her mission, Holly ascended the great staircase as rapidly as her feet would allow. The exertion, not to mention her own trepidations, caused her heart to pound wildly in her chest, until she felt its reverberations in every limb. The thought of seeing Zachary again caused such excitement inside her that she nearly felt ill. Trembling all over, she went to his door, which had been left slightly ajar. She considered knocking, then decided against it, as she did not want to give him the opportunity of shutting her out.

Gently she pushed the door open, and it gave a faint, almost unnoticeable squeak. She had never actually stepped inside Zachary's bedroom during the period of her residence at the estate. Rich blue brocade and velvet draped the massive mahogany bed. Dark cherrywood paneling gleamed from the light shed by the row of four tow-

ering rectangular windows. Zachary was standing at one
of the windows, having parted a fringed velvet curtain to
stare down at the front drive. He held a glass of liquor in
his hand. His hair was still wet and gleaming from a morning bath, and the scent of shaving soap lingered in the air.
He was dressed in a plum silk robe that reached nearly to
the floor, bare feet protruding from beneath the hem. Holly
had forgotten how impossibly large he was. She was glad
his back was still turned, so he wouldn't see the yearning
shiver that ran through her.

"What did she say?" he asked in a low growl, evidently
thinking she was Mrs. Burney.

Holly fought to keep her voice steady. "I'm afraid she
insisted on seeing you."

Zachary's broad back stiffened, muscles bulging beneath
the thin covering of silk as he realized the identity of the
intruder. It seemed to take him a moment to find his voice.
"Get out," he said quietly, without heat. "Go back to Ravenhill."

"Lord Blake has no claim on me," she whispered, her
throat clenching, "nor I on him."

Slowly Zachary turned around. There was a slight
tremor in his fingers that sent the amber liquid in his glass
sloshing against the sides. He took a deep swallow of the
liquor, his cold black gaze never leaving her. He looked
composed, though his face was undeniably haggard. There
were circles beneath his eyes, and the healthy bronze color
of his skin had turned ashen from too much time spent
drinking indoors. Holly's gaze swept over him hungrily,
and she ached to run to him, stroke and soothe and hold
him. *Please, God, don't let him send me away,* she thought
desperately. She hated the way he looked at her, the black
eyes that had once been filled with teasing warmth and
passion now so flat and indifferent. He regarded her as if

she were a stranger . . . as if he had no feeling left for her.

"What does that mean?" He spoke in a monotone, as if the subject held no interest for him.

Marshaling her courage, Holly closed the door and approached him, then stopped a few feet away. "Lord Blake and I agreed to remain friends, but there will be no wedding. I told him that I could not keep my promise to George, because . . ." She paused and nearly shriveled from dismay as she saw Zachary's complete lack of reaction to the news.

"Because," he prompted in a monotone.

"Because my heart is otherwise engaged."

A long, nerve-wracking silence followed her admission. Oh, why didn't he say something? Why did he look so callous and indifferent?

"That was a mistake," he finally said.

"No." She stared at him beseechingly. "My mistake was in leaving here . . . leaving you . . . and I've come to explain things and ask you—"

"Holly, don't." Zachary let out a taut breath and shook his head. "You don't have to explain a damned thing. I understand why you left." A self-deprecating smile touched his lips. "After a month of reflection—and swilling like a pig at his trough—I accepted your decision. You made the best choice. You were right—it would have come to a bad end between us. God knows it's better to preserve a few enjoyable memories and leave things as they are."

The finality in his voice stunned Holly. "Please," she said unsteadily, "don't say another word. Just listen to me. I owe you the complete truth, and after you hear it—if you still want to send me away—then I will go. But I won't leave until I've said my piece, and you'll stand right there and listen, and if you don't . . ."

"If I don't?" he asked with a ghost of his old smile.

"Then I'll never let you have a moment's peace," she threatened in suppressed panic. "I'll follow you everywhere. I'll shout at the top of my lungs."

Zachary finished his drink and went to the night table, where a bottle of brandy awaited. The sight gave Holly a tiny thrill of hope. He wouldn't still be drinking if he had lost all feeling for her, would he? "All right," he said brusquely, refilling his glass. "Say your piece. You have my attention for the next five minutes, after which I want your troublesome little arse off my estate. Agreed?"

"Agreed." Holly bit her lip and lowered her hands to her sides. It was difficult to strip her soul bare before him, but that was precisely what was required if she was to win him back. "I loved you from the beginning," she said, forcing herself to look directly at him. "I can see that now, although at the time I didn't realize what was happening. I haven't wanted to face the truth, that I am exactly what you called me—a coward." Her gaze searched Zachary's dark face for a reaction to her admission, but there was no sign of emotion. He downed another two fingers of brandy, consuming the distillation with slow, deliberate swallows. "When George died in my arms," Holly continued raggedly, "I wanted to die, too. I never wanted to feel such pain again, and I knew the safest thing would be to never let myself love anyone that way. And so I used my promise to George as an excuse to hold you at bay."

Holly paused uncertainly, realizing that for some reason her words had caused a flush to rise from Zachary's throat to his ears. Taking courage from that telltale wash of color, she forced herself to go on. "I was willing to use any reason I could find to keep from loving you. And then . . . when you and I . . . in the summerhouse . . ." Too distraught to look at him any longer, Holly lowered her head.

"I had never felt that way before," she said. "I was utterly lost. I had no control over my heart or my thoughts, and so I was frantic to leave you. Ever since then I've tried to step back into my old life, but the fit isn't right anymore. I've changed. Because of you." Suddenly she could barely see him through a scalding rush of tears. "I've finally realized that there is something worse than possibly losing you . . . and that is never having you at all." Her voice cramped and faltered, and she could only whisper. "Please let me stay, Zachary—on any terms you desire. Don't make me live without you. I love you so desperately."

The room was as quiet as a tomb, with no sound or movement from the man standing several feet away. If he still wanted her, if he still cared, she thought, he would have taken her in his arms by now. The realization made her want to shrink into nothing. A dull, pervasive pain began to seep from her chest. She wondered what she would do after he sent her away, where she would go, how she would go about building a new life for herself and Rose, when all she wanted to do was draw into a ball and howl with bitter regret. Staring hard at the floor, she shuddered with the effort not to break into humiliating sobs.

Zachary's bare feet came into her vision, and she started in surprise, for he had come to her as silently as a cat. He took her left hand, paused and stared down at it wordlessly. Suddenly Holly understood what he was looking at—the gold wedding band that she had never removed since the day her husband had placed it on her finger. Making a wretched sound, she snatched her hand from his and tugged at the ring. It was difficult to remove, and she twisted at it in a spasm of panic before it finally slid free. Dropping the circlet to the floor, she looked at the pale mark it had left on her finger and raised her tear-filled eyes to Zachary's blurred face.

She heard him murmur her name, and then, to her utter astonishment, she saw him sink to his knees and felt his huge hands clutching the folds of silk at her hips. He buried his face against her midriff like an exhausted child.

Shocked, Holly reached down to his dark hair. The thick, slightly curling strands were damp against her fingertips, and she stroked them lovingly. "Darling," she whispered over and over, touching the hot nape of his neck.

Suddenly he rose in a fluid movement and stared into her upturned face. He wore the expression of a man who had journeyed through hellfire, and been scorched in the process.

"Damn you," he muttered, wiping at her tears with his fingers. "I could throttle you for putting us both through this."

"You told me not to come back," she sobbed in painful relief. "I was so afraid to try . . . Y-you sounded so final . . ."

"I thought I was losing you. I didn't know what the hell I was saying." He crushed her against his pounding heart, running his hands over her hair and completely disheveling it.

"You said no s-second chances."

"A thousand chances for you. A hundred thousand."

"I'm sorry," she wept. "I'm so sorry—"

"I want you to marry me," Zachary said in a guttural voice. "I'm going to bind you with every agreement and contract and ritual known to man."

"Yes, yes . . ." Eagerly she pulled his head down to hers, kissing him with all the aching longing she had felt the past month. He made a rough sound and savaged her mouth with brutal passion, hurting her a little, but she was too wild with emotion to mind.

"I want you in my bed," he said thickly. "Now."

A crimson flood of color swept over her, and Holly
barely managed a nod before he picked her up and carried
her to the bed with the single-minded intensity of a starved
jungle cat with its prey. It appeared she hadn't much
choice in the matter—not that she had any thought of de-
nying him. She loved him beyond propriety, beyond morals or ideals or sanity. She was his utterly, just as he was
hers.

He undressed her swiftly, pulling hard at rows of buttons
and hooks, tearing cloth when it would not yield quickly
enough to his plundering fingers. Gasping at his urgency,
Holly tried to help him, sitting on the bed to unlace her
shoes, peeling away her garters and stockings, lifting her
arms as he tugged her chemise over her head. When she
was completely naked, her blushing body reclining back
on the mattress, Zachary shed his robe and lowered himself
beside her.

The sight of his magnificent body, long and powerful
and supremely masculine, caused Holly's eyes to widen.
"Oh, Zachary, you're such a beautiful man." She gathered
herself against the wonderful wealth of hair on his chest,
playing with the dark curls, brushing her mouth and fingers
through them.

A faint groan came from over her head. "You're the
beautiful one." His hands moved gently over her back and
hips, savoring the texture of her skin. "I never recovered
from my first glance at you, at the Bellemont ball."

"You saw me then? But it was dark outside."

"I followed you after I kissed you in the conservatory."
He pushed her to her back, his gaze sweeping over her
naked body. "I watched as you went to your carriage, and
I thought you were the loveliest thing I had ever seen."

He pressed a kiss to her shoulder, his tongue touching the fragile curve, and Holly trembled.

"And you began to scheme," she said breathlessly.

"That's right. I thought of a hundred ways to get under your skirts, and I decided the best plan was to hire you. But somewhere in the middle of my efforts to seduce you, I fell in love with you."

"And your intentions became honorable," she said, pleased.

"No, I still wanted to get under your skirts."

"Zachary Bronson," she exclaimed, and he grinned, bracing his forearms on either side of her head. Holly felt her pulse quicken with anticipation as the length of one hard, hair-dusted leg insinuated between her thighs, and the burning silken weight of his sex pressed intimately against her hip.

"That afternoon in the summerhouse was the best damn thing that ever happened to me," he said. "But the way you left me right afterward . . . it was like being cast from heaven straight to hell."

"I was afraid," she said remorsefully, pulling his head down and kissing his cheeks and brandy-flavored mouth.

"So was I. I didn't know how I was going to recover from you."

"You make me sound like an illness," she said with a wavering smile.

A hot glow appeared in his sable eyes. "I've discovered there's no cure for you, my lady. I thought of going to another woman, but I couldn't. The hell of it is, you're the only one I want."

"Then you haven't . . ." Holly was filled with relief. The thoughts of Zachary making love to other women in her absence had tormented her, and she was overwhelmed with gladness that he hadn't.

"No, I haven't," he informed her, his tone lowering to a growl that was only half-feigned. "I've gone a month without relief, and you're going to pay for it." Holly's eyes closed, and all her nerves sparked wildly as she heard his threatening whisper in her ear. "For the next few hours, my lady, you're going to be damned busy taking care of my needs."

"Yes," she whispered. "Yes, that's what I want, too—" Her words were cut short as Zachary bent his head over her breast. His hot breath fanned over the tender nipple until it contracted, and then he took it in his mouth. Holly's entire body tensed as he used the tip of his tongue to feather and tickle the sensitive peak. She put her arms around his shoulders, her fingers splayed wide over the hard slopes of muscle. He drew the taut nipple deeper into his mouth, suckling for long minutes, until he felt her thighs closing rhythmically on either side of his leg.

His hand slid between her legs, expertly finding the touch of moisture hidden among the springy curls. Whispering softly, he parted the soft feminine flesh to discover the peak that ached so sweetly. He teased her, sliding his fingertip around the tiny nub but never quite touching it, until she gasped and lifted her hips beseechingly. "Please," she whispered through lips that felt swollen and hot. "Please, Zachary . . ."

She felt his mouth brush hers, a delicious pressure that made her surge upward in an eager search for more. He kissed her again, his tongue exploring her mouth while she responded with utter abandon. His body shifted over hers, and she felt his sex nudge against her, the broad head nestling in the triangle of dark curls. Encouraged by his hoarse murmur, Holly reached down to the heavy shaft, her hand trembling a little as she closed it around the hardness. She stroked him hesitantly, and her face turned scar-

let as his own hand covered hers and moved it in a
rougher, harder caress.

"Shouldn't I be more gentle with you?" she asked,
somehow mortified and excited at the same time.

"Men aren't like women," he said raspily. "You prefer
gentleness . . . all we require is enthusiasm."

Wordlessly Holly demonstrated her enthusiasm until he
removed her hand with a curse and a groan. "Enough," he
managed to say. "I don't want this to end too soon."

"I do." Holly threw her arms around him and spread
kisses over his chest and throat. "I want you . . . oh, Zachary, I want . . ."

"That feeling I gave you in the summerhouse?" he whispered, his eyes gleaming with wicked knowledge.

Holly nodded against his throat, and spread herself beneath him, her body taut and trembling with the need to
be taken, claimed, possessed. He drew his hand in a slow,
searching path over her breasts, stomach, abdomen, and
she made an excited sound as his palm brushed over the
small, curly patch of hair at the apex of her thighs. His
fingers were clever and maddeningly elusive, dipping into
the curls with light touches, never quite reaching the place
that had become hot and embarrassingly saturated. Her
hips lifted urgently, searching for the stimulation he with-
held, and then she felt his mouth slide over her skin in a
trail from her breasts to her stomach. His hands closed over
her hips, squeezing and steadying, and Holly jumped in
surprise as she felt his mouth drift over the moist curls.
She exclaimed something, an incoherent sound that could
have been either protest or encouragement, and Zachary's
dark head lifted as he glanced at her flushed face.

"My sweet, proper lady," he said softly, "have I shocked
you?"

"Yes," she whimpered.

"Put your legs over my shoulders."

She stared at him in helpless mortification. "Zachary, I couldn't . . ."

"Now." And he breathed between her thighs, making her entire body quiver.

She closed her eyes and did it, resting her calves and heels on his muscled back. His fingers stroked and opened her, and then she felt his mouth, the slide of his tongue, and the pleasure of it seized her in a swift, scorching whirl. It did not seem possible that this could be happening to her, this terrible sweet intimacy that threw her into utter confusion. She felt him nibbling, licking, and the sensation thickened and spread inside her until she made sounds she had never made before. Her mewling gasps and pleas seemed to excite her bold lover. He growled a little and gripped her buttocks with his hands, urging her higher against his mouth. His tongue swirled and teased until she felt the pleasure rushing too fast and hot to bear . . . she gave a wild cry, the torment flowing into quivering release. His mouth remained upon her until the last exquisite tremor had faded and she was left weak and dazed.

Easing her trembling legs away from his back, Zachary moved over her, his powerful sleek body settling into the cradle of her hips. She felt the big, insistent shape of his sex pressing against her. "Zachary, have mercy," she whispered through dry lips.

"No mercy for you, my lady." He cupped her head in his hands, kissing her as he pushed inside her wet, swollen flesh. She inhaled sharply, writhing to accommodate him, the plundering invasion stretching her tight. He spread her legs with his own and filled her more deeply, until she moaned into the depths of his mouth. The feel of him excited her, and despite her weariness, she arched in welcome. He began a steady rhythm, his hips delving into hers, the hair on his chest brushing over the hardened tips of her breasts. She tilted her head back in ecstasy as she felt him cover her neck with kisses and gentle bites.

"You're mine," he whispered, riding her faster, his rhythm turning impatient. "You belong to me . . . Holly . . . forever."

"Yes," she moaned as he drove the sensation to another peak.

"Tell me."

"I love you, Zachary . . . oh . . . I need you so much . . . only you . . ."

He rewarded her with a thrust that reached the tip of her womb, and she convulsed with pleasure, shuddering, pulsing, overwhelmed by a physical joy that had been, until now, unimaginable. His body went incredibly taut over hers, muscles bunching into steely curves, his throat catching on a groan. Her flesh worked sweetly on his, closing around the invading hardness as he pumped and throbbed inside her.

Sighing deeply, Holly wrapped her arms and legs around him, holding him tightly as the sensations subsided to a warm glow. She felt him try to move off her, and she murmured a protest.

"I'll crush you," he whispered.

"I don't care."

Smiling, he moved to his side and kept her with him, their bodies still joined.

"That was even better than in the summerhouse," Holly said wonderingly.

A quiet laugh rumbled in Zachary's chest. "There are many things I'm going to enjoy teaching you."

Her faint smile dissolved as she considered the prospect. "Zachary," she said gravely, "I can't help but wonder if a man like you will be content to stay with just one woman."

He cupped her face in his hands and pressed his lips to her forehead. Drawing back, he stared into her questioning brown eyes. "I've been searching for you my entire life," he said seriously. "You're the only one I want, now and forever. If you don't believe me, I'll—"

"I believe you," she said hastily, touching her fingers to his lips. She smiled into his dark face. "There's no need for proof or promises."

"It would be no trouble to prove it again." He nudged deeper inside her, making her gasp a little, and she cuddled against him with a pleasured moan.

"No, I want to talk," she said breathlessly. "I want to ask you something . . ."

"Mmmm?" He stroked her buttocks, seeming to delight in the soft shapes in his hands.

"Why did you turn away Mr. Somers when he came to ask for Elizabeth's hand in marriage?"

The question distracted him, and he glanced alertly into her face. His black brows lowered in a slight scowl. "How did you know about that?"

Looping her arms around his neck, she shook her head with a faint smile. "Answer my question, please."

He swore a little and dropped his head to the pillow. "I turned him away because I'm testing him."

"Testing him," Holly repeated. Considering the words, she drew apart from Zachary, wincing a little as his heavy shaft slipped from her body. "But why? You can't possibly think he only wants to marry Elizabeth because of her—your—fortune."

"It's not outside the realm of possibility."

"Zachary, you can't manipulate people as if they're pawns in a chess game. Especially people in your own family!"

"I'm only trying to protect Lizzie's interests. If Somers

still wants her without my approval—and the dowry that comes with it—then he'll pass the test."

"Zachary." Holly shook her head with a disapproving sigh. She drew the bed linens over herself and contemplated him while he lounged unabashedly naked beside her. "Your sister loves this man. You must respect her choice. And even if she and Mr. Somers do pass this test of yours, they will never forgive you for it, and you'll have caused an irreparable breach in the family."

"What do you want me to do?"

"You know," she murmured. Cuddling closer to him, she blew gently into the curls on his chest.

"Dammit, Holly, I've spent my whole life doing things a certain way, and I can't change that. It's my nature to protect myself and my family from all the bastards who'd try to take advantage of us, and I'll admit, I've become set in my ways. If you're going to try and turn me into some kind of milquetoast—"

"Of course not." She drew her tongue over the jutting edge of his collarbone, and delved into the hollow where his pulse beat strongly. "I wouldn't want to change you in any way." Pressing her face against his throat, she let her long eyelashes tickle his skin. "But I want so much for your sister to be happy, Zachary. Would you deny her the same joy that you and I have found? Forget this wretched test, and send for Mr. Somers."

She sensed his inner struggle, the desire to control the situation warring with the gentler side of his nature. As she continued to entreat and caress him, however, he gave a reluctant laugh. His hands came up to her soft white shoulders, pressing her back to the flattened pillow. "I don't like being managed," he grumbled.

She smiled at him. "I'm not trying to manage you, my darling. I'm only making an appeal to your higher nature."

The endearment caused his expression to become hungry and absorbed, and the argument seemed to lose interest for him. "As I once told you, my lady, I have no higher nature."

"But you'll send for Mr. Somers?" she prompted. "And settle things for Elizabeth?"

"Yes. Later." He dragged away the layers of linen that covered her, and settled a hand over her breast.

"But Zachary," she said, gasping a little as he spread her knees. "You can't possibly do this *again* . . . not so soon after . . ." The feel of his hard length sliding inside her caused all words to fade into an astonished moan.

"Damned if I can't," he muttered tenderly against her breast, catching a flushed nipple between his teeth, and for a long time all conversation stopped.

Holly held Zachary's hand as they wandered along the wilderness walk of his estate garden. Her skirts brushed clumps of purple and white crocuses, while a light spring breeze stirred through yellow irises and gleaming white snowdrops that were strewn along the borders of the grassy walk. Long, thick ribbons of fragile yellow aconites led to vast groves of honeysuckle and Japanese apricot. Breathing deeply of the fragrant air, Holly felt happiness welling in her chest until it spilled into an irrepressible laugh. "Your house may be an architectural horror," she said, "but oh, this garden is a glimpse of heaven."

Zachary's hand tightened on hers, and she saw a smile cross his face. The afternoon had been the most blissful either of them had ever known, the hours filled with lovemaking and soft laughter, and even a few tears as they shared the secrets of their hearts. Now that they had reconciled, it seemed there were a thousand things to discuss, and not nearly enough time. However, Holly was eager to return to the Taylors' home and share with her daughter the news of her impending marriage. The Taylor family would be outraged, of course, and added to their unhappiness over the match would be the complete surprise of realizing that George's wife was rejecting his last wishes. They would hardly understand that the decision was not a cavalier one. She simply had no choice. The fact was, she couldn't live without Zachary Bronson.

"Stay with me," Zachary said quietly. "I'll send for Rose, and you'll both live here while we arrange for the wedding."

"You know I can't do that."

He frowned and guided her carefully around a small marble and brass sundial set in the ground. "I don't want to let you out of my sight."

Holly diverted his attention by bringing up the subject of the wedding ceremony, stressing that she wanted it to be accomplished with discretion and expediency. Unfortunately, it seemed that Zachary desired something far more grandiose. Upon hearing of his ideas for a large church, a thousand doves, a dozen trumpeters, a banquet for five hundred and various other appalling schemes, Holly firmly stated that she would have nothing to do with such an event.

"We'll have something private and very quiet, and above all, *small,*" she said. "It's the only choice, really."

"I agree," he said readily. "On second thought, we don't need to invite more than three hundred guests."

Holly gave him an incredulous glance. "When I said 'small,' I had a different number in mind. Perhaps half a dozen."

His jaw set obstinately. "I want all of London to know that I've won you."

"They'll know," she said dryly. "I'm sure the *ton* will

talk of little else . . . and it's a certainty that none of my scandal-avoiding former friends would attend the wedding, extravagant or otherwise."

"Nearly all of mine would," he said cheerfully.

"Undoubtedly," she agreed, knowing that he was referring to the crowd of ruffians, dandies and social climbers who ran the gamut from being bad *ton* to complete wastrels. "Nevertheless, the wedding will be as discreet as possible. You can save the doves and trumpeters and such for Elizabeth's wedding."

"I suppose it would be faster that way," he said grudgingly.

Holly stopped on the graveled path and smiled up at him. "We'll keep our wedding small, then, and get on with it." She slid her arms around his lean waist. "I don't want to wait a day longer than necessary to belong to you."

Needing no further encouragement, Zachary bent his head to kiss her thoroughly. "I need you," he muttered, pressing her against his aroused loins to emphasize the fact. "Come back to the house with me now, sweet love, and let me—"

"Not again until we marry." Breathing fast, she rested her ear against his thundering heart. Despite her own eagerness to make love with him, she wanted to wait until they were properly wed. "I've been compromised quite enough today, I should think."

"Oh, no, you haven't." His hands wandered over the bodice of her gown, and he kissed the side of her throat. With a coaxing murmur, he led her to an old stone wall covered with rare yellow camellias, and began to reach for the hem of her skirts.

"Don't you dare," Holly warned with an unsteady laugh, skittering away from him. "A gentleman should treat his beloved with respect, and here you are—"

"The size of this cockstand is ample proof of my respect for you," he interrupted, pulling her hand to his swollen crotch.

Holly knew she should have rebuked him, but instead she found herself pressing close against his long, sturdy form. "You're impossibly vulgar," she said against his ear.

Zachary cupped her hand more tightly around himself. "That's one of the things you like best about me," he whispered, and she couldn't help smiling.

"Yes."

He nuzzled into the little space between her lace-edged neckline and the soft, warm skin of her throat. "Let me take you to the summerhouse. Just for a few minutes. No one will know."

Reluctantly she wriggled away from him. *"I'll* know."

Zachary shook his head with a groaning laugh, turning to brace his hands on the flower-covered wall. Dropping his head, he breathed deeply, striving to master his rampaging desire. As Holly approached him hesitantly, he glanced sideways with smoldering black eyes. "All right, then," he said in a softly threatening tone underlaid with smoke. "I won't touch you again until our wedding night. But you may be sorry you made me wait."

"I already am," she confessed, and their smiling gazes locked for a long moment.

Although Zachary had intended to send for Jason Somers the very next day, the young man surprised him with an early morning call. Zachary had slept deeply for the first night in a month and awakened at the hour of eight, unusually late for him. He couldn't remember when he had felt so relaxed. It seemed that after decades of striving and struggling, he had finally reached the pinnacle he had sought. Perhaps for the first time in his life he could truly be happy . . . and the reason was at once extraordinary and commonplace. He was in love. He had finally relinquished his heart to someone and found that she loved him in return. It seemed too miraculous to be true.

In the midst of his solitary breakfast, the visitor was announced, and Zachary bade the housekeeper to show the young man in. Grim, handsome, pale and dressed as if he were attending a funeral, Somers appeared as the tragic hero of some overblown romance. Zachary actually felt a prickle of something that might have been remorse as he recalled his last meeting with the fellow, during which he had met Somers's earnest request for Elizabeth's hand with a quiet, crushing denial. No doubt Somers remembered every detail of the unpleasant scene, which would account for his resolute expression. It was the expression, in fact, of a valiant knight daring to approach an evil dragon in his lair.

Unshaven and still wearing his dressing robe, Zachary sat at a table in the breakfast room and gestured for Somers to join him. "Pardon my appearance," he said mildly, "but it is a bit earlier than the usual visiting hour. Will you take some coffee?"

"No, thank you." Somers remained standing.

Relaxing in his chair, Zachary took a long, hot swallow of his coffee. "Convenient that you should choose this day to call on me," he remarked, "as I had planned to send for you this morning."

"Had you?" Somers's green eyes narrowed intently. "Why is that, Mr. Bronson? Something to do with the Devon estate, I suppose?"

"No, actually. It concerns the matter we discussed the other day."

"As I recall, there was no discussion," Somers said

flatly. "I asked for your consent to marry Elizabeth, and you refused."

"Yes." Zachary cleared his throat gruffly. "Well, I—"

"You've left me no choice, sir." Although Somers flushed slightly with obvious nervousness, his voice was steady as he continued. "Out of respect for you, I came to inform you in person that I intend to marry Elizabeth with or without your approval. And despite what you or anyone else thinks, I'm not doing it because I have an eye on your damned fortune. I happen to love your sister. If she'll have me, I'm going to provide for her, work like hell for her and treat her with all the respect and gentleness a man can give his wife. And if you require more than that of any man, you can go to the devil."

Zachary felt his brows lift slightly. He couldn't help but be impressed by the young man—it wasn't often that someone dared to stand up to him this way. "If I may ask," he said quietly, "why do you love Elizabeth?"

"She's my perfect match in every way that matters."

"Not socially," Zachary pointed out.

"I said," came the young man's calm reply, "in every way that matters. I don't give a damn what her social status is."

The answer satisfied Zachary. His instincts told him that Somers was a decent man who truly loved Elizabeth. "Then you have my approval to marry Lizzie—if you'll do one thing for me."

Somers seemed too stunned to reply at first. "What is it?" he eventually asked in a suspicious tone.

"I have another project for you."

Somers shook his head immediately. "I won't spend the rest of my career taking commissions from you and being accused of nepotism. I respect my own abilities too much for that. I'll do well enough designing for other men—and

I'll recommend another architect to suit you."

"It's a humble project, actually," Zachary said, ignoring the refusal. "I'm tearing down some tenement slums on a block of real estate I own on the east side of town. I want you to design a new one, like nothing that currently exists. A large building to house dozens of families—rooms with windows—decent housing where they can cook and eat and sleep. And a facade attractive enough that a man can enter or exit the place without shame. On top of all that, I want it to be economical, so that others will be inspired to imitate it. Can you do something like that?"

"Yes, I could," Jason replied quietly, seeming to grasp the importance of the idea, the number of lives it could change. "And I will, although I may not want my name attached to the project. You see—"

"I understand," Zachary said without rancor. "You'll never get commissions from the aristocracy if they perceive that you design for the commoners as well."

Somers regarded him curiously, a strange expression entering his green eyes. "I've never met a gentleman in your position who gave a damn about the living conditions of the ordinary man."

"I *am* an ordinary man," Zachary pointed out. "I just happen to have had a bit more luck than most."

A half-smile played on Somers's lips. "I'll reserve opinion on that, sir."

Taking it for granted that the arrangement was settled, Zachary unlaced his fingers and drummed them idly on the desk. "You know, Somers, you could do worse than spend the rest of your career accepting my commissions. With your talent and my money—"

"Oh, no." A sudden laugh escaped the younger man, and he regarded Zachary with the first flicker of real friendliness. "I respect you, Bronson. But I won't be owned by you. I don't want your money. I just want your sister."

A hundred admonitions came to Zachary's mind, concerning how he wanted his sister to be treated, about all that Elizabeth needed and deserved, about the dire consequences if Somers ever disappointed her. But as he stared into Jason Somers's handsome, self-assured young face, the words remained locked inside him. Zachary realized he could no longer control every detail of his family's life or manage every minute of their days. It was time for each of them—including himself—to lead their own lives. A strange feeling came over him as he contemplated the novelty of handing his sister into someone else's care, and trusting that she would be happy and loved.

"All right," he said, rising from the desk and extending a hand. "Take Lizzie with my blessing."

"Thank you." They shook hands heartily, and Somers seemed unable to repress a grin.

"Regarding the dowry," Zachary said, " I would like to—"

"As I told you," Somers interrupted, "I don't want the dowry."

"It's for Elizabeth," Zachary said. "A woman should have a bit of independence in a marriage." Not only was this his personal view, but he had witnessed such circumstances in *ton* marriages, when wives who had come into the union with their own property and money were accorded far more consideration by their husbands. Moreover, women were legally entitled to keep their own property when their husbands died, regardless of what the deceased's will might stipulate.

"Very well. I want whatever is best for Elizabeth, naturally. If you don't mind, Bronson, I'll take my leave now. Regardless of the matters you and I should still discuss,

I'd like to share the good news with your sister."

"Thank you," Zachary replied in a heartfelt tone. "I'm damn tired of being painted as the unloving ogre she has accused me of being for the past few days." As Zachary exchanged a bow with Somers and watched the architect stride toward the door, one last thought occurred to him. "Oh, Somers . . . I trust you'll have no objections if I arrange the wedding."

"Arrange it however you like," Somers replied without breaking stride, clearly eager to find Elizabeth.

"Good," Zachary muttered in satisfaction, and seated himself at his desk. Picking up his pen, he dipped it in an inkwell and began to make a list. "One thousand doves for the church, five orchestras for the reception . . . fireworks, a dozen trumpeters—no, better make that *two* dozen . . ."

Seventeen

As Holly had expected, none of the Taylors could bring themselves to attend the small chapel wedding held on the Bronson estate. Understanding their feelings about her marriage to Bronson, and their disappointment over her failure to carry out George's wishes, Holly did not blame them at all. In time, she thought, they might come to forgive her, especially when they saw how Rose would benefit from the alliance. And Rose, certainly, had made little secret of her joy.

"Are you going to be my papa now?" the child had asked Zachary, sitting with her arms looped around his neck. She had flown to him with shrill cries of delight when Holly had brought her to visit the estate, and he had swung her in the air until her little petticoats and white stockings had been a white blur. Touched by the obvious happiness of the pair, Holly had felt a great settling of comfort and peace inside. If she had had any lingering doubts about the rightness of this new life for her daughter, they dissolved at the sight of Rose's beaming face. The child would be spoiled, undoubtedly, but she would also be loved wholeheartedly.

"Is that what you'd like?" Zachary said in answer to Rose's question.

She wrinkled her face thoughtfully, and her doubtful gaze flickered to Holly before returning to Zachary. "I should like very much to live in your big house," she replied with all the candor of a young child, "and I don't mind that Mama will marry you. But I don't want to call you Papa. It would make my papa in heaven sad, I think."

The words stunned Holly, and she fumbled for a reply. Helplessly she watched as Zachary touched the little girl's round chin and turned her face toward him. "Then call me whatever you like," he said matter-of-factly. "But believe me, princess, I'm not going to replace your papa. I'd be a fool to try, fine man that he was. I just want to take care of you and your mother. I imagine—I hope—that your papa will be somewhat relieved to see that someone will be looking after you down here while he's unable."

"Oh," Rose said in obvious satisfaction. "I think that's all right, then, as long as we don't forget him. Isn't that right, Mama?"

"Yes," Holly whispered, her throat tight with emotion, her cheeks flushed with happiness. She stared at Zachary with glittering brown eyes. "You're absolutely right, Rose."

On the day of the wedding, they were accompanied by Elizabeth, Paula, and Jason Somers, as well as Holly's own bewildered parents. They had traveled from Dorset for the occasion, and while they did not seem disapproving of the match, they were obviously astonished that their eldest daughter was marrying into a world so different from the one she had been destined for. "Mr. Bronson appears to be a decent man," her mother whispered to her before the ceremony, "and his manners are pleasing enough, though they may lack polish . . . and I suppose he is fine-looking, albeit a bit too coarse to be considered truly handsome . . ."

"Mama," Holly asked with a wry smile, long accustomed to the woman's diffidence, "are you trying to say that you approve of him?"

"I suppose I am," her mother admitted, "although Mr. Bronson certainly bears no resemblance in appearance or character to your first husband."

"Mama . . ." Impulsively Holly embraced her and smiled against the feathery plumes of her mother's hat. "In time you'll come to realize, as I have, that Mr. Bronson is a wonderful man in every regard. His character is a bit tarnished in some places, but in other places it shines more brightly than George's or my own."

"If you say so," her mother said doubtfully, and Holly laughed.

As they gathered in the chapel, Holly being flanked by Elizabeth and Rose, and Zachary by Jason Somers, who had agreed to stand up for him, they were all surprised by a last-minute addition to the wedding party. Holly smiled brilliantly as she saw Lord Blake, the earl of Ravenhill, enter the chapel. After stopping to make a precise bow, Ravenhill moved to stand beside Holly's parents. His warm gray eyes seemed to contain a quiet smile as he glanced at Holly and then at Zachary.

"What is he doing here?" Zachary asked beneath his breath.

Holly reached for his tense arm and held it lightly. "It's a very great favor," she whispered back. "By attending our wedding, Lord Blake is publicly showing his support of our marriage."

"More likely taking his last opportunity to ogle you."

Holly cast Zachary a shaming glance, but he seemed not to notice her disapproval as his gaze wandered avidly over her gown. She was dressed in pale yellow *gros de naples*, a finely textured silk with a tiny bouquet of spring flowers pinned at the center of her straight banded neckline. The short puffed sleeves were overlaid with long transparent ones made of *crêpe lisse.* The effect was youthful and fragile, requiring no ornamentation save a few orange blossoms pinned in her dark upswept curls.

The vicar began to speak: "Wilt thou have this woman to thy wedded wife, to live together after God's ordinance in the holy estate of matrimony? Wilt thou love her, comfort her, honor and keep her in sickness and in health; and forsaking all other, keep thee only unto her, so long as ye both shall live?"

Zachary's reply was quiet and steady. "I will."

And as the ceremony progressed, Holly was changed from a widow to a bride once more.

They exchanged vows, placed rings on each other's fingers and knelt together as the vicar began a lengthy prayer. Holly tried to focus on the vicar's words, but as she glanced into Zachary's serious face, it seemed the world had vanished except for the two of them. His grip on her hands was warm and strong as he pulled her to her feet, and hazily she realized that the vicar was finishing the ceremony: ". . . those whom God hath joined together, let no man put asunder."

They were married now, Holly thought in wonder, staring at her husband in the suspended silence, her fingers lacing tightly with his. Suddenly Rose's voice broke through the stillness, as the little girl apparently felt moved to add to the vicar's closing words. Her tone exactly mimicked his grave monotone. "And they lived happily ever after."

Laughter rippled through the small gathering, and Zachary pressed a brief, hard kiss on Holly's smiling mouth.

The wedding supper that followed was a lighthearted affair, with music supplied by violinists and conversation seasoned by flowing bottles of expensive wine. Rose was allowed to sit at the adults' table for a short time. She was clearly dismayed when Maude appeared at the hour of eight to take her up to the nursery, but her protests were forestalled when Zachary murmured quietly to her and placed some small object in her hand. Exchanging a good-night kiss with Holly, the child went happily upstairs with Maude.

"What did you give her?" Holly asked Zachary, and his black eyes glinted with mischief.

"Buttons."

"Buttons," she whispered in surprise. "From where?"

"One from my wedding coat and one from the back of your gown. Rose wanted them to commemorate the occasion."

"You took a button from the back of my gown?" Holly whispered, casting him a shaming glance as she wondered how he had managed to accomplish the small feat without her notice.

"Be thankful I stopped at just one, my lady," he advised.

Holly did not reply, her blush heightening as she reflected that she was anticipating their wedding night fully as much as he.

At last the long supper and the endless rounds of toasts came to a conclusion, and the men remained at the table to enjoy their port. Holly slipped upstairs to the bedroom adjoining Zachary's, and with Maude's help, she removed her wedding clothes. She changed into a nightgown made of fine, thin white cambric that had been intricately pleated and ruffled at the bodice and sleeves. Dismissing the servant with a smile of thanks, Holly brushed out her hair until it fell in long, loose locks over her shoulders.

It felt strange, to once again be waiting for a husband's conjugal visit—strange but wonderful. How fortunate she was to have been blessed with two loves in her life. Sitting at the dressing table, she bent her head to whisper a silent prayer of thankfulness.

Eventually the quiet click of the door interrupted the silence, and she glanced upward to find Zachary approaching her.

Slowly he removed his wedding coat and tossed it over the back of a chair. He came to her and settled his hands on her shoulders while their gazes met in the mirror. "No doubt I should have waited longer." His fingers slid over her shining hair, then lightly touched the sides of her neck. Holly shivered pleasurably at the gentle brush of his fingertips. "But the more I thought of you up here . . . my sweet, pretty wife . . . the more impossible it became to stay away." Continuing to stare at her reflection, Zachary carefully unfastened the little covered buttons at her throat, working down the long row until the cambric sagged loosely over her chest. His dark hands slipped beneath the thin fabric, their shadowy outline visible as he fondled the round shapes of her breasts.

Holly's breathing deepened as she leaned against her chair. Her nipples contracted from the sliding heat of his palms. He used his thumbs and forefingers to pull gently at the tips, until the sensation chased all the way down to her toes.

"Zachary," she said unsteadily, "I love you."

He knelt beside her chair and urged her forward, his mouth capturing the tip of one breast through the cambric and tugging urgently. She quivered, her hands coming to his head, and she rubbed her mouth over his thick black hair. Releasing her breast, Zachary smiled and cupped her small face between his palms. "Tell me," he said, "do you still think that good wives pander to their husbands' desires but should never encourage them?"

"I'm sure I should think so," she said ruefully.

"That's too bad," he informed her, laughter shimmering in his eyes. "Because there's nothing I enjoy so much as watching you struggle with your improper desires." He picked her up easily, and she curled her arms around his neck as he carried her to the bed. A few flickering candles illuminated the room with soft pools of light, causing Zachary's skin to gleam like bronze as he removed his clothing. He tugged Holly's gown to her hips, spreading kisses on each newly revealed inch of her body, then pulled it off completely. She turned toward him, gathering herself against him with a sound of mingled greed and pleasure that made him laugh softly. But his flaring amusement dimmed as she touched him, her hands inexpertly searching his shoulders and back and smoothing over the hard slopes of muscle. His chest moved in uneven breaths, and he pressed his face in her hair.

"Zachary," she whispered near his ear, "teach me all the things you like. Tell me what you want. I'll do anything for you . . . anything."

He lifted his head and looked into her warm, trusting brown eyes. His own expression became fierce with adoration, and he bent to take her mouth hungrily. Grasping her hand in his, he drew her fingers slowly over his body, lingering on the places that gave him pleasure, showing her ways to stroke and caress him that she had never imagined.

Murmuring hotly against her throat, he spread her thighs and slipped his fingers inside her, and kissed her stomach and navel and rested his thumb lightly on the peak hidden in the damp clustered curls between her legs. She strained upward with a smothered moan, and he circled his thumb once, twice, while his fingers flexed deeper inside her body. He bent his head over her loins and slid his tongue over her swollen flesh, and gnawed softly with his lips and the edge of his teeth, and her fingers went to the back of his neck in a frantic grasp.

"Please," she moaned, inflamed and ready, every muscle in her body tensing in anticipation. "Now, Zachary—"

But he rolled off of her and pulled her stiff limbs over his, and made her straddle his hips so that his erection rubbed into the place he had made so wet and hot. Understanding what he wanted, Holly reached down with trembling hands and pushed the taut length of him into place. She tried to sink down on him, but in her inexperience she could not find the proper angle. He guided her to lean deeper, until her breasts swayed over his face. The hard shaft slid more easily then, and she gasped at the luscious invasion.

Rising upward on his elbows, Zachary caught one nipple in his mouth, and then the other, taking little stinging bites that caused her hips to jerk against his. Holly pressed herself on him urgently, then rose and did it again, finding a rhythm that caused his powerful legs to quiver beneath hers. He gritted his teeth and grabbed huge fistfuls of the bed linens, while sweat beaded on his face. He did not reach for her or guide her, only let her do as she wished, until the pleasure in her core surged in a great throbbing tide. Letting out a low cry, Holly ground herself against him, crushed her mouth on his, fused her body to his, while the fiery delight raced through her. Only then did he touch her, gripping her buttocks in his hands to pull her down even harder as his own passion exploded.

Holly rested against his shoulder for a long time afterward, occasionally reaching up to stroke his face with gentle fingertips. When Zachary's breathing returned to normal, he moved to blow out the candles, then returned to her arms. She didn't know whether they slept for minutes or hours, but she awakened in the darkness to feel his hands on her once more. He kissed her mouth and breasts, while his coaxing hand teased the tender place between her thighs until she was ready for him again. She gave a little start as he rolled her to her stomach and wedged a pillow beneath her hips. "Trust me?" came his devilish whisper against her ear. She relaxed and offered a moan of encouragement, opening herself completely to whatever he desired. She felt his legs slide between hers, and he took her from behind, fitting himself deeply into her body. She wondered dizzily if this was immoral, if she should allow it, and then soon she didn't care. His long thrusts caused guttural cries to rise from her throat, and she felt his teeth gently score the back of her neck as his climax followed hers.

They made love once more as dawn approached, every movement languid and dreamy, their mouths clinging in unbroken kisses as Zachary cradled her in his arms. "I never want to leave this bed," she whispered to him, stretching beneath the stroke of his hand on her lower back.

"I'm afraid you'll have to, my lady. But from now on, there's always another night for us."

She trailed her fingers through his chest hair, found the little point of nipple and rubbed it gently. "Zachary?"

"Yes, my love?"

"How often do you usually, er . . . that is, what do you prefer . . ."

Her attempts to phrase the question delicately seemed to entertain him. "How often would *you* prefer?" he parried, drawing a fingertip over her blushing cheek.

"Well, with George, I . . . that is, we . . . at least once a week."

"Once a week," he repeated, and beneath the laughter in his eyes there was a hot flicker that made her toes curl.

"I'm afraid I'll require your wifely compliance a great deal more often than that, Lady Bronson."

In a rush of tingling embarrassment, Holly reflected that he was a man of strong appetites—she should not have been surprised by his rampantly sexual nature. And the prospect of sharing most of her nights with him was not exactly a hardship. "I've been taught my entire life to be moderate in all things," she said. "And I have been . . . except when it comes to you."

"Well, Lady Bronson," he murmured, his wide shoulders rising above hers, "I think that bodes well for our future. Don't you?" And he kissed her before she could answer.

Holly thought she had come to know and understand Zachary Bronson quite well after abiding beneath his roof for the better part of a Season. However, she soon discovered the vast difference between simply abiding with him and living as his wife. As the first month of their married life passed, she gradually became accustomed to sharing astonishing intimacy with him. She learned many things about Zachary: That although he could be callous or harsh toward those who displeased him, he was never completely without mercy. That he was not a religious man, nor was he particularly spiritual, yet he had a code of honor that led him to be unflinchingly honest. That he was embarrassed by open praise from others, and made light of the favors that he did for them.

Although Zachary tried mightily to conceal it, he possessed a vein of compassion that led him to be kind to those he perceived as vulnerable or weak. He drove hard bargains in his business dealings, but he slipped lavish tips to street sweepers and match girls, and secretly funded a multitude of reformist causes. When any of his charitable impulses were discovered, he disclaimed any good motives and pretended that everything he did was for purely mercenary reasons.

Perplexed by his behavior, Holly approached him in the library on a day he had chosen to work at home. "The pensions for your workers, and the new safety standards at your factories, and the workingmens' college you're funding," she mused aloud, "these are all things you've done only because it will eventually bring you more profit?"

"That's right. Making the employees intelligent and reasonably healthy will result in greater productivity."

"And the bill you're secretly sponsoring in Parliament to outlaw all employment of orphans in mills and factories," Holly continued, "that is also purely for business reasons?"

"How do you know about that?" he asked with a faint scowl.

"I overheard you talking to Mr. Cranfill the other day," she said, naming one of his political friends. Sitting on his knee, Holly loosened his starched necktie and played with the dark hair at his nape. "Why does it embarrass you for other people to know about your good works?" she asked softly.

He shrugged uncomfortably. "It serves no purpose. You know what they say."

Holly nodded thoughtfully, remembering the article published in the *Times* the previous day that had criticized Zachary's support of the workingmens' college:

Mr. Bronson has made it his ambition to see that the middle and even lower classes are allowed to run the country. People who haven't the slightest understanding of responsibility or morality are to be given

power over the rest of us. He wants the sheep to lead
the shepherds, and in this pursuit, he is actively
working for uneducated brutes like himself to be elevated above men of intellect and refinement.

"Everything I do causes controversy," Zachary said
matter-of-factly. "In fact, there are times when my patronage almost becomes a liability for the causes I'm trying to
help. I've been accused of everything short of trying to
lead a great lower-class conspiracy that will end up overturning the monarchy."

"It isn't fair," Holly murmured, feeling a wash of guilt
as she realized that there were respectable men of the upper
circles she used to frequent who were actively fighting
against measures that would educate and protect people so
much less fortunate than they. How strange that she and
George had never discussed such problems, had scarcely
been aware of them. It had never occurred to them to
worry about children being forced to work in mines at ages
three and four . . . that there were thousands of widows trying to support their families by selling matches or braiding
straw . . . that there was an entire class of people who had
no chance to rise above their circumstances unless someone fought for them. Sighing, she rested her head against
her husband's shoulder. "How selfish and blind I've been
for most of my life," she murmured.

"You?" Zachary sounded surprised. He bent to kiss the
curve of her cheek. "You're an angel."

"Am I?" she asked wryly. "It's becoming clear to me
that I've done very little in my life to help other people
. . . but you . . . you've done so much, and you're not being
given any of the recognition you deserve."

"I don't want recognition." He shifted her in his lap and
kissed her.

"What do you want?" she asked softly, a smile playing on her lips.

His hand curled around her ankle and began to roam farther beneath her skirts. "I should think it's fairly clear to you by now."

To be certain, Zachary was far from a saint. He was not above manipulating others to obtain the results he desired. Holly was both amused and appalled as she uncovered evidence of his maneuvering, such as the invitation they received to the annual after-Season country weekend party held by the earl and countess of Glintworth. The invitation was wholly unexpected, as Glintworth, Lord Wrey, was a member of high standing in the *ton,* and the Bronsons had earned too much notoriety to merit a place on the exclusive guest list. But once they were received publicly at a ball given by the Glintworths, it would be difficult for anyone in first society to cut them afterward.

Holly brought the invitation to Zachary with a questioning frown on her face. He was lounging in the music room while Rose plunked the keys of the gleaming little mahogany piano that had been installed specifically for her use. For some reason Zachary claimed to enjoy hearing the child's efforts at learning scales, and he spent at least two mornings a week listening to her.

"A messenger just delivered this," Holly told him quietly, showing him the invitation while he listened to Rose's cacophony as if it were a performance of some heavenly choir.

"What is it?" he asked, sprawling more comfortably in the chair near the piano, while Rose began yet another set of scales.

"An invitation to the earl of Glintworth's country weekend." Holly stared at him suspiciously. "Did you have something to do with it?"

"Why do you ask?" he countered a little too blandly.

"Because there is no reason we should be invited. Glintworth is the greatest snob in the civilized world, and he would never voluntarily condescend to invite us to anything, even if it were merely to watch his boots being shined!"

"Unless . . ." Zachary murmured, "he wanted something I could do for him."

"Listen to this, Uncle Zach," Rose commanded. "It's my best one!" The piano fairly vibrated from her enthusiastic playing.

"I'm listening, princess," Zachary assured her, then spoke to Holly in a soft undertone. "I think you'll soon see, my love, that many in the *ton* will be forced to overlook our little transgressions. There are too many peers who are financially entangled with me—or would like to be. And friendship, like anything else, has a purchasing price."

"Zachary Bronson," Holly exclaimed in horrified disbelief, "do you mean to tell me that you've somehow *coerced* the earl and countess of Glintworth into inviting us to their weekend party?"

"I gave them a choice," he said indignantly. "The fact is, Glintworth is in debt up to his ears, and he's been after me for months to let him invest . . ." He paused to applaud for Rose as she launched into an unsteady rendition of "Three Blind Mice," then turned back to Holly. "He's chased me like a dog after a rat about letting him invest in a rail line I'm planning. The other day I told him that in return for letting him have a piece of my business, I wouldn't mind a public demonstration of friendship from a man as estimable as himself. Evidently Glintworth convinced Lady Wrey that it would be in their best interests to send us an invitation to her party."

"So you gave them the choice of entertaining us or facing financial ruin?"

"I wasn't quite that blunt."

"Oh, Zachary, what a pirate you are!"

He grinned at her disapproving expression. "Thank you."

"That was not intended as praise! I suspect if someone were drowning in quicksand, you would extort all manner of promises before throwing him a rope."

He shrugged philosophically. "My sweet, that's the entire point of having the rope."

As it happened, they did attend the weekend party, and were received by the *ton* with a sort of grim courtesy that made one thing clear: They were not exactly welcome, but neither were they going to be excluded. Zachary's prediction had been correct. He had countless financial affiliations with ambitious peers who owed him favors—they would not dare to risk his wrath. A man could have fine heritage and a great deal of land, but if he had no money to maintain his estate and his lifestyle, he was eventually bound to lose everything. As the economy lurched slowly away from its agrarian roots, too many impoverished aristocrats had been forced to sell their property and ancient holdings for want of cash, and no associate of Zachary Bronson's cared to find himself in such a position.

There was a time when Holly might have been distressed by the cool reception her former friends gave her, but she was surprised to find that now it did not matter to her at all. She knew the things that were being said about her: that she had been Zachary Bronson's paramour before their marriage, that the wedding had taken place as a result of pregnancy, that she had married him for mercenary reasons, that she had been brought low by association with a family of bad blood. But gossip and social disapproval and the taint of scandal affected her no more than harmless darts flung against a suit of armor. She had never felt so secure, so cherished and loved, and it seemed that her happiness only grew each day.

To her relief, Zachary had slowed the reckless pace of his life, and although he was still constantly busy, his relentless energy did not exhaust her as she had once feared. Even Paula had remarked on the change in him, pleased that he now usually slept eight hours instead of five, and that he spent his evenings home instead of carousing in town. For years he had gone through life as if it were a battle, and now he had begun to regard the world around him with a new sense of comfortable ease.

Zachary drank less and spent fewer hours indoors poring over contracts and figures, choosing instead to spend afternoons accompanying Holly and Rose on picnics or open carriage rides. He purchased a handsome yacht for them to enjoy at water parties, escorted them to pantomimes at Drury Lane and bought a seaside "cottage" with a dozen bedrooms at Brighton for summertime trips to the shore. When friends joked about what a family man he had become, Zachary only smiled and replied that he found no greater enjoyment than spending time in the presence of his wife and daughter. Upper society was clearly puzzled by his behavior. It was generally considered unmanly to dote so openly on one's wife, not to mention a child, and yet no one dared make a critical comment in Zachary's presence. His attitude was written off as yet another of his many idiosyncrasies. Holly herself was surprised by the extent of his devotion, but she couldn't help feeling a twinge of pleasure at the obvious jealousy of other women, who teasingly asked what magic potion she had employed to keep her husband so enthralled.

Often Zachary brought friends home for supper, and

their table was filled with politicians, lawyers and wealthy merchants who were very different from the company Holly was accustomed to. They talked freely about money, trade, political issues, all the things that would never have been mentioned at aristocratic tables. These people were foreign to her, often rootless and rough-edged, and yet she found them fascinating.

"What a crowd of scoundrels," she exclaimed to Zachary late one evening, after the last dinner guest had departed. She walked upstairs to their bedroom, while Zachary kept one arm loosely around her waist. "That Mr. Cromby and Mr. Whitton are barely fit for decent society."

"I know." Zachary lowered his head repentantly, but she caught his sudden grin. "Seeing them makes me realize how much I've changed since I met you."

She let out a skeptical snort. "You, sir, are the biggest scoundrel of them all."

"It's your job to reform me," he replied lazily, stopping just one step beneath her so that their faces were level.

Holly linked her arms around his neck and kissed the end of his nose. "But I don't want to. I love you just as you are, wicked scoundrelly husband."

He caught her mouth with his, kissing her deeply. "Just for that, I'm going to be especially wicked." His lips roamed across her soft cheek and down to the edge of her jaw. "You'll have no gentleman in your bed tonight, milady."

"In other words, a typical evening," she mused, and gave a shriek of laughter as he suddenly tossed her over his shoulder and carried her up the stairs. "Zachary, put me down this very . . . oh, you barbarian, someone will see!" He carried her past a gaping housemaid, disregarding Holly's mortified pleas, and headed into his bedroom, where he proceeded to provoke and tease her for hours.

He made her laugh, made her play and struggle and groan with pleasure. Afterward, when she was exhausted and sated, he made love to her with gentle tenderness, whispering to her in the darkness that he would love her for eternity. It humbled her to be loved so greatly, and she could not fathom why he thought her so special when she was so very ordinary. "There are very many women like me, you know," she murmured as the morning approached, while she lay with her hair streaming across his neck and chest. "Women with my kind of upbringing, ones with older titles and nicer faces and figures."

She felt him smile against her cheek. "What are you trying to say? That you'd rather I'd married someone else?"

"Of course not." She tugged at a curl of his chest hair reprovingly. "It's just that I'm not the great prize you make me out to be. You could have gotten any woman that you had set your heart on."

"In my entire life, there's only been you. You're every dream and wish and want I've ever had." His hand played gently in her hair. "Mind you, I don't always like feeling this damn happy . . . It's a bit like king of the mountain."

"Now that you've reached the top of the pile, you're afraid to be knocked off?" she asked perceptively.

"Something like that."

Holly understood exactly how he felt. It was the very reason she had once refused to marry him, fearing the risk of losing something so precious, until the fear had stood squarely in the way of what she had most wanted. "Well, we won't live that way," Holly murmured, kissing his bare shoulder. "We'll enjoy each moment to the fullest, and let the morrow take care of itself."

* * *

Having taken an interest in one of the reform societies Zachary had donated to, Holly attended a meeting of the gentlewomen who had founded the group. As she learned more about the group, which was a children's aid society, she became enthusiastic about helping in ways other than merely donating money. The women in the society were busy organizing charity bazaars, lobbying for social legislation and founding new institutions to help care for the multitude of children who had been orphaned from recent epidemics of typhus and consumption. When it was decided to write a pamphlet describing the conditions of child labor in factories, Holly volunteered for a position on the committee. The next day, she and a half-dozen women went to visit a broom-making factory that had been deemed one of the worst offenders. Suspecting that Zachary would not approve of the factory visit, Holly decided not to mention it to him.

Although she had braced herself for an unpleasant sight, Holly found herself unprepared for the misery of the conditions at the factory. The place was filthy and poorly ventilated, with many children working who were clearly younger than the age of nine. Holly was moved to quiet anguish at the sight of the thin, wretched creatures with blank faces, their small hands moving in ceaseless tedious work, some of them missing fingers from accidents while using sharp knives to cut bundles of straw. They were orphans, one of the adult workers explained, gathered from orphanages and moved to a narrow, dark dormitory next to the factory. They worked fourteen hours a day, sometimes longer, and in return for their relentless labor, they were given a minimum of food and clothing, and a few pence a day.

Gravely the women of the children's aid committee remained at the factory and asked questions until their presence was discovered by a manager. They were quickly ushered from the premises, but at that point they had already learned what they needed to know. Saddened by what she had seen, but filled with resolution, Holly returned home and wrote the committee's report to be presented to the society at the next meeting.

"Tired from the meeting?" Zachary asked at supper that night, his perceptive gaze noting the signs of strain on her face.

Holly nodded, feeling more than a little guilt about not telling him where she had been that day. However, she was fairly certain of his displeasure should he find out, and she reasoned privately that there was no need to confess.

Unfortunately, Zachary did find out about the factory visit the following day, not from Holly but from one of his friends whose wife had also gone. Unfortunately, the friend had also related that the factory was in a particularly unsavory part of town, surrounded by streets with names like "Bitch Alley," "Dead Man's Yard" and "Maidenhead Lane."

Zachary's reaction astonished Holly. He cornered her the very moment he arrived home, and she realized with a sinking heart that he was not merely displeased. He was irate. He strove to keep his voice controlled, but it actually shook with fury as he forced words through his clenched teeth. "Dammit, Holly, I'd never have believed you'd do something so harebrained. Do you understand that the building could have collapsed around you and those henwits? I know what condition those places are in, and I wouldn't let a dog of mine venture past the threshold, much less my wife. And the men—good God, when I think of the low-living bastards who were in your vicinity, it makes my blood curdle! Sailors and drunkards on every corner—do you know what would happen if one of them took it into his head to snap up a little treat like you?" As the thought seemed to temporarily render him incapable of speech, Holly took the opportunity to defend herself.

"I was with companions, and—"

"Ladies," he said savagely. "Armed with umbrellas, no doubt. Just what do you think they would have been able to do, had you met with bad company?"

"The few men we encountered in the neighborhood were harmless," Holly argued. "In fact, it was the very same place you lived in during your childhood, and those men were no different from you—"

"In those days, I'd have played merry hell with you, if I'd managed to get my hands on you," he said harshly. "Have no illusions, milady . . . you'd have ended face-to-the wall in Maidenhead Lane with your skirts around your waist. The only wonder is that you didn't meet that fate with some randy sailor yesterday."

"You're exaggerating," Holly said defensively, but that only roused his temper to a higher pitch.

He continued to blister her ears with a lecture that was furious and insulting by turns, naming the various diseases she could have contracted and the vermin she had likely encountered, until Holly couldn't bear another word.

"I've heard enough," she cried hotly. "It's clear to me that I'm not to make a single decision without asking your permission first—I'm to be treated as a child, and you will act as a dictator." The accusation was unfair, and she knew it, but she was too incensed to care.

Suddenly his fury seemed to evaporate, and he stared at her with an inscrutable gaze. A long moment passed before he spoke again. "You wouldn't have taken Rose to such a place, would you?"

"Of course not! But she is a little girl, and I'm—"

"My life," he interrupted quietly. "You're my entire life.

If anything ever happens to you, Holly, there is nothing left for me."

Suddenly his words made her feel small and petty and, as he had accused, irresponsible. And yet her intentions had truly been good. On the other hand, she had known that visiting the factory had not been the wisest thing to do, or she wouldn't have tried to keep it secret from him. Swallowing back further arguments, she stared at a fixed point on the wall with an unhappy frown.

She heard Zachary swear beneath his breath, the ugliness of the word causing her to wince. "I won't say another word if you'll make me a promise."

"Yes?" she said warily.

"From now on, don't go anywhere that you wouldn't feel perfectly safe taking Rose. Unless I'm with you."

"I suppose that's not unreasonable," she said grudgingly. "Very well, I promise."

Zachary nodded shortly, his mouth set in a grim line. It occurred to Holly that this was the first time he had ever exerted his marital authority. Moreover, he had handled the situation far differently than George would have. George had set far greater limits for her, albeit in a gentler fashion. In the same circumstances, George would undoubtedly have asked her to leave the committee altogether. True ladies, he would have pointed out, did little more than carry baskets of jellies and soups to the poor, or perhaps contribute a bit of needlework to a bazaar. Zachary, for all his fire and thunder, actually asked very little of her in the way of wifely obedience. "I am sorry," she brought herself to say stiffly. "I didn't mean to worry you."

He accepted the apology with a single nod. "You didn't worry me," he muttered. "When I realized what you'd done, it scared the living hell out of me."

Although their quarrel was made up and the atmosphere

became easier, Holly was aware of a certain constraint between them that lasted through dinner and afterward. For the first time in their marriage, Zachary did not come to her bed at night. She had a restless sleep, tossing and turning, waking frequently to realize that she was alone. In the morning she was frustrated and bleary-eyed, and to compound her discontent, she discovered that Zachary had already left the house for his offices in town. It was difficult to summon her usual vitality during the day, and the thought of food was singularly unappealing. After consulting a looking glass to view her own fatigued appearance, Holly groaned and wondered if Zachary had been right, that she might indeed have caught some sort of illness during her factory visit.

She napped late in the day, pulling the curtains closed in her room to block out all trace of light. After sinking into an exhausted slumber, she awoke to find Zachary's outline near her as he occupied a bedside chair.

"Wh-what time is it?" she asked groggily, struggling to rise to her elbows.

"Half-past seven."

Realizing she had slept longer than she had intended, Holly made an apologetic sound. "Did I make everyone late for supper? . . . Oh, I must have—"

Zachary hushed her softly, moving over her, pressing her back to the pillows. "Megrims?" he murmured quietly.

She shook her head. "No, I was only tired. I didn't sleep well last night. I wanted you . . . that is . . . wanted your company . . ."

He laughed softly at her awkward admission. Straightening, he unbuttoned his waistcoat and dropped it to the floor, then tugged at his necktie. The low, vibrant sound of his voice in the darkness seemed to gather and tickle at the top of her spine. "We'll have supper sent up for you."

The white banner of his shirt fluttered from view as it, too, was cast to the floor. "In a little while," he added, and shed the rest of his clothes to join her in bed.

Over the course of the next fortnight, Holly was aware of not quite being herself, the fatigue having settled deep in her marrow and refusing to leave no matter how much she slept. Retaining her usual good humor took a great deal of effort, and late in the day she often felt irritable or melancholy. Her weight began to drop, which she rather liked at first, but unfortunately her eyes had begun to take on a sunken aspect that was not at all pleasing. A family doctor was sent for, but he was unable to find anything wrong with her.

Zachary treated her with extreme gentleness and patience, bringing her gifts of sweets and novels and amusing engravings. When it became clear that she no longer had the stamina for lovemaking, despite her willingness, he settled for other intimacies, spending the evenings bathing her, rubbing scented cream into her dry skin, cuddling and kissing her as if she were a treasured child. Another doctor was sent for, and then another, but neither had been able to come up with a diagnosis other than "decline," the word all physicians used when they were unable to identify an illness.

"I don't know why I'm so weary," Holly exclaimed fretfully one evening, while Zachary brushed her long hair as they sat before the fire. The air was warm—stifling, almost—but she felt chilled in all her limbs. "There's no reason for this decline—I've always been perfectly healthy, and nothing like this has ever happened to me before."

The motion of the brush paused, then resumed its gentle stroke. "I think you're over the worst of it now," came his

soft voice. "You seem a little better today." While he
brushed her hair, he made a hundred promises of all the
things they would do when she was well again: the places
they would travel, the exotic pleasures he would show her.
She fell asleep in his lap with a smile curving her lips, her
head resting heavily in the crook of his arm.

The next morning, however, she was much worse, her
body quivering and light and burning hot, as if every part
of her had been transmuted from flesh to flame. She was
only vaguely aware of voices, of Zachary's gentle hand on
her head and Paula's light cool fingers moving a cool rag
over her scorching skin. It seemed that if that gentle cool-
ing stroke ever ceased, she would not be able to bear the
heat that would surely overtake her. She heard herself
whispering words that made no sense, then some moments
everything was clear enough that she could speak. "Help
me, Mother . . . don't stop, please . . ."

"Dear Holly," came Paula's kind, familiar voice, and the
cloth moved diligently over her, ceaseless and untiring.
Somewhere amid the delirium she heard Zachary as he
snapped out orders to servants and sent a footman for the
doctor, and there was some new hoarse note she had never
heard in his voice. He was afraid, she thought dully . . .
She tried to call for him, to reassure him that she would
certainly get well again. But now that was only an elusive
hope. It seemed this terrible inner fire would always be
with her, burning and charring until she was nothing but
an empty shell.

A new doctor arrived, a handsome blond man who
wasn't much older than herself. Having always been attended by gray-whiskered old physicians of renowned experience and wisdom, Holly wondered if Dr. Linley would
be of any use at all. However, his cool competence was
immediately apparent, and during his examination she felt

her delirium receding somewhat, as if storm clouds had been driven at bay by an emerging sun. With a gentle briskness that somehow reassured her, Linley left behind some brandy tonic and sent for some broth from the kitchen, advising that she must eat to preserve her strength. He left to confer with Zachary, who waited outside the room.

Finally Zachary came in to see her. Carefully he took the bedside chair and moved it to the edge of the mattress.

"I like that Dr. Linley," Holly murmured.

"I thought you would," Zachary said dryly. "I nearly turned him away at the door when I saw his appearance. It was only because of his excellent reputation that I let him inside."

"Oh, well . . ." Making an effort, Holly dismissed the subject of the handsome doctor with a feeble gesture. "He's moderately attractive, I suppose . . . if one likes that golden Adonis sort."

Zachary grinned briefly. "Fortunately you prefer Hades."

She made a sound that, given more breath, would have been a chuckle. "At this moment, you bear the god of the underworld . . . more than a passing resemblance," she informed him. She watched his face, which was calm and self-assured as always, except that he couldn't conceal the skull-white color of his skin. "What is Dr. Linley's verdict?" she asked in a scratchy whisper.

"Only a bad case of influenza," he said matter-of-factly. "With some more rest and time, you'll be just—"

"It's typhoid," Holly interrupted, a weary smile curving her lips at his deception. Naturally the doctor had advised him to keep the news from her, to prevent worry from hindering her possible recovery. She lifted a slender white arm and showed him the small pink blotch on the inside of her elbow. "I have more of these on my stomach and chest. Just as George did."

Zachary stared thoughtfully at his shoes, hands shoved deep in his pockets as if he were deep in concentration. However, when his gaze lifted, she saw the gleam of hideous fear in his black eyes, and she made a crooning sound of reassurance. She patted the mattress beside her. Slowly he came to her and rested his dark head on her breasts. Encircling his powerful shoulders with her arms, Holly whispered into the thick locks of his hair, "I'm going to get well, darling."

He trembled all over and then recovered with startling quickness, sitting up and regarding her with a shadow of a smile. "Of course," he muttered.

"Send Rose away to protect her," she whispered. "To my family in the country. And Elizabeth and your mother—"

"They'll be gone within the hour. Except my mother— she wants to stay and help care for you."

"But the risk . . ." she said. "Make her go, Zachary."

"We Bronsons are a damned hardy breed," he said with a smile. "Every time some plague or epidemic went through the rookeries, we came out completely untouched. Scarlet fever, putrid fever, cholera . . ." He waved his hand in the same gesture he would use to shoo away a gnat. "You can't make one of us ill."

"I would have said the same for myself, not long ago." She shaped her dry lips into a smile. "I've never been really sick before. Why now? I wonder. I nursed George all through the typhoid and never had a single symptom."

The mention of her former husband caused Zachary to turn whiter, if that was possible, and Holly murmured contritely, understanding his terror that she would come to the same end as George. "I'll be all right," she whispered.

"Just need rest. Wake me when the broth is sent up. I'll drink every drop . . . just to show you . . ."

But she had no memory of the broth, or of anything distinct, as fiery dreams engulfed her and the entire world dissolved into swirling heat. Her tired thoughts tried to break through the shimmering hot wall, but they were battered away like moths, and she was left with no sense, no words, nothing but the incoherent sounds that rose endlessly from her own throat. She was tired of her own ceaseless droning, and yet she couldn't seem to make it stop. She had no power over anything, no sense of day and night.

There were times when she knew that Zachary was with her. She clung to his big, gentle hands and listened to the soothing murmur of his voice, while her body was racked with pain. He was so strong, so effortlessly powerful, and she tried in vain to absorb some of his vitality into herself. But he could not give her his strength, nor could he shelter her from the waves of fiery heat. It was her battle to fight, and to her weary despair she felt her will to recover fade, until all she was left with was the wish to endure. It had been like this for George. His gentle spirit had withered from the harsh demands of typhoid, and there had been no fight left in him. She had not understood until now how difficult it had been for him, and finally in her heart she forgave him for letting go. She was so close to letting go herself. The thought of Rose and Zachary still had power to entice her, but she was so tired, and the pain was pulling her irresistibly away from them.

It had been three weeks since Holly had become bedridden—weeks that would forever blend in Zachary's mind as one long interval of exhaustion and misery. Almost worse than Holly's delirium were the intervals when she was lucid, when she smiled at him affectionately and murmured concerned words. He was not eating or sleeping properly, she said. She wanted him to take better care of himself. She would be better very soon, she told him . . . how long had it been? . . . well, typhoid never lasted longer than a month. And just as Zachary allowed himself to be charmed and convinced that she truly was improving, she would sink back into her feverish ravings, and he was cast into worse despair than before.

It surprised him at times when a newspaper was occasionally placed before him along with a plate of food. After a few mechanical bites of bread or fruit he would glance at the front page of the paper, not to read but to marvel bleakly at the evidence that the rest of the world was going on as usual. The events in this house were catastrophic, soul-consuming, and yet business and politics and social events continued at their customarily brisk pace. Not that this trial of endurance was going unnoticed, however. As the word of Holly's illness had spread, the letters had begun to arrive.

It seemed that everyone from the highest social circles to the lowest wished to express their concern and friendship for the ailing lady. Aristocrats who had treated the newlyweds with everything short of actual disdain were apparently now anxious to prove their loyalty. It seemed that as Holly's illness progressed, her popularity climbed, and everyone claimed to be her closest friend. What a great sodding mass of hypocrites, Zachary thought sullenly, staring at the great hall filled with floral bowers and baskets of jellies and biscuit tins and fruit liquors, and silver trays heaped with messages of friendly sympathy. There were even a few callers, despite the contagious nature of typhoid fever, and Zachary took savage pleasure in turning them away. There was only one that he allowed inside the house, one that he had been expecting: Lord Blake, the earl of Ravenhill.

It somehow made Zachary like Ravenhill more for not bringing another useless basket or an unwanted bouquet. Ravenhill called unannounced one morning, dressed soberly, his blond hair gleaming even in the subdued light of the entrance hall. Zachary would never be friends with the man—he could not bring himself to forgive someone who had been a rival for Holly's hand. However, he had felt a grudging gratitude ever since Holly had told him that Ravenhill had advised her to follow her heart rather than adhere to George Taylor's wishes. The fact that Ravenhill could have made Holly's decision difficult, but had chosen not to, made Zachary feel a bit more kindly disposed toward him.

Ravenhill approached him, shook hands, then stared at him intently. The light gray eyes missed nothing as they swept over Zachary's bloodshot eyes and huge, gaunt frame. Suddenly Ravenhill averted his gaze and ran a hand over his jaw with several slow repetitions, as if considering a weighty problem. "Oh, Christ," he finally whispered. Zachary could read his thoughts easily: that Zachary's appearance would not be so ravaged were Holly not in grave, perhaps fatal, danger.

"Go up to her if you want," Zachary said gruffly.

A bitter, self-mocking smile curved Ravenhill's aristocratic mouth. "I don't know," he said, his voice nearly inaudible. "I don't know if I can go through this a second time."

"Do as you like, then." Zachary left him abruptly, unable to stand the twitching pain in the other man's face, the flash of fear in his eyes. He did not want to share feelings or memories or platitudes. He had coldly told his mother, Maude, the housekeeper and any servant within earshot that if they resorted to fits of weeping or other displays of emotion, they would be banished on the spot. The atmosphere in the household was calm, quiet and oddly serene.

Not caring where Ravenhill went or what he did or how he might locate Holly's room without assistance, Zachary wandered aimlessly until he came to the ballroom. It was dark, the windows covered in heavy draperies. He shoved one of the velvet panels aside and secured it, until long shafts of sunlight scored across the shining parqueted floor and illuminated a green silk-covered wall. Staring into a huge gold-framed mirror, he remembered the long-ago dance lessons, the way Holly had stood in his arms and earnestly murmured instructions to him, while at the time all he had been able to think of was how he desired her, loved her.

Her warm brown eyes had danced as she had teased him: *I wouldn't suggest applying too many of your pugilistic skills to our dance lesson, Mr. Bronson. I should dislike to find myself engaged in fisticuffs with you . . .*

Slowly Zachary lowered himself to the floor and sat, his back against the window ledge, remembering—his eyes half-closed and his head drooped in weariness. He was so tired, and yet he couldn't seem to sleep at night, his entire being locked in suspenseful agony. The only peace came when it was his turn to watch over Holly and he could reassure himself every minute that she was still breathing, her pulse still beating, her lips moving ceaselessly as she floated through fragments of dreams.

After what could have been five minutes or fifty, Zachary heard a voice echo in the dark, gleaming cavern of a room. "Bronson."

He lifted his head and saw Ravenhill standing in the doorway. The earl looked pale and grim, almost unnaturally self-controlled. "I don't know if she'll die," Ravenhill said curtly. "She doesn't look nearly as sunken and emaciated as George did at this point. But I do know she's heading into the crisis, and you'd do well to send for the doctor."

Zachary was on his feet before he had finished the last sentence.

Holly seemed to awaken in some blessedly cool dream, the pain and heat lifting, leaving her relaxed and more alert than she had felt in weeks. *I am better now,* she thought in surprise, and looked about eagerly, wanting to share the wonderful news with Zachary. She wanted to see him, and Rose, and to make them understand that the torment of the past days was finally over. But she was perplexed to find herself alone, standing in a cool, faintly salty fog that reminded her of the seaside. She hesitated, not certain of where to go or why she was here, but she was lured by faint sweet sounds ahead . . . it almost sounded like water splashing, birds chirping, trees rustling. She wandered forward, her limbs invigorated, her senses refreshed by the soft atmosphere. Gradually the veil of mist faded, and she found herself in a place of sparkling blue water and gentle green hills, with lush exotic flowers everywhere. Curiously she bent to touch one of the velvety peach-colored blossoms, and its fragrance seemed to surround and intoxicate her. Despite her puzzlement, she wanted to laugh in pleasure. Oh, she had forgotten how it had felt to be so purely happy, in the way that innocent children were. "What a beautiful dream," she said.

A smiling voice answered her. "Well, it's not precisely a dream."

She turned with a bewildered frown, hunting for the source of the tantalizingly familiar voice, and saw a man walking toward her. He stopped and stared at her with the blue eyes she had never forgotten.

"George," she said.

Holly's fair, fresh skin had a plum-colored cast, and her breathing was alarmingly fast and shallow. The fever burned unbelievably hot, and her eyes were half-open in a strange, fixed stare. Dressed in her white gown, with only a light sheet to cover her legs, she looked as small as a child as she lay alone in her bed. She was dying, Zachary thought numbly, and he could not seem to think of what would happen afterward. For him there would be no hopes, no expectations, no future pleasure or happiness, as if his own life would end when hers did. He waited in the corner of the room silently while Dr. Linley examined Holly. Paula and Maude had also entered the bedroom, both of them obviously struggling to mask their grief.

The doctor came to Zachary and spoke very softly. "Mr. Bronson, there are several techniques I've been trained in, most of which I believe would finish your wife off quickly rather than save her. The only thing I can do is give her something that will make her passing easier."

Zachary did not require an explanation. He knew exactly what Linley was offering: to drug Holly so that she would sleep peacefully during the last painful stage of the typhoid. He heard himself breathing in a too-rapid, too-light fashion that was not unlike Holly's. Then he heard the sound change, and he glanced toward the bed as Holly's breaths came in difficult, fitful sighs.

"The death rattle," he heard Maude say fearfully.

Zachary felt his sanity snap, and he flinched under Linley's steady regard. "Get out," he said hoarsely, almost giving in to the temptation to bare his teeth at them all and growl like an enraged animal. "Leave me alone with her. Leave, now!"

It almost surprised Zachary that they complied without argument, his mother weeping into a handkerchief as she closed the door. He locked the door behind them, secluding himself in the room with his wife, and went to the bed. Without hesitation he sat on the mattress and gathered Holly in his arms, disregarding her weak, protesting moan. "I'll follow you to the next life if I have to," he whispered harshly in her ear. "You'll never be free of me. I'll chase you through heaven and hell and beyond." He continued to whisper without stopping—threatening, coaxing, cursing—while his hands gripped her body close to his as if he could physically prevent the life from flowing out of her. "You stay with me, Holly," he muttered savagely, his mouth sliding over her hot, wet face and neck. "Don't do this to me. You stay, damn you." And finally when no more words would come from his aching throat, he sank down to the mattress with her, burying his face against her still breasts.

It was indeed George, but his appearance was altered in some way from how it had been in life. He looked so very young, his skin and eyes and hair radiant, every aspect of him glowing with strength and health. "Holly, darling," he said with a quiet laugh, seeming to enjoy her surprise. "You didn't realize I would come to meet you?"

In spite of her pleasure at seeing him, Holly held back, staring, fearing for some reason to touch him. "George, how can it be that we're together? I . . ." She considered the situation, her happiness ebbing as she realized that she might have lost the life she had always known until now. "Oh," she said, her eyes stinging and aching suddenly. No tears came, but she was filled with desolation.

George tilted his head and regarded her with loving sympathy. "You're not ready for this, are you?"

"No," she said in growing desperation. "George, have I no choice? I want to return at once."

"To that prison of a body, and all the pain and struggle? Why not come with me instead? There are places even more beautiful than this." He extended his hand invitingly. "Let me show them to you."

She shook her head violently. "Oh, George, you could offer me a thousand paradises, but I could never . . . There is someone, a man, who needs me, and I need him—"

"Yes, I know about that."

"You do?" She was amazed by the lack of accusation or recrimination in his face. "George, I must go back to him and Rose! Please don't blame me, you must understand that I didn't forget you, or stop caring for you, but, oh . . . how I've come to love him!"

"Yes, I understand." He smiled, and to her relief, his hand fell back to his side. "I would never blame you for that, Holly."

Although she had made no effort to step backward, it seemed that her anxiety had pulled her several yards away from him.

"You've found your soul mate," he commented.

"Yes, I . . ." A wash of clear, bright knowledge swept over her, and she was relieved that he seemed to understand. "Yes, I have."

"That's good," he murmured. "It's good that you realize how fortunate you are. I had only one regret when I came here. I had done so little in life for other people. So much of what we concerned ourselves with was immaterial. There's only love, Holly . . . fill your life with it while you can."

Her emotions tumbled over and over as she watched him

walk away. "George," she cried unsteadily, longing to ask him so many things.

He paused and looked back with a loving smile. "Tell Rose I'm watching over her."

And then he was gone.

She closed her eyes and felt herself sinking, falling much too fast, back into the heat and darkness, where the air reverberated with savage, snarling words that caught around her like chains. The vehemence frightened her at first, until she understood its cause. She moved, her arms feeling wretchedly heavy, as if they had been encased in iron. After the wonderful floating lightness of her heavenly vision, it was difficult to accustom herself to this pain and illness once more. But she accepted it gladly, knowing that she had gained more time with the one she loved most, in this world or the next. She reached out and stilled the words on her husband's lips, and felt his mouth tremble against her fingers. "Hush," she whispered, glad that his violent litany had quieted. It was so difficult to speak, but she concentrated fiercely on making herself understood. "Hush . . .'s all right now."

She opened her eyes and stared into Zachary's pale, wild face. The black eyes were fathomless with astonished wonder, the lashes spiked with tears. Slowly she stroked his hard face, his cheek, watching as sanity and awareness crept into his expression.

"Holly," he said, his voice shaking and utterly humble. "You . . . you'll stay with me?"

"Course I will." She sighed and smiled, keeping her hand on his cheek, though the effort demanded all her strength. "Not going anywhere . . . dearest Zachary."

Epilogue

"*Higher, Mama, higher!*"

Holly unrolled more string and the kite dove and soared in the cloud-ribboned sky, its green silk tail fluttering amid a strong breeze. Rose trotted beside her, shrieking her approval. Somehow their skirts and legs tangled and they fell together in a wildly giggling heap. Bounding up immediately, Rose took the roll of string and continued to run, her brown curls flying in shining banners behind her. Holly remained on the ground, resting on her back. Smiling, she relaxed on the crisp green lawn while the sun shone full on her face.

"Holly." The anxious note in her husband's voice pierced her reverie. She rolled to her side with an inquiring smile. He was coming toward her from the house, his stride purposeful, his hard face set with a frown.

"You must have been watching from the library window," Holly murmured, crooking her finger for him to join her on the grass.

"I saw you fall," he said curtly, squatting beside her. "Are you all right?"

Holly wriggled to her back, heedless of possible grass

stains, knowing she looked far more like a tumbled country
lass than the grand lady she had been reared to be. "Come
closer and I'll show you," she said throatily.

A reluctant laugh escaped him as his gaze traveled over
her abandoned posture, the skirts flipped up to reveal her
white-stockinged ankles. Holly lay still beneath his pe-
rusal, hoping his reticence with her was finally beginning
to fade. In the past six weeks of her recovery from typhoid,
she had regained her health in full measure, until she was
once more pink-cheeked and lively, and even a bit plump.
She knew she had never looked or felt better, and along
with her health had come all her natural desire to be physically close with her husband.

Ironically, Zachary's recovery had been somewhat
slower than hers. Although he was as affectionate and teasing as ever, there was an unbreakable restraint in his manner with her, an undue carefulness in the way he touched
her, as if she were still so fragile that he might accidentally
cause her harm. Although he had regained some of the
weight he had lost, he was still a bit too lean, too watchful
and tense, as if he were waiting for some unseen enemy
to pounce.

He had not made love to her since before the typhoid
fever. There was no mistaking the fact that he wanted her,
and after the past two months of celibacy, a man with his
sexual appetite must be suffering mightily. But he had
greeted her recent advances with careful, gentle rebuffs,
promising that they would be intimate again when she was
better. Clearly his opinion of her health was far different
than her own, or even Dr. Linley's. The physician had
tactfully informed her that she was ready to resume all
normal marital activity as soon as she felt able. However,
she didn't seem able to convince Zachary that she was
more than healthy enough to receive him in her bed.

Wanting him to relax, to be happy, to lose his restraint in her arms, Holly slid him a provocative glance. "Kiss me," she murmured. "There's no one here but Rose . . . and she certainly won't mind."

Zachary hesitated and bent over her, brushing his mouth gently over hers. She slid a hand around the back of his neck, fingers curving over muscles that were as hard as steel. Holding him to her, she touched her tongue to his lips, but he would not share his taste with her. He took her wrist carefully and pulled her hand away from his neck.

"Have to go back," he said unsteadily, and let out a panting breath. "Work to do." Shivering and laughing briefly, he stood in an easy movement and threw her a glance of tortured love. He returned to the house while she raised herself to a sitting position and contemplated his tall, retreating figure.

Clearly something must be done, Holly thought with mingled amusement and exasperation. Of all men, she had never thought Zachary Bronson would be so difficult to seduce. He seemed almost afraid to touch her. She had no doubt that he would make love to her again someday, when he finally realized that he would not inadvertently hurt her. But she did not want to wait. She wanted him now, the vigorous full-blooded lover whose lusty advances made her mad with pleasure—not this careful, considerate gentleman who seemed entirely too self-controlled for his own good.

Returning home from a long day spent in his town offices, Zachary entered the house with a sigh of relief. It had been an unexpectedly difficult negotiation, but he had finally acquired the largest interest in a Birmingham metalwork factory that produced chains, nails and needles. The difficult part had not been in setting the financial terms, but in convincing his would-be partners that from now on the factory would be run by his managers, his way. There would be decent hours for the workers, no children employed and part of the profits would be reinvested in ways his partners had called foolish and unnecessary. He had nearly walked away from the deal entirely, and when they had realized he would not yield an inch, they had agreed to all his terms.

The day of patient, persistent debate had left him agitated. He was still tense with battle readiness, longing for a way to expel his pent-up energy. Unfortunately, his favorite method, that of tumbling his wife, was still not available to him. He knew Holly would welcome him if he approached her that way. However, she still seemed so small and fragile, and he was terrified that her health might undergo a setback if he pushed her too hard. Moreover, his own feelings for her overwhelmed him. It had been so long since he had made love to her that he half-feared he would fall on her like a rabid animal when he finally approached her.

It was Thursday, the usual night off for the servants, but the household seemed far quieter and emptier than usual. As Zachary wandered from the entrance hall to the family dining room, he discovered that the cold supper that the cook always set out on these evenings was not to be found. Checking his pocket watch, he discovered that he was only a quarter-hour late. Was it possible that the family had already eaten and retired? Mysteriously, there wasn't a single person in view, and no one responded to his casual call. The house seemed deserted.

Frowning, Zachary strode to the grand staircase, his pace quickening as he wondered if something had gone wrong . . . and then he saw it. A rose with crimson petals, laid carefully along the bottom step. He picked up the flower, the long stem carefully denuded of thorns. As he ascended the stairs, he found another on the sixth step, and another on the twelfth. His gaze progressed upward, discovering that a trail of red roses had been laid out for him to follow.

A smile pulled up from deep inside him, and he shook his head slightly. He wandered along the path of roses, in no particular hurry as he added to his growing collection. The blossoms were lush and fragrant, the sweet smell teasing his senses as he carried them. After retrieving more than a dozen, he found himself standing before his own bedroom door, with one last bloom dangling from the doorknob by a red ribbon. Feeling rather dreamlike, he opened the door, crossed the threshold and closed himself inside the bedroom.

A small table laden with covered silver dishes and candles in silver holders had been set in the corner. His gaze traveled from the cozy supper for two to the sight of his pretty dark-haired wife, who was dressed in something filmy and black. Her body was visible through the wickedly revealing negligee, and he stared at her in stupefied silence.

"Where is everyone?" he asked with difficulty.

Holly waved a rose as if it were a magic wand. "I made them all disappear." Smiling mysteriously, she came forward to embrace him. "Now, which will you have first?" she asked. "Supper? . . . Or me?"

The roses dropped to the floor in a rustling, sweetly aromatic heap. He stood amid the cascade of blossoms as she pressed against him, silken and fragrant and utterly female. Zachary's arms went around her. The feel of her warm flesh beneath the transparent black silk was enough to make his mouth go dry and his aching loins wake in a rapid, twitching surge. He tried to control the bursting excitement that filled him, but he was so hungry with longing, his body so damn deprived, that all he could do was stand there and gulp for air. Her small, clever hands roamed busily beneath his coat, tugging at buttons, pulling at fabric until his shirt hung free of his trousers. Her palm brushed lightly over his rock-hard erection, lingered in a squeezing caress, and she smiled against his shirtfront. "I suppose this answers my question," she murmured, and set about freeing him from the tight constriction of broadcloth.

Somehow in the midst of his turmoil, Zachary was able to make his stiff mouth form words. "Holly, I'm afraid . . . oh, God . . . I can't control myself."

"Then don't," she said simply, and tugged his head down to hers.

He resisted, his face drawn with torment. "If I should cause you a relapse . . ."

"Darling." She stroked his cheek with her soft hand, smiling tenderly at him. "Don't you know that your love only gives me strength?" She touched the corner of his taut mouth with a gentle fingertip. "Give me what I need, Zachary," she whispered. "It's been far too long."

Groaning, he took her sweet mouth with his, delving deeply with his tongue, and the pleasure of it drove him wild. He kissed her endlessly, sucking, stroking, devouring, while his hands cupped over her silk-covered breasts, her round hips, her bottom. The feel of her made him dizzy. He dragged her to the bed and tossed her on top of the mattress, and tore at his own clothes until most of them were gone. He crawled on top of her, his hands and mouth searching for the white skin left uncovered by the veil of black silk, while she whispered urgently for him to unfasten her gown. "There are some buttons," she gasped. "No

. . . not there, over here . . . yes, and a ribbon that ties over my . . . oh, yes . . ."

His growing desperation made it impossible to dispose entirely of the intricate network of fastenings. Finally he settled for pushing the filmy skirts up to her waist and lowering himself between her open thighs. He pushed himself inside her, lunging, sliding, until he was deeply encased in her silken heat. She moaned and wrapped her arms and legs around him, her hips pressing firmly upward against his weight. Framing her face in his hands, he kissed her open mouth and began to thrust without restraint, taking her in primitive, impatient drives that made her whimper against his lips. The delicate crescents of her nails pressed into his back, and he shuddered and pumped harder, until the eruption of sensation caught up with him at last. For a moment the release seemed too intense to bear, white-hot and consuming as it blazed through his body. Just as his climax began to ease, he felt her inner muscles tighten around him in a long, exquisite ripple. He took her cry into his mouth and held himself as far inside her as possible, riding her until the last tremor had faded.

They lay together, winded and relaxed and steeped in pleasurable aftermath. Zachary drew his fingers over his wife's alluring body, unfastening what was left of the negligee and stripping it away. Finding a rose poised on a nearby pillow, he retrieved the soft open blossom and drew it over her damp pearly skin, tickling her breasts and navel, gently stroking it between her thighs. "Zachary," she protested, delighting him with a blush.

He grinned lazily, feeling at peace for the first time in months. "Witch," he murmured. "You knew I wanted to wait longer before doing this."

Holly levered herself over him with a triumphant smile. "You don't always know what's best for me."

He tangled his hands in her hair and urged her to kiss him. "And what is best for you?" he whispered when their lips had parted.

"You," she informed him. "As much of you as I can have."

Filled with adoration, Zachary stared into her smiling face. "I believe I can oblige you, my love." And he pulled her deep into his embrace and loved her once again.

Suddenly, You

Coming in June 2001
Only from Avon Books

Lisa Kleypas
has transported readers
to a world where a single glance
sometimes means more
than a stolen kiss.

Now, meet Lisa's most dynamic heroine
and enigmatic hero as they enter
into a sensuous bargain that was
greater than either expected . . .